WINGS UNFURLED

REBECCA GOMEZ FARRELL

Meerkat Press
Asheville

ISBN-13 - 978-1-946154-64-4 (Paperback)
ISBN-13 - 978-1-946154-65-1 (eBook)

Cover and book design by Tricia Reeks

Printed in the United States of America

Published in the United States of America by
Meerkat Press, LLC, Atlanta, Georgia
www.meerkatpress.com

Praise for the Wings Rising Series

"War, treachery, and star-crossed lovers abound in this high fantasy novel . . . Farrell's book is imaginative, filled with detailed worldbuilding."

—Kirkus Reviews

"Rebecca Gomez Farrell weaves together a brilliant fantasy adventure about love, power, and destiny."

—Seattle Book Reviews

"*Wings Unseen* is an enthralling female-driven fantasy debut. . . . Compelling, entertaining, and enlightening, *Wings Unseen* is a fantastic read!"

—Jeffe Kennedy (Author of The Twelve Kingdoms Trilogy)

"With a talon-like hook, *Wings Unseen* will grab you and not let you go."

—Mur Lafferty, award-winning author of *Six Wakes*

"*Wings Unseen* marries intrigue, unique worldbuilding, and political machination in a fast-paced story that will surely appeal to high fantasy and historical fantasy readers."

—Jaym Gates, author of *Shattered Queen*

"*Wings Unseen* is the fantasy I've been waiting to read for a long time. Vibrant, intense, but underscored by a weight that makes the characters jump out at you, this is not a book you will put down."

—Jay Requard, Author of *The Saga of The Panther* and *War Pigs*

"An intricately woven coming-of-age tale full of magic and intrigue. *Wings Unseen* presents a vivid world populated with a wonderful collection of characters to love and despise."

—Dominica Phetteplace, award-winning author of "Gin Is Stronger Than Witchcraft" and "Project Entropy"

*For those who've fought back the darkness that
dimmed your light.*

CONTENTS

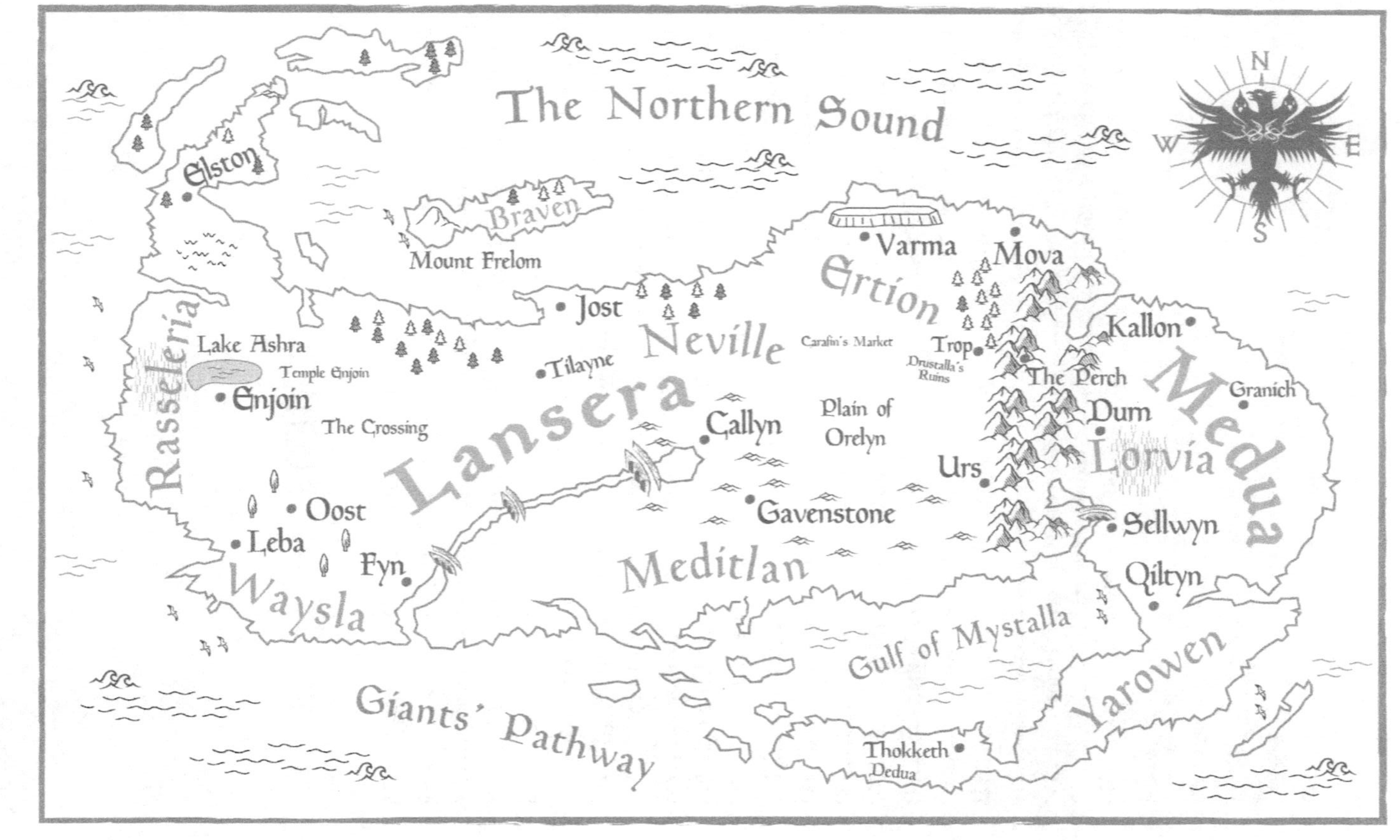
The Northern Sound
N
W
E
S
Elston
Braven
Mount Frelom
Varma
Mova
Ertion
Rasseleria
Lake Ashra
Temple Enjoin
Enjoin
The Crossing
Jost
Tilayne
Neville
Carafin's Market
Trop
Drustalla's Ruins
Kallon
The Perch
Granich
Lansera
Callyn
Plain of Orelyn
Dum
Medua
Oost
Urs
Lorvia
Leba
Gavenstone
Fyn
Meditlan
Sellwyn
Waysla
Qiltyn
Gulf of Mystalla
Giants' Pathway
Yarowen
Thokketh
Dedua

Izmareld

"Okay, you can go," Daddy said.

Izzy had been such a good girl for such a long time, sitting on that cold stone bench with the adults. Daddy gave her shoulder a squeeze, and she dashed away with a delighted "Whee!"

At home, Mama sometimes let Izzy run around the garden for hours. The meadow here was similar, except droopy trees bordered it instead of hills. Izzy's boots slid like skis over the slick wet grass. Maybe she'd run to the nearby village where her great-great-great-grandfather had been born, like Grammy said. Or was it her great-great? Izzy couldn't remember. Running was so much fun!

"Don't let her out of your sight, Evon!"

Daddy sounded stern, but Izzy could tell the difference between his serious and poking-fun voices. Evon, the son of Daddy's friend Rall, was nice, but he'd have to catch her if he wanted to play too.

"Slow down, Izzy, or your father will kill me," Evon huffed from behind, but he was a big nine-year-old. He could catch up if he wanted.

Izzy stuck out the tip of her tongue. Maybe she could taste the air like the Razzy people did, if they were her great-greats. "Razzy" wasn't really their name, but "Izzy" wasn't her name either, and everyone called her that anyway.

Her tongue felt thick, hanging out of her mouth, or maybe the air tasted thick, like in the kitchen back home when Mar Jeffyr baked bread rolls. Izzy wished she could have one of those now. With crunchy lemon sugar on top.

Crr-owk.

What a funny noise! The swans in Grammy's pond sometimes honked so loud, Izzy laughed. She dashed to the swamp forest, hoping to find the creature that made that sound. A rainbow fluttered past the tree trunks. Izzy's breath caught. Its colors were so much bolder than the ones in the sky!

"Whoa!" Evon tumbled over her, landing in a patch of mud. Izzy wanted to laugh, but she knew better now that she was four. So she put her hand out to help Evon up.

"A Lanserim always helps their enemies to their feet," she said, reciting one of her father's favorite sayings.

Evon chuckled, "I didn't know we were enemies. But thank you, Izzy." Looking down at his clothes, he scowled. Mama did the same when she couldn't find her pants and had to wear a dress. Evon sighed, "I'll be right back, or someone else will, okay, Izzy? Don't go far."

"Okay," she said. How far could she go during a *right back,* she wondered. Evon took off toward her father and his important friends, gathered around the table. From here, their big heads bobbed like a caterpillar's body.

The rainbow waved again through the trees, its colors fanning out. Izzy giggled when she heard another funny call. She had to find it! She moved into the woods, following the sound until she couldn't anymore because there were too many branches. But the rainbow appeared just ahead of her, then hopped away and a cluster of leaves fell, blocking her view.

She wanted to tell Daddy about it, but she couldn't see Daddy anywhere. Only trees with roots as tall as she was rising out of the soggy ground. Izzy scrambled up one and reached her hand out as far as she could. Maybe she could touch the rainbow . . .

PLOP! Izzy toppled into a shallow pond and heaved half a cry, until she remembered how tough Mama was. So she fought away the ouch by rolling back onto her legs. Her clothes were so dirty, but unlike Evon, she didn't mind. Dirty was fun.

Izzy scrambled over the roots, careful not to tangle her feet. The rainbow came into sharper focus. It was more like a mass of rainbows, glittery and dazzling as the wings of chorna moths in the moonslight.

Lansera had four whole moons. Mama had taught her a rhyme to remember them. Izzy sang,

"Copper Tansic in the sky.
Golden Oro likes to fly.
Black Onsic plays a game.
Silver Esye casts my flame."

The moons always glowed so strong, but these colors were brighter. Suddenly, so was everything else around her but the trees! Those turned pastel gray, like faded tapestries that had seen too much sun.

Izzy's eyes widened.

The sunlight pulsed with gold and silver and copper—the colors of the metallic threads Mama had laced through her special long tunics. The light shimmered and shifted around her, and a deeper color, a blue that made her feel cool and safe, hung like a haze in the air.

Izzy smiled big, and the rainbows ruffled. They weren't floating after all, but feathers attached to something gigantic!

Daddy called her name, but he sounded far away, as though yelling through a very long pipe. The rainbows danced, and Izzy reached for them, felt downy fluff softer than a baby woranbird.

She took one more step, and—

PART ONE

MOONFALL

When leaps the mighty cantalere,
the dark brother drains his foes.
The Guard must ring the beastly lair
Where battles end their roam.

CHAPTER ONE

Serra

Serrafina Gavenstone could not believe her eyes. Gone was the comfortable armchair that had stood guard in this hall for nearly two decades, outside the door to her old bedroom. Her dear handmaid, Bini, had sat there so many times during Serra's childhood, waiting to be called upon. A bare chair of blonde Wasylim wood rested in its place on the stone floor.

Serra shook her head, blinked three times, and only then was certain she viewed reality and not the spiritual realm, which was always a distinct possibility. She had the sight, a supernatural gift from Madel, Lansera's goddess, who inhabited that other plane of existence. Serra could slip the sight on faster than reading glasses. With it, she could glimpse Madel's realm and its color-rich gossamer that overlaid reality like a decorative veil over a gown.

Such a small change, that chair, but it added to her unease. Lately, dark patches flickered at the edges of her sight. Which was why Serra had come to Callyn—to tell the king. Any such change in her vision could be a sign of a threat emerging, as the claren scourge had six years ago. Claren swarms had attacked the peoples of Lansera, consuming all beings from the inside out and leaving husks of skin in their wake. They'd been invisible to everyone but Serra, as they'd come from the spiritual realm.

"Can I help you, Lady . . . ?"

A young man touched Serra's shoulder, a castle servant she had not met in the months of her latest absence.

"Mar Gavenstone," she corrected him, then shushed him as he gaped at her name and form of address. "Not 'Lady Gavenstone,' that's my Aunt Marji. Just 'Mar' suits me fine. Not Seer Serra, either. That's plain silly."

His color returned to a healthy shade. "Well, yes, all right then. Can I help you, Mar Gavenstone?"

"I'm here to see King Albrecht. Please tell him I've arrived." She shook her head then touched his arm. "You must tell him it's Lady Serra, not *Mar* Gavenstone." Chagrin colored her cheeks. "I shouldn't have corrected you in the first place, I'm sorry. It was just a . . . a wish." The king would admonish her, again, for not taking up her claim to Gavenstone Manor, the ruling house of the nearby Meditlan region. Serra hadn't lived there since she was eight, when her parents had drowned and the royal Albrechts had taken her in to foster. "I'll wait right here. No refreshment is required."

The servant clasped his hands together and raised his elbows to her, holding the gesture long and high enough to indicate the appropriate amount of deference. Then he hurried off across the courtyard. Were it spring, Serra'd steal away to the queensgarden to wait. Walking the spiral labyrinth through its fragrant balac vines had brought her peace many times in her childhood. But it was winter, and the branches were bare.

The bejeweled tapestry on the wall had also disappeared, she noticed. A simpler, but perhaps more appropriate, rug of woven feathers hung in its place. It displayed the form of the mythical three-headed bird of creation that had protected Lansera from the claren. As the seer, Serra had been one of the bird's figurative three heads. Janto Albrecht, the prince and her former fiancé, became the slayer and second head after defeating the legendary silver stag in the flesh. His wife, Vesperi, was the weapon and the third. Her silver flame could burn through a claren swarm in seconds.

Janto had dubbed their trio the "hunting party" soon after they'd begun systemically clearing the countryside of claren. The task complete and people saved, he and Vesperi had returned to Castle Callyn four years ago. Serra had too, for a time. But her life had changed so completely from the one she used to dream of within these walls, that *home* no longer applied to them.

"Serra, I am so glad you're here."

Janto swept her up in an engulfing hug that lasted longer than perhaps appropriate.

"Put me down!" she scolded with a smile. Though it'd been six years since she'd released Janto from their engagement, Serra remained ever vigilant of appearances. "What if someone starts a rumor about the prince seeking comfort away from the princess?"

Vesperi was from Medua, a region of Lansera that had been its own country for two generations. The advers, false priests of a fake god, had ruled the Meduans through fear. Brutality was prized, and placing one's self-interest first? A virtue. Their people had been reunited since the clarens' attack, but the Meduan and Lanserim ways of life had grown so far apart, some doubted they could ever truly be one again.

"I'm just so glad to see you," Janto said. His hand trembled. "Father's . . ."

Tears brimmed in Serra's eyes before she knew why they came. "What's wrong?"

"Father's sick." Janto stared at the stone floor. "Very sick."

"No." He couldn't be sick. She was here to seek his guidance. King Dever Albrecht's stalwart competence had calmed so much of the political upheaval since the Conjoining, the day their claren hunting party had toppled Mandat Hall and reunited the two countries. He was their steadfast waypost. She needed him. They all did.

What shall we do without him?

The words slipped out from a smooth-tongued voice beside her. Serra turned her head to find an empty hall. *A thought?* But it had sounded so corporeal.

Your fears are very real.

Serra gasped. The voice again. Her sight revealed nothing but the dark patches encroaching on her vision of Madel's realm. They'd shifted some, looked more like pockets that puckered open and closed before evaporating.

"Serra, are you okay?" Concern flooded Janto's amber eyes.

Surely, her worries had merely made her imagine it. "I'm fine, I promise."

With a finger, Janto lifted her chin. "I'm so glad you're here. He's not doing well. You . . ."—he choked back tears—"you should see him right away."

Serra nodded, her mind racing. "Will Vesperi be there?"

His answer held a bitter edge. "No. She's not at Callyn. Hasn't been in two months."

"What? With the king sick . . ." Serra's protective impulses bristled. For the sake of their people, she'd brokered a truce with Vesperi long ago. But getting along with Meduans, and their often brash and selfish ways, could be a challenge. Serra's own romantic life proved that—she'd broken up with Lorne Granich, the son of a Meduan lord, for the fifth and final time just a few months ago.

Janto gave her a warning glance. "It's complicated, Serra. After Izzy—"

Of course. Learning the king was sick had pushed her goddaughter's disappearance to the back of her mind. Not being a mother herself, Serra could not, and would not, hazard a guess as to the complicated emotions Vesperi and Janto felt. Whatever was going on with Serra's sight could wait—she was here, and the Albrechts needed her.

Perhaps the darkness in Serra's sight had been Madel's way of impelling her to come.

Janto led her past the throne and council rooms. Memories of the king in both sprang to mind, especially the day he had guided their hunting party down the path toward toppling Mandat Hall, the seat of the advers' power, which had enabled the Conjoining. Vesperi's absence at the castle spoke volumes—if even Janto, their prince, couldn't get along with his Meduan bride, how could the rest of the Lanserim?

Serra pushed the memory of Lorne's pale blue eyes, flashing with betrayal, from her mind.

He is unworthy of you.

The thought was as insidious as the beating of claren wings. Still, she'd tried to convince Lorne it was true. That last day together, his flaxen hair swept up into a handsome bun and his jewels freshly shined, he'd proposed spending their futures together, perhaps even marrying, though he hadn't pressed that far. She'd panicked, couldn't picture that future, any future, really. Not since she'd sacrificed the one she'd had as a child of marrying Janto and becoming queen.

Such a coward, Serrafina.

That was much closer to truth than the voice had come before. Her spirits drained as Janto gripped her hand and they bypassed the stairs leading up to the king's study. To not be at his desk, Dever Albrecht must be gravely ill. He rarely kept to his quarters in daylight.

Her throat tightened, though Janto's hand felt as reassuring in hers as it always had. She noted fresh archery calluses on his fingers. From the courtyard, sunlight streamed into the walkway and highlighted his strawberry-blond curls and the green cast of his warm brown skin. The angles of his muscles had sharpened, no doubt from the months he'd spent scouring the mangrove swamp between Wasyla and Rasseleria for Izzy. No one had found a trace.

"I've had a letter from Ryn Cladio," Janto said. Ryn Cladio was the highest priest in the Order devoted to serving Madel. "He speaks of strange animal corpses found in the marshlands—"

"Not the claren returned?" Serra gasped. It had been two years since any reports. She'd seen none in her recent scourings.

"Not the claren. The bodies are intact, but long decayed. They've identified horns thus far, and many hooves—too many for the number of carcasses."

Extra legs? And horns? What new madness did they have to contend with, and with the king sick?

"He sent me a couple lines of verse, too. Said an old tome he was unfamiliar with had surfaced in the rooms beneath Temple Enjoin. The ryns and rynnas are stumped as to what to make of its old alphabet. He's sent me what they translated thus far. I'm hoping it sounds familiar to Father."

Serra said nothing in response. Their fulfillment of the silver stag prophecy had quelled whatever doubts she had about the power of old rhymes and chants.

Against the wall outside the king's quarters hunched the normally erect form of Ser Allyn. To see the king's most trusted advisor in any state but composed? Serra's throat clenched.

"Lady Serra," he raised his elbows in greeting, "I am glad you're here. The king will be pleased to see you."

"What are you doing out here, and not inside, Ser Allyn?" Janto asked.

"I shouldn't intrude, my prince. Not on the time you have left." He held himself tall, composed, though he choked on the words.

Serra paled. *Is the king so far gone as that?*

"Allyn, don't be ridiculous. You are coming back inside with us. With Father." Janto reached for his arm, but the advisor stepped back, his form rigid.

"I couldn't." Tears formed in his eyes, though he tried to blink them away.

"Nonsense. You are family as much as I," Serra interjected, and Janto nodded.

Ser Allyn made a desperate sound, like a woranbird that had lost its mate.

Janto clutched his shoulder. "Consider it my first command, if you must. But there is no one else Father would rather have by his side, in death or in life."

He assented, allowing Janto to wave him in.

"Oh good." Queen Lexamy's golden voice filled the room as Ser Allyn entered. "I'd begun to worry you thought we could handle this without you."

The queen smothered the advisor in a hug, dimpled arms reaching easily around his slender figure. Then she caught sight of Serra, and heavy wrinkles smoothed from her brow. She held out her other arm, and Serra filled it with gladness.

The embrace ended, and Serra slipped into a chair beside the queen. A beam of light highlighted her dusky skin and exposed smears of moisture from recent tears. Janto moved to close the curtain, as the same light fell against the king's closed eyes.

King Dever Albrecht spoke in rasps. "No, open them more." Instantly, all attention was on him. "I want to see my daughter."

Serra could count on one hand the number of times he'd called her that. Most of them had come in the years since she'd left Janto at the altar. The king had known Serra, orphaned and rootless, needed assurance that *they* had not parted ways, that she was part of the Albrecht family in spirit, though not in name.

She leaned over him as his eyes, the same color as Janto's, fluttered open.

"Still not in your rightful hold, I see," he said with a wet cough.

Many times, Serra had described King Dever Albrecht as stern. But today, his voice held humor. She shook her head. To return to Meditlan, walk its halls devoid of her family, was another future she could not imagine. They'd all passed away, except for Aunt Marji and her husband, Jehos, who ruled in Serra's stead.

"Someday."

He patted her hand. Perhaps the need for performative command had shrunken away with the fat on his bones. He was far too thin, and that, too, was hard to take in. Her eyelashes wet, Serra kissed his cheeks. The warmth in them gladdened her.

"What are you doing in this bed?" she teased. "Don't you know you're supposed to be the strong one?"

The king laughed, and it rattled down his throat, coins tossed in a well. The queen reached for something in a nearby chest—a honey and eucalyptus candy, Serra guessed. It would soothe his throat. The queen had encouraged Serra to study herbology in Oost, and Serra practiced it now in her travels.

"Oh, Serra, you have always been the strongest of us." The king winked. "Don't tell my son."

-He does not know you as well as he thinks.

Serra pushed the harmful thought away; there were more pressing issues at hand than her own failings. She peeked up at a smiling Janto. "I promise."

This man had acted as her father for most her life, given her structure and discipline. Once, he'd trusted her with his son's heart, and after, with their people's lives. But he wasn't prone to such sentiment as now flowed from his lips.

"I am so glad to have raised you, child." He leaned forward and she ducked down so he could kiss her forehead.

"Father, I have received a letter from Ryn Cladio," Janto started.

"Oh?" The king struggled to straighten against his pillow. The queen helped him rearrange himself.

"He believes Madel revealed a set of old verses to him—they have had odd sightings in the marshes, and—"

"People have had odd sightings in marshes for millennia," the king jested. Then he groaned, and Queen Lexamy dunked a towel in iced water to wipe his sweat. Serra wondered that he took Janto's news so lightly. He normally treated anything to do with the Order with the utmost seriousness.

"May I?" Ser Allyn asked, and the queen handed him the rag. "I used to, when we were children. Do you remember, Dever?"

"Allyn," the king's voice grated, gravel crunched underfoot, "of course I remember you taking care of me. Although I had a few years on you."

Ser Allyn chided, "Two at best. You've always been so proud of that age difference."

The king smiled, though his eyes fluttered closed.

"Father, the verses—"

"Yes, yes. I'm sorry. What are they?"

Janto retrieved a rolled parchment from his cloak. Serra tried not to reflect on why he pushed the issue—it was clear enough in the weariness that lined the king's face. *I have been gone too long.* To be this far advanced, King Dever must have been sick for months.

"*When leaps the mighty cantalere, the dark brother drains his foes,*" Janto read. "Ryn Cladio says the carcasses they found in the swamps might be canteleres."

"Cantaleres!" the queen gasped. The mythical beasts were rumored to have three pairs of legs and mighty horns for spearing their prey. Serra shivered, remembering the bedtime stories that her handmaid Bini had read to her of the fields of slain rabbits left behind by their rampages. After the claren and the silver stag had proven real, most Lanserim had little doubt that other legendary creatures might be as well.

"Father, I'm thinking of asking Sielban for his interpretation." Janto regarded the king with a mixture of concern and impatience. "I can think of no other person in Lansera who has Madel's ear, if you have no ideas, and neither does the Order."

The king stirred. "You must not bother Sielban. His focus must be on the murat. It's a sacred calling, training our boys into men—he must not be distracted from his task."

Janto had slain the silver stag during his murat, an annual competition between young men on the remote island of Braven in the northern sound. The long-lived Sielban was Braven's sole year-round inhabitant. Janto, and many of the others who had been there, spoke of the Rasselerian with reverence. He argued, "But Sielban will have no task, for there will be no men to train if Lansera is in peril."

Vexation animated the king, and he rose half up in bed. "The Albrechts have never bothered Sielban for advisement. Do you think I have not been tempted? Son, you must have faith Madel will show you Her plans, as She has always done for me."

He grunted again, an anguished sound so unlike him, Janto rushed to his side. They all did, joining hands. The king deflated against his pillow. "Time's close."

"Don't say that," the queen tried, a useless sentiment. Serra breathed deeply, comforted by the familiar smell of the Meditlan cloves studding the necklace she wore. She prayed time might somehow be frozen and the king's words proven untrue, but she feared he was right.

"Madel hasn't seen fit to hide it from me," he continued. "That's why I'm not as concerned as you'd like about these supposed cantaleres, son. I know we are in Her hands."

He gestured for a drink, which the queen provided, pressing it to his lips. "She's given me a new vision."

Once before, during his own murat, Madel had granted the king a vision. He'd held onto it for four decades, dreaming of a better future for their peoples. Through the fulfillment of the silver stag prophecy and the Conjoining, that dream had come true.

Might this mean something bigger being asked of Serra, Janto, and Vesperi? That potential was part of why Serra didn't want to be tied down to anywhere or anyone. Dangers could arise at any moment, sacrifices be asked. *Is that why I broke it off with Lorne?*

A safe choice. Better to spare yourself that pain.

Serra agreed, accepting the thought as her own. It eased smoothly into the swirl of her emotions.

"Go on," Janto prodded his father. "Share it with us."

Serra rested her chin in her hand. The king struggled to raise himself higher on his pillows, so Ser Allyn gave him an extra lift. Gray stubble grizzled the king's face. The queen tilted the water glass again to his lips.

"I saw a land covered in mist," he said. "The mist shifted over its surface liked smoke captured in a glass. The most brilliant colors flashed through it—shimmers from heaven, I thought. Purples and oranges and greens and every color in between, maybe even ones we have no name for."

Madel's realm. Hearing someone else describe how it looked was surprising—and surely a sign his vision was from Madel and not the ravings of a sick man, Serra hoped.

"I felt peace gazing at the mist's graceful movement in harmony with the land. But something grew beneath the mist and deepened into an abyss. It had been there all along, I think, blending in. This abyss drew the mist's colors into it, and as it did, those shimmers of heaven arced like lightning over the land. The life the abyss had consumed flashed from within it, and somehow, its darkness blinded me."

Could he be talking about the darkness she'd seen? Relief washed over Serra. Her burden might already be known to the king. He would know what to make of it.

"When I could see again, the mist was gone, and the colors and the abyss. I could see down into our world, recognize it as Lansera from our maps. The sight grieved me at first; its trees were barren, though no snow covered the ground. The world was ravaged worse than how the claren would have left it—"

Serra and Janto exchanged glances.

"—worse even than the plain of Orelyn before Turyn's Peace. At least the corpses left in that battle's bloody wake had offered proof that people had once been there."

The image was frightening—what could be worse than such carnage? During the Meduans' rebellion, a thousand warriors had died on that plain. To avoid any further loss of life, King Turyn, Dever's father, had brokered his peace and ceded the rebels the land east of the mountains to live how they wished, outside of Lansera's governance. And thus, Medua had come to exist.

King Dever continued, pale, but his fervor energized him. With her sight, Serra glimpsed the familiar electric blue of Madel's presence enveloping him like the mist he'd described. As always, it both awed and heartened her.

"As I scanned the land," he said, "silver sparks crackled over its surface. Not all in the same place, nor at the same time, but twinkling into existence and flaming strong. One at Mount Frelom, another at the Perch. More from the Lorvian riverlands to the Rasselerian huts. Even on the Deduin plains, though no ice was left to mark them as such. As the silver rays strengthened, they flowed together into one big light. I had to turn away from their brilliance.

"A hand graced my cheek, and I peered again at the world. Lansera and the colorful gossamer had been restored. My fear melted away. All was not lost. All would be as it was. Madel finds a way."

The king closed his eyes, and his smile conveyed his peacefulness. The blue glow subsided. But the vision had not calmed Serra's fears. If this was indeed a prophetic vision, and she had no reason to doubt it, then Lansera was under a great threat, one also affecting Madel's realm or why else the dark patches in her sight?

A threat that will bring a future not worth the living.

She did not want to think such dark thoughts. But a quick perusal of the others' countenances confirmed she was not alone in that reaction. She opened her mouth to share what she knew, but Janto first kneeled by his father's bedside and clasped the king's forted hands.

"Father, what do you make of this vision?"

The king did not stir. Queen Lexamy caressed his hair. "My love," she said gently, loathe to disturb him, "we do not understand this vision as you do. Can you share what Madel intended us to make of it?"

Serra wondered how it felt to love someone that deeply.

The king coughed as though woken from a nap, and his eyes fluttered open, one at a time.

"No?" he said, "I had thought its meaning obvious."

Serra gave a pained laugh. "I've learned, my king, that what the devout find obvious can sometimes take a while for the rest of us to understand. Some never do, I fear."

"Hm," he considered. "It was Madel's hand that touched my face. She was telling me not to fear what might come after my death. Life would go on, the country return to itself." He chuckled, "I have sometimes given myself too much credit for Lansera's prosperity. It is Madel who sees to that."

Perhaps. But Madel chooses Her servants well. Or at least Serra believed as much when she felt confident in her own abilities. That confidence had yet to be strong enough to send her back home to govern Meditlan. *Not that I want to.*

"But what of the mist and the colors, Father?" Janto asked. "And the silver? Is Vesperi to play a role in this future?"

Serra could hear Janto's yearning. Who else but Vesperi could the silver refer to? She possessed the flame.

"I have no doubt she will," the king answered. "Unless you think a queen holds so little sway over her people?" He gave his wife a peck. Then he poked Janto's side with more vigor than Serra had thought he still possessed. "Maybe the vision was to encourage *you* to bring your wife home. We don't need to interrupt Sielban's work to see the need for that."

Serra suppressed a scoff. Vesperi loved Janto, which was why she'd gone away, no doubt. The Meduans who wanted to be better people, to resist their ingrained behaviors and become more like the Lanserim, recognized that their impulses were sometimes best dealt with away from those they risked hurting. She'd seen Lorne do the same many times. *Is that why he hasn't tried to contact me?* That he'd yet to extend an olive branch had surprised her. Not that she'd accept it.

"I hope the vision comforts you, Father," Janto said. Serra prayed the king missed the pity those words conveyed. They were the words of a son who didn't accept his father's interpretation but believed

Madel capable of giving a dying man reassurance that those he left behind would be fine.

The king nodded, hands coming back to his chest. "And it will comfort you when needed. When things seem grim, know Madel has us in Her hand. She will bring balance again."

What sort of balance could there be without the king to lead them? *None.*

One syllable, yet the smooth, fluid voice that spoke it reverberated through her head. King Dever Albrecht was dying. Serra could imagine nothing darker lurking on the horizon than that.

CHAPTER TWO
Vesperi

Princess Vesperi Albrecht raised her right index finger high to Esye, the silver moon. She took solace in the moon's presence, the source of her silver flame. Esye's light wavered through the fog that rolled in from the northern sound. Cloudless days revealed Esye's boldness, the moon's power undulating in waves of pure energy. Overcast ones like this masked that power, made the moon appear soft and gauzy. Vesperi—the weapon, wielder of the silver flame, and mother of one brilliant, fiery, and *missing* daughter—knew womanhood sometimes demanded such subterfuge. And that she'd failed to find that balance within herself, or she wouldn't be here in far-flung Elston, staring down a line of thrushberry hedges.

At this distance, the bushes appeared harmless enough. They bore clumps of evergreen, rounded leaves in defiance of winter's freeze. Hidden thorns protected their purple berries, prized for ink. Vesperi recalled the first time Izmareld had pricked her finger on such a bush. Her daughter had screamed and screamed, and Vesperi's heart had almost stopped. But Izzy's hands had been covered in purple stains rather than blood.

Vesperi seized on the memory and how it had made her feel. How dare anything, even a shrubbery, harm her daughter? She reached into her core, cast her anger at Esye and received that anger back in the form of the flame. The certainty that when she flipped her palm, its silver power would be churning in her hand, ready for casting, soothed

Vesperi. Of late, nothing else could do the same. Her daughter had been missing for three hundred and twenty-two days. Izzy was five now, a whole birthday celebration she'd missed and so much else every day.

Seven months after Izzy had disappeared into the mangrove swamp bordering Wasyla and Rasseleria, the new life growing in Vesperi's womb went still. After another survey of the swamps, Janto had returned to Castle Callyn. Vesperi told him of the miscarriage, and his eyes filled with so much sorrow and tenderness, she could not bear to look at them. Not when he was responsible for Izzy's disappearance, so busy giving his fancy lords so much attention, he'd failed to notice his daughter run off into those dismal woods alone.

Vesperi released the silver flame with a finger jab, directed it at the hedges separating Elston Manor from the rugged, oh-so-quaint village that took its name.

A pleasant laugh, one might even call it tinkling, came from the manor's back porch. Lady Rufalyn called out, "What did my thrush-berries do to you, my princess?"

Her hostess's good humor only made Vesperi want to wreak more destruction. Oh, the stories Janto would hear if she did, of his wild, unstable Meduan wife blowing up half this cowpoke village. That he might cast her aside was honestly appealing. *How ironic a thought.* Once upon a time, Vesperi had wanted nothing more in this world than to rule her family's holdings as liege-lady. Now, she would someday be queen of a country exponentially greater than Sellwyn had ever been. And she might give it up because she couldn't tolerate her husband's presence.

"Come, I've found some more of Elston's old books in the base-ment. It's freezing out here." Lady Rufalyn was a beautiful woman whose laugh lines had deepened into a badge of elegance as she'd aged. But Vesperi hadn't come to her manor for company or even to "heal" in Elston's many hot spring baths, as Lady Rufalyn's invitation had suggested. She'd come to escape the absence of Izzy's laughter between Callyn's stone walls, the lack of her footfalls padding over the rug before climbing into bed with her parents.

Vesperi didn't reply. Instead, she burned a line of constrained silver fire into the hedge, singeing leaves and branches while leaving the bush intact. Its burst berries tinged the char lines deep purple.

Lady Rufalyn laughed again. "You have graced Elston Manor with a piece of royal art!"

Vesperi chuckled, too, at such ludicrousness. She charred an impression of a duckling's feathers into the hedge. "A royal gift that'll grow out by summer's end." Her silver flame, first used to murder her enemies and then to fumigate the claren, had become artistic. Even worse—therapeutic. But the silver flame was still a weapon, and she, *the* weapon.

A part of Vesperi had feared that power when she became a mother. This hobby of craftily burning bushes had been an escape, a way to redirect her temper when newborn Izzy would scream and cry, which morphed into roiling tantrums until well into toddlerhood. Vesperi had never been patient. Raising Izzy had given Vesperi the sparest ounce of compassion for her father, knowing she'd been far worse.

"Did you like ducks as a child?" Lady Rufalyn asked, taking a seat with a warm mug of something in her hand and a lush scarf of stained-glass crochet wrapped around her shoulders.

"As a child, I liked avoiding the leers of my father's guards and the kitchen he tried to banish me to." Vesperi had come to Elston, especially, to escape that younger version of herself, the one who'd dared to dream life could be better than it had been in Sellwyn. That it could be more than dodging blows dealt by the egos of men less worthy of power than she. Yet she'd trade her current life for that one in an instant, if it meant no more silence in Callyn's crowded halls.

"Come join me." Lady Rufalyn was tenacious. "I have tea."

"I don't want tea," Vesperi retorted, then teased, "If only it were hot chocolate." She'd been at Elston Manor for a month—long enough to know there were no chocolate stores in the pantry.

Though she'd admit it to no one, Lady Rufalyn's companionship did sound appealing. There were a few hours left to read, and Vesperi could make use of them. Many Lanserim histories were housed in the manor's collection, and she hoped to stumble upon something explaining Izzy's disappearance or hinting at ways to get her back again. If she'd learned nothing else from being the fulfillment of prophecy herself, it was this: answers could be found in books.

But Lady Rufalyn's eyes were those of a woman who understood, who had been through Vesperi's pain and come back to herself again, and not just because she'd been widowed. Some shared experiences didn't need to be spoken to be understood, and Vesperi tiptoed on the edges of grief and anger. If she leaned too hard into either, she'd be consumed.

Her last silver strike into the bush raised a tail feather high on the duckling's leafy body, about to waddle out for its first swim. A quaint country scene, but Vesperi knew innocence could be lost too soon at too high a cost. It had been the Meduan way, and she prayed that Izzy's disappearance had been from some other cause.

Her breath caught at the thought, though it had come to her many times before. She choked, emotion overcoming her careful control. Tears sprang from her eyes, which she wiped with the heavy sleeves of her cloak.

No, she would *not* be conversing with Lady Rufalyn right then. "I'm going to the temple," she shouted, her back already turned to her hostess. "Won't be gone long."

Chair legs scraped against the porch's cobblestones. "The books will be waiting, and dinner, on your return."

Lanserim courtesies had become enough ingrained in Vesperi that she remembered to grant Lady Rufalyn a "thank you" before continuing toward Elston's temple on the far side of town.

She marched through the biting winds until the temple's circular dome came into view. It rose higher than any other construction in the village of brick-built homes and shops. From the dome, a giant hand stretched skyward, painted in a vivid blue: Madel's hand, the goddess's symbol.

Vesperi had once scoffed at the idea of a female god. That had been before the claren, before she'd met Janto, and before her life had taken its impossible turn that proved Madel was real in every way the false god, Saeth, whom the advers had used to control the Meduan populace, was not.

Vesperi squinted; on the dome, a poor soul fought off the wind as he applied a new coat of paint to the hand. Just looking at him, chained by a rope to avoid being blown off, made her shiver.

As she reached the temple's entrance, the sun broke through a passing cloud and shone on a section of mural painted on the building's outer wall. She could have sworn it wasn't there the last time she'd visited. It featured the bird of creation with its three heads as outsized as Madel's hand on the dome. The bird was portrayed as outlandishly fat, probably couldn't fly a foot, though Vesperi had to admire how each feather had been painted a different color. Her topiary amusements had taught her that such detail required much patience.

She examined the mural more closely, a vain impulse she felt no guilt over. The bird spread its wings over a trio of symbolic images danc-ing near its feet. Janto's sigil, the silver stag, was drawn well enough, though its half-prance, half-leap in the air made for an entertaining pose. Vesperi was portrayed as a quartet of differently sized lightning bolts, though the real weapon could not fling multiple flames at once. But what made Vesperi laugh, guffaw even, was poor Serra painted as a pair of eyeballs, veins and all. They were fried worse than Izzy after a lemon cake spree.

"Do you like it, Princess?" A hopeful voice spoke from the temple's entrance. "Mer Werno finished it last evening. He's been working on it the past two days. He's our best painter, don't you think?"

Vesperi couldn't deny the painter's eye for anatomy—the bloodshot eyes made her fear they'd burst. But the irises were purple, not Serra's becoming green.

"He's made her into a Deduin," Vesperi answered the woman she'd come to see: Rynna Lourda, an old friend of Serra's.

Rynna Lourda's big, black eyes opened wide and embarrassment flamed her cheeks. "You're right! How did I miss that? And Mer Werno doesn't have time to fix it—he's to finish the hand's new coat, then head home to bring inside his fallowent bushes to protect them from this freeze. Oh dear." She clutched at Vesperi's arm. "Do you think Serra will mind terribly?"

A few years back, the prissy and self-righteous Lady Serrafina Gavenstone would have minded a lot. But chasing down a horrific pestilence and learning to live outside castle walls had done Serra a world of good—more than learning to live within them had done Vesperi, some might say. Never mind that both of them would sooner live among street rats than with the Deduins again, and their other-worldly irises and steady diet of salt-cured sheven flesh.

But Serra had more tact than that. "I'm sure she'll understand," Vesperi guessed, "if she comes this way before Mer Werno can fix it. I'll warn her about the rumors she was a Deduin this whole time." Vesperi winked, knowing the power of conspiratorial bonding.

Rynna Lourda exhaled a loud puff. "Oh good." She drew a gloved hand over her brow. Somehow, sweat droplets had managed to form, rather than freeze, in her pores. "Now, I suppose you'll be wanting more feed for those swans of yours?"

Vesperi nodded, a genuine smile on her face for the first time that day. What she enjoyed most in Elston was visiting a pair of swans that lived in a pond near the manor. She was glad they hadn't wintered in the warmer climes of Lake Ashra.

Her chest cinched. She ought to be headed back to warmer climes herself. But that would mean heading home to a castle full of courtesans that felt emptier than the casket she knew most of them believed Izzy would come home in, too, someday—a possibility Vesperi would not accept. Not even with her flame could she see how to burn a path forward through such vacant tundra. That future was barren as the Deduin ice plains.

Though she could take steps twice as long as Vesperi's, Rynna Lourda's plodding gait made her easy to follow. They crossed the temple floor that was covered in a mixture of prayer mats and wooden pews dark as marsh reeds. Vesperi glanced up at the dome's apex, where the glass allowed worshippers to gaze upon Madel's hand. She stifled a laugh; Mer Werno's flat bottom was splayed across it, his paint tray nearby. Were she a goddess, Vesperi would declare such a scene utmost blasphemy and revel in smiting him. Instead, she hurried off after Lourda, and decided not to mention the dome's need to be cleaned of smears. They entered a warm kitchen.

"Princess Vesperi!" Two ryns, working at the stove, stumbled over each other's greetings as they raised their elbows long and high. A spoon clattered to the floor. "May Madel's hand guide you."

"And you also," Vesperi returned, though she thought Madel's hand would be better served swatting Mer Werno's ass off Her temple dome.

One of the men hurried over with a bowl of oat gruel. Vesperi waved it away. "Oh, I couldn't." She'd had little appetite since Izzy's disappearance. Even less since early winter, when eating for two had ceased to be necessary.

"The princess is just here for her swans, boys," Lourda explained, ducking her head into the cellar. She said "princess" as though the word were imbued with glitter and spun sugar threads. Vesperi rolled her eyes, considered informing Lourda of the things this princess had done in Medua before the Conjoining, the least of which was murdering Serra's brother in her own bedroom—Vesperi doubted Serra had ever caught her friend up on *that* detail. But she held her tongue, because well, she rather liked the idea of sparkling. The flame did shimmer in her palm when she called on it.

She loosened the ties of her pouch, and Lourda scooped hulled millet into it from a burlap bag. Vesperi enjoyed the *shlssh* of the grain as it poured into the dark green velvet. The rynna added a pinch of infinitesimally small and black fallowent seeds and instructed Vesperi to shake them together.

"Even the birdies should get extra protection from the claren, just in case," Lourda declared, as she did every time they completed this ritual. Fallowent had been instrumental in the battle against the claren. Their hordes had an aversion to it, so a steady dietary supplement repelled them. Most everyone in Lansera had taken to eating a pinch a day, and growing fallowent bushes near entryways.

Vesperi did as instructed, though there'd been no reports of claren in at least two years. If there had been, she'd be among the first to know. *Mankind is done without me,* she mused, remembering a line from the silver stag prophecy that had made the importance of her weapon plain.

She tied the pouch with a bowline knot and gave it a tug to ensure it held. Sar Mertina would be proud to see how swiftly she'd done it. Mertina, a knight, had protected the royal family for a generation—and taught Vesperi how to tie knots.

"I must be going," Vesperi said. "I have more studying I'd like to get done before the dinner Lady Rufalyn has planned this evening."

Vesperi braced herself for the bone-crunching hug Lourda would direct her way. The hug came, Vesperi survived, and she bid the strange woman of endless smiles farewell for the afternoon.

Back on the road, Vesperi made quick work of the distance between the temple and the pond hidden in a grove of black-trunked trees. Croaking frogs quieted as she neared a small beach. She crouched down low and made a clicking sound with her tongue while shaking the millet in her pouch.

On a tiny island near the pond's western edge, a barrel-sized bush with oblong leaves rustled. One orange beak appeared through the foliage, easy to miss for an unexperienced eye. Another ducked out below the first's head—the female swan, white, though speckled with black dots. Vesperi fancied it recognized her as it pushed into the water with a slight splash. Its mate followed, his coat glistening as sunlit snow. He fluttered his wings to stretch them out.

The swans were majestic creatures. In part, she enjoyed their company because of the lucent demarcation of their relationship: the swans graced her with their presence in exchange for the free treats she provided. Vesperi welcomed such clear expectations, living among Lanserim whose ways so often mystified her.

The male swan comported itself with head held high and neck lengthened in full, except when lowered to eat her proffered food or twined with its mate for an afternoon swim. Swans were the Albrechts' family sigil. Droves of them took to the lakes and ponds that formed off the River Call in late spring.

This particular one reminded her of her father-in-law, the king. Such awe she'd felt the first time she'd met him. Vesperi had been in a prison cell then, for good reason. Yet the king had shown her concern and trust, and most of all, he'd shown her himself. King Dever Albrecht was a good man, a smart man. But above all, he was a man who believed in Madel and had dedicated his life to amplifying Her goodness. In his presence, Vesperi had first glimpsed a truth: that life wasn't meant to be an unending power struggle for survival, as the advers had taught. That it could be full of people loving each other and helping each other become better versions of themselves. He'd given her acceptance when her hopes that her own father might do the same had been irrevocably dashed.

A swan inspiring her the same was silly, of course. But when she caught sight of that bird and the sun reflecting from its wings, the dark cloud hovering always close by brightened a bit. Madel willing, one of these days it would dissipate entirely.

And what then? Return to the Albrechts and my husband? Vesperi gazed at the sky. Even muted by the fog, the moon Esye shined. *When I'm ready. If I ever am.*

It felt silly to bid birds adieu with elbows raised. Vesperi did it anyhow, once the cold had chilled her through her cloak. Spring was a still a month off, so that didn't take long. She would return to the piles of books at Elston Manor, seek a prophecy that might provide clues on how to bring home the heir to Lansera's throne.

"What does the mama snake say to the baby snake?" Vesperi used to ask Izzy, to calm her daughter down when a tantrum had gone so long, Vesperi feared she might, in a rage, lose her temper like Lord Sellwyn had with her. The Sellwyn family sigil was a viper, and they struck deadly fast. But Janto had taught Vesperi that sharp edges could be softened with patience and tenderness.

"Ssssnuggles, ssssnakelet!" her daughter would respond, crawling into her lap. Vesperi would run her hand through Izzy's tousled black curls to soothe her. When her child's breathing calmed into an inevitable sleep, even after all the abuse Vesperi had lived through, she marveled at the wonders Madel could create.

As the swans drifted off, Vesperi marveled instead at how much beauty remained in a world where such terrors existed. None had been worse than Izzy disappearing without a trace.

CHAPTER THREE

ESYE

Esye reclined in the morning sun. Her hips were round as an apple, her upper body narrow as its stem. Through the fronds of her favorite fern cluster, light speckled her pale, pale skin.

The cluster was Esye's favorite because she had counted each and every fern that grew up and faded away within it. The giant fern fans formed a nearly complete circle, their branches supporting each other, fronds interwoven. The perfect place for a nap.

Inside this den, Esye feasted on rays of color fluttering down. Some caught like feathers in the fern fronds; she pinched those with two fingers before slurping up their wiggly hues. Others danced an endless reverie, chasing each other on an unfelt wind.

The sky itself, once electric, had become a powdered blue of late. Esye tried not to think of it. A vibrant yellow ray burst on her tongue, sending girlish giggles rolling out of her. She loved how pure the color tasted, remembered how, not so long ago, the crunch of claren shells had polluted her sustenance. Her eyes flashed at the memory of their poison inside her, how the brutes' wings had sliced into her body and she'd itched and screamed and raged at their insolence. Each time her anger had surged against them had been a blessed release.

A shadow blocked the color rays and Esye shivered. If she dwelled too long on the claren, a new darkness might breed. But this shadow was a different sort of visitor, one she knew well. With fingertips that sparked silver, she stepped from the ferns into the brightness.

Esye beamed at the shadow. "Dear brother," she said, "it has been too long since we last spoke. You've kept yourself to the other horizon."

Her brother's human-shaped form shimmered into being. The shadow coalesced into a cape at his back, and a blackness dark as ink flowed in his veins. "Aren't you the one who's been keeping to herself?" Onsic said. "I've come from the others, and they mentioned your evening visits have ceased."

Esye tipped her head and searched her memories. Was he right, had it been a while since she'd visited Tansic and Oro? Time for the moons was sometimes a filament, hard to grasp or twist. And she'd needed to recover a long time after the claren, the weapon having used so much of Esye's essence to combat it. Maybe she'd been among these ferns, resting, for longer than she'd meant. "I am sorry if I have caused offense."

"Of course not," Onsic said. He sounded tired, and Esye wondered if he might be sick. The last time he'd fallen ill, Madel had filled him with Her breath and sent a storm of needles to heal his soul affliction. That had drained his darkness for a time, so it might be made pure again.

His finger wisped over her skin, imposing a line of his cold, dark universe onto it. "I'm just surprised you've been so indisposed. Are you weak? Have you felt . . . choleric?"

She peered into the minute galaxy he'd birthed on her wrist. The stars beckoned as she considered the question. After Madel called on her or one of her siblings to restore harmony, returning to full strength took time. She had thought herself healed, but maybe she'd been wrong. Maybe this time, she was the one with a deeper ailment.

Madel would take care of it. "I have felt fine. At least I think I have."

The cosmic impression he'd left faded once he broke the touch. "Oh, good. I am glad to hear it."

His expression, full of brittle worry lines arrayed like dried fern fronds, did not match his words. Was he humoring her? "It's just," he said, "some of the plants have been faltering. Have you seen the balance boughs?"

Esye loved tending those boughs, encouraging their delicate tendrils to latch up with others nearby. Once they formed a vine, the leaves and blossoms released color rays all their own, in constant waves sweet as honey.

"Not since . . ." Why, she couldn't say when she'd last pruned them back. "I will visit them tomorrow."

"And the jurgen nests," Onsic tittered. "I've come across so many mangled ones. That only happens when you're not at your best."

That couldn't be. She had sealed some of the jurgen nests just that morning, and they'd looked well protected. Jurgen eggshells were notoriously thin, and Esye formed metallic domes over the nests to hold heat within them. Reinforcing them, down by the riverbank, was one of her favorite daily tasks. "Madel would tell me if I'd gotten something wrong with the jurgens. She's fast to right our mistakes."

Her brother sighed, and the stars his form contained twinkled with less brilliance. "But Madel's not here is She? Or haven't you noticed?"

Esye raised her head heavenward. A suffocating sensation choked her—fear.

He was right, the sky had lightened to a glacial blue in just the last few minutes. The last time Esye had seen it that shade was back when the giants took their steps and Madel had withdrawn to allow it.

"But She'll be back, won't She?" Esye's stomach clenched.

"Will She?" Onsic's crescent twisted to a frown and his lips, glimmering with stars, hung heavy. "I wish I had your confidence." He drew something forth from his cape of shadows: a hardened brown hunk that wept with sap.

"This will help you remember your tasks better," he said, "until you're feeling yourself again. I made it from the calls of the rhini swinging in their trees and distilled them down with honey and agar. Break off a piece and suck on it until the clarity you seek returns."

Esye could not remember the last time Onsic had gifted her anything. He'd never been the most thoughtful of brothers. She plopped a portion of the lozenge into her mouth. As it dissolved, it dragged a rhini's hoot from her throat, which made Onsic laugh, a deep and filling sound.

"Thank you," she said.

He patted her shoulder and slipped away. With him went the last of the mark he'd pressed onto her arm. Where once had been a universe, there were now no stars, no life at all but her own pale radiance.

The faint blue of Madel's receding light gave her skin a sickly cast. Maybe that's why she'd felt something was off with Onsic. Without the sharpness that Madel's presence brought, many things appeared a different hue. Maybe Esye *had* overlooked some of those jurgen nests. Something was affecting the celestial balance.

Esye could feel Onsic's lozenge working, though it left a nasty aftertaste, like oil gone rancid. She vowed to check on the jurgen nests right away, and the balance boughs, too. Those plants were even harder to breed, should anything upset them.

A gloomy feeling settled over her as she replayed Onsic's words, and she withdrew into the ferns. Maybe she should remain here awhile longer, until it passed. *If* it passed.

She plopped another lozenge fragment in her mouth and lay back against the grass. The evergreen fern fronds closest to her had noticeably dry tips. Another problem she'd overlooked? She shriveled in on herself, tugged a blanket of woven feathers over her head. Perhaps she would not leave today at all, not while she felt like this.

The cold vanes of the blanket's feathers touched her skin, and she wondered, did feathers know the exact moment when their maker discarded them?

Looking up at fading blue sky, Esye did.

CHAPTER FOUR
JANTO

In the far western corner of Castle Callyn, in a courtyard full of people, a shadow undulated. Prince Janto Albrecht, who'd seen a great many strange things, could not look away. Near the shadow, Eddy, master of horse, taught a group of young folks from the city how to inspect horseshoes. From the center well, kitchen servants drew water for the midday meal's cooking. Sar Mertina, one of the Albrechts' longest-serving guards, stood at Janto's elbow, waiting for his command. Her long braid had aged to a palomino twist of black and gray.

None of them reacted in the slightest to the shadow's flickering dark waves. So Janto shook his head to clear his vision. *It's nothing. Just the worry catching up with me.* Indeed, nothing was there when his gaze returned to the spot. Maybe it'd been a manifestation of his guilt—one word spoken from Janto to Mertina would mean a disruption to everyone's day. But he needed the distraction, and his bow arm itched.

Sar Mertina carried out his order, clearing the courtyard of its occupants. If Vesperi were here, perhaps angry sex with his wife would have sufficed—Vesperi was always delighted by the invitation. It had taken Janto time to grow comfortable with that. He hadn't wanted to be yet another man she bedded because she had to, no matter how much pleasure she feigned from it. They'd talked, and she'd singed not a few pillows and bedsheets. Eventually, he'd understood that she'd reclaimed sex for herself and viewed the pleasure it could bring as a gift when the rest of the world demanded too much. He trusted her word that she loved it. He certainly did.

But she wasn't there. So Janto retrieved his bow, the Old Girl, from his quarters and stepped into the courtyard for fresh air and a fresh round of target practice. His friend and advisor, Ser Napeler of Wasyla, waited against the courtyard's stone well. Despite the wintry weather, Nap had stripped off his cloak and changed into one of his rattier tunics. Of course, by Nap's standards, "ratty" was a loose thread or two.

"I thought you could use a challenger," Nap said, wrapping his flaxen hair into a bun. He spent a good two hours a day at exercise, whether training with army recruits or running back and forth from the city. Janto had half a mind to make Nap an army commander some-day, but he wanted his friend nearby rather than traveling to inspect battlements or lead forays against the raiding parties of Meduans who refused to leave violence behind. Nap wasn't the strongest strategist, but he had plentiful common sense, and a plainspoken manner Janto admired.

Janto had wanted to shoot targets by himself, loosing arrows fast as he could string them and maybe his worries with them. But Nap was right, what he needed was a friend's company, and Serra was no good with bows. "You? A challenge? Maybe six years ago on Braven . . ."

Nap chuckled as he kicked off the stone ring. They'd met during their murat, where archery had been one of many feats in which the chosen men competed. Janto's father held the record for archery targets hit.

He glanced at the king's quarters, but its curtains were drawn. Perhaps the sound of their efforts might rally his father for another day. Janto would not give up hope that something would. He didn't want to become king like this, not after having lost his daughter, and maybe his wife. His father, too?

He shook his head. "Let's shoot."

Nap retrieved his bow from the wall by the stairwell to the king's study. Its polished shine showed off its deep cherry-red coloring. Green veins ran through it, the markings of kratomwood.

Though it was much taller, the Old Girl was far less showy of a bow. It had been loaned to Janto by Hamsyn, another of their murat mates. Janto had used it to slay the silver stag, enough of an accom-plishment to earn the Old Girl a lifetime of reverence. Hamsyn did not have the same luxury. He'd died, trapped by the advers in a room full of claren on the day their little band had assaulted Mandat Hall and fulfilled the prophecy.

The Old Girl meant a lot, and she was a very fine weapon. Nap, with his wide chest and strong abdominal muscles, would match her better. But Janto was nearly a foot taller than his friend, so he reasoned things worked out.

They stood about four feet apart with two targets placed against the kitchen's back wall, a good twenty yards away. The high windows there let out heat, and an arrow was not apt to stray that far. The targets—Janto laughed. "Silver stags? Really?"

Two matching scarecrows had been stuffed with straw and painted gray. Out of each head sprung thick branches covered in dead leaves. They were a far cry from the stag's majesty, especially that antler attempt. The stag's real ones sprang from its head like an elaborate candelabra, nearly fifty tines pointing straight ahead.

"Well, you thrashed those koparin dummies near to pieces." Nap grinned, pleased with himself, which gave Janto hope his friend might grow a sense of humor yet. "Had to pick something else."

He raised a brow, daring Janto to argue otherwise. But Janto *had* shredded those cute straw critters with glee. He knew how dangerous real koparin could be, having spent summers hunting them on the plain of Orelyn with his father. The ruthless wild cats lived among the ruins of Janto's great-great-grandmother Drustalla's summer palace near the foothills.

"Let's begin?" Janto raised an eyebrow, and Nap strung his first arrow in answer. He released it with a twang that woke Janto's senses. A hit, but above the eye rather than centered on the scarecrow target's forehead. Janto strung his own arrow in answer. He took a deep breath, steadied his arm, released his finger . . .

. . . and stumbled back from the force of the bowstring's release. Luckily, his head hit a patch of the cold, hard dirt rather than the stone path.

"Are you all right, my prince?" Nap extended a hand. *Lanserim always help their enemies to their feet.*

Janto's ears rang, but that would soon pass. He took Nap's hand and examined the target. The arrow had bounced off the stone wall and landed on its back. "I had Ser Irven restring the Old Girl," he explained, "and I forgot to check for tautness. I'll do better next round."

Such a stupid oversight. Sometimes it seemed he'd never stop making such mistakes. What sort of king would he be then? Not the sort his people deserved.

String and release.

Janto wished decisions came easy for him like they did for the king. Part of him wanted to insist Sielban be consulted about the rhyme Ryn Cladio had discovered, and those carcasses in the marshlands. Another part worried some of the remains might be Izzy's.

String and release.

He did better on the next round. Arrow after arrow landed right where he intended. Nap kept up, circling the bullseye a few times until he began to split arrows. Then Janto blinked—another shadow wavered overhead, just above the targets. Steel glints reflected off it like moonslight over a lake. His skin grew cold despite his long sleeves.

Another blink, and the illusion disappeared. *That's what I get for hitting my head.* Janto took stock of his aching arms, and how his fingers reverberated from the constant bow release. His calluses had lost a few layers of skin. "What's the score, challenger?"

"Ten bullseyes to twelve," Nap declared. "Sure you want to leave it there?"

"I'm sure I don't want to give you the chance to catch up." Janto clapped his friend's back. "And I'm sure I want a nice warm mug of mulled wine." *And to use my clearing head to figure out who else to consult about Ryn Cladio's message.*

Nap grunted his assent. He wasn't one for exclaiming over food and drink but partook, nonetheless.

They found Janto's other old girl—Serra would chide him for such a nickname—sipping from a mug in the kitchen. She welcomed them with a quick elbow raise. Nap's eyes widened as he took in her presence.

"Lady Serra, I didn't know you were here." He raised his elbows rapidly. He'd been part of their hunting party that had destroyed Mandat Hall, so he knew her well, but he'd never been comfortable around women.

Serra laughed as she pulled him into a hug rather than let his courtesy suffice as greeting. She stood a few inches taller than Nap, but disappeared in his bulky, muscled arms. "It's good to see you. I rest better knowing you're here to help Janto with his duties."

"It's an honor." Nap raised his elbows again.

"So's having you in my service, Nap," Janto said, as he had many times before. Loyalty was another quality Nap had in spades. It was eerie, sometimes, how like Ser Allyn he was, and how Janto hadn't realized it until Nap came to Callyn to serve as his right hand.

Janto removed his cloak on which the stag had been embroidered in pounded silver threads. Nap went to the fire to warm his tanned skin. Serra looked beautiful, as she always did. Seeing her here in Callyn, Janto was reminded of the girl he'd grown up with rather than the woman she'd become. Maybe that was just the finery she'd changed into. Metallic threads of dark gray levere adorned her skirt overlay. The Meduans had mined a levere vein in Durn for a few decades, discovered during the divide between their lands. The metal resisted Vesperi's flame. If struck with one of her bolts, it reflected the magic right back.

Serra patted a seat beside her, commanding, "You too," when Nap hesitated to join them at the high counter.

Mar Jeffyr, the head cook, filled their cups with mulled wine and her hearty smile, and Janto realized something else. He hadn't expected Serra in Callyn anymore than Nap had. Her presence during this time of crisis felt natural, but she couldn't have known how sick the king was. With the Meduans' reintegration into Lanserim society so fragile, the king had made sure no news of his illness had spread. If the people knew how serious things were, his father reasoned, some of the more reticent Meduans might not be so cooperative. Or some of the Lanserim, either, who'd held their peace to honor the one he'd dreamed of for their reunited country.

"What did you come here for anyhow, Serra?" Janto said. "I didn't think to ask earlier."

She startled, as though woken from a dream, and he supposed it might be like that, coming home to Callyn to discover the king's condition. "Sorry, my sight slipped on right then. For a moment, I thought I glimpsed a fissure right here in the kitchen."

The shadow? It had been right on the other side of that wall. Fast as a reflex, Janto scanned the space, though he wouldn't be able to see a fissure if one were there. Only Serra could see those rifts between Lansera and Madel's realm, portals the claren had used to seep into their world. But could it be a coincidence that he'd also seen something in the same area?

Serra gripped her mug with white knuckles. She whispered, "It's dark, different than they usually are. More of a pucker than a portal."

She pointed to a shelf full of sparkling clean pots and pans above the sink where Mar Jeffyr washed dishes. Other cooks assembled sandwiches nearby—a cold lunch that was Janto's fault for choosing target practice over their chores.

"It's gone now." Her face scrunched up with confusion. "I must have imagined it."

The thought of that shadow raised Janto's arm hairs. But why? A shadow was hardly out of the ordinary, so why did this one seem remarkable? *What isn't these days*, his mind supplied. Janto wanted his wife at his side, but she wasn't there. He wanted his daughter, to know she was alive and well and to teach her to string her own bow. He wanted his father to not be dying. And he didn't want to deal with the mystery Ryn Cladio had reported.

He didn't realize he was crying until Serra wiped tears from his face with her gray handkerchief. Her family's sigil, grape leaves, was embroidered on it in pressed gold thread.

"What would you have said to your parents," he asked her, "if you'd had the chance?" Lord and Lady Gavenstone had drowned when she was eight, and Serra had moved to Callyn and away from her brother, honoring their last wishes, shortly after.

Serra tilted her chin up. A faraway look grew in her eyes, similar to her expression when using the sight, but less focused. "I don't know that I understood death then. Maybe I'd have told them I loved them. That's what I would tell Agler, if I could."

Her brother, Agler Gavenstone, had been murdered six years ago by Vesperi. Sometimes, how that reprehensible act had started all three toward their shared destiny, was still unbelievable. *Remarkable, even.*

A knock came from outside one of the kitchen's open doors. Ser Allyn slipped in, his features forlorn, his wispy, gray-brown hair a mess. "It's time," he said gently.

Panic descended, a pulse in Janto's temple that tremored through his limbs. Serra gave him a brave smile and offered her hand. He wrested courage out of that familiar touch as Ser Allyn led them back to his parents' quarters. Nap trailed behind, thrumming with a nervous energy that neither Janto, nor his family, needed.

"Go on," he bid his friend. "Get some lunch, get the courtyard open again. I'll call you when I need you."

Nap raised his elbows, relief evident as his stance relaxed. He was a great friend, but not everyone was suited for moments like this.

Each step was a dreaded one toward Janto's reign as king of a reunited Lansera. He wasn't ready.

Once they entered the bedchamber, Janto wasn't bothered by any of that. His father still breathed, though coughs wracked his body. His mother lay beside her husband, head resting on his chest.

The king reached for his son with his free hand, and Janto stepped close, Serra's hand clenched in his other.

"Father," he croaked. "I love you."

"I love you too, son." The king smiled, and Janto swore a radiant blue light pooled in his irises, normally the same amber as Janto's own.

The king covered Janto and Serra's held hands. "And you, daughter."

Serra was crying. "I love you, too."

He blinked slowly, his hand and head shaking with the effort of speech. He had clearly deteriorated over the past two hours Janto had left his parents alone.

"Tell that irascible wife of yours that I love her also," the king managed. "Vesperi needs to hear it; it's the only way she'll believe it. And you know my new vision—you know how important she is to it."

Janto gulped and nodded, but his father wasn't done yet. His eyes peered deep, his voice as firm and steady as it had been before this illness.

"And tell her the flame must fly to be found again."

The words struck a chord within Janto, like the verses of the silver stag prophecy once he'd realized they were more than a nursery rhyme. His father's smile gave Janto hope—not for recovery, but that his worries would work out in the end. For him and Vesperi. For their family. For Lansera, too.

His mother gasped, and his father's body slumped against the cushions.

He was gone. His father was gone.

Queen Lexamy draped herself over her husband of thirty years and sobbed. Janto knew no one tougher than his mother, but he also knew she wasn't prepared for this. No one ever was. Janto knew that too, sure as his daughter's room remained undisturbed since the fateful morning they'd left on caravan to Rasseleria ten months ago. Maybe his father would take care of Izzy now—no, Vesperi would smite him out of existence for such a thought.

Serra gripped his hand and took deep breaths. Ser Allyn lowered himself into a chair by the bed and lowered his head, too. His body shook as he cried. Seeing his father's oldest friend overcome, a figure who'd been as steadfast as anyone in his life, Janto realized action needed to be taken.

In that moment, Janto Albrecht became king.

He made a mental note to have Allyn's daughter and wife be brought up from their home in the city to comfort the advisor. He made another that his mother was to be left alone as long as she needed in this room. Not until the embalmers insisted otherwise would he consider asking her to move. Then he left his loved ones, crossed the hall, and entered his own bedchamber to see to the tasks at hand.

A knock came at the inner door to the bedroom chamber, the one opening into a corridor between the castle proper and its outer wall. The passage wasn't secret, per se, but it was an additional route of egress should a siege be launched against Castle Callyn. The corridor was also used by the family for passing into each other's quarters outside the prying eyes of castle staff. Izzy had run down it many times to sneak into bed with her parents.

The knock came again, and a desperate hope surged in Janto's veins, though it had been so long since he'd felt anything resembling it regarding his daughter's disappearance. He swung the door in, and . . .

. . . found Pic, a serving boy of fourteen whom Janto had known his whole life. Janto schooled his features, though he could not keep a flush of disappointment from his face.

Pic shriveled, deepening his pockmarks. "I'm s-sorry, Janto . . . P-Prince Janto. I didn't mean—"

Janto rescued him with a well-practiced muss of his chestnut hair. The boy had grown up in Callyn—he'd likely been traveling the passage since he could crawl. "What is it, Pic?"

"I j-just wanted to see if you needed anything. If I could bring something for your father, or—"

He didn't know yet. Neither did the realm. Janto focused his thoughts again. "Tell Mer Olen to ready forty pigeons for travel tonight."

The lad's eyelids fluttered fast, realizing what Janto's order meant.

Janto gave him a calming clap on the shoulder. "Then bring forty sheets of parchment here."

Pic nodded. "May I?" he queried toward the room's proper door.

Janto granted him access, and the boy sped off to the aerie. Each bird would likewise speed Janto's message to Lansera's manor houses and town councils, along with a funeral invitation. He'd send one to Elston with a head start; Vesperi ought to know what had happened before anyone else. Janto spared himself some hope it would bring her back, but other tasks took precedence over worrying about their relationship now.

He needed Serra. So he returned to his father's bedroom and kissed his mother's cheek, where she remained on the bed beside his father, who was dead. His father, who was dead. Janto stroked the still-warm brow, a caress he never would have made were he alive. Then he asked Serra to please come with him.

Nap waited outside his quarters, having carried out Janto's earlier commands. Janto invited him in. Serra opened the curtain near the bed and stirred up dust devils on Vesperi's trunk. She'd always preferred the light.

"My father has died," Janto said. Strangely, the words didn't catch on his tongue.

Nap bowed while raising his elbows. "Janto, my sincerest condolences."

"See, you *can* say my name," Janto kidded, accustomed to giving Nap a hard time for his formality. "A hug would do."

The request caught Nap off guard, but he held his arms out. Janto eased into them and appreciated the back clap Nap improvised.

Serra sniffled close by. "Can I get one of those too?"

Janto soaked up his friends' comfort for a moment, tried not to think of how he wished Vesperi were here to hold him in their stead. "I'll miss you both in the coming weeks," he said, moving to the window. Hills rolled west from the castle and continued on to the Mount, where he'd bury his father in the tombs built into its hillside. How long would it take for the funeral guests to arrive? A week?

Serra's tone was questioning. "I'm staying through the funeral, of course. You need me."

He did, but that didn't matter. Serra would understand. They hadn't been raised to put themselves first. "You heard what Father said yesterday." Janto watched the sky, wondered what other signs he might be missing. "We need to learn more about his vision and Ryn Cladio's old chant. And we need to do it without alarming our people, which means I need *you* to share it with someone who can help."

"Surely it can wait." Serra spoke at a higher pitch. If he looked, he'd bet she was crossing her arms.

"Can it?" He spun around. "Are you not seeing 'shimmers from heaven' as my father described them?" The potential fissure in the kitchen qualified, he guessed.

That quieted her. "Since when did you get so good at deciphering prophecy?"

"Since it became my responsibility." Janto waited until she lowered her arms before continuing. "You know I'd rather you were here. But you, of all people, also know how important it is we heed that vision and act before there *is* a threat. We must get ahead of this, not wait until another swarm of claren manifests. Or something worse. I need you to make that clear to Jerusho."

Lead Councilman Jerusho of Mova, another of Janto's murat friends, was more known for his smarts than his swordsmanship. Not Janto's first choice for discernment, but his father had been adamant Sielban not be disturbed. Outside of the Order, Jerusho was the most devout person Janto knew. He'd encouraged Janto to hunt the silver stag, right after catching the granfaylon himself, a legendary fish rumored to be paper-thin and translucent. Believing Madel wanted him to, Jerusho had gone to the murat to prove it real, and had hoisted the great fish from Braven's streams.

"Jerusho!" Nap yelped the name, though he swiftly schooled his features back into his practiced, attentive stance. "I mean, of course, as you wish."

Janto chuckled. Jerusho and Nap couldn't be more different. Nap was a true believer in his own discipline, and Jerusho, in things unseen. "No man I know, except perhaps Ryn Cladio, has a better understanding of Madel's precepts and the old prophecies. Nap, you remember his stories around the campfire about the ones his dear ryn shared with him? And the Order has had no luck so far."

"Sielban—" Serra started.

"—is off the table," Janto finished. "I will not betray one of my father's last wishes." The decision didn't sit well with him, but perhaps that was the grief bubbling out of his chest. Besides, who was Janto to second guess his father's wisdom, especially now?

That's right, listen to your father.

The voice came so close to his ear, it could have been his own. Janto looked up to find a shadow in the corner of the room.

"Do you see that?" he prodded Serra.

She wasn't listening, her arms crossed again, obviously displeased with his command. "I don't get to bury him? People who don't even know him will be coming to pay their respects, and you are denying me that?"

Janto was sorry he'd put that hurt in her haughty tone. Maybe it wasn't the right choice, but it was the only one he had. Ignoring the shadow for now, he said, "I trust you alone to do this for me, Serra."

She curtsied, elbows raised. "For my *king*, anything."

The words stung. "Please don't ever say that again," he complained, though Serra recognized it as more of a plea. She knew him too well.

"You must get used to it," she said. "You are the king now, Janto." Her voice softened, new tears springing from her eyes.

"Nap," Janto addressed his right-hand man, "Serra will need your assistance. She should not travel alone to Mova with those vandal bands about. And Madel knows, Jerusho will need your protection on the way back."

Nap nodded his assent while Serra gasped, "Vandals! I thought those troubles had died down after the Wasylim offered to teach them how to weave?"

"They have," Janto confirmed. That maneuver was one of the last brilliant things his father had pulled off, teaching new skills to some of the Meduan immigrants who'd depended on robbery and threats in the past. Yet caution was reasonable for dealing with people who'd endured what they had. Not all Meduans were satisfied simply because they no longer had to grovel for their subsistence. "I'm not willing to risk you regardless."

Serra gave him another hug. Her head tilted as an idea struck. "May I stop by Terella's glasshouses on the way? I'm always interested in what she's researching. If something's brewing, she might know, in the way she did with the fallowent."

Janto nodded. Terella was the fallen Hamsyn's sister and an expert botanist at eighteen. She'd discovered fallowent's usefulness in repelling claren. "But don't stay for long. This is pressing."

"I know." Serra squeezed his hand. "I'll share Ryn Cladio's prophecy and the vision with Jerusho, then send him your way. We'll leave on the morrow?"

Janto agreed, and his friends made to leave, granting him space to grieve, though Janto knew he'd return to his mother as soon as he could. "Nap, would you check on the scribes, please? They should be headed here."

Nap tipped his head and hurried into the hall.

Janto caught Serra's arm, having forgotten something important she needed to know.

"What is it?" She looked spooked and worn down and he regretted adding anything to her plate. But the day his father died did not allow for such considerations. Not when it was also the day Janto ascended the throne.

"Lorne is there, in Mova." The Meduan playboy had been essential in helping the hunting party—they may not have succeeded without him. Janto did not always enjoy his company, a lingering jealousy perhaps of anyone Serra took up with. But he trusted the man and had been surprised to hear news of their breakup from Jerusho of all people, who'd been "soothing the battered soul" per his last letter.

Serra's face paled, and she peered at the rug-covered floor. "It doesn't matter."

"It does." Serra had seemed happy, finally, the last time Janto had seen them together. But Lorne was Meduan, and Janto knew what it could be like, loving a Meduan. "I'm sorry. I wouldn't ask it if I saw another way."

Serra nodded. "Thank you for the warning."

And because he couldn't bear to have his oldest and dearest friend in the world mad and sad at the same time, he embraced her again, and Serra laughed and they both cried and laughed until the scribes arrived.

Then King Janto Albrecht carried out his first official duty: dictating the news of his father's death. After the scribes left, he felt a void in the room.

From a forgotten shadow, a king-sized specter grew.

"Listen to your father," it said, billowing like a sheet of pressed metal in decay.

"You are not my father," Janto argued.

"But I am what's left of him."

Despite his instincts screaming no, Janto wished it were true.

CHAPTER FIVE
VESPERI

Elston was home to over twenty hot springs, each with a stone bathhouse built around it. Every dawn, Vesperi sought a different one out, having no desire for the populace to become too familiar with her body. After an adolescence in which she'd had to share it with others to survive, she only granted Janto the privilege now. To have that choice was exhilarating.

Moonslight filtered through the fog as Vesperi walked the swept road through Elston. Tansic's copper and Oro's gold commingled, with Esye's silver a ways off. Onsic hung full and round in the sky, a gaping black disc that gave off no light of its own, though it had a blue halo. Rather, when the others strayed close, Onsic appeared to swallow their radiance. The trick of the eye had always given Vesperi the creeps, like so many of the men she'd grown up with who took and took and didn't give back.

By the time she reached the bathhouse, Vesperi's skin was cold to the touch beneath her layers of fabric. She strode to the dressing room, bidding the attendant silent with a finger to her lips. Once unclothed, Vesperi opened the heavy door to the women's spring. Two townspeople bathed within its waters. She *could* demand the attendant cordon off a private portion for her use, but Vesperi did not wish to add to her reputation. Being feared and despised had been currency in Medua, but in Lansera, such behavior only offered more reasons to fight with her husband. More reason to be here in Elston, rather than home with Janto, and she already had enough of those.

The women averted their eyes as she entered, continuing their conversation. Obviously, they found little of interest in Vesperi's form, which simultaneously delighted and annoyed her.

One woman, short, and with skin as wan as Vesperi's had grown in Elston, remarked to her friend, "Can you believe Old Feron, going on about a jurgen he claims ruined his winter greens?"

The women chuckled, scoffing at the notion of a jurgen on the loose. But Vesperi knew a thing or two about the likelihood of mythical beasts gallivanting about. Jurgens, with their squat, scaly bodies that hugged the ground and their wide, spiked tails, could easily batter down a farmer's gate. They'd done just that in an old tome of fairy tales she'd read back at the manor house.

The water's heat pricked Vesperi's body like a barool's spike. She'd had the displeasure of stepping on barool worms many times in her journeys over the mountains. Within seconds, the pain morphed into the gentler thrum of massage. She reached for a sand bar to remove dry skin.

The second woman wrapped her long hair into a loose bun. "Imagine blaming some squirrels on a jurgen! Does Feron think he's the prince, that the silver stag will come prancing out of the forest for him to spear? Menfolk."

Vesperi hid a grin. She'd have to remember to tell Janto about this conversation. If she ever returned home, that was.

The first woman's eyes glinted. "At least Feron's younger brother still has his wits. Think he'll come by your house again, with that persimmon wine from Meditlan?"

"Oh hush," the second replied. "Don't know as I'd let him. With a brother half-mad?"

Vesperi knew a thing or two about brothers like that. Though her own, Uzziel, was merely rotten, not dull-witted. Their father, Lord Jahnas Sellwyn, had always spoiled him despite his wasting illness. Others in Medua would have killed Uzziel for that weakness, but Lord Sellwyn had drenched the boy with sentiment, something Vesperi never received despite her worthiness. Lacking that familial warmth, how could she have known losing a child would ache with such fierceness, that her flame could not rival it for destructiveness?

She grimaced with fleeting shame at having abandoned Uzziel years ago, when Lorne Granich had brought the child to his father's holdings in Lorvia after Sellwyn Manor had been ravaged by the claren. But the little cretin would no doubt do the same in her shoes—*was* doing the same. Uzziel had sent her no correspondence. And Vesperi had been busy living her new life in a new country where she was prized for her strength of will and what her powers could do, instead of her curves and the flesh between her legs.

But how had that new life turned out? Without Izzy, she lived a nightmare, not the dream she'd let herself believe she could have.

She rose from the waters, skin soft as a newborn. She smelled like one's soiled clothes, too. Something must be done about the hot springs' odor, noxious as the craval ranches in Neville. If they found a way to mask the scent, perhaps Elston would grow to be more than a hovel.

The two women bid her adieu with a "May Madel's hand guide you." Vesperi repeated the courtesy as she'd been trained, though she didn't understand why Lanserim dropped kindness around as though an infinite resource. She moved into one of the small, wooden rooms built next to the spring. Bergamot and sandalwood-scented steam enveloped her. Periodically, the bathhouse workers poured water over hot stones kept in a brazier that fed into four separate rooms.

Vesperi had figured out that reciting the silver stag prophecy twice took about as long as she could endure the sauna's heat.

When the silver stag runs free,
blessed will he who binds it be.
Rise up, ye treasured bird of three.
Wing him what boons ye foresee.

When evil spawns and overruns,
from silver the weapon comes.
Without her sight, mankind is done.
With it, all will again be one.

The awe she'd felt at being part of that prophecy had long since dulled. Reciting it now was a calming mechanism. Once finished, she headed to the dressing room, glad to find herself alone. She pulled on her thick, woolen pants and tucked a shirt of the same fabric into them. Then she made quick work of buttoning her boots, having spent many years tending to such needs for Uzziel. Over her shoulders went her green velvet cloak, the surest giveaway that she *was* Princess Vesperi Albrecht, if anyone cared to look. On it, tail feathers lined a swan, each a different color so they formed a rainbow against her back. The feathers' colors reminded her of the king's cloak, though his was of the three-headed bird itself.

Vesperi nodded at a new clerk as she exited. His eyes lit up at the sight of her cloak, and he raised his elbows. Outside, her breath puffed in white clouds she feared might freeze. She didn't like the cold, but Izmareld had loved it. That was part of the reason Vesperi had chosen Elston for this sojourn. Any chance to understand her daughter better, to connect with her in some way.

A cup of fresh hot cocoa waited for her on the desk she'd been using at Elston Manor. She sighed, unsure how much longer she could take the kindness with which Lady Rufalyn battered her, including special ordering chocolate for her stores. Her torrent of niceties tore at Vesperi's defenses. She decided not to drink the cocoa out of sheer stubbornness.

Then she imagined Izzy's disbelief, writ large in her reddish-brown eyes like her father's. *But it's chocolate, Mommy!*

"Fine," Vesperi said, defeated again by the mothering instinct that had so beguiled her at first. "Familial guilt wins."

She took a sip and sighed faster and more genuinely than she had during her last orgasm. Janto was no inadequate lover, but Madel's hand, the cocoa was good. And mixed with Yarowen jersey milk, a taste of home for Vesperi, from very far away. Yet another example of Lady Rufalyn going out of her way. Vesperi ought to thank her for them both.

She smothered that sentiment under an avalanche of velvety chocolate bliss and turned the next parchment page. Green ink made her eyes cross. They watered while she blinked, trying to read through the blur. It was her fifth day at this tome, a record of the festivals thrown in Lansera, beginning a hundred years ago. *Such a bore.* Vesperi fantasized about reducing the book to ashen memory with her flame, its prose more tedious than wiping Uzziel's slobber had ever been. More tedious, even, than maintaining her silence with Janto.

Vesperi loved the fool, she did, but Izzy shared his eyes and the freckles that peppered their faces. When she'd gaze on her husband at home, his face would melt away, be subsumed by hers. Then she'd remember that Janto was there when Izzy went missing, and that he didn't save her. In her heart, she knew it wasn't his fault, knew that his and Lord Sydley's party, all those *nice* and *kind* people from villages near the mangrove swamp, had searched day and night those first two months. None of it had helped.

Vesperi had been raised to view life as a battle. People prospered when they were smart, fast, and cruel enough to take what they wanted from someone else before that someone else could use it to hurt them back. Being surrounded by Lanserim, these people who loved and laughed and tried to be good—was wearying. Especially without Izzy tiptoeing down the hidden passage outside their bedroom, or clinging to her hip for hours at a time, something she'd once thought a fault.

For a time, knowing the new baby was coming, someone sweet and pure who had never known and would never know what Vesperi's life had been like, was enough. But after waking on that bed covered in blood, and dark tissue, and the body, oh, the body—

Vesperi tugged her shawl back up to cover her arms. She returned to the history of Lady Gella Xantas's raccoon festival. As she flipped the brittle parchment page, a corner of it arced with silver flame. Vesperi cursed, dropping the book to the ground. The flame extinguished, but the tome's binding split, scattering parchment like the feathers of a rufior, its constant beating of wings disturbed.

"I didn't do that," she said aloud, though there was no one to apologize to. At least no one in Elston. *Ryn Cladio will kill me when he learns the state of his book.* With kindness. *Even worse.* And she *hadn't* done it. The silver flame had flared to life without her calling it. A sudden pulse had released from her hand of its own free will.

She flipped her palm, and a firework of silver dust erupted, forming a crownlike ring, then went out. She felt nothing. Vesperi brought to mind the image of Esye, raised her hand to where she imagined the moon's light might trail into the room, were there a window, and—

Nothing. Not a fizzle of the silver flame. Vesperi shook her hand. Again, nothing. Panic compelled her out the door and into the street. The frigid air surged through her unsecured shawl, and she cursed with every step. Her hand stretched toward Esye, barely visible in the afternoon light. No stream of its power came to her, no silver energy as familiar to Vesperi as the feel of Janto's hand on her breast. She yelled, whether in grief or anger, she did not know.

"It's not right." Someone spoke, a child.

"Excuse me?" Vesperi spied a young boy piling rocks nearby. Did he know who she was? What she could do? Well, what she'd been able to do two minutes ago.

"The moons," he said. "Onsic is bigger than the others now." He went back to his pile, humming a tune under his breath.

Vesperi gasped. Dark Onsic hung high to the right of Elston Manor, far from where it had appeared earlier that day. Its corona made the blue sky around it pale and the void of light within it feel ominous. It dwarfed the other three moons, though they'd been the same size before. Esye hung in the east, but appeared dimmer by the second.

Vesperi felt cold. Someone screamed, others yelled, and Elston's cobblestoned roads filled with people gaping at the sky.

"What happened?" A merchant rolled his cart next to her, not noticing several sweet cream buns bounce off its wheels to the ground. A swarm of birds surrounded them.

So many feathered beasts in the world, Vesperi thought. But one was missing now, the male swan at the pond. Vesperi could feel it in her bones. A prayer fell from her lips in case she was wrong, and she ran that way to check. Not a bird stirred over the waters.

How could swans live this far north in winter, she'd wondered. Vesperi had her answer now—they could not.

The merchant placed a hand on her shoulder, must have followed her, concerned. She realized she was crying, shaking in a stranger's arms. Once before in her life, Vesperi had felt this thoroughly at sea, when she'd held her father's corpse, drained of all life and matter by the claren. Janto had been the one to rock her grief away, then.

"What happened?" the merchant asked again, this time of her rather than the heavens.

Vesperi's voice held steady, though she couldn't breathe. "The king is dead."

His eyes widened, and he glued them to the moons, unbelieving. Vesperi ducked out of his arms, her flesh numbed from the cold and the lack of flame within her palm. She had to go home—her real home. She had a husband to comfort, and a kingdom to support.

Vesperi prayed that Madel would help her be the person they needed, because she had no idea who she was on her own.

Her palm remained empty, not a flicker of magic on its surface.

CHAPTER SIX
SERRA

In a tavern in the Nevillim town of Tilayne, Serra tore one of her favorite shawls into mourning ribbons. She drank a dark ale she wished were wine. Moments earlier, a shouting match over a disagreement on who'd sat where almost went to fisticuffs. Ser Napeler had discreetly positioned himself inside the tavern, but the men came to their senses, raising elbows to each other before departing, though grumbling under their breaths.

People were on edge. Serra knew the feeling.

They don't even know what's coming yet.

She covered a gasp at the return of such thoughts. Her neck hairs raised as they had done in the presence of the Brotherhood, a band of ghosts that Madel had animated to see Her purposes through. Was the unfamiliar voice one of them? Or just the grimmest outcomes she could imagine given weight inside her head?

The foreboding she felt increased tenfold, though she would *not* let such darkness dominate her mood. When tearing mourning ribbons, however, it was hard not to. The last time she'd worn them was when their hunting party had arrived in this same town to tell the same young woman she was about to meet that her brother, Hamsyn, had died saving the kingdom. They'd had no body to bring with them; it had been consumed by fire after the claren consumed its innards. So Serra and her companions had brought their grief tied in ribbons around their arms.

The shawl was lace, easy enough to rip, though Serra started each strip with a small nick from the utility knife she carried. Her surgeon's knife was sharper, but she kept that in its own case to maintain its edge and avoid contamination, should her skills be needed. Mourning ribbons weren't meant to be pristine anyhow, much like the condition of their bearers.

Her mood was bleak as she recalled memories of King Dever. He had given her a good life, a family when she'd had none, and the preservation of her honor by pardoning her brother Agler of his attempted murder, and giving him a nobleman's rest in the Mount after his death.

His death at Vesperi's hands. A part of Serra would always add that coda when she thought of Agler, though she'd long chosen to blame the advers for the crime, and the cruel society they'd engendered, rather than the woman who'd committed it. Serra was a long way from the child who saw right and wrong so clearly when she'd wanted Vesperi's head.

Terella Norvyn entered the inn, her blonde hair graying prematurely, like her brother's had. It made her appear frailer than she was. Her gray eyes met Serra's over the tabletops and lowered pointedly at Serra's mug. Serra laughed and shook her head. The ale would last her half the evening. A few minutes later, Terella placed a glass tankard filled with a pickle-green beverage beside it.

"What's that?" Serra resisted sticking a finger down her throat.

"Something new the innkeeper has been brewing. She uses those pickled reed shoots the Rasselerians like so much."

Serra knew a thing or two about the digestive power of those reeds, which was why she kept a small jar of them in her pack in case someone swallowed something poisonous. She was glad she'd passed on the refill.

"Are you old enough to hold your liquor?" Serra teased the eighteen-year-old.

Terella smiled. "I snuck sips from Hamsyn's ale before I was ten. Ma swears that's why I've such a strong constitution." She took a sip and licked her lips.

With a *thrilch,* Serra tore another ribbon from her shawl.

"Would you like me to tie that for you?" Terella offered.

Serra extended her arm. "Thank you."

Terella's voice went quiet. "It's for the king, isn't it?"

There'd been plenty of time for a pigeon to carry the message to

Tilayne, but not enough that hearing someone else say it made it any easier to accept.

"Yes." Serra took a sip of her ale for solace. Spiced with clove, it tickled as it traveled down her throat. "Tomorrow, I'd like to stop by your glasshouses to resupply some of my stocks."

"Of course."

The subject was effectively changed, as intended. Serra wasn't ready to talk about the king's death, and Terella understood such reticence. Luckily, Serra was no longer famous enough that others in the tavern would have also guessed why she'd been tying the ribbons. The people would mourn their king as news spread, but such personal expressions were left to family and friends.

"I'm not sure if they'll be as potent as usual," Terella continued, speaking of the plants.

"What do you mean?" Serra took another sip.

"The moonslight."

Serra's brow furrowed. The change in the moonslight had made riding disconcerting the past two evenings since Onsic's form had enlarged. And silver Esye hadn't joined copper Tansic and golden Oro in the western sky, where it was due this time of year. As a result of the light shift, shadows cast seemed darker, and Serra had been glad of Nap's presence. With the king's death, and that portal unlike any others she'd seen in Callyn's kitchen, and the invading blackness in her sight . . .

All is lost, lost, never to return.

Or perhaps the cloud cover had just been strong. Serra would not give in to such hopelessness.

Terella leaned in close to whisper. "Some of the plants have developed strange black spots over the last two days. I fear the change is affecting their nutrient absorption. It's not the claren, is it? We've been shipping fallowent all the way to Thokketh, as I promised Prince Janto, and there's a thousand new seedlings growing in the glasshouses."

Not just the cloud cover, then. Serra shook her head. "I've seen no sign of claren." She had, of course, done a habitual sweep of the tavern before entering. "I think your fallowent has made our whole realm as abhorrent to the claren as water to a cat." If Madel were faithful, that would hold true. She sighed. "Are you sure there's more to Esye's dimming than bad weather?"

Terella nodded. "One of my aides thinks the moonslight change is setting the Meduan laborers on edge."

After two generations' worth of torment, some of the Meduans were like Terella's plants, their balance easily upset. Add the spreading knowledge of the king's death, and . . . Serra checked for listening ears before asking, "Have you had any raids?"

Terella rested her chin on her fist. "There was a crack in one of our glass panels one morning, the one facing south. A hammer hit might have made it, but so may have happenstance—a bird dropping a rock from its beak, perhaps. We keep our thorny plants there, which thieves are not so inclined to steal."

"If the thief knew how important soothprickler juice was, they might be," Serra mused. But not many folks had the time or inclination to learn herbology. Serra had barely scraped the surface of the study, and sometimes felt its application was its own form of magic, one easy to miss in day-to-day life.

What else are we missing? There had to be an explanation for the phenomena occurring in Lansera. The last time, it had lain with the Meduans' suffering, that they'd inflicted on each other and the Lanserim had overlooked. "What about the Meduans in your employ, Terella? Are you happy with them?"

"Quite." Her head nodded with enthusiasm. "Especially the ones who've come over from Durn. They tell us how hard they worked in the mines, day and night, yet had to scavenge for food in their fern forests. Can you imagine? Worked to skin and bone with nothing to show for it but a lord's full coffers?"

Serra had seen it. The claren hunts in those mines had been oppressive.

"They're amazingly patient and helpful," Terella continued. "Every once in a while, one sneaks back to bring me an extra cutting of peculiar plants."

"Sneaks back?" Serra leaned forward. "There is no ruling house left in Durn, just the family alone in their manor. Are they afraid of the Durnish councils? I can notify Janto—"

Terella pressed her hands. "I just meant they return here as soon as possible. Too many memories."

"Ah." Serra sunk into her seat. If returning was so bad, however, would those workers undertake the journey just to please their boss? Terella's blind faith in her Meduan workers might be misplaced.

Certainly, most of the immigrants had the best of intentions . . . and the worst of a foundation to build upon. If they interacted with the Meduans who'd chosen to stay on their lands, the ones who expressed chagrin over their malfeasance when a royal delegation visited but reverted as soon as they left . . .

Some people are incapable of reform. Better to cast them away. Like Lorne.

Serra had never had such a thought. Certainly, she and Lorne were incompatible. But to cast him away? Or the other Meduans who tried so hard to learn? She used the sight again, to check if anything might be amiss and making her think such things, but the tavern was perfectly normal, minus the lack of silver in its hues.

Or you've just placed more trust in the Meduans than you should.

Like cold fingers to the neck, the idea shocked her senses, but she couldn't deny the potential. Perhaps her better sense was weighing in, giving voice to ugly truths. She whispered, "Don't you worry about them, that they might stab you in the back?"

"And grind up my bones to feed the giants?" Terella rolled her eyes like the teenager she was. It was easy to forget. "Is that why you won't get back together with that riverland man of yours?" she teased. "Has he threatened to chop you up for bits? Or perhaps the weapon did herself? I hear our new queen can be quite dangerous."

"That was unfair of me." Serra's cheeks flamed, some of it due to Terella's admonishment and some to the reminder, yet again, of the king's death. She had difficulty picturing Vesperi presiding with Janto in the throne room over feasts or court sessions, when she returned to Callyn. *If she returns.*

"Yes," Terella agreed, eyes flashing. "I don't understand how Lanserim hold such grudges against people who've been through so much. If anything, it's *us* who scare me, not them."

Serra wished she could agree fully, but part of her knew the girl was naive, no matter how competent her botany skills. Terella's brother had been a hero. Serra's? A traitor who'd fallen under the spell of Meduan advers and tried to poison the king. Six years did not undo a generation of justifiable suspicion anytime Meduans came over the mountains. Even the hunting party had needed to travel with a guard when they eradicated the pestilence from Meduan holdings, if not a unit from the army.

Back then, it'd felt like they were on the frontlines of a societal shift, but Lanserim like Terella, whom destiny had not forced into it, were doing the true hand-to-hand combat. They shared their lives with Meduans, every day. Serra need only think of Lorne to know how much she'd failed at that. The thought made her chest ache.

He is not worth such agony.

And she could serve Madel's plans better unencumbered, without loved ones tying her back to home.

That's right. Madel needs you alone.

When Serra took stock of her life, she had to agree with that conclusion.

"Want to know more about the Meduans, do you?"

An elderly woman leaned into their conversation, uninvited. Her short-cut hair was tucked under a feather-lined bonnet. She wore a heavy gray shawl clasped at her throat with an ornate bronzed button. "When I was newly married, they killed my brother when he tried to talk one of them from rising up against King Turyn. Most the ones who did it are dead by now, but it makes me wary, so many around again."

"They killed my brother, too," Serra said, squeezing the woman's mitten-gloved hand.

"And mine," Terella reminded her.

Serra held her tongue at the dare Terella's tone implied.

"What's your name?" she asked the woman.

"Mar Koma, you may call me. Only my husband called me Frella."

Serra raised her elbows in welcome, and the woman chuckled.

"No need for such formality, dearie." She lifted a soup spoon to her mouth, slurped up the stew broth, and dabbed at her lips. "Want to see a trick?"

Terella and Serra exchanged a bemused glance. "Please."

The woman scooted her chair closer and flipped up a palm. Silver light crackled over it and puffed out with a flash. Serra gasped. *Like Lorne's echo.* He had a modicum of the power Vesperi possessed, and he'd claimed others did too, but Serra hadn't come across another who did.

Terella's eyebrows shot high. "What was that?"

Nap hastened to her side, hand on his hilt. "Lady Serra, are you safe?" He kept his eyes trained on Mar Koma, though the rest of the tavern hadn't noticed the feeble display.

The older woman let loose an uproarious laugh. "Oh, no wonder you don't like Meduans! You're Lady Gavenstone. That prince passed you over for one."

"That's not what happened," Serra angry-whispered. They had the attention of a few tavern guests now. "And I don't dislike Meduans."

They are not worthy of your affection. Why pretend?

I am often not worthy of other's affection, Serra retorted, to whom or what, she did not know.

Maybe so.

She twisted her mourning ribbons.

"*Hmph,*" Mar Koma said.

Terella tucked her hair behind her ears. "Was that magic?"

The voice? Oh, no, Terella was talking to their guest. *What is wrong with me?* The voice wasn't real. It couldn't be.

Mar Koma took a long, pointed slurp of her stew then steepled her hands on her stomach. "I lured a fly into it once and *ZAP!*" She clapped her hands together. "It fizzled right up."

Crackled was more apt. Serra had spent years with such sounds for company, that of insects roasting in their shells.

Mar Koma narrowed an eye. "Think Madel wants me to use it to defend against those Meduans, Lady Gavenstone?"

That the echo was Madel's gift was true enough, but their goddess did not distinguish between Her peoples like that, despite what those peoples might sometimes think. And this woman made her bristle— Serra was as guilty of Meduan distrust as anyone, but that didn't give others the right to threaten her friends.

"I know a Meduan with the same talent," Serra said, wondering what Mar Koma would make of that. "Not to mention the weapon, our new queen. Your flame wouldn't last a second against her strength."

"New queen, eh?" The woman rocked back on her chair's legs. "So good King Albrecht is dead like the rumors say, is he?"

Serra hadn't meant to bring up the subject. She raised her elbows to the woman, having had enough of her and the tavern for the evening. "May Madel's hand guide you, Mar Koma. See you tomorrow, Terella."

Her mourning ribbons fluttered like ravens' wings as she went out the door, Nap filing in beside her.

‡

The next morning, rainbows of sunlight spiraled inside the angled ceilings and walls of the glasshouse complex. Nap did a quick march around the closest building as Serra waited for Terella to appear. She watched him make a circuit, his features relaxed. But they morphed to a frown as a rainbowlike gossamer appeared *outside* the farthest wall.

Serra slipped on the sight.

"There was something . . ." Nap muttered, and Serra watched that *something* shear through reality's curtain with the force of a knife. A fissure came into existence, growing a stroke at a time. Through it, she glimpsed whirls of the spiritual realm's color-heightened environment. What had happened in Callyn's kitchen was no one-off. Yet that portal's manifestation had felt different, empty and foreboding, and disappeared quick. Whereas, the brilliance of Madel's realm gleamed from this, as it was revealed bit by bit.

"Strange new morning ritual in Callyn?" Terella teased, having walked up beside Serra, who'd pressed her nose against the glass.

"Not quite." She held up her hand, and Terella gave her silence, though her eyebrows quirked. The new fissure grew until it reached about a foot's length and maple leaf's width. It hung high in the sky, but what might fly through . . .

"You should have that section of meadow roped off. It's not safe." Serra pointed to the portal, though no one else could see its flicker.

Not safe indeed. Wouldn't want to stumble in through one of those.

The suggestion of a giggle tickled the skin behind her left ear. She clasped a hand over it.

Terella's face went ashen.

"No, not claren," Serra reassured her, dropping her hand. If it were claren, they could have entered her body through her earhole, so Terella's reaction was fair. "But a way they might use to come here, if they weren't all dead. And it didn't exist a moment ago."

"I saw it," Nap confirmed, "for that moment." His eyes shined.

"I'll tell the council." Terella wrung her hands. "And order a circle of fallowent bushes planted by it."

"It can wait," Serra apologized. "I didn't mean to scare you." Yet the precaution was smart. Terella intrigued her for many reasons. She'd been the first person to recognize fallowent's effectiveness in repelling claren, and she'd been only twelve then.

Faint blue orbs danced above Terella's head when Serra focused on her with the sight. *I knew it.* The same orbs had alighted on the king's head as he shared his vision, and on her brother Agler's when he'd recounted the king's forgiveness. *Madel's favor.*

Serra observed the younger woman. "Show me your new Meduan plant acquirements?"

"Certainly. And this is for you."

Terella offered her a tall mug with a ceramic lid Serra could slide off when ready for a walking sip. She took it with gratitude. One sniff assured her it was brewed tachery, Serra's favorite beverage.

"I love you," she said.

"Oh, Lady Serra, you seduce me," Terella laughed, and Serra gave her a good-natured cheek peck. She followed the botanist into the nearest glasshouse, one of five in a Nevillim meadow of frosted grass. About thirty workers tended the plants in shifts, twice as many as the last time Serra had visited for twice as many buildings.

As she strolled the well-tended rows, Serra rolled leaves between her fingers to release their fragrances. Terella led the way to the far side of the second glasshouse. A child and an adult worked together down one of its rows, misting a plant with broad, hand-sized leaves.

Terella introduced them. "Mer Drenyl and his daughter, Koren."

Serra clasped her fingers and raised her elbows to the father-daughter pair. "How long have you been working here?" she asked.

Mer Drenyl, perhaps thirty, answered with a sniff. "About a year, I think. The council here, they're good. Make sure we have plenty to eat and a roof over our heads." Clearly, he'd been used to inspections when he'd lived in Durn, so the praise spilled out. "But I like to keep busy. And Koren likes to keep me company."

"No interest in school, Koren?" Serra inquired. The girl looked about seven—old enough for a Meduan child that Mer Drenyl couldn't be her actual father. Only Meduan nobility had been allowed families during the divide, and to many of them, only sons had counted.

Koren sidled closer to him.

"It's okay." Serra understood her apprehension. Whether or not they were blood, Mer Drenyl had assuredly rescued her from a bad situation, and she needed the safety of his nearness in the presence of a nosy stranger.

"What are you two tending?" Serra asked, softening her tone. She reached for one of the mottled leaves, but Mer Drenyl caught her hand.

"Don't do that unless you want to be sneezing for a week anytime you go to scratch an itch."

Her hand fell to her side. "That does not sound pleasant. What's it used for?" She cast the sight at it: no blue mist or orbs.

"Well, if someone gets something stuck up their nose and needs to sneeze . . ."

Koren dissolved into giggles, and Serra had to guess whether Mer Drenyl had meant it or was joking. He shrugged his shoulders. "I'm not rightly sure it has that effect, as I'm not willing to try it myself."

"An herbalist must know every sensation her salves create before offering them to others," Serra declared, repeating the lesson Queen Lexamy had taught her with a hidden pouch of itching powder. She reached again for the plant and watched as Koren's pupils enlarged with surprise, and maybe alarm.

Serra withdrew her hand. "But maybe we'll let this one alone and not tell anyone?" She winked and Koren giggled again, leaving a smile on her face.

"There's a rainbow," the girl said. "Did you see?"

That startled Serra—could the girl see the fissure too? Nap had for a second, but minutes later? That was impossible, wasn't it?

Another glimmer caught Serra's eye, and she released her breath. The glimmer came from a plant with black-spotted blossoms hanging from the ceiling a row behind them. The light arced between its mostly transparent petals and delicate silver, copper, gold, and black-veined leaves on a looping vine. The vine appeared thick, but as she drew close, Serra realized it was an intertwined collection of thin stems veined with the same colors as the leaves. By joining, they'd created strength, much as the metallurgists did when braiding threads of pounded metals into fortifications.

The plant's beauty was dazzling, though the colors faded into various shades of green as her sight dimmed. Serra broke off one of its leaves, and a calm she hadn't felt in some time enveloped her. Oh, this plant had plenty of potential for herbalists. "Is this also from your foraging, Mer Drenyl?"

He shook his head, and Terella spoke up.

"It's from mine, actually. I . . . I wanted to see the sea." Her cheeks colored a curious shade of pink. "I never had, so I went to the coastline near Jost and waved to Mount Frelom's peak across the sound. It's somewhere my brother had been—"

"Of course," Serra cut her off. "May I take a cutting to study it more?"

Terella snipped off a gnarled twist of the plant. Serra tucked it into her pack, noting the puff of basil-like fragrance it released.

She raised her elbows to Mer Drenyl and Koren, hoping they'd forgive her rudeness, but she needed to talk with Terella alone. "It was a pleasure to meet you both. May Madel's hand guide you."

After a stilted pause, little Koren returned the courtesy. "And you also!" Her cheeks flushed with pride at having remembered the full greeting.

"Terella," Serra said, "would you walk me out?"

They strolled in silence. Terella led the way, stopping almost without thinking to direct workers to mist some plants a second time and prune others back to their first growths. She was the embodiment of "green thumb," but the other color that trailed her tweaked Serra's interest more.

Outside the first glasshouse's door, Serra tugged Terella out of others' earshots, startling her.

"I don't think I've ever known you to lie before," she explained.

"Wha–what?" Terella's chin quivered.

Serra's disapproving frown silenced her. "While I have no doubt you thought of Hamsyn at that shore, he was not the reason you went there."

Terella mouthed a silent "no."

"Was it Madel?"

Surprised eyes met Serra's.

"My sight isn't just for the claren," Serra explained. "It allows me to see other things. The area I told you to fence off—I can still see an opening from Madel's realm there, a 'shimmer from heaven' if you will." Echoing King Dever's words brought a smile to her lips. "I can see signs of Madel's presence, too. I've suspected before, but I confirmed today that you have Her favor."

Terella's guilt at lying melted away. She smiled sweetly, as though a crush had been exposed. "You can see that She speaks to me?"

"Do you mean through ritual chants? I've heard people describe it that way."

Terella shook her head. "No, directly. In my ear, sometimes. It's not often, and I don't understand why, but sometimes."

Is that what's happening to me, Serra wondered. It did not feel the same.

A mixture of doubt and awe filled Terella's voice. "I haven't told anyone. I don't think even Ma would understand."

Serra did. The Lanserim believed in Madel and Her protection, but most didn't have the personal connection to their goddess that Serra's sight allowed.

"That's why I went north," Terella continued, "to find the plant. She sent these . . . fireflies, maybe? Maybe angels, I don't know. Whatever they were, they showed me where it hung in the forest near the shore. A patch of black sand marked it, like on Braven."

Maybe Janto should reconsider a visit to Sielban. If even the island's sand was a sign from Madel, surely She would provide him with insight there. "And She told you to cultivate the vine, like the fallowent?"

"I didn't need to be told."

Serra gave her a tight smile of understanding. "I wish I could say the same for myself. It took a great many tellings before I understood what Madel asked of me." *And I have no idea what that is anymore.* "Would you pray, Terella, that Madel reveals Her will to me, and to the royal family?"

"Of course." She gave Serra a full hug. "I don't know why She chose me for this work. Guess it's a good thing I liked pulling weeds as a kid." She laughed.

"Most of us never do know why She chooses us, I think. For someone who loves Her people so much, She doesn't spend much time explaining Herself."

Then why give Her your faith? Why not trust in something more . . . dependable? Something that will always be with you.

Like doubt? Serra huffed. She'd seen Madel's hand with her own eyes, had been granted the sight and used by Her to defeat the claren scourge. Doubting Madel was not part of this equation.

They walked over to the horses Nap had saddled and watered. He raised his elbows to Terella in farewell. Serra did the same.

"Grow the plant," she instructed, though Terella needed no prodding. "The king will give you whatever resources you need to do so." She'd write Janto of it and the new portal once she and Nap reached Mova.

Nap boosted her onto her horse, and Serra asked, "What's it called? The plant?"

"Symphony," Terella declared. Perhaps Madel has whispered the name in her ear, just then. She waved as Serra kicked her horse into a gallop, wondering what song Madel had them blindly strumming this time around.

At least the voice in her head had quieted, for now.

CHAPTER SEVEN

VESPERI

With fair weather, the journey from Elston to Callyn by carriage took five days. Yet the weather had *not* been fair since Vesperi left Lady Rufalyn's estate. A pigeon had confirmed the king's death, just as her things were loaded for a morning departure. Vesperi had learned to trust her instincts a long time ago—her survival had sometimes depended on it.

If only she'd done so the day she'd allowed Janto to take Izzy on his caravan to those Wasylim backwaters. They were no place for a child, especially not one who'd spent the winter with a lingering cough. But Vesperi had been asked to host a delegation of teachers from all over the kingdom, an unexpected honor that had delighted her. They wanted to incorporate Meduan history into their lessons. And Vesperi had agreed that Izzy might be better off away from the castle for the conference. The child didn't need to hear Vesperi recount her years of prostitution at the nunnery. Nor her descriptions of the false Saeth's worship ceremonies—the advers' torture of their sacrifices, their bets on how many screams a given victim would last. The Lanserim teachers, grown adults, had been aghast to hear her words. Vesperi had wanted to smite them all, then and there, for their obliviousness to their neighbors' torment.

I couldn't do that now if I wanted to. Flexing her useless fingers made her angry, and that anger was close to frustration, which was close to grief. Vesperi was a mother no longer, hardly a wife, and stripped of the power she'd had as the weapon. *What's left?*

She tried not to think about it, having had enough of those emotions. So she took up another useless exercise instead: holding her breath and straining to catch the barest hint of a child's cry. They traveled through Rasseleria's northeastern edge, leagues from the swamp-plagued border between it and Wasyla where Izzy had disappeared, but she couldn't help herself.

The carriage stopped rolling and a knock came at the thin wooden door.

Her tone was not royal. "What is it?"

One of the knights—Jyndala might be her name, if Vesperi had to guess—gave her a fearful look that made Vesperi question how useful the woman would be if a need for her warrior skills came up. Two days ago, Vesperi needing a defense at all wouldn't have occurred to her. But flameless . . .

"I'm sorry," Sar Jyndala stammered, and Vesperi gestured to hurry her up. "There's a group of Rasselerians up ahead and . . ." The knight peered beyond the carriage door, then ducked her head back in. "No, they've caught up to us now. Do you wish to speak with them?"

No. Vesperi took a deep breath, recalled the meditation sessions she'd undergone with Serra and Callyn's Rynna Hullvy. Being Lanserim royalty wasn't as peaceful an experience as she'd imagined it to be. It required so much decorum. Luckily, telling lies came naturally to her from years of necessity.

"Yes," Vesperi strained to smile. "Tell them I'll be out in a minute."

Janto needed her right now, the only person in existence who did with Izzy gone. She didn't want to spend an hour exchanging pleasantries with these Rasselerians. She wanted to offer her husband what comfort she could, send these others away with a flashing silver threat for daring to waylay her a minute, and—

She took measured breaths, and when she was ready, opened the door again. Three Rasselerians waited in a huddle, their heads pressed together. None rose taller than her shoulders. They each had red hair and tongues that flicked out as soon as her foot met the grass-sodden earth. Frog men, she used to call them, though courtesy training had been effective enough that she refrained from it now. Plus, Janto's own skin held a hint of their greenish hue, as had Izzy's. *As does Izzy's.*

"Our Queen." The Rasselerians spoke in unison, raising their elbows. Vesperi's mouth fell agape at the greeting, though she ought to have expected it. Clearly, they knew of the king's death. Clearly, Vesperi's life had changed in ways she did not yet understand. *Will it ever stop?*

Sar Jyndala held open a pouch containing a supply of fallowent. Vesperi swallowed a fingerful, and the Rasselerians followed suit, a new custom some of the people had taken to practicing. She waited on them to speak, but lost patience.

"What can I do for you?"

The nearest Rasselerian reached inside his cloak, made of the same fabric as their bodysuits, a thin material that mimicked its surroundings. At the moment, that was muddy snow and yellowed grasses.

Vesperi felt a rush of apprehension, remembering another trio of Rasselerians who'd produced a rosewood box bearing her family's sigil, the Sellwyn viper. It had exposed her murder of Agler Gavenstone to the rest of the hunting party, and threatened to undo them before Janto had even realized they needed to rejoin their countries to defeat the claren.

These Rasselerians brought out a glass carving of a swan in flight. Its neck stretched toward a convergence of the four moons, and its beauty mesmerized her.

"Is this glass from the ancient days?" she asked.

The Rasselerians collected such shards from the Battle of the Gods, when Madel first raised up the three-headed bird to defend Lansera, or so the creation myth went. Vesperi held the carving up to the sun, noted its pearlescent sheen—yes, it was from that age. That sheen distinguished the relics from the everyday discards in the sands around Lake Ashra.

The Rasselerian this group had designated as their speaker nodded, either in answer to her question or from hearing her thoughts. Many of them possessed that talent, though they were polite enough not to make a show of it. She respected that, and the weight of the figurine, heavy in her palm. Its craftsmanship was exquisite, each feather detailed and the backsplash full of a patterned sky and a lined pool . . . just like the one in Elston she'd frequented.

"A gift," the lead Rasselerian spoke. "For you to remember the king in his final form."

Had they been spying on her in Elston? There was no way this object could have been carved in just the past few days. Perhaps Madel had granted them foreknowledge of the king's death. But why? Surely not to complete an art piece. She rubbed a finger against its smooth edges. "I will give it to my husband."

The man's tongue flicked out, an admonishment. "It is for you," he insisted. "To help you believe."

"I don't understand." Perhaps speaking in riddles was the result of following a goddess who spoke through prophecy and ritual chants. It would be so much easier if Madel just appeared at their temple gatherings.

"Pray that you will." Another Rasselerian spoke, a woman per her shapely form. She drew something else from her cloak: a small chapbook adorned with Madel's handprint.

"*This* is for the king," she explained. "We've been gathering Rasselerian sayings for centuries and pass them to the Albrechts now."

More riddles. Vesperi tired of them so.

The woman said, "Do not wait for the coronation to give it to him, no matter what your Ser Allyn says."

Vesperi laughed, and the woman smiled, eyes blossoming with shared amusement. Ser Allyn must have been to these parts before, poor people.

Coronation. Oh wow. Wow. Yes, they'd called her "queen," and Vesperi knew she'd married a prince. But day-to-day life in Callyn had been routine, at least in contrast with her Meduan worries. In Sellwyn, Vesperi's thoughts had been taken up with guessing what guard she might be forced to seduce next, what taunts her brother would fling her way, what would happen if Father banished her for not taking a suitor. Then Lord Sellwyn had, and she'd run away, and ended up wed to Prince Janto Albrecht. And she'd become a mother, which was hard but wonderful, and Vesperi had never known such joy. That had gone with her daughter, and now, so was King Dever Albrecht, who'd given her grace, and the flame that had won her place in the family.

Vesperi couldn't justify being Lansera's queen. She could barely justify returning home to Janto. She wiped a tear and cursed herself for showing such weakness before these commoners.

The Rasselerian woman gazed up to the heavens. "He must get it right away. Time is short."

"I'll give it to him myself," Vesperi promised before dashing back inside the carriage. Sar Jyndala could handle the farewells well enough.

She positioned the glass carving in a gap between seat and wall.

The carriage lurched, and Vesperi untied the ribbon binding the book, hoping she could reproduce its intricate looping knot later. The pages opened with a crack:

When leaps the mighty cantalere,
the dark brother drains his foes.
The Guard must ring the beastly lair
Where battles end their roam.

Vesperi groaned. *More prophecy.* The lines continued, but she wasn't in the mood to guess at blurred ink. The book was too delicate for her to slam with satisfaction, but she tried anyhow.

CHAPTER EIGHT

JANTO

An eerie silence settled in the throne room after Janto had welcomed the last few noble families to arrive in Callyn. They'd come for the funeral the next day, and to pay their respects to the king, laid on a dais that obscured the throne. The throne itself was an ornate metalwork meant to mimic the briar patches on the plain of Orelyn, complete with thorns.

Janto yearned to hear his father's commanding voice fill the room. But he wasn't there. Just his corpse, over which his blue velvet cloak was spread.

And his shade lurking beyond Janto's reach. If he acknowledged the presence, Janto knew what he'd see—a grayscale mimicry of his father's form, with vacant pits for eyes. The shade haunted him, but Janto had not the time, nor the reserves, to deal with it just yet.

The Albrechtian swans swam on the black collar of his real—and dead, still dead—father's cloak. The cloak's bulk featured an intricate embroidery of the bird of creation, done in multicolored threads. Another rich blue fabric covered the dais. That one would soon be transformed into a tapestry depicting his father doing . . . Janto didn't know what it would depict his father doing. Not another choice he'd have to make, he hoped.

On the floor, gifts were nestled in an ocean of feathers from Callyn's citizens. They, and other people from villages within a few days' ride, had laid the feathers down one by one. The gifts had arrived with the noble families and town councillors. A potted orange tree, its roots braided to mimic intertwined swan necks, was Lord Sydley's contribution from citrus-rich Wasyla.

Janto marveled at the large bear rug from Lord Cino Xantas of Ertion, folded neatly beside the potted plant. The bear's head rested over its arms and legs, the pile high as Janto's waist. It must have been a great beast, striped gray, white, and black.

He wondered if any of the presents came from the formerly Meduan lands—their remaining lords had not come to pay their respects. A familiar worry sprang up, that letting any Meduan nobles keep their lands had been a mistake. Raids had begun to flourish again between their estates, and a new wave of immigrants fled east over the mountains, bringing conflict with them.

Perhaps the large, spiked club with a sharp metal halo had come from Vesperi's brother, Uzziel. Janto remembered her description of something similar called a tornian—Uzziel had threatened her with one once. Janto had never met the invalid boy, now under the care of Lorne Granich's father, Cavallen, who ruled a portion of the riverlands.

He drew close to where his father's body rested. Janto hadn't wanted to see him this way, but a king shouldn't be afraid to look upon difficult things. He'd seen many dead people thanks to the claren, and had brought death to a few when needed. Yet Janto had no desire to observe the soul missing from eyes that had held such strength.

The king's head rested on a satin pillow, yellowed from years of use in his bed. It was a gesture toward the comfort the servants wished him in the afterlife. His gray hair had been shortened, but it was too straight, too flat. His cheeks had hollowed from illness, and his frame was not as muscled as it once was. But what Janto couldn't allow was the stubble that grew more pronounced as his skin had dried. Had the embalmers not seen any of his portraits? Dever Albrecht hadn't worn a beard, preferring the clean-shaven style of the Order.

"Is there a servant nearby?" Janto asked the empty hall.

Silence, from even the ghost. Janto's orders for quiet were taken more seriously now than they had been when he was merely a prince.

He opened a side door and asked for his father's shaving kit and a basin. Then he took in the rest of the corpse. Minus the cloak, Dever Albrecht was dressed in battle gear, a helmet topped with a long swan feather tucked under his right arm. He'd never ridden to war, his greatest achievement maintaining Turyn's Peace between

Lansera and Medua for decades during the divide. How strange that Dever Albrecht, soldier, would be the final image many of his people had of him.

Pic entered, wearing black ribbons as all the servants did. Typically, such a gesture was reserved for family and close friends, but Janto knew his father would have approved of the castle's staff taking up the custom. The boy set up a tray, placed a ceramic basin on it, and filled it with steaming water from a kettle. He positioned King Dever's shaving implements beside it: a razor made of silver pounded into sheets as fine as any whisker, a brush of tough koparin hairs for sloughing away dry skin, the queen's special blend of oils and creams, a towel, and another brush meant for a final sweep of hair from the face.

"Thank you." Janto tousled Pic's hair. He wondered what it would have been like if his parents had had another child. He wondered, too, if perhaps they did and never told him. Vesperi's miscarriage had been so challenging. With Serra and Nap sent away, and the distance between him and his wife growing—Janto was painfully aware a king did not have many people he could confide such tragedies in.

You can confide in me, son. I will always be here.

Pic startled, and his glance bounced around the room.

The shadow stilled its undulations.

"What did you hear?" Janto asked, surprised.

"N-n-nothing. For a second, I thought . . . a raven's screech, at most."

Proof enough that this ghost was something more than a hallucination. Janto filed that detail away, one more mystery to be solved after the funeral.

The door creaked shut behind Pic. Through the throne room's glass ceiling, the sun lit the king's face. So many things came to mind that Janto might ask him, if he could.

You can.

You are not my father.

Janto picked up the koparin brush, its bristles yellow-white with a black ring on each tip. He grimaced, crunching feathers underfoot to get close. As he swished the brush over his father's skin, he used a lighter touch than he would on his own face.

If I could, I would ask you how I'm to help my wife through our losses, Father. They grieved so differently, and he did not know how to reach her. He'd been able to before, when they'd discovered Lord

Sellwyn's drained corpse in Sellwyn Manor, another claren victim. And a few times when her new life in Lansera had overwhelmed her sense of self, her everyday existence here so different than under the advers' rule. He'd learned from Vesperi that those differences ran deep as her thought processes. How had he reached her then, when he knew her less well than he did now? The divide between them felt as though an unfathomable chasm. They had been so close, chasing each other through his silver dreams once.

Janto plunged his hands into the basin, the water musked with roasted coriander seeds. He splashed the king's face to dampen it. The cold skin's give felt wrong, sluggish, but he proceeded to massage water into it. *I would ask you how to be a father.* Janto had thought he was managing with parenting Izzy, but he'd failed her utterly, and the void she and their miscarried child had left would never be filled. Yet once he and Vesperi got past this, they must have other children . . . *if* they got past this. For the kingdom, yes, but also for each other. The pride Janto had felt beholding his wife and his child was immense, whether crouched over a book in their study or learning knots from Sar Mertina in the stables. But how could they try? How could *he* have enough ego to think any child could be entrusted to his care? His father had not been an affectionate man, but he had kept Janto safe. Janto could promise no future children the same. Izzy's disappearance proved that.

With three fingers, Janto scooped cream from the tray. Pic had placed a ramekin of hot stones beneath it, and the warmth nourished him. A peppery scent complemented the coriander's toasted notes. Janto breathed comfort in as he spread the cream onto his father's neck and chin.

I would ask you how to rule a country. On that, his father had not been silent while alive. But who could ever be prepared to be king? Janto wanted nothing more than to turn to him for advice on every decision, little and big, that he had made over the past week. Should Rynna Hullvy perform the funeral ritual as he asked, or should he have sent for Ryn Cladio? They'd had another report of a raid on travelers yesterday. Should he send troops to patrol the roads in Neville? Would doing so spur the marauders to rebel?

Why had Esye gone dim? Why did this specter torment him?

Janto dipped his fingers in the wash basin and dried them on the towel. With a steady hand, he took the razor and shaved a long, slow swipe down the left side of his father's face. The routine of dipping the razor to remove cream and shaving a new line was comforting. *I would ask you how to commune with Madel, Father. I need to know what threat we're under.* The king had trusted in Madel's divine benevolence, that She'd always guide Lansera to safety. Janto would feel surer of his choices if he had Her insight to guide him.

Janto laid the razor down. He wiped his father's face of cream dribbling down his neck. With the second, softer brush, he whisked the shavings from his face and the blue blanket beneath. Then he placed one hand over each cheek and wiped, checking for smoothness as his father had taught. *I would ask you how I'll manage without you.*

The throne room provided no answer, and even the shade had disappeared. He sighed with relief before taking it all in: the water he'd splashed on his father's armor, the broken feathers needing a fluffing, the cream flung onto his own tunic, which only a wash would get out. Someday, he'd stop making messes everywhere he went, but he'd done the right thing here. For himself, at least.

"Goodbye, Father," he said, gazing on Dever Albrecht's countenance for the last time. Come morning, the casket would be closed. "I'll take your answers in Madel's realm."

"In the cobalt flame, you mean."

His wife's rich alto filled the throne room as easily as his father's had.

"Vesperi," Janto gasped.

She wore her customary pants, though these were a crushed brown velvet more suited for Elston's cold. Her tunic was lightweight, and the knife belted at her waist matched the silver glint in her eyes, though that was not present now, perhaps from the tiredness of the journey.

"That's what your chants say, don't they? 'Let them rest in the cobalt flame,' not Madel's realm. Unless you'd have me believe those dusty old tomes are wrong?"

Vesperi's raven hair was bound loose in a braid, and her customary smirk in place. He'd want it no other way.

He bridged the space between them fast as he could. "They are one and the same: Madel's realm and the cobalt flame. We just didn't know about the realm before the portals opened up." Janto needed her, had ever since the moment they'd met in a silver dream.

She flinched when his arms wrapped around her, but eased her own over his, holding him close. Janto laid his head against her breast and tears spilled out, his body shaking.

"I'm so sorry for you." She kissed the top of his head. "He was the best man I knew." She tilted his chin up, her smirk replaced with worry lines. "Save one."

It felt like forgiveness, or a chance at it. Janto would take solace in whatever grace given him, solace in his wife as long as she allowed. He sunk onto one of the throne room's benches and laid his head in her lap.

On the dais, a shadow blinked back alive in the space behind his father's coffin. Janto's eyelids fluttered closed. His wife was home—what greater wonder could there be than that?

‡

A ritual bell rings, resonating through the amphitheater, which is empty, strangely, as Janto was sure hundreds would turn out to mourn his father. But only he and Rynna Hullvy are here, outside the tomb chiseled into the Mount's hillside. The rynna strikes the bell again, and the sound it makes echoes from rock walls at the far end of the amphitheater. The echo is louder than it should be for a construction open to the sky.

Rynna Hullvy touches his arm, and it's cold, like an unseen presence. Her blue eyes flash silver, as Vesperi's do when she releases the flame. The priestess lifts her head to the sky, and Janto follows.

Lightning bolts in the deep cobalt blue and is captured—a rift! The new portal's edges lose their sharpness as it expands. Electrified charges wriggle out of the opening and spill into sky, smooth as silver fish. They eddy outward, as though repulsed from each other, and swirl into the sky beyond. Above his head, all is silver, beating, pulsing, until the charges disperse, flying fast.

Rynna Hullvy touches his arm again, and Janto is flying. His hands grasp feather tufts, and he holds tight as his ride tracks one of the silver charges. It's a chase, as thrilling as his first time hunting koparin. Janto yells into the wind, and the sound is swallowed by the speed they travel.

Callyn's loping hillsides give way to Nevillim fields shining straw gold. Sun glints off Terella's glasshouses, and Janto veers away from the brightness. His mount does also, following the silver. Janto thinks they must be headed to Braven, can see Mount Frelom rising in the distance, but that doesn't make sense. Mount Frelom is always covered in clouds. Yet its snow-capped peak gleams, beckoning.

They veer to the east and the frigid Ertion plateaus. The silver charge veers down, and Janto strengthens his grip, his fingers grasping skin beneath the feathers. They plunge. Janto's heart leaps into this throat, but he keeps his eyes on the silver. It flows through an open window of a modest hut roofed with thatched bark and reinforced with yellowed geese feathers.

Janto blinks and finds his ride is gone, his feet planted on the ground beside the window. He peers into a bedroom: the silver charge touches a young man, and its spark grows into an outline that dazzles the boy awake. A giggle, and he sits up in bed. His hand opens to reveal a dancing spark of silver.

Janto is whisked away to another scene and another and another. A teenage girl with neat hair pulled back and a pair of raven's wings stands tall, puffing out her chest as silver arcs between her hands. A round man in a ryn's light shift cups Lake Ashra's waters in his hands. It sizzles into steam. Near the icy walls of Thokketh, a Deduin mother lays her child in a heavily blanketed crib. As she returns to her cooking fire, silver light flashes from her violet eyes and sears to a crisp the sheven meat she'd been roasting.

A dozen such scenes flash by, and Janto cannot keep them straight, nor understand what he's witnessing. A hand clutches his shoulder—

Beneath their bedcover, Vesperi stroked his trembling skin. Her eyes were full of concern, but not the silver glints Janto was used to seeing in them. The absence of Esye's moonslight, perhaps. Janto did not dwell on it.

"I dreamt—" he started.

Vesperi rose up against the pillows. "A silver dream?"

"Yes."

She sunk in on herself and Janto let his worries back in. Though Vesperi's power had been there in the dream, she had not, nor had the silver stag or its doe, which had acted as her ciphers in the past.

Why wasn't she there? Janto panicked, clutching her shoulder.

She gently unhooked his fingers. "Go on. Tell me."

He recounted as much of the dream as he could find words for. Her eyes widened, and her brow furrowed. Janto ran a finger though one of her curls as he finished his tale. "You saw none of it?" She had always been in his dreams before.

She hit his hand away and shifted her back to him without a word. He knew better than to try to engage further, being well familiar with his wife's temperament. It was enough that Vesperi had come back, that she shared his bed. And the grief of *why* she'd come was enough to send Janto retreating back to sleep. *Father, I miss you.*

The ghost flickered into being, then looked down from the foot of their bed.

It comes when called. Perhaps Pic had simply heard a bird. What else could this be but his mind playing tricks?

I am well-versed in tricks. The shade's lips curled up into a slim crescent. *Sleep well, my son. I will not be far.*

Vesperi groaned and flipped positions, tucking her head under his chin. Janto stared at the blackness across the bed until his eyes closed against his will.

CHAPTER NINE
Serra

Winds roiled over Mova's arid steppes. Most of the town's cabins lay far to the east, no more than a line of dots on the horizon. Serra and Nap neared a solitary cabin situated closer in. On its porch, the winds tossed the long, lustrous blond hair of one Lorne Granich to maximum effect. He'd likely positioned himself just so in anticipation of their arrival.

Serra laughed. *Of course he did.* In this weather, why else would he be reclining in a chair outside without a hat? Lorne was little accustomed to winter having grown up in the riverlands of Lorvia. As he'd remarked when they'd visited the region on a hunting trip, "Granich Manor's ice boxes are hotter than an Ertion's armpits."

Serra had pondered this moment since leaving Callyn, guessed Lorne might ignore her, give her the cold shoulder as Janto had done when she'd broken off their engagement. But that wasn't Lorne's style. As she and Nap rode in, he stood, a smile breaking across his face. It held a hint of danger, she thought. Or was that pain? Serra would take neither bet just yet.

When silver arced between his fingertips, she laughed again. Such a courtesan, always performing for his audience.

"My echo's brighter, don't you think?" he said. Lorne had been born with a weak facsimile of the power Vesperi possessed, like Mar Koma in the tavern in Tilayne. It couldn't fly farther than his own hands, most days.

Serra rolled her eyes as Nap helped her down, glad the knight had moved fast enough to stop Lorne from offering. Though Lorne was far too preoccupied with showing off, anyhow.

"Ah, and the good Ser Nap, too!" Lorne raised his elbows with a flourish. "Janto's letter did not mention you'd be coming." Amusement shone from his eyes, deepening their pastel blue. Or maybe that was the absence of Esye's silver in the daylight mix. The moon had gone nearly out.

"More raids in Neville have been reported. The lady needed protection." Nap took a moment to stretch his legs before leading the two horses to a nearby water trough.

"Meduans on a rampage!" Lorne appeared aghast, clutching a hand to his chest. "Why, we are such a rowdy bunch, what'll we do next?" He sent another spark traveling through his fingertips. "But I doubt you've come to see my parlor tricks?"

"No." Serra kept her composure. She was here on the king's business. No time for bantering with Lorne—there was too much at risk.

And Lorne is not worth the risking.

Ah, there it is. That voice that made her innards crawl, amplifying her own worst instincts.

"I need to speak with the king's murat companion, Jerusho," she said.

"The 'king's murat companion?' Oh dear." Lorne's grin held strong, but some light drained from his eyes. "Are we so far gone that your formality training reappears in my presence? Nap," Lorne turned to the quiet man who displayed none of the awkwardness he must be feeling at this exchange, "has she been like this your whole trip?"

Nap garbled a reply, and Lorne huffed before making a show of extending Serra a hand to help her up the porch steps. "Jerusho is right inside, preparing for tonight's council meeting, my lady."

"My lady" was a common address; why did her heart flutter when it came from Lorne's lips? Not for the first time, she wondered if this mission were wise.

Lorne led them through solid, creaky doors carved with the plumage of local birds. Though his hair flowed free, a bundle of gray and brown furs subsumed his lanky figure.

"I'm surprised you didn't choose koparin fur to complement your coloring," she jested. Lorne had enjoyed keeping up with Lanserim fashion trends since immigrating right after the Conjoining. He'd groaned every time she showed up on his doorstep from a trip, wearing simple sheaths or plain clothes fit for riding. But once he had them removed, the complaints ceased.

Serra hid her blush behind a cough.

"Oh, the markets sold out of those furs months ago," Lorne laughed. "Though I appreciate the attention you're giving my accoutrements." He winked, no stranger to taking advantage of the openings she gave him.

Serra cursed herself for blushing again, but when her eyes lifted, she gasped. A familiar blue haze surrounded a dark-haired, portly man seated at a large table in the next room. He wore a heavy, fur-lined tunic that even the haze could not penetrate, though Serra had rarely seen Madel's presence so thick. Janto had been right to send her here to seek Madel's guidance.

"He has a suitor," Lorne *tsked*. "Stop gaping."

The man, Jerusho, no doubt, laughed heartily. "Oh, I don't think Dorella would mind so much. It'd make her proud to know I'm such a catch." He squinted up from the pile of parchments on his desk and spotted Napeler. In a half-second, he'd enveloped the much smaller man in a great hug.

"Jerusho," Nap's voice was muffled by furs, "I can't breathe."

Jerusho clapped his back before giving him room. "It's been too long, friend. I haven't seen you since our murat. And this must be—"

Lorne trumpeted, "Behold, Lady Serrafina, once of Gavenstone, once betrothed to the mighty prince and now betrothed to the freedom of the open road."

Serra jabbed him hard, but the furs swallowed her intent.

Jerusho clapped his hands together, his smile growing, "Oh, delighted to—"

Lorne cut him off, raising elbows his way next. "And this is Jerusho of Mova, whose presence you seek, unlike my own."

"Oh-h-h." Realization dawned on Jerusho's face, like biting a fruit whose flavor he'd forgotten. "This is *her*. I didn't realize your Serra was the same as Janto's."

"I'm not Janto's, nor am I *his*." The bite in her voice borrowed some panache from years spent riding with Vesperi.

Jerusho acknowledged the correction with an inquisitiveness that reminded her of Ryn Gylles, her mentor during her days with the

Order. He dipped his elbows. "My apologies, I was remembering the times Janto spoke of you on our murat. They were . . . well, I suppose they weren't so different from the conversations I've had with my new friend Lorne this winter."

Serra chose not to dwell on the comparison, and not to waste time, with all they needed to research to protect Lansera. "The king—Janto needs you to read this letter. There's danger—"

"More claren?" Lorne touched her elbow, his voice filled with concern.

She met his eyes, shook her head. "No. Not yet, at least. Madel willing, never. But that's part of this. New fissures are opening. And Ryn Cladio has found unusual animal carcasses outside Lake Ashra. Here."

She handed Jerusho the letter, and Lorne went to the other side of the table to read over the Ertion's shoulder. Jerusho's countenance grew pale as a granfaylon as he read, which amused Serra despite the circumstances. His steadfast belief that Madel had meant him to catch that mythical fish was why Janto placed so much trust in him. Jerusho's faith had yielded a feast of granfaylon flesh.

"These words," Jerusho said, mouthing the verse Ryn Cladio had sent. "They're familiar, but I can't place why—might just be that they rhyme. What does Janto make of them?"

"He has no idea." Serra slunk into a chair. "That's why I'm here— he hopes you will." Through her thickest pants, she could feel the bristles of bear fur from the chair's cushion. Her bones ached, suddenly, from the trip. Or perhaps from her dashed hope that Jerusho would instantly recognize the words as prophecy. Perhaps they were just a forgotten chant, and the animal carcasses a coincidence.

"Do you have anything to drink?"

"Oh, how uncharitable of me!" Jerusho rose gracefully. "Lorne has kept hot tachery brewing all morning, and there's also bombal draught, if you'd prefer?"

"Tachery, please." She'd yet to brave bombal draught; the Ertion liquor smelled worse than the hot springs in Elston. That Lorne had made sure fresh tachery awaited her arrival? She wasn't brave enough to think about that, either. He didn't even drink it, claiming it too bitter for his delicate sensibilities.

How foppish.

The thought chilled her. Lorne held himself to no particular notion of manhood. It was part of what she'd found so attractive about him. Did her innermost self disagree with her outer one that much?

Nap followed Jerusho from the room to gather the beverages. Lorne took the opportunity to slink into the seat beside her and loop one of her mourning ribbons around his thumb. She expected him to brag about his latest exploits or preen for laughs, but instead, he asked "Are you okay?" in the soft voice he only used when they were alone.

Her eyes lifted and found his own held a mixture of affection and concern. "I'm fine." She covered his hand for a moment to provide assurance.

"No. You don't get to 'I'm fine' me." His voice gentled. "The king is dead, and I know how much he meant to you. And something new is threatening us, and it must be something big to bring you here, hundreds of miles away from the royal family and the responsibilities you left me for in Meditlan."

Oh, the lies we weave. Go on, tell him the truth. He can take it.

"Quiet!" Serra shouted at her traitorous brain.

Lorne jerked back and a scowl leapt to his face.

Oh no. "I didn't mean you—mean it. I didn't mean it. I'm sorry." She pulled her hand away, ashamed. Returning to Gavenstone had been her excuse for breaking things off with Lorne that last time, when she'd run. Serra shrunk in her chair, ashamed of the lies.

Lorne masked his features with nonchalance. "Didn't mean it? So you want me back then?" Sarcasm spilled forth. "Think I'm ready to join you at Gavenstone? That I can be trusted not to swim in the wine vats or corrupt the town councillors?"

She tried to speak, but he shushed her. "I'm sorry, I hadn't meant to start a fight." He sounded contrite. "I had just wanted you to know someone sees you, Serra, that you're not fine, no matter how much you claim otherwise."

So very far from fine indeed. Think you'll ever find "fine" again?

A silencing of her inner monologue would certainly help. When Lorne touched her brow, like he'd done a hundred times before, she couldn't keep the tears in. Her chest shuddered, and a moan rose from deep within her, where she'd stowed it away this past week of traveling and mourning on the road.

"I didn't go to Medit—" she started.

The grounding scent of roasted tachery wafted from a steaming mug placed before her. Jerusho, features crestfallen, said, "I am so sorry about the king. You were close?"

She nodded, putting space between herself and Lorne. Confessions could wait. Jerusho's return was a reminder it wasn't her future at stake right now, but Lansera's.

Yes, self-sacrifice. That's a noble choice. You don't need companionship getting in the way.

Jerusho took his own seat with a groan. "It's so terrible," he said as Nap brought bombal draught for Lorne and a water glass for himself. "What will we do without King Albrecht?" The councilman sniffed and rubbed tears from his eyes.

"Why are you so aggrieved," Serra wondered aloud. "You did not know him." *That was unkind.*

"No." Jerusho took out his handkerchief. "Though of course I know Janto, and now you." He wiped his face. "But the king . . . Dever Albrecht was not just a man in some castle to us. He was an example of what we could be, you know? That's why Mova's council is meeting tonight, to discuss how we might honor his memory in the square."

She didn't know. Exchanges like this reminded her, no matter how much time she spent traveling among Lansera's people, that she was not fully a part of them. To her, King Dever Albrecht was very real, not an ideal. He was a man she knew, a man whose sense of duty she'd sometimes bristled against but always respected. A man who'd forgiven her brother of traitorous actions when she could not and who'd understood when she'd had to place country before her own happiness, breaking his son's heart.

Lorne touched her arm, a man so very different from the king. But one she longed for, nonetheless. *I miss you. I might need you, and I'm afraid of what that means for me, for my self-respect.* She gritted her teeth to gather back her wits and focus on the task at hand.

"That's a lovely thought," she said. Her face relaxed with the first sip of tachery. It had been steeped with cardamom, clove, and cinnamon, just as she liked it. "I'm sure your council will come up with a fitting tribute. And believe me, I'd be mourning him too, in Callyn, if I could. But Janto's very concerned about Ryn Cladio's report, and so am I."

Should she tell him everything? Madel's haze wrapped around him still, as though swaddling clothes. She found it reassuring. "The sight's revealed more than new rifts into the other realm," she continued.

"When I use it, I've been seeing these dark patches—pockets, almost— in my peripheral vision that flash open, then disappear. And King Dever had a dream recently, about a dark abyss overtaking Lansera. And the words in the letter—"

"*When leaps the mighty cantalere, the dark brother drains his foes,*" Jerusho supplied.

"Well, that's a fancy trick," Lorne said. "I didn't know you were such a fast memorizer."

"Not memorizing, but remembering," Jerusho explained. "In the kitchen, it came to me . . . poor Nap here had to clean up the mess as I dropped a saucer in my shock."

Nap sipped his water without comment.

"My old ryn, he used to tell me stories—nearly raised me, such a fine man. Anyhow, he'd recount some of the old myths, you know, the ones about the Silver Guard and the giants and the Battle of the Gods. And he'd say those words when he'd close one book and move on to another. There was more to it . . ." Jerusho grimaced. "I don't remember the rest. But maybe it'll come to me if I try hard enough."

"Maybe the horse ride to Callyn will jostle it out of you," Serra said.

Jerusho quirked his head. "What?"

"Our lady said you're headed out to advise Janto at court about this matter." Lorne crossed over to Jerusho's side of the table to give him a consoling shoulder pat. "You've proven yourself invaluable, my dear man. Writing letters will not suffice—Janto will need to move fast to act on whatever you remember next."

"And he'll need your old ryn's books," Nap proposed.

That would be wise, Serra agreed.

Jerusho's brows knit. "I don't rightly know that I can go. I just became head council a few months ago. And what of Dorella? And our families? Callyn is awful far away."

"It is. I know it's a big ask, and we should move fast, too. Leave in no more than a couple days." Serra hesitated, remembering how it felt to have the ghastly Brotherhood command her next move rather than trust her to make the right choice. "I will not force you, Jerusho, but I do believe Janto needs you in Callyn. With his father gone . . . he needs someone as immersed in Madel's presence as you are."

"What do you mean?" The councillor's confusion deepened. "I've studied the chants, of course, and I was close with my old ryn, but . . ."

"I mean I can see it, Jerusho. Physically. A blue mist about you glows with more intensity than all the quartz of Callyn's bridge." With the sight, the color's brilliance was almost too much to take in. "It's a sign that Madel's working through you, and a sign for me that I should not leave this place until you've agreed to come."

Jerusho glanced about as though a swarm of bees surrounded him.

Lorne laughed, a genuine one, loud as a honking goose. "Oh, Jerusho, you dear man. Only she can see it. Not until Vesperi struck at the claren where Serra pointed, could the rest of us view their carcasses clattering to the ground."

"I'm not sure I want to be covered in some sort of goddess goo."

Serra laughed too. "It's not like that." But a chill came over her, remembering how very tangible some of what bled over from Madel's realm could be. She needed to impress on Jerusho the importance of this, no matter how nebulous the threat. "You never doubted you'd find the granfaylon, did you? Janto told me you believed in the realness of things you'd never seen—you have faith. You taught him the same, and thus, he became the slayer. Without you, he wouldn't have." Janto hadn't said that, exactly, but Serra was confident he'd allow her some leeway.

Jerusho smiled and her heart lightened—she'd made progress.

"This is a real, present threat," she argued. "We must figure out what's going on. We need you to do that, Jerusho."

"I . . . I'll talk with Dorella." He took a step to the door. "And you'll be coming, too, Lorne? I bet Janto can use more advisors with a Meduan perspective."

Lorne managed to keep the sarcasm from his voice. "Oh, I'm not suited for court, or so I've been told." A quick peek her way seared like an ember blast. "Wouldn't want to cause a distraction when the important people have so much to decide."

Her chin quivered, but she couldn't bring herself to deny his statement. That would be admitting something she wasn't ready to confront. As would giving voice to how much she wanted him to come.

He wouldn't come for you, *anyhow. Not anymore.*

She cringed at the truth of that, while Jerusho raised his elbows and hurried out the door.

Lorne stood. "I'll show you to the guest bedroom, Serra. Nap, you'll have to room with me—there is no palace of accommodations here. And Jerusho isn't one for servants, but the skins are fresh enough. I think he had them aired a whole year ago."

He winked, and Serra allowed herself a smile in response—nothing was more Lorne than a wink. And few things were more enticing than the way he strolled down the hall, showing off the lines of his figure despite the furs and leathers. That her attraction to him remained was no surprise. But she had other problems on her mind. A kingdom's worth of them.

CHAPTER TEN

ESYE

)

Were you maybe too attentive?

Onsic's voice crowded Esye's thoughts as she took in the cracked eggs and infantile limbs of jurgens smashed to nothing but skin and dried muck. Another nest stomped, the third she'd found destroyed that day. It had taken so much effort to leave her safe fern den; she'd only done so at Onsic's prodding when he'd visited that morning, worried she kept herself too hidden away. And now, to find this?

Perhaps you left them alone too long?

He hadn't said those exact words, but with the cantaleres riding, he hadn't had to. She'd heard their horns clanking as they battled each other, their cries bellowing. Still, she had not mustered the willpower to come out and reinforce the jurgen's nests. Not since the last of the silver had seeped from her skin and the dark patch on the floor of her fern glade had drunk it in.

She'd tried to stem the loss of her essence, to wrench it back from the ground after that first burst had funneled out of her in a rush. But her command had failed, as though it too had been sucked in and absorbed. The essence drained from her in trickles and drips over the course of a week. Esye doubted there was any left, so how could she reinforce the jurgens' nests? And if she couldn't do that, why bother to rise at all?

But Onsic had been so convincing, so certain she would be

motivated by her daily tasks. So after he'd left, she'd turned another bit of his rhini lozenge in her mouth and tried not to gag on its slimy texture. Her spirits lifted long enough for her to lift herself.

To come here. And find this.

Even the cantalere's hooked hooves could not have broken through the defensive shells she'd built around the eggs so easily. Maybe her strength had already been sapped when she'd raised them up, and she hadn't realized it yet.

Like Onsic had suggested. He'd said so many things to her the last few days.

Maybe you should have someone else tend them. For now. Until you feel better.

A solitary jurgen drank from the stream, and Esye shooed it away to the far bank. There, the armored, low-rising creature battered a patch of springy groundcover with its spiked tail and wallowed in the freshly turned dirt. In a similar manner, the jurgens dug the shallow recesses in which they laid their eggs, sometimes as many as five in each. And if those eggs were lucky, the adults went far away for months, as they were apt to crush their young themselves in a rage. The jurgens were not particularly self-preserving in their pursuits. Without help, they'd bring about their own destruction, and Madel could not abide the loss of Her creations. Each had a purpose to serve.

Esye sighed. So much pride she'd taken in tending their nests. One day—sometime before the giants had stepped across the sea but after the balance boughs first bloomed—one day Madel's hand had guided her to them as she'd chased a colorful breeze. Esye had gasped at the beautiful eggs, exposed to the elements. They contained so many hues within their scaled shells.

Madel had smiled, pulsing with pure blue energy, and Esye had smiled back, accepting the task. In a few weeks, after the heat she'd contained within the silver shells had dissipated, the little jurgens cracked their ways out with thorny tails barely larger than her thumb. They'd chirped, and grown jurgens had rustled out of the ferns to lead them to the stream for their first drinks. Little Esye did brought her more satisfaction than witnessing that scene time and again.

Would you, brother? I know you are busy, but the nests, they need protection—

I am always willing to help you, dear sister.

When had she asked him to? Had she at all? She couldn't have, or this wouldn't have happened. Esye must have misremembered it; he'd said she was doing that a lot lately, too.

The broken shells bore scorch marks. Had Esye flamed too hot when she'd sealed the nests? She'd never made such a mistake before. She closed her eyes, breathed deep, and probed her core. Silver stars burned within her: her essence, her power. But rather than fill her with relief and pride that she contained such might, it terrified her.

Malice pulsed within each silver flicker. It wouldn't be safe to dip into that power, to send it out from within. *Not safe, I'm not safe!* She wanted to wrench out what was left of it herself—that she could have done such damage to the jurgens, to the creatures Madel had trusted her to protect, was terrifying.

In a panic, she took a draught of ambrosia. The golden liquid felt pleasing as it worked its way through her system, but it didn't provide the lighter-than-air feeling it normally did. Her limbs dragged as she made her way back to the fern glade. She coughed, and the coughing grew into a wracking fit. Esye reached for Onsic's remedy.

A hot fire blazed within her. Esye doubled over, stomach clenching. The pain seared her flesh, her tenebrous hold on this form. She might have screamed, but the sensation, for all it hurt and burned and lanced every inch of her, was a welcome one. If she could have observed herself writhing, Esye knew what she'd see: electric blue light arcing through her, slicing at her core as a knife whittles soft wood until a new creation is born.

Madel. Esye forced her eyes open through the pain, but the sky looked the same, that pale blue of glacial dust, a mere remnant of Her presence. Yet she could see Madel's energy out the corner of her eye, a storm of blue lightning. The part of herself Esye had feared moments ago, her essence, poured out through her skin and gathered into a great silver ball of gleaming barbs and knobs. A cobalt fireball engulfed it, launching it into the woods she could not see, the ones beyond her comprehension. The ones in the Lanserim realm.

A chorus of squawks sounded, and a great rush of wind swept past Esye, swooping after the silver flame and carrying her awareness of Madel with it. She felt empty, so much more so than before, when she hadn't thought there anything left of herself to take. This was not the first time Madel had borrowed her essence, but it was the first time she'd felt grateful to be relieved of it.

You are but a shadow of yourself, dear sister. It's irresponsible to pretend you're the same as before.

A feather's vane plonked her on the head, and a waterfall of them rained down after. She eased herself back toward her den, laid down on the spongy ground, and let another hunk of Onsic's remedy dissolve in her mouth. The oily taste wasn't so bad once you got used to it.

Her hands flexed, and something crunched between her fingers. A dead frond. She gasped—all brown, the whole stalk. But these plants only stopped growing when they reached the maturity they were meant to have. *Did I wither them, too?* The fronds' edges appeared tipped in dull bronze or . . . or sucked clean. Esye ran a finger on their undersides, felt spores that had shriveled for lack of nutrients. Could she have burned them unknowingly, given off radiant heat as she slept?

Can't you manage anything anymore?

She'd laughed away her brother's concern when he'd asked her that. But now, she shivered. Their world was changing, and Esye had not changed with it. She brushed a pile of the bristly, fallen fronds over herself, closed her eyes, and hoped on waking, she'd find herself in a chrysalis. Until then, withdrawing seemed her surest bet, for herself and for all that she loved.

CHAPTER ELEVEN

Janto

The chilly breeze poked through every crevice Janto's fur-lined coat allowed. His boots crunched over a path where fresh gravel had been lain. The path led to the Mount, where the Lanserim nobility took their eternal rest. Esye's light, so rare of late, came out to guide them, adding silver highlights to their surroundings that he had missed.

Last time he'd taken this journey was to bury Agler Gavenstone. To say times had been simpler then would be a farce, but Janto had a king's burdens on his shoulders now, not merely those of a young man unsure how to comfort his fiancée.

He needed the comforting now. Vesperi squeezed his gloved hand, the pressure slight but appreciated, nonetheless. She was not the wife his younger self would have imagined, but he was grateful she was the one he had, despite the unacknowledged rancor in their interactions. They would deal with this new, more recent grief, first, add it to the ones they already mourned.

Queen Lexamy marched on his other side. Behind them, six pall-bearers hoisted the casket. And beyond them, the specter masquerading as his father lurked. Whenever Janto let his doubts creep in, it solidified.

He craved the reassurance of his mother's hand, but she gave him a strained smile and shook her head. Vesperi also kept her thoughts to herself. Had his parents ever struggled as he and she did now?

The specter grew to his father's height. Janto looked away.

The procession slowed as they reached the Mount's open

amphitheater. His mother entered first to greet Rynna Hullvy. The priestess waited by the ritual bell, her long silver hair braided. She brushed gravel from her skirt, evidence she'd been meditating until hearing their caravan draw near. Members of the Order typically communed with Madel before such tasks.

The rynna's countenance was more peaceful than it had appeared in his dream. His vision of Mount Frelom's exposed peak also sprang to mind.

Queen Lexamy hugged Rynna Hullvy. They touched heads before his mother took her seat on the stone stairs. Janto and Vesperi sat beside her. They bundled themselves under blankets left on the seats earlier that morning.

The caravan of mourners filed in after them, quieter than they'd been at Agler's funeral. Was that due to the cold or the reverence they granted his father? At least eight hundred people had come, most of Lansera's nobility and a strong contingent of citizens from Callyn and nearby villages. It took fifteen minutes for them to fill the amphitheater's grounds. The standing crowd at back was many rows thick.

Janto instructed Ser Allyn, "They will need warm beverages. Send a horse back with instructions to have warmed ale brought as soon as possible. I don't want my father's funeral marred by any reports of frost-bitten limbs."

"Of course." Ser Allyn waved over Pic, who ran off for a mount as the last mourners found a place.

The ritual bell's resonance rang through the air. The small amount of conversation ended. Vesperi sat quietly beside him. He whispered, "I'm so glad you are here for this."

She nodded, her face drawn. His father had meant a lot to her, too.

Janto closed his eyes, as the bell commanded. Rynna Hullvy spoke:

"Madel, protector of the earth and sky, ruler of the heavens and the vanquished gods, we thank You. To You, we give an offering. We return to You one of us, one of Your own: King Dever Albrecht of Callyn, son of Turyn and Golinda, brother of Gelus. All his life, he served You."

The rynna paused long enough for the congregants to repeat her words. They rolled them backward in whispers, a tide returning to the sea.

"Dever Albrecht was well-known to me. He was king longer than he was a novice in the Order, but his soul was ever with our goddess.

His devotion to Her was evident in how he ruled, forty years of peace and prosperity for Lansera, and six years of reunion with our lost family over the mountains."

She paused, letting the statement linger longer than seemed necessary. Janto wondered if she were about to end the ritual already. Had she so few words to memorialize a man as remarkable as his father had been?

Her gasp compelled his eyes open and upward. More gasps released all around him, and exclamations of fear turned to wonder.

Above the amphitheater, the cloud-covered winter sky had transformed into a most extraordinary blue. Except the clouds hadn't gone away. They could be seen through the blue haze, which spread wider across the firmament. It floated outward, a lace coverlet over an extraordinarily large feasting table.

Vesperi exclaimed, "It's a rift," and Janto agreed. What else could such a wonder be but Madel's realm leaking through to their own? The color was so brilliant, so uplifting, it was hard to imagine anything as horrible as the claren had existed within it. His mind jumped to the grim discoveries Ryn Cladio had made.

"The day he came to me in my prison cell," Vesperi said, "your father glowed with that blue. That and the three-headed bird on his cloak were why I trusted him, trusted you, too. And our destiny." She gifted Janto with a watery smile, and he clutched her hand. The shadow was nowhere to be seen.

Rynna Hullvy's eyes twinkled as she proclaimed, "Madel reaches out to us to honor King Dever." The crowd murmured its approval, bathing in the extraordinary sight. Janto's whole body relaxed as he breathed in, the sensation rolling through him much like the congregants' words had rolled back a minute ago, when the world had seemed normal despite the surrealism of his father's death.

But something else caused him to stand at attention, hand on his sword hilt. The blue mist puckered at its center, like a curtain pinched. It revealed a deeper blue beyond, pulsing and electrified. His eyes crossed, and he could have sworn the shape of a gigantic hand, palm facing forward, was evident for a blink. A glowing ball of silver energy spikes pulsed within it. And then the spikes broke off, dozens at a time. They burst through the veil and entered the world, as though silver birds no bigger than doves.

There was no mistaking how close this wonder was to his dream.

Nor how little Janto understood it. He could think of no one else but Sielban who might.

The crowd gasped anew at the development. Their delighted murmurs grew as more of the silver "birds" took flight. The streaks of energy dove down almost to the amphitheater's awning before veering away in multiple directions.

Vesperi withdrew her hand, though her smile remained, a wistful one, which surprised him—Vesperi had plenty of her own silver energy to draw upon. Queen Lexamy laid an arm over Janto's shoulders. "Madel's hand sends birds to guide your father's spirit home. What a joy."

He nodded, though he struggled to find that joy again. Perhaps that was how grief worked. Dozens, if not a hundred of the silver flashes must have been released in the minutes since Rynna Hullvy had stopped the ceremony. A last few trickled out of the fissure, and the blue haze dispelled. In its wake, the crowd's conjectures increased in volume. Lord Xantas's belly laugh was easy to pick out. It spread, as always, among them.

"Amazing!" the people said, and "A good portent, the king be blessed!" Many more sentiments reached Janto's ears, but he didn't begin to think again until Rynna Hullvy struck the ritual bell. The crowd fell silent, remembering the reason they'd come.

Rynna Hullvy continued, "Clearly, Madel saw fit to open our eyes to Her glory today. If any of our countrymen here are Meduans, I hope you can take solace in the realness of Her power. Madel loves Her children."

"Hear, hear!" echoed Lord Xantas and others among the crowd.

"May he rest in the cobalt flame," the rynna called out, moving on to the end of the funeral ritual. The congregants took up the chant in rounds, though they lingered barely long enough to finish them, too consumed by the miraculous sights of the day.

"May he rest in the cobalt flame.

May he rest in the cobalt flame."

Not Madel's realm—Janto remembered Vesperi's words when she'd arrived—but in a flame the same color as the mist that had come through that portal. Was the difference significant? One was Madel's presence, and the other, Her realm, was it not?

Janto looked back up and realized Esye was gone entirely, the moon's earlier reappearance already fading from memory.

Fueled by their excitement, the crowd's dispersion was not orderly. Janto wished he could share in their amazement, but something felt amiss. And Vesperi had been quiet for so long a stretch. That was worrisome, but his next task needed to take priority.

"Go with my mother," Janto encouraged Vesperi, after pressing his lips against hers. She'd colored them black as the ribbons on their arms. "I need to finish this."

"Okay," she agreed. "But I need to talk with you."

"I know."

Her head jerked up; she had thought she'd better hidden whatever bothered her.

The servants arrived with steaming jugs on carts. "Make sure you walk back with a cup of that ale," he said. Her lips had been cold.

She took a mug, waved farewell. And Janto took a few steps toward the coffin. The other lieges of Lansera in attendance joined him: Lord Xantas for Ertion, Lady Gransyl Farami of Neville, Lady Rufalyn on behalf of Rasseleria and Elston, and Jehos Gavenstone, Serra's uncle in place of her aunt. They each took a place behind a pall, Janto included.

"Lord Sydley," he called as the elderly commander and liege of Wasyla attempted to take one too, despite leaning heavily on his cane, "please guide us to the Albrecht tomb. Ser Allyn will take your place."

Lord Sydley raised his elbows along with his cane in acknowledgment, and Janto handed over the large set of engraved keys that opened tombs for each noble house. Ser Allyn's cheeks colored with the unexpected honor, and Janto felt proud of finding a quick solution to the problem. Plenty more waited for him that would not be so easily solved.

Janto halted the pall bearers. "Rynna Hullvy."

The rynna took a moment to answer, bliss lingering on her face. "Yes, Prince—King Janto."

"I need you to turn to your books—spiritual, historical—and scour them for references of cantaleres and openings between the realms." A sudden hunch came upon him. "The Silver Guard, too." What else might an army of silver sparks be? "And send a bird to Ryn Cladio, asking him to do the same."

Rynna Hullvy raised her elbows in acknowledgment of the command.

Lady Rufalyn, who wore a feather-covered shawl despite the cold, regarded him with hawkish eyes. "Now tell me, young king, do you look for darkness among the light, as much as your wife?" She winked. "I admit there are times we could do with more cynicism, but after a sight such as this? Take joy in knowing Madel so eagerly welcomed your father to Her realm."

"I will try," Janto said.

Lord Sydley opened the creaking, gated door that led into the Mount. "On three, gentle folk. One . . . two . . .three."

Janto shouldered his pall. The group marched in sync. The cave's relative warmth was a relief from the late winter freeze. Sydley halted them before the Albrechts' tomb, placed close to the opening. He fished out a dark key engraved with entwined swans, and lit a torch quick as he could, mindful of the burden they bore.

Inside the tomb, the torchlight flickered on the white marble plates that kept Janto's family's coffins in their places, six generations of Albrechts. He and the nobility hefted the second member of the sixth generation onto the shelf beside Janto's uncle Gelus. Gelus had died of a wound taken on the plain of Orelyn that had festered years after the fighting was done.

The pallbearers lowered the casket and crouched against the tomb's walls, waiting on Janto. He lifted a newly chiseled nameplate from where it'd been leaned and read the words it held: "King Dever Albrecht, sixty-four years. For four decades, he ruled Lansera and reunified its peoples. Beloved father, husband, and man. May he rest in the cobalt flame."

"May he rest in the cobalt flame.

May he rest in the cobalt flame."

As the round died down, his father's image came to mind. Gray hair cropped short, brown eyes that revealed wit and duty in equal parts, and a regal presence Janto would ever aspire to and fall short of. But no cobalt flame surrounded the King Dever Albrecht he conjured. Rather, a rainbow of feathers fluttering in an unseen breeze.

And to its right, an inverse image in black and gray that dissipated as fast as Janto spied it.

My doubts remain. The Lanserim people had witnessed Madel's hand and taken heart, yet for Janto, it had engendered fear of the danger She'd extended that hand to combat. The extraordinary visual of the dream Mount Frelom, shining bright in the sunlight, stayed at the forefront of his mind.

‡

Back at the castle, Janto asked for a piping hot mug of ale and more parchment.

Dearest Serra,

I trust Jerusho will soon be on his way. If he has not left, please ask him to scour his old ryn's collection for any mention of the Silver Guard. I have had a new dream, and Madel displayed a wondrous sight at Father's funeral that has convinced me the old tales are key to understanding this. Perhaps Vesperi's weapon will not be enough on its own, this time.

I dreamt of silver flashes going out into the world and saw much the same while awake yesterday at the Mount. I would ask that you use your sight to investigate. The silver went so many places, but few I recognized. The one closest to you is the Perch.

He had more than half a mind to head north to Braven instead of waiting for his friends' return. Janto had glimpsed plenty of silver energy on that astonishing island himself. But his father had advised against it.

Indeed, I did, son.

The shadow again, wavering in and out of sight like Jerusho's granfaylon had before they caught it and wrested it from the other realm.

I am here to guide you. You should not trust your instincts right now. Lean on mine.

Was it his subconscious? A trick of the grief? Or perhaps . . . perhaps his father's spirit had returned to aid him, answering Janto's innermost wish. To think himself wiser than a man who'd ruled for decades *was* folly, after all.

Eyes he could not see lingered with a hunger that Janto would not feed with further recognition. His pen stroked the paper:

I await your next missive from there, Serra. Beware dark brothers, cantaleres, and even the shadows. Anything feels possible right now.

My seeing glass is trained to the east,

Janto

CHAPTER TWELVE

SERRA

Morning frost glazed the plateau like an iced gingersnap. Where the sun shone directly, the light blinded, though it lacked a certain steely quality. Esye was missing from view.

Serra sipped her tachery and rocked back in a chair on Mer Jerusho's front porch. A scratchy, beaver's hair blanket covered her legs—she tucked it in snugly after pondering whether one made of jurgen fur would feel the same. More spikes, she mused.

Lorne slunk into the seat beside her, and she thought for a moment that they might just enjoy the morning. The notion was quickly dispelled.

"I should go with you." His silver echo was a good argument for that, as Serra was now charged with gathering up others who possessed the same quality. But Serra and Napeler would move faster to the Perch on their own. And Serra did not know what might happen in such close quarters with Lorne on the journey.

Nothing. He's moved on, just as you wished.

The thought made her heart clinch, but that *was* how she wanted it. Wasn't it?

How pathetic. A Lanserim of your stature lusting after a wretched Meduan.

Serra grit her teeth. "It wouldn't be wise, Lorne. Jerusho needs you to help with the Mova council."

"Why, I didn't know you had such faith in my capabilities," he spoke with fake surprise, before resuming his normal tenor. "Do you really think a token Meduan will be able to convince that lot of Lanserim that nothing's amiss when their chief takes off on a sudden journey before spring's even hit?"

"*You* are a Lanserim, too. All Meduans are Lanser—"

Lorne gagged on his mug of tea. "Yes, yes." He waved his hand. "Have you always been this insufferably correct and I've forgotten? How *did* I endure it?"

She sucked in her cheeks at the sting of his retort. "And yet you claim not to know why I ended this."

He paused, perhaps realizing he'd dug the divide between them a little wider. Did he regret it or celebrate it, she wondered, staring off across the plateau. *Do I?* It didn't matter—there was more at stake than her romantic life. She was reminded of that every time she used the sight. The dark pockets had multiplied, each popping open on the horizon for a moment, before blinking out of existence.

More bad news coming. Best curl up with that mug of tachery and never move again.

Serra bit her lip, driving the thought away. She took another sip and grimaced. There was something unusual in this blend, perhaps a spice from Ertion unknown or forgotten to her. It made her gums tingle.

"Ginseng," Lorne supplied. "It grows in the foothills. Gives the mountain folk an extra push through their winter lumbering."

She tilted her head.

"I know how to read your expressions. I spent a lot of time memorizing them while you slept. After our trysts," he added, almost as an afterthought.

Serra blushed to her fingertips, which she closed around the cooling mug. Part of her hoped Lorne didn't share such details with others, but another part of her did. Having been so ensconced with a Meduan—it *would* cause her trouble if she returned to Meditlan rule. But getting past such biases, including her own, would do a lot to secure Lansera's future as well.

Lorne leaned closer, his eyes glinting. Then alarm leapt into them.

"What is it?" Serra asked, already turning. To the north, a pine forest rose higher than the plateau's edge. She could see nothing of interest, minus birds swooping and rabbits hopping about. Beyond the dark pockets in her periphery, the sight revealed nothing either.

Nothing red, black, and swarming like the claren. Yet she could feel the menace approaching.

"Lower," Lorne guided her. "The birds are circling in anticipation, and the rabbits . . . they're fleeing."

Serra directed her gaze as instructed. Indeed, the rabbits' blurry forms leapt closer, and there were many more than she'd come across in a meadow, much less an exposed plateau. "A fire?" she wondered.

"I don't think so." Lorne moved to the porch's edge. Serra followed, then gasped as the threat came into view.

"Green as rufior's feathers," she said, using the sight to glimpse the lumbering beast headed their way, "and something like a staff is giving off spurts of reddish-brown energy from its head."

"A cantalere." Lorne's voice was reverent, though he pulled her inside, slamming the door.

Jerusho looked up from his papers, startled. "Got that cold that fast, did it?"

Serra uttered a sentence brand-new to her. "A cantalere is chasing rabbits over the plateau. It'll be here soon."

"What?" The Ertion moved fast. He opened a side cabinet and drew out a bow and arrow. "I don't suppose either of you are good at this? I'm better with a fishing net."

Serra shook her head, deciding right then that she ought to start training with arms, if life was always going to be this unpredictable. Lorne did likewise—swordplay was his forte, and she was not about to let him rush out there to stab a cantalere in the ribs.

"You ought to have brought Janto," Jerusho joked. "He's much better at this part."

And Nap had gone into town to replenish their stores for the unforeseen trip to the Perch. Jerusho went to a window, drew back the heavy drapes. Light brightened the room and livened her senses.

The cantalere was not yet close, but rabbits covered the plateau, claws clattering as they propelled themselves forward. Serra's thoughts raced. What resources did they have? A swordsman and a fisherman, neither great for this task.

A fisherman!

"Do you have any fish traps big enough for a cantalere?"

Jerusho scratched his chin and frowned. "I fish in rivers, not . . . wait. A delegation came from Varma with Lord Xantas last spring. They brought a tribute . . ."

. . . to the great granfaylon fisherman, her thoughts filled in. Plenty of fish large as she was were harvested from Varma's seaward waters every year. It would make sense they'd present him a ceremonial trap large enough to catch a sheven, should he be so inclined to repeat his feat.

Jerusho scrambled through double doors leading down to the cabin's lower level. Lorne followed, knowing anything that large would need two pairs of hands to maneuver. From below, Serra heard crashing and banging loud enough to obscure the great clatter of rabbit claws. Through the window, she could make out the cantelere's form, appearing about as large as a dog at this distance. It would not remain so for long.

"Hurry, boys!" she yelled down the stairs. Occasionally, the cantalere slowed its approach to toss a rabbit in the air, flinging it from the sharp, jagged horn on its head. She shuddered, picturing it running loose through the streets of Mova. Without the sight, the animal's green hue was more of a tinge to its brown fur, the color harder to see in this realm. Nor did any energy rush out of its horn, though that too, looked plenty threatening.

Jerusho and Lorne reentered the room, hoisting an oblong cage of corded metals thick enough to withstand the cantalere's horn. Not that any of them knew how thick that might be. No one living likely did.

The brave fools continued straight out the front door, and Serra followed, a brave enough fool herself to remain nearby if they needed help.

They waded through the rabbits easily enough.

"Now what?" Lorne's hands fell to his sides as the cage clattered to the damp ground.

"I don't know," Jerusho groaned. "I haven't fished with a trap this big!"

Serra kept one eye on the creature whose huffs she could now hear, too close for comfort. Too close to attempt something like this. But they must. "It doesn't matter that it's not a fish," she said. "How would you approach this if it were? Think quick!"

"Bait!" Jerusho grabbed Lorne's arm. "Let's get some rabbits in here."

A few of the furry rodents already flopped dramatically against the inner bars. Jerusho and Lorne each herded another pair in. She hated that they had to sacrifice the poor bunnies, but what other choice did they have? The cantalere whinnied, close enough to raise the hairs on Serra's arm.

Jerusho fumbled with a latch on the trap's door, while Lorne scrambled to secure it to the ground.

"It's almost here! Get back!" Serra yelled. The cantalere gave off a horrendous smell, or maybe that was the rabbit carcasses torn to shreds by its horns. Bits of fur stuck to its hide. It had an extra pair of legs, making six.

"Please, please, please," Serra prayed. What she wouldn't give for Vesperi's flame right now. Lorne and Jerusho jumped back onto the porch just as the cantalere . . . ran right past the cage they'd so heroically improvised.

Desperate, Lorne cast his magic to catch the beast's attention. As the silver light flashed, a few nearby rabbits crackled into crisps. The strike stopped short of the cage, though much farther than Lorne's echo had ever reached before. He glanced her way with utter shock before their attention returned to the cantalere.

Two of the beast's spindly legs swung it around a few yards past the cage. Its back legs dug into the ground, apparently hooked rather than hooved. They braced the large animal against the sudden change in direction and speed. The cantalere raised its flat snout and sniffed the air.

"Please let it prefer charred rabbit to a human's scent," Lorne prayed. Serra hadn't considered that possibility. She took a step toward the cabin door, but the cantalere ambled over to the trap, taking deep sniffs and releasing a string of whinnies that panicked the contained rabbits. They flopped against the bars.

The cantalere speared one of them through a hole in the trap, and its prey let loose a scream, forcing Serra's face into her hands. When she looked again, the cantalere was struggling to get at the carcass. The rabbit's body caught against the cage, and the cantalere's jagged horn shredded it while the beast grew more incensed. The other rabbits had fallen silent. They shuddered so intensely, Serra could hear their fearful breathing.

Lorne started playing a lute next to her ear.

"What are you doing?!" Serra half-whispered, half-yelled. "Try your echo again!"

He winked at her over the wooden instrument and continued

blowing, a light, soothing song. The rabbits' ears quirked up, and one raised its head.

"Keep playing!" Jerusho encouraged, hands gripped on the porch railing.

Lorne repeated the soft melody, and a pair of the poor things made a run for it, lunging through the cage opening. The cantalere reacted nearly as fast, pulling the rest of its horn back out and showering rabbit parts everywhere. It hefted its bulk toward the trap's entrance, though the escaped rabbits were black streaks many yards away.

The music stopped, and the cantalere's snout careened back to the trap, where the other rabbits remained. It dug its gangly limbs in the ground again and readjusted, knowing a good thing when it had it. Then it lunged in at the rabbits, and Serra's breath skipped, her eyes on the trap door's latch.

The latch released and the door clunked down with a heavy swing. The cantalere jumped, catching its horn in the wires above its head, and panicked. The remaining rabbits screamed but could do nothing to avoid being trampled. The latch held, but the trapdoor strained, bulging out, as the cantalere headbutted it.

"We've got to reinforce that." Serra pivoted to Jerusho for ideas, but the councilman had disappeared back inside when she wasn't looking. He re-emerged, head glistening with sweat and a cord of thick, sturdy rope hefted on his shoulder. He grunted with determination, and Lorne and Serra moved out of the way.

Jerusho dashed to the cage. It was a wonder, seeing someone in their element. He didn't flinch as he crisscrossed the rope over the trap door and made two loops around the trap to strengthen it. He tied off the coil with a fancy knot and gave it several satisfied tugs.

The cantalere, having exhausted itself, settled in for a nap among the trampled carcasses.

"Now what?" Jerusho asked.

Lorne and Serra exchanged glances, and she collapsed onto the porch chair where she'd been drinking tachery an eon ago. "I have no idea," she said. Then she pressed her palms to her brow. "A lute?"

Lorne smiled as he wiped sweat away. "I've needed to direct my attention to something new—beyond matchmaking for Jerusho here. Seemed like an easy instrument to pick up."

Serra looked elsewhere, knowing why he needed the distraction. She was proud of him for directing his energy to less destructive behaviors. After one of their breakups, he'd seduced half of Fyn. Oh, he'd claimed he'd only been flirting, but tell that to the herbalist's son who'd stumbled half-dressed into a well in the middle of the night, on his way to what he'd misread as an invitation.

Had she decided she'd had enough of Lorne's condescension that time, or had Lorne had enough of hers?

But that wasn't what she meant. "No, why did you use the lute and not your magic on—" she pointed at the cantalere, "that? You might have been able to kill it."

"Or send it into a fury when I singed its neck hairs. I had no idea if it would work that way again. It's never been that strong before."

Jerusho interjected, "Do you think we *should* kill it?"

Serra shook her head. "Not if you think your companions can keep it caged on the journey to Callyn. Alive would be best for studying how to protect ourselves against such creatures. We have to expect more."

She need not say out loud how real that danger now felt.

It's more than you can handle.

Enough! I've seen a cantalere in the flesh, and I know Madel has a plan to defeat them. I will listen to your poison no longer—I don't care if you're merely inside my head. Be gone!

I will always be here, Seer. When you let me in.

That I will never do. Not when my people need me.

But when they don't, and you're left with yourself?

"Are you okay, Serra?" Lorne touched her arm.

"Fine. Just cold." She closed whatever door in her mind she could and prayed it would be enough.

"I'll find a cart." Jerusho disappeared into his stable.

"Follow me," Lorne suggested. "Let's go find something warm."

Serra shivered in agreement. He led Serra into the cabin and down the hall to his bedroom. She began to protest, but one eyeroll was enough to convey he'd try nothing. He opened another thick, wooden door, this one adorned with flower carvings. Too much of Lorne's current favorite musk filled the room, but it felt cozy, with a four-poster bed made of dark wood and an end table the same shade, skirted with matted velvet. The tapestry on the wall displayed a muscled, extremely tall Jerusho catching the granfaylon in the woods of Braven.

Serra had to laugh, and that she could felt like confirmation that the voice plaguing her had been banished.

Lorne joined her in the merriment. "It's the only thing he's spent money on in the four months I've been on this blasted plateau," he said, "and let me tell you, he *has* riches—or at least items he could have sold in Medua for true wealth. The people in this town keep giving him their valuables. They stare at him like he's the coming of the three-headed bird itself. Like he's as important as you are."

Serra did not comment on the compliment. "He is a murated man; that's no small thing in Lansera."

"I've gathered," Lorne replied. He removed her outermost coat and laid it folded on the end table. Serra wondered when he'd developed such manners.

"About the echo," he handed her a fresh mug of tachery from a pot left steeping beside his bed, "that was a much stronger burst than typical. But it's nothing near what Vesperi has. The weapon could burn a cantalere to ashes, nearly as fast as the claren. I lived through the fall of Mandat Hall. I've seen how powerful she is."

"You're not the only one," Serra agreed. Lorne had been integral to their victory then, having joined up with the hunting party on Madel's behest.

Serra claimed a corner of his bed but was careful to keep distance between them. "But she can't be everywhere at once. If more come, or the claren return, or—" She shuddered to consider there might be worse creatures than those horrors that sucked life and flesh from their victims. But if the cantaleres came in force . . . "We need to be able to fight them. It makes sense Janto is sending me chasing after more people like you. Especially if their magic has strengthened too."

Lorne took her free hand in his and met her eyes. Before she could reproach him, he said, "I think you should go collect Uzziel Sellwyn after the Perch."

Serra gaped. Uzziel lived with Lorne's father in Granich Manor in the Meduan riverlands. She had no desire to go there without a larger guard than Nap, nor to meet Uzziel. Vesperi rarely spoke of her brother, and when she did, it came coupled with a curse. Lorne had said little more, though he'd spent time protecting the child before the clarens' attack.

Which meant Madel had wanted Uzziel to survive, Serra realized. Perhaps for this.

"He had something, Serra. I saw it when I carried him out of

Sellwyn. Whatever it was, it flew from his hand and burnt a branch of his father's hanging tree as we fled to the east. I'm not sure he was aware it happened, and our safety was too pressing for me to expend much thought on it. He never mentioned it, but the boy had just left his bed for the first time in his life to flee his home, knowing his father hadn't survived. He had plenty already to process."

"I'll write Janto to ask for more protection from the Perch. I'm sure Ser Swalus can spare a few of his Ravens." The Perch was the headquarters for Lansera's network of spies, the Ravens. They served primarily to report information on Medua back to the crown during the divide. *And now.* The Ravens had not been disbanded. No matter how much she wished it, there was plenty of reason not to trust people from the Meduan regions.

Vesperi will not be thrilled to learn I'm planning to retrieve the one person she hates most in this world. But Serra sat now beside the one person *she* hadn't wanted to see anytime soon, either. Vesperi could manage.

She gasped, realizing something else. "The cantaleres are a literal threat, not a prophetic allusion, like the three-headed bird. Maybe the dark brother is too. Do you think it could be Uzziel?"

Lorne waved his hand. "He's just a kid."

"So were we both, not so long ago. That didn't stop Madel from using us. We don't know who the dark brother's foes are, whether to protect against him or them." She ran a hand through her hair, then took another calming sip of tachery—no ginseng in this pot.

"I know this gets harder every moment, not knowing what we're up against . . . well, what we're up against *in addition* to that monster outside with a horn that could gore a man clean through." Lorne shuddered. Then he stood and rummaged through a drawer in the end table. "But I have a favor to ask."

"Okay?" Serra watched his movements, glad to be with someone who understood so well the difficulties of trying to protect the Lanserim from unseen threats. It would be so easy to take solace in his proximity, but what good would that do either of them? It would muddy their focus. *And I don't want to,* she reminded herself. *I am done with Lorne that way.*

Lorne opened his palm, revealing a minuscule representation of a river dividing into many parts, carved on a square of ancient purple glass. Such artifacts could be found on the banks of Lake Ashra—relic glass.

"What is that?" Serra pored over the unfamiliar sigil, though the answer seemed obvious when Lorne spoke next.

"The sigil of House Granich." A shy, proud smile curled his lip. Serra denied how enticing it was. "Some Rasselerians brought it here after a trip to Varma. I'd never seen it before—how ridiculous is that? Never having seen my family's sigil? Father hid it while I was growing up. He viewed it as a relic of the old Lanserim ways—not that he'd have given up our historic holdings, had anyone challenged them, mind you. But he paid lip service to the advers' creed that might meant right, not heritage."

Lorne met her eyes. "I'd like you to give it to my sister."

He rarely spoke of Cora Granich. She'd been raised as a servant in his home, a better lot than that of many Meduan women. Growing up, he hadn't known who she was until another of his servants had pointed her out.

"Of course." Serra took the smooth glass pendant and wrapped it for her pouch. Cora had decided not to come over the mountains after the Conjoining, and though she had appeared treated well on Lorne's rare visits home, he'd been worried his father's new house rules were for show. Even if they weren't, many Meduans found it hard to believe they really had a choice to make their own way in the world once granted it. If never taught how to spin a kaleidoscope's rings, one never saw more than painted glass.

"I have a favor to ask you, too." Serra rebuttoned her pouch. "Please remain here, so I—we—the king can contact you if needed. Let us know if anything changes with your echo? Or if anything else comes stomping its way into the countryside."

"Of course. Let me know if I can ever kiss you again?"

She smiled sadly and closed the door, not risking another glance. Then she sunk to her feet against his door as a new wave of grief overcame her. Even if she did take him back, there was no promise it would last. Lansera was in danger again, and would it ever truly be safe? Were any of them ever?

Serra waited in the stable with her things for Nap's return. She'd insist they leave for the Perch right away. Because they had a king- dom to save, yet again, and because she had so recently been a king's daughter. That nothing lasted was all she was sure of now. Not peace, not love, and not the safety Madel had promised.

The cantalere, asleep on its blood-stained hooves, was her proof. She needed no extra voice in her head to tell her that.

CHAPTER THIRTEEN

VESPERI

Through a crack in a side door leading into the throne room, Vesperi watched as her husband rested his head on a hand. He stared, entranced, at the early morning's sunrays splashing the throne room's floor, almost as though something held his attention. Yet there was only stone and dust.

Should his head dip much lower, the throne's metal briars might scar his face, and Vesperi would smite him if he allowed so much as a scratch. *Not that I have the option any longer.* Her empty palm twinged sharp as a phantom limb.

She entered, the side door creaking.

That prodded Janto to speak, though he did not glance up. "What is it?" Annoyance tinged his voice. That wasn't a good sign. His first full day of court lay ahead. He looked regal enough on the throne, but something more than grief marred his features.

"I could ask you the same thing," she said. "You look as lively as that craval beast Mar Jeffyr served up last night."

"Vesperi." He flashed her a tired smile that emphasized his dimples. In the light, his freckles were more pronounced. She'd missed his face, and not just the way it conjured memories of Izzy or that she'd imagined their miscarried child would share his strawberry-blond hair. She'd missed *him* while she'd been holed up in Elston, licking her wounds. And she wanted to do something to make that already disappeared smile reappear. So she did what she knew best.

Weaving her way in to avoid the metalwork, she licked the space between his earlobe and jawline. Janto sighed with the pleasure she aimed for. She moved a hand to his chest and—

"I appreciate the sentiment." He closed his fingers over hers. "But I'm not up for that yet." He grinned, his eyes deepening to a maple brown. "Especially not in the throne room. You're lucky it's early."

"Like that would have mattered to me." Vesperi pressed forward for a lingering kiss, which Janto gave her a show of enjoying. Had he ever resisted her seduction before? Not since their first journey together, when she'd been a prisoner rather than an equal.

Though she'd deny it if asked, she wished she knew how to give him comfort. Janto had given it to her many times, though she hadn't been willing to accept it in recent months. Now, she circled him with her arms and was pleased when he nestled into them, pleased even more that she'd tried this much—she had not known she was willing to be intimate again with him.

That's something. She imagined what Serra would do in this circumstance. Maybe whisper "How can I help?" in plaintive tones, offer to . . . to . . . *something.* The Lanserim were always offering to do something for each other. It galled her, that impulse to consider others' needs first, though as a parent, she'd done so without thinking.

"Are you just grieving?" she asked, forgetting tact. Janto worried her, yes, but so did her missing magic. And the king had been important to her too.

He wasn't the only one who needed comforting.

The words burned like a confession, but she admitted them anyhow. "I've lost the silver flame."

Janto pivoted toward her, his voice raised. "What?"

His angry tone surprised her. She matched it. "It's gone. I don't know what happened."

Janto scowled. "When? Why are you just sharing this with me?"

"In Elston, the day your father died."

"Over a week ago? What if we'd had news of a claren attack? What if the army needed your assistance handling bandits? What if—"

"Your father died!" she yelled back. Her speech echoed through the cavernous room. "I was trying to be considerate." She hated how her next words came out like a whine. "I didn't want to make this about me."

Janto's voice filled with self-reproach. *He deserves it. Can't he see that I'm trying?* "I'm sorry," he said. "It's just, well, you're a matter of national security, and not because you married me."

"I know," Vesperi sighed. "I hadn't thought of it like that. I hadn't thought of it much." Except for yesterday, when she'd spent two hours in the queensgarden trying to get so much as a whiff of silver smoke to spark. She'd channeled all her past anger into her palm but couldn't find Esye in the sky. Without the moon's silver light to provide the spark, she'd succeeded only in smashing a patch of clover to death with her pacing.

"I should have known," Janto reflected. "Your eyes . . ." He drew her close by the arm. "I don't want you to think this in any way makes you less beautiful, Vesperi. But they've lost their silver."

That wasn't news to her. Him noticing felt reassuring. "I knew the king had died right then. I don't know how, but the moment the flame went out, I knew. It's connected somehow, Janto."

He nodded, his face solemn. "It is. I'm sure what happened during the funeral rites is part of it, too. I don't know what you felt during that—"

"Buoyed, refreshed. It's lessened now, except maybe the grief doesn't feel as strong."

"I felt that, too. But also a gnawing sense that something wasn't right. What happened was so like my dream. It has to mean something, and I don't think it's good."

A knock came at the side door. Janto acknowledged it and Ser Allyn stepped in. The wiry old man's frown prompted Vesperi to step aside, but Janto held her hand.

"What is it?" he asked Ser Allyn.

"Some of Rynna Hullvy's oldest books on history and theology," the servant explained, standing tall. "As you asked."

Ser Allyn motioned, and another servant wheeled in a cart laden with at least ten tomes of many-inch-thick bindings. Two were familiar from Lady Rufalyn's collection.

"Did Rynna Hullvy send a summary, perhaps?" Janto asked.

Vesperi laughed. Ser Allyn shook his head.

"Please ask her to send an expert on the morrow," Janto said. "I can't imagine I'll have time to read it all myself."

"Your highness," Ser Allyn raised his elbows with respect. "As you asked, I remain on to advise you. This morning, you receive your first supplicants after you break your fast. You need to be energized, make a good impression in your first few months as Lansera's ruler. Don't spend your hours hunting for koparin in these hills," he motioned to the books. "They will not help you achieve that."

Janto grumbled but acquiesced, "I want those experts, Ser Allyn. Jerusho will be here soon, but I don't know if this can wait. I want them right away."

Vesperi wondered if she qualified. She'd read a few tomes twice over in the last month, retained plenty of knowledge about do-good Lanserim fighting wave after wave of reprehensible, and admirably powerful, foes. And there was that chapbook from the Rasselerians—she hadn't thought to give it to him yet, not with the funeral the day after she'd arrived. "Janto, I could—"

"Of course." Allyn raised his elbows to acknowledge the command. "And another letter arrived from Lady Serrafina in the last hour." He handed it over and exited the room.

Vesperi scoffed. When things proved difficult, Janto always reached out for Serra's advice. And who could blame him? Vesperi had no means of providing comfort, solace, all these things people seemed to expect of each other in Lansera. She couldn't even promise the silver flame's protection anymore. Why *should* Janto trust her, after her self-exile, with matters of state?

Guilt reflected from Janto's eyes. *Good.* But the concern on his brow outweighed it. "I think whatever is affecting Lansera involves the three of us," he remarked, the letter in hand. "I've sent her to cast about, investigate where I saw the silver flashes in my dream. If others have such magic, we'll need it." His downturned head conveyed contriteness. "Especially knowing you've lost yours."

He skimmed the letter speedily, and his eyes ballooned. "There are cantaleres rampaging through Mova."

Cantaleres? Hadn't the Rasselerians' book said something about them? "Janto, I've another—"

"Vesperi," the parchment fluttered in Janto's hand, "she won't be alone when she returns to Callyn."

"Who? Lorne?" She quirked an eyebrow, surprised Janto would consider Serra's dalliance with the Meduan of any concern to her. But nothing could have prepared her for the words that came next.

"Your brother."

Uzziel. Vesperi reeled at the onslaught of memories her brother's name stirred. Years at his bedside, being forced to tend his needs rather than her own and beaten when she'd refused. Expulsion to the nunnery when she'd lost her ability to withstand it any longer. Her father's preference for him, despite how much more capable she was, how much more she could have done to further the greatness of their house than that ungrateful whelp in his bed. The torture he'd inflicted on her personally, with words, with deeds, with his very existence. Uzziel was the symbol of all Vesperi had left behind in Medua.

To have him come here, stomp his way into her . . . Vesperi laughed. "He'll never make it this far. He won't make it from his bed. You've sent Serra on a fool's errand."

Janto's grasp was tender. "He may prove stronger than you think, Vesperi. We should hope for it, if he'll help against what's coming."

Her eyeroll conveyed well enough how likely she thought that possibility. She stood, needed to get some fresh air, strike some bushes with . . . with shears.

"You'll be back for court?" Janto asked.

Vesperi nodded her way out the side door. Oh, she'd be there. She wasn't about to let Uzziel usurp her queenly duties as well.

‡

The room was fuller than usual, fuller perhaps than any day except the one she'd wed Janto. Half that crowd had been there to gape at a Meduan becoming a princess, the other half at seeing two heads of the bird of creation joined in matrimony.

Their interest wasn't so different now, Vesperi considered. Maybe some of the nobility and citizens from Callyn filled the benches to pay their respects to King Dever. But most wanted to gape at their new king. And queen. The Lanserim were excellent gapers.

Whatever their reasons, the magnetism of two hundred people rising at her presence was electric. Vesperi soaked it in as she stepped through the doors at the far side of the room. She wore one of the few dresses she kept in her possession. Over its green velvet, the skirt overlay consisted of silver thread and emeralds. Part of her felt a pretender, keeping up her association with the flame, but the other part knew the colors complemented her features, set her black hair to shining.

She was late, and Janto strode down the aisle to meet her. He kissed her lips briefly and gave her a smile, half-pride, half-pretending he hadn't been worried at her absence. Her own smile in exchange was cautious.

"What do I say?" she whispered low enough for only him to hear.

Janto chuckled into her neck. "'My king,' should suffice," he whispered back.

"Presumptuous," Vesperi winked. She performed as instructed, and he took her hand, guiding her to his mother's perch on the left bench nearest the throne. She watched as he returned to the throne, maneuvering himself away from the barbs. He looked the part, no slouching in the chair.

He took a sip from his goblet and waved the next plaintiff in. Vesperi wondered if it would reflect badly on herself if she asked for a pillow to sit upon. Court could last hours.

"Pinch your wrist," Queen Lexamy whispered from her left. "Whenever you start to feel drowsy."

Vesperi was unsurprised her mother-in-law answered an unasked question—her Rasselerian heritage came with a bit of their telepathy. Unlike the frog people, however, the queen's use of it didn't creep Vesperi out.

The book. I must get him that book!

One of the guards admitted the next supplicant. With a practiced nudge, Janto repositioned his crown of silver brambles on his head. The queen wore her golden and grander version of the same circlet, and Vesperi wondered what her own would be like. Callyn's metallurgist was no doubt at work on it already—the coronation would take place next week.

The plaintiffs came in a group of three, councilmen from somewhere in Meditlan, if she judged correctly from the dried grape leaves stuck in their cloaks. Vesperi straightened, proud she'd learned the sigils—the Gavenstones' was a grape cluster.

"Your highness," the tallest man said, raising his elbows in deep regard. The others, a man and a woman, followed suit.

Janto bid them stand up. "What can I do for you, citizens? Did the grapevines freeze this winter? You'll cause many in the kingdom despair if they don't have Meditlan's first fruits to celebrate with next fall."

The joke drew a few chuckles from among the wings, but none from the Meditlan party. Vesperi would need to speak with Janto about his comedic timing.

"We had intended to report on that to Lady Marji, your highness," the tall man continued. "And on a number of our new workers who have been slipping off in the night."

The emphasis he placed on *new* made it quite clear he spoke of Meduan immigrants. Vesperi refrained from an eyeroll. Despite the Lanserim's best intentions, Janto was fooling himself if he thought their two cultures would ever fully enmesh.

"But the morning we were to depart, something remarkable happened."

"Remarkable enough it brought you here, two days' farther ride, instead?" Janto tented his fingers.

The party nodded. The woman spoke next, removing her straw hat. "I was sharpening the tills, your highness, when something in the bushes beyond the barn caught my attention. It made a terrible ruckus—lots of huffing and scratching, so much I feared a drasmo had crossed the bay from Yarowen."

Attendees exchanged excited chatter at the prospect. The fast-moving drasmos were notorious for leaving a mess as they hunted, without rest, for insects.

"Go on," Janto prodded, his creased brow already trying to puzzle out how to eradicate the vermin, if needed. Vesperi, on the other hand, would prefer a nice warm bath to such rote troubles. *Commoners.*

"Except it wasn't a drasmo. It had a big, flat tail like a creek beaver. But it was twice as big." The woman spoke louder, caught up in the memory. "And that tail had spikes all over it."

A jurgen. Like the women in the bathhouse had talked about. Gasps of disbelief rebounded through the throne room. Someone to Vesperi's right muttered the word.

The third Meditlan plaintiff displayed a piece of fragmented wood, pockmarked with holes. "And this is what it did to my front gate."

The chatter increased in volume, and someone shouted, "The Meduans' handiwork, after running off, more like!" Similar sentiments could be heard on both sides of the aisle.

The spokesman made to speak, and Janto raised a hand for quiet. His mouth fell slightly open as the crowd obeyed him, though King Dever had regained control that way many times in the past. Vesperi imagined living her whole life knowing she would someday be queen and still being amazed when it happened. *Would I have taken such pride in following in my father's footsteps?* She didn't like the answer.

Lord Jahnas Sellwyn was to King Dever as the moon Onsic's void to Esye's fire.

Janto asked the spokesman, "Did you see the animal as well? And what are your names?"

"Yelen Fora, your highness," the man raised his elbows again, "chief farmer of Orun village, on the coast. And I didn't see it."

The crowd took that as proof it hadn't happened, but Janto used his "magic" trick a second time, waiting for the silence to reply. "But you believe them?"

The man nodded.

"Then so do I." A flabbergasted uproar followed, but Vesperi caught Queen Lexamy encouraging Janto on with a wave of her hand. Subtlety was an art Vesperi still needed to master. Part of her wanted to ask why Janto didn't just tell them right then about Serra's cantalere. But she held her tongue.

"I have experience with creatures once thought legend, as you know," Janto said. "As king, I choose to believe my people's word."

Someone else shouted, "Slayer of the stag!" and Janto's cheeks colored. He continued, "I'll send a small team of soldiers and researchers to investigate."

Ser Allyn noted the order on parchment.

"They'll capture it and bring it back for study. But if needed," Janto pointed to the battered piece of wood at his feet, "they'll kill it first."

Then he offered the Meditlans rooms for the evening so they could be questioned more about the experience.

The next plaintiff was a woman alone. She walked slowly, but surely, every step an eternity. Her movement felt familiar to Vesperi—she'd moved much the same when Izzy first went missing. And sometimes still on waking. This woman was deeply grieving.

"What's your name?" Janto asked once the woman drew close enough. He sounded querulous, and Vesperi had a premonition: this was not a story she wanted to hear. But she must.

"Hinta." No town or region name, no title. She was Meduan. The woman raised her head enough that tear trails, through her travel-dirtied face, became evident. One hand closed tight around something Vesperi couldn't see.

"And what can your king do for you, Mar Hinta?"

She made a noise, one Vesperi knew well, the sound of mourning gathering itself into speech. "I don't know."

Janto paused, gave her time to gather her thoughts. If she had come from over the mountains, it had been a long, hard journey already, even without whatever spurred her on. "You came here for a reason. Tell us what it is."

Mar Hinta stood a little taller, and in so doing, unfolded her fist. What she clutched was a ribbon. It reminded Vesperi of the ones the Lanserim used to dangle feathers for children to chase.

"This is my son's belt. It's all I have left of him."

Vesperi's heart sank. Oh, she knew this woman's pain well.

Janto prodded, "Please go on. And someone get her some water, please."

The woman sniffled. "He was born after . . . after you came to Qiltyn. I saw you both"—she gestured to Vesperi, who acknowledged her with an elbow raise—"that day, when Mandat Hall burned. I'd thought myself mad, Lanserim soldiers all around and a Meduan woman with their prince."

Mandat Hall had fallen maybe less than an hour before Janto addressed the people of Qiltyn, formally taking back their country and regranting them Lanserim citizenship. About an hour before this woman had first laid eyes on a Lanserim.

"He was mine, my Pityr," she continued. "No one was supposed to take him from me, not anymore, not after you killed the advers. But something did."

The woman's pain cast a pallor over the court. Vesperi ached with each syllable.

"He disappeared before my eyes. His hand first, where he'd grabbed at some butterfly over my shoulder. And then something . . . something pulled him in and I grabbed madly, but all I got was this."

She held the belt up high, turned in a circle so the people could see it. The crowd whispered amongst themselves, unsure what to make of her story. Was it easier or harder to believe than a jurgen's appearance, Vesperi wondered. She hadn't considered how it must have been for Janto, to have Izzy in his sight one second, and then gone the next. Months of scouring the mangrove swamps—she'd ignored how deep his cuts from the sawgrass had been.

Queen Lexamy squeezed her hand, startling Vesperi. The Lanserim impulse to provide comfort, yet again catching her off guard.

Janto spoke, "I know a bit of what that's like, Mar Hinta. I am sorry for your loss, I truly am."

"He's not lost." The woman spoke sharply, and Vesperi felt, rather than heard, the reproach. "He's just gone somewhere else. He was right in front of me, like you are now. And then . . . then he wasn't."

A sob wrenched from her throat. She collapsed, clinging to the shred of fabric, sobs echoing in the throne room.

Janto descended from the throne. "I'm so sorry." He slid to his knees and wrapped her in a hug. Her eyes went wide as she scurried out of reach and lifted her arm to protect herself.

"Oh no, I didn't mean to—" Janto righted himself and backed away. Meduans had been taught to fear their leaders. This woman was no more likely to respond to that sort of comfort than Vesperi had, years ago.

Vesperi sighed and caught Janto's eye. He nodded.

Her ways were direct but effective. "We will not hurt you," she said, lowering the woman's arm. She spoke firmly and held her head high. "We will find out what is stealing our people. I promise you."

"There have been others?" the woman gasped, and hope lit her countenance. "You can find him, bring him back?" She searched Vesperi's face like a woman sighting a campfire through a needlestorm.

"There have." Vesperi touched her shoulders. "And we will find out how to rescue them. I guarantee you, we will not forget your son—how could we? We lost the princess the same way last spring."

The courtiers gasped, though Vesperi could not reason why. It wasn't news that Izzy was gone. Did they think her dead, not merely disappeared? Even after hearing this woman's story?

Ser Allyn made to quiet them, but Vesperi silenced him with a hand to his wrist.

"We will find the princess, this Pityr, and anyone else who's disappeared. And we'll stop the jurgens, too," she threw in for good measure. Her voice was shriller than she liked, and her heart raced—why wasn't the court quieting down? Hadn't she done what a queen should, reassure them?

Queen Lexamy cast worried green eyes her way. She gathered up the folds of her skirt and stepped away from the benches. "This will be enough for today, citizens of Lansera," Lexamy said. "The king thanks you for holding an audience with him. If you were not heard today, rest assured, he will see to you tomorrow. Ser Allyn," she beckoned him over, "please provide Mar Hinta with a room so she can rest until we can glean more details from her about her son's disappearance."

"Of course," Ser Allyn guided the woman out a side entrance into the courtyard. Queen Lexamy and Janto raised their elbows and bowed as the rest of the looky-loos filtered out. Vesperi stood motionless, flummoxed. Once alone with the castle staff, the queen took Vesperi by the elbow and led her to the throne.

"Janto, Vesperi," her voice was equal parts exasperation and worry, "bringing your loss into this is not going to aid that woman."

"But you heard what hap—"

She silenced Vesperi with a raised hand. "Oh, I am not deaf. And if I were your father," she gave Janto a hint of a smile, "I'd already be praying for guidance, reaching for a ritual bell to chime and hoping Madel might answer. But I am not your father. I am a mother, and I know how your hurt aches. But I also know you cannot act on this woman's tragedy for yourselves. You must do it for her. For your people."

Vesperi wrested her arm away. "Is Izzy not 'our people's' princess? I fail to see the difference. How can we search for that woman's son without having Izzy in the forefront of our thoughts? We have to help her—it could give us answers, too!"

Queen Lexamy placed a gentle but firm arm on her shoulders. She leaned forward to include Janto in the embrace, while avoiding the brambles. "How can you search at all," she said, "without your sight here?"

Janto blinked rapidly. "I shouldn't have sent Serra away. She saw a new fissure in the kitchen, and I sent her to collect Jerusho rather than stay here until we worked it out."

Vesperi flared with anger. "New fissures? That could be what happened to Izzy! If there are rifts opening and people slipping through because we can't see them . . . What else have you 'forgotten' to fill me in on yet? Did you and Serra discuss jurgen mating habits while she was here?"

"Be thankful she's lost her flame, son," his mother said before kissing his head. "Because you're about to get burned regardless."

Queen Lexamy exited quick as she could, while Vesperi pointed a finger into her husband's nose.

"You told your mother already? And what other secrets are you and Serra keeping, hmm? What else is she privy to that your own wife is not?"

Vesperi paced in front of the throne, tired of this. Of sitting on a hard bench, listening to people's problems when she had enough of her own. Tired of being left out of important developments, important to *her*, because her husband didn't trust her enough.

Tired of being told she should keep a lid on her emotions, should be over Izzy's disappearance, and move on. *I shouldn't and I won't ever.*

"Vesperi," Janto's tone landed somewhere between pleading and exasperated, "I wasn't trying to leave you out of the loop. You haven't been available until now."

Oh sure, use her need for space against her. Wasn't that typical?

"Can you try to trust me on this?"

Trust him? When he kept proving he didn't trust her an inch? *Ridiculous!* Why should she trust him? He lost their daughter! During a picnic in the woods. A picnic! The epitome of ridiculous Lanserim notions, that eating a meal outside was nicer than indoors, with the plates and napkins and servants—

"You're worrying me." Janto half-stood, but thought better of it, sinking further into the throne.

Good. You can't handle me. She stomped her feet as she paced. A memory sprang to mind of Izzy doing the exact same thing last spring. She'd been denied another go at Lash the Feather during a feast lasting well past her bedtime. Izzy had clenched her little fists so hard, Vesperi worried her fingernails might pierce her skin.

She opened her hands, observed the imprints of her nails against her own palm. The memory and sudden deceleration of her emotions made her sway. Janto jumped to his feet, and she cursed herself for welcoming the reassurance of his steadying hand. And for the tears coming, too, and the fading anger. Maybe she hadn't lost the flame. Maybe she'd become too much of a Lanserim to hold onto the malice needed to wield it.

But it was more than that. Vesperi peeked up through the glass ceiling to where Esye should be but was not. Tansic and Oro's intertwining copper and gold halos remained the same as ever, but Onsic loomed ever larger in the sky. *We should be worried about the moons.* But Vesperi couldn't bring herself to rank celestial bodies higher in priority than her daughter's absence. *We can find her, why can't he see that?*

"Hey," Janto snuck his arms under her shoulders from behind, "I didn't have time to tell you all about Serra's visit—with everything happening. I'm sorry."

Vesperi wanted to keep up her front, but she'd made mistakes, too. She twisted to cradle his cheek with a hand. "I know. I do. I understand. On my trip back home, a Rasselerian delegation gave me a book of old chants they'd gathered for you. It mentions cantaleres. I forgot to tell you." Her facial muscles had such a hard time expressing contrition. It pained her. "I don't understand what you're going through or how to help. Dever wasn't *my* father."

Then why did her tears flow so freely? What right did she have to grieve like this, forcing the king's own son to comfort her? It was so hard being in these halls—her body ached with Izzy's absence. She wanted to read to her, play with her, cradle her to sleep. Maybe Vesperi grieved for that, too, for all the affection she wanted to give her daughter that she'd never had.

She sunk onto the closest bench. Janto followed.

"Hey," he said, peeking through his mussed hair. His face was as wet as hers, his beautiful white cloak damp from catching tears. Janto was her partner in this grief, her partner in everything. She felt gratitude for that.

She picked strands of her hair from his lashes. "I don't think she's dead, Janto. I would know it." Vesperi had never been so connected to anyone in her life as she was to Izmareld. Not even to Janto and Serra and their prophecy, a connection she couldn't sever when she'd wanted to.

"Maybe you're right." He pressed lips to her forehead. "Maybe the two disappearances aren't a coincidence. I'll think about it, okay. Send Ravens to investigate. Perhaps we've missed some sort of evidence that could explain it."

"You had more of it reported already today." Sometimes, Vesperi wondered if all men were blind to everything but sex and food.

Her husband's perplexity gave way to understanding with a hint of panic. He opened a door. "Send Ser Allyn," he commanded, "and our guests from Meditlan."

As he retook his seat, Vesperi mused, "I can't blame you for assuming those farmworkers ran away." She knew her people, and if they'd been Meduan guards in the past, or worse, nobility, hard work was not in their make-up. But chances were they'd been peasants who'd never return to Medua, and their "running away" was stumbling through another portal accidentally.

"I'll blame myself enough. Don't worry."

"Can I go with your investigators?" Vesperi felt guilty asking the question, but the desire to be anywhere Izzy might reappear outweighed the knowledge that Janto wanted her near.

He slumped, chewed on his lip, then took her hand. "I'm not saying no. I wouldn't. But—"

She swooped up to meet his lips, silencing him. "I'll stay."

Doing so felt right, as surely as today's events had renewed her hope they'd find Izzy. Vesperi needed to believe in her instincts as a mother, a lover, a companion. They were all she had left without the flame. She hoped they were enough.

A shadow passed over the throne, and Janto shuddered, nearly jumping back in fright.

How typical of a man. Vesperi gazed up. "Look," she pointed at the dark form passing over Tansic. A cloud, but—

His countenance lightened at once. "Almost seems like wings, doesn't it?" He put his arm back around her shoulders.

Whatever it was moved on toward the fog where Esye should be. For a moment, a silver corona shone through.

CHAPTER FOURTEEN

Janto

The strange cloud's appearance was a much more heartening portent than the specter that'd been wearing Janto down for days. Luckily, a glance at the shadows confirmed that that too had dissipated.

Ser Allyn entered from the hall. "Your highness, your murat friend, Mer Jerusho of Mova, has arrived."

Janto shifted his view to a window looking out on the courtyard. Many of the departing courtiers had gathered around a strange cage on a cart. *The cantalere.* Two unfamiliar men and a woman helped Jerusho off his horse. For a few days' travel, their garments appeared rather harried with several holes and tears.

Janto hurried outside, beckoning Vesperi to follow. A gash was evident on Jerusho's arm, flaming red with purple bruising around it. But that didn't stop Janto from embracing his friend. He'd not seen the man since their murat. Despite the beard he wore, and that gash, he hadn't aged a day.

"It's so good to see you." Janto clutched his shoulders. "And Vesperi tells me she has another book to add to our research. Let me intro—"

Vesperi was examining the animal from a distance. Introductions could wait—Janto also wanted a look. The creatures from Madel's realm that he'd seen before had an ethereal, compelling quality, even the claren.

The crowd parted like curds from whey to let him through. Jerusho followed close behind. The cantalere appeared asleep, perhaps a ruse with so many eyes on it. Its flat, broad head rested over many legs that Janto hoped made it clumsy in a chase. Part of him relished the idea of finding out, the same part that had surged seeing the giant bird-shaped shadow in the sky. Were they calls to action for the hunting party?

The cantalere's jagged horn glinted in the sunlight, and its greenish brown fur shimmered depending on where Janto cast his gaze.

The cold silver of his crown pressed against his forehead. He nudged it back into place. "Is that why you looked so beat up, my friend?" he asked Jerusho in jest. "One cantalere can't pose that much of a threat to the great granfaylon fisher."

He said the last part as loudly as he could, and the courtiers surrounding them stepped back, impressed with the traveler in their midst. No doubt the novelty of Janto's own presence had already faded.

"I wish it were 'one,' Janto," Jerusho rubbed the back of his neck. "We encountered a herd of them outside Carafin's Market."

A herd? Someone shrieked, while others in the crowd swiveled in closer to listen. Carafin's Market was Neville's largest city, and the biggest trading post in Lansera. One of these could do a lot of damage there.

One of Jerusho's companions, a canteen in his hand, reported, "And you can add 'cantalere slayer' to the councilman's credits now. He handled himself nicely in the melee."

"Melee?" Vesperi whirled around, her focus broken. "More Meduan raids? My countrymen have grown homesick."

"No," explained Jerusho. "The cantaleres, fifteen at least. They stampeded past the market, goring and flinging animals and . . . and people caught in their paths."

The courtyard environs blurred as Janto focused in on his friend. "How many people dead?"

"A dozen, maybe. We did not stay for the count, but continued here in all haste. I knew you'd want to know right away."

"And how many cantaleres remain?" Janto took a step in the direction of his quarters.

"Six," said one of the Movians, her braids loose from their bindings. "We and the villagers slaughtered at least five. They were organizing a hunting party when we left."

Vesperi's hand slipped into Janto's, which he knew better than to comment on. She matched his stride. "They are not the only hunting party on its way," she announced with confidence.

Janto was grateful she could read his thoughts so easily, but he wondered if she realized she wouldn't be able to help. Not without her flame. How to stop word of *that* from spreading?

The crowd was growing unruly, but Janto made sure his voice was heard, channeling his father's gravitas as best he could. "We will bring a troop of soldiers with us for the protection of the Nevillim plains. Pic," he called out to the serving boy, always at his heels, "bring the Old Girl to my quarters."

Pic nodded, but Janto paused his momentum with a hand to the elbow. "Please see to their lodgings also, and bring Jerusho to my mother to tend that wound." To Jerusho, he said, "I need you, even more than I did before. Learn what you can from the books once you've been refreshed. Send me anything you think may help, while I'm gone. Especially on how best to kill them."

Any notion Janto may have entertained of capturing the cantaleres had vanished the instant he'd learned Lanserim were dead. The threats from Madel's realm were more pressing than its wonders.

Pic scurried off and Jerusho and his party shifted course to follow. Janto and Vesperi continued through the courtyard arch closest to their quarters. His pace was rapid and thoughts full of preparation and yes, the thrill of reclaiming the slayer's role, one he knew how to fulfill.

Vesperi jerked his arm and Janto lost his balance. Which was a better option than what would have happened: ramming into his mother who blocked their door.

"Get inside."

Janto hadn't heard that tone since, at twelve, he'd made the mistake of borrowing the castle's satin curtains to slide down Callyn's grassy hills.

They entered their quarters in silence, Janto bristling. He opened his trunk to begin packing, while Vesperi stood beside the closed curtains.

"There's no need for that." His mother placed a hand on the trunk's whittled surface. "You will remain here."

"I should be out *there*, Mother." He pulled a pair of riding pants from the trunk. He had no desire to have this argument with her, not when his people were hurting and he could help. "I can be of use with the Old Girl out there, killing these menaces. I'm the bloody slayer—I'm meant to do it."

"You're meant to be king, Janto. You could get yourself killed out there." The discipline in her voice annoyed him.

She paused before landing the next punch. "You have no heir."

An agonized sound escaped Vesperi's throat. Janto slammed the trunk lid down and it shattered. The force of his anger rattled him.

"I'm sorry," his voice cracked, annoying him more. He was twenty-seven, a husband, father, king, and his mother still got the best of him. "I didn't mean that as a threat. But that was a low blow."

"Did you see me flinch?" She gentled her tone. "I know you better than that."

"I don't understand why you think we should stay here. I'm the slayer. That doesn't end because I'm king. My lack of an heir didn't matter the last several years—and I had no siblings then, either. Why does it now?"

"A different time, a different prophecy. Your people have different needs of you."

"Different needs of me? There are herds of cantalere in Neville and likely Ertion, too. Jurgens rolling their way through Meditlan farms."

"Elston, too," Vesperi added, a reminder that Janto should take every report heard at Callyn as only one instance of potentially many in his kingdom.

"Elston, too," he said. "And people are disappearing! If we don't find out why, you know"—he pointed a finger to his mother—"they'll blame the Meduans for it. The councils will clamor to banish them, throw them out with winter's last dregs, as the madness spreads. And then we'll have another civil war on our hands."

"And how will you, with one bow, stop that?" The queen poured the three of them wine from a pitcher on the dressing table. The chalices were made of rosewood, which had been rare on this side of the mountains during the divide. Queen Lexamy had seen to it that the pink-hued, sturdy wood from the forests surrounding Sellwyn made its way into the castle over the years.

"You can organize your army from here," she said. "Send hundreds of soldiers out after those creatures, if you must. That'll do more good than you and Vesperi in the field."

"You mean because I'm useless now?" his wife barbed.

Janto didn't know which cut sharper, Vesperi's spite or self-pity. His mother had a point. Sending her out among their people, feeling useless . . . weapon or not, she could cause plenty of damage.

"So you'd have us remain here, trying to make sense of a new prophecy?" Vesperi said.

"*Old* prophesy," Janto corrected and Vesperi huffed at him. "She's right, Mother. If our people need us, we should be out there, helping them, not directing them from behind closed walls."

The queen sighed overloud. "The people need their king, alive and well, after having just lost one. They need to know they can depend on you to be steady, to see them through this. Not to charge recklessly out there, aiming your sword at a foe you don't understand."

Vesperi gulped her wine rather than savor it. "I don't know what Lanserim need. But Meduans respond to force, to shows of strength, not power shielded from public view. That's why they came so fast to your side after we burned Mandat Hall; they knew then that King Ralion was nothing but an expensive figurehead. Real power came with swords and horses."

"You're not helping," Queen Lexamy said between gritted teeth.

Vesperi tilted her head. "Was I supposed to be helping you or him?"

His mother had four decades of ruling experience to back her up. She was too shrewd to speak solely from a mother's concern. Vesperi's perspective was very different, which was why it was also valuable. She understood what Meduans respected, which was not instinctive to Janto. As king, he needed to serve all their needs.

If only he could ask his father's advice.

As if on cue, the specter materialized at the foot of the bed, above the shattered trunk. Janto's goose flesh rose, and he jumped up, shifting his mother away from the area and onto the pillows.

"Janto, are you all right?" Vesperi asked, at his side.

Go on, son, tell them what your father says.

He would do nothing this marauder suggested. Rather, he sat guardedly on one of the bedroom's plush, tatted armchairs. The cushion's whoosh of air added indignity to his despair, and Vesperi leaned against the armrest.

"How could Madel let this happen, Mother?" He wished the wine were a stiffer drink, perhaps bombal draught. Maybe then he could pretend that voice whispering to him was all in his head.

Madel is not here, now. Madel has left you on your own. The silver specks within the shadow glistened, making its dark angles all the sharper by contrast.

"What do you mean?" Queen Lexamy relaxed against the pillows, sensing her battle won for now. Her head cocked, unsure for once of his thoughts.

"Send the cantalere and jurgen to threaten us, with everything else going on? Father's death." The words caught in his throat. He avoided looking at that spot, at that presence which only made his father's absence more pronounced. His speech gathered speed and fury, "Taking the flame from Vesperi, the baby from us . . . Izzy. And our people's losses too. It's like everything we worked for, sacrificed for, balances on the tip of that cantalere's horn. The Conjoining, all of it."

He sunk his face into his hands, wished for the day his mother could solve any hurt by producing a piece of sour shornal taffy from the folds of her gown. His frustration seemed to fuel the otherworldly presence. It wafted closer.

Yes, that's right. It is *all too much.*

Janto measured the distance to the door. He wouldn't be able to get any of them out, not without passing through that sinister being. Pulsing molten silver framed its vacant eyes and dripped down its raiment. All resemblance to his father had gone.

The queen regarded him, deep bags under her own eyes. "I'm trying to come up with a story from your father's reign, Janto, something to put this into perspective or show you how much he, too, wrestled with times of crisis when there seemed no way out."

Literally no way out, Janto worried. How could they edge past it?

The queen sighed. "But the truth is, I can't. Because what I want to do right now is run up the steps to your father's study and find him there. I want him to hold me, and tickle me under the chin, and tell me not to worry so hard. But he isn't there." Tears overcame her practiced resolve, and wine sloshed over her glass's rim. "The truth is, I don't know what any of us are going to do without him. I don't have any idea how we're getting through anything else again."

"Oh, Mother, me too." Janto reached for her, right through the shadow, which burst as soon as he did. *Father would never run away from his family's sorrow.* He steeled his resolve—whatever it was had clearly been preying on his fears. He would no longer allow that.

Vesperi moved to give them space, but Janto wouldn't have it, embracing them both. Soon, all three were crying. The queen accidentally dropped her chalice, and then Janto did too, and Vesperi followed suit on purpose. They laughed through their tears at the absurdity of it, faces flushed hot as apples roasting in their skins.

Once they'd calmed to wheezing sniffles, Janto took in his wife's heartening smile. Their marriage reflected the tenuous peace between their peoples. Sometimes, it felt destined to clatter down around them as rapidly as those cups. But in moments like these, he had no fear of that, at least.

She went to peck his cheek, an impulse she caught and refrained from, lest Janto forget how much work the two of them still had to do on themselves. "We stay," she said. "We'll manage this kingdom of yours from here. I've learned to be quite fast at reading through tomes. When we know something more concrete, we'll do that instead."

For now, they'd study books instead of cantalere tracks. Janto would make do with that.

‡

When leaps the mighty cantalere,
   the dark brother drains his foes.
The words swirled through his head as he carried Vesperi's book to the council room. Two new lines that she'd memorized on the journey home gave validation to his hunch about the Silver Guard:
The Guard must ring the beastly lair
Where battles end their roam.
On the parchment, those lines were a blurry mess along with the rest of the prophecy. Janto didn't know how Vesperi had deciphered them.

At the green-veined table made of dark kratomwood that filled the council room, Jerusho camped with a sling around his arm. Janto put the book down, but the Ertion halted him, running a finger over the tabletop, then holding it to the light. Janto braced himself for a lecture on keeping Castle Callyn clean, but Jerusho's *humph* soon dispelled the notion.

"Just making sure the wood hasn't been oiled recently." He plopped the book on the table. A cloud of dust rose like flour from punched bread dough. "I made as many notes as I could before we left Mova," Jerusho said, "but I couldn't take as many books on the journey as I'd like, not at the speed you requested."

"Of course." Janto wished there was a faster way to travel. He remained unconvinced he best served Lansera from here, but his mother had been right about Serra; they needed her sight here, too. And at the farm in Orun and where that woman's son had disappeared, and at the Perch. Serra could tell if a rift had opened in the vineyard or at least better guess what else might have caused those harvesters to vanish. But he'd already sent her to collect potential Guard members. And she'd need him for instructions on what to do once they'd gathered.

He wished he had more to work with: more understanding, more resources, more anything than questions. *More of my father's wisdom, perhaps, or at least someone's who's lived long enough to gain some.* Once again, his thoughts landed on Sielban, who could flit about the island of Braven in a flash. He should ask Sielban how he managed to travel those distances. Maybe Serra could be taught.

The shadow seeped into the room, thick as oil through a sieve.

I told you to leave Sielban alone.

Janto ignored its presence with firm resolve.

Lest it get trapped in the pages of another book, Jerusho pushed his beard aside. "I brought this one because you asked about the Silver Guard. It records a number of their heroic feats, though it's been at least a decade since my old ryn read one to me. I was surprised by your request, honestly, when Serra relayed it." He asked, "Where is your wife, anyhow? If this involves prophecy, then it involves her too, does it not?"

"Likely," Janto admitted, sliding into a chair beside his friend. His rightful place was at the table's head, but he didn't feel ready for that yet. "We're not so sure this time."

"Why's that?"

Janto hesitated, knowing Vesperi wouldn't take well to her vulnerability being discussed with yet another person, but they were running out of options. His kingdom was at risk; he'd face her wrath if he had to. He'd face that thing across the room, too. "She's lost the flame. Since Esye went into shadow, she hasn't been able to call it."

How delightful!

A pause. Then quickly, as though to cover the first reply:

How delightful to have your friend to guide you on how best to rule at home, where it's safe.

Janto made no reaction to the slip. Perhaps he could find a way to get the phantom to make another.

Jerusho spoke thoughtfully, "The weapon doubts her strength, does she? Let us help her find it again."

Janto was glad of his companionship. The Ertion raised his glass for a clink, and Janto obliged after pouring some honey mead into his own.

A knock came at the door. Janto's command to enter revealed Rynna Hullvy, her braided hair askew, eyes glazed over. She raised her elbows to him. "My king."

"Seen the cantalere, have you?" Janto returned the gesture.

"I have no words. What wonders Madel sends us."

Janto doubted the malevolent wonder haunting him or the cantaleres came from Madel. This one certainly didn't want him to believe She could save them.

Jerusho opened another book as Rynna Hullvy took a seat. Janto handed her a cup of hot water sprinkled with calming libtyl leaves. The book's aged cover was woven of dulled silver threads displaying a leaping fish—a good sign, Janto hoped, as the Silver Guard was every bit as legendary as the granfaylon.

Jerusho turned the cover, and Rynna Hullvy leaned over to brush the page with some sort of transparent liquid that gave the faded lettering clarity—they would need to try that on the Rasselerian prophecy.

Janto strained to read the passage, but old Lanserim spellings were beyond him. He hadn't tried to decipher any such script since his schooling. *A king should learn how to do such things,* Ser Allyn's voice chided, but his father's advised, *or keep people close who can.*

I said no such thing.

You are not my father.

The specter wavered.

"What does it say?" Janto asked. If this research disturbed the presence, he was determined to keep at it.

Jerusho was silent for a moment, considering. "Nothing of use to us, I think." He turned the next page and stroked his chin. "Ah, now this is familiar. It's the first account I remember seeing of the Silver Guard." He read the page over a few times. 'Descended from the skies,' it says, to save the people from an invasion of cantaleres."

"Well, that sounds promising." Janto leaned in, though it did not grant him comprehension of the penmanship.

Rynna Hullvy squinted at the text. "Didio Albrecht used the Silver Guard to fight off the cantaleres, last they were seen. I had heard no report of their return until today." She asked Janto, "Do you think this is connected to what happened at your father's funeral?"

How odd to have a rynna look to him for answers. As the priestess of Callyn, she held considerable sway over the populace of Lansera's largest town. Should he tell her everything and risk her sharing it, spurring on a panic? Though if a moon's disappearance from the sky hadn't done that yet, what could?

"I think those flashes were Vesperi's silver flame, disbursed to create the Guard."

How ridiculous.

The derisive response buoyed his theory. "The night before, I dreamed a version of what happened that morning—a silver dream, the ones that bonded me with Vesperi before we even met. But as to what that means . . ." Janto raised his hands with a shoulder shrug.

"It appears that account is not the first instance of cantaleres coming to Lansera." Jerusho had moved farther ahead. "This story is from before the Albrechts ruled—my ryn said the book was five hundred years old, at his best guess."

"Does that mean these threats are cyclical?" Janto would grasp at feathers if he must, anything to make things make sense. *And bring Izzy back*, said a quieter, hopeful voice in his head. It kept growing louder, but he hadn't the heart to listen, not yet.

"We have more reading to do, before we can decide that." Jerusho freshened his cup but thought better of more alcohol before taking a sip.

Janto knocked on the door for a servant. "Bring us fresh tachery ever hour until we're done, and no other disturbances, unless it's my wife. We'll be in here for a while, I fear."

"Sometimes fears are justified," Jerusho grinned. "But there are worse ones than being shut up with stuffy old books for hours."

Janto could think of some. Jerusho did not have a shade glaring pure darkness his way before disappearing.

‡

The knock on the door was Pic's familiar two-rap. "Your highness," he smiled wide, as though Janto's rise to power were his own, "your tachery."

Their fourth refill, and though they'd made progress, they were no closer to understanding the prophecy in the Rasselerians' book or why jurgens, canteleres, and rifts were appearing and people dis-appearing fast as Esye from the sky. Luckily for Janto's sanity, the phantom stayed away.

Vesperi had come and gone twice, staying for a couple hours before retreating lest she rip the parchment apart. Jerusho had nearly had a heart attack when she'd handled his book with the granfaylon on the cover.

"And some treats from the kitchen." Pic produced another platter from behind his back with a sly grin. Not so long ago, Janto would have been able to see anything he hid. The boy's unbridled growth spurts would make him tall as Ser Allyn, soon enough.

"Let Mar Jeffyr know we appreciate it." Janto gave Pic a head tousle before closing the door. The platter's contents were full of delicious smells. His companions let out appreciative groans before he laid it on the table. The dishes had a theme of spring, though they were a few weeks off from that yet. Perhaps the green-dyed leaves on the tarts and the pink rosewood blooms on the cookies were meant to inspire them to continue their foraging.

Thus far, they'd established that the Silver Guard had come several times to Lansera, usually in pursuit of creatures from Madel's realm. Once, the Guard had welcomed the giants on their first journey across the glacial pathway from the Deduin peninsula. Another time, they'd arisen to combat a strange plague of spores that slimed crops all over the land, stopping them from absorbing water and nutrients. A great famine had followed, and the Silver Guard worked to eradicate the spores for many years before the land was cleansed.

Janto rolled his empty mug between his hands. "Can we go back to the account of the giants? 'Ascended' is what you translated, but I'm wondering what the exact words were."

The whole poem had a more celebratory feel than Janto had expected. Though there were no official histories of giants in his schooling, terror had laced all previous references to them that he'd heard.

Rynna Hullvy turned back a few delicate pages at a time, to where they'd been an hour ago. She read:

Steppe to steppe, the giants went
Over the frozen waters
Riding the barren waste
Like waves, a river otter.

The final footfall; oh, radiant sight!
The Silver Guard ascending
Sent to wash the giants' feet
Great Madel's fiery blessing.

"It's clearly 'ascending,' my king." Her tone was apologetic.

"But the next word? 'Sent'? Could it mean 'sent *down*'?"

Jerusho and Rynna Hullvy peered again at the words and exchanged looks. "It could."

Jerusho stroked his beard. "And that would change the meaning of 'ascending,' too. In cases when the suffix is subsumed, a paired verb means its opposite: 'came down.'"

Janto felt recharged, and it wasn't from the tachery; he could drink no more of that without choking. "Maybe they were washing those giants' feet with fire, a silver one. Maybe the blessing was Madel saving the Lanserim from the giants! Wouldn't you describe what happened at the Mount, Rynna Hullvy, as silver coming down? Why, I bet you could ask any of Callyn's citizens what they saw at the funeral, and they'd answer, 'Birds came down from the skies! Silver ones!'"

Rynna Hullvy rubbed her forehead. "But that was a sign of honor from Madel for your father."

"Can't it be both?" Janto asked. "How best to honor him than to send us the means to keep his country safe? I think we're on the right path."

A knock came at the door, though the knocker did not wait for it to be answered. Vesperi entered in her night clothes, a pair of silken pants and matching tunic in a ruddy green.

"My queen." Janto's companions spoke in unison, averting their eyes from the rather casual dress for royalty. Janto, however, loved that she displayed her curves with such ease.

Vesperi laughed, a welcome sound. "Why such modesty? I'm a married woman, and surely no Lanserim would dare betray the king with me." A hand raised to her head and mouth opened to an "*o*" of false scandalization.

She went behind Janto's chair and rubbed his shoulders. "Come to bed. You've been at this"—she glared at the books—"all day. Ser Allyn forced me to entertain the noble pissants who haven't the sense to realize their welcome is wearing thin. I'm rather impressed I managed it without a stabbing."

"Quite impressive indeed," Janto's eyes glimmered with amusement. "But I can't rest. Not until we figure out what's happening."

"Well," she took a seat to his left. The chair squeaked against the stone floor, "what've we learned so far?"

"That Olde Lanserim grammar is a bloody mess," Rynna Hullvy

laughed, glad for the interruption, it appeared. "And that the king thinks the Silver Guard is among us."

Vesperi gave him a quizzical expression. "Is that what happened at the funeral? The Silver Guard returned?"

Janto lifted his shoulders.

"Mm." Vesperi fell silent.

Jerusho's brow creased. "You think they're connected, don't you? With your loss of the flame?"

She bolted upright. Her shock shifted to pure fury, directed straight Janto's way. "You told them?"

He wanted to apologize but stopped himself before he could. This was too important for Vesperi's pride to get in the way. "Yes," he stated. "This is bigger than us, Vesperi, or you'd have your weapon. Those flashes have gone to other people, and—"

"Those flashes were *my* flame. Madel took it from me, and She gave it away."

Her voice petered out, while possibilities Janto hadn't considered sent his mind reeling. If Madel had scattered Vesperi's flame, then the intended use was for good. But that meant an unknown number of people out there had just discovered they had a special talent for destruction, and—Janto observed Vesperi as she fumed—some of them were Meduan. A time might come when he would yearn for the days when only one bedeviling woman from those lands possessed such power. But yearning for the past wouldn't accomplish anything. Living in the present and gearing toward the future were a king's duty.

The king. "The flame must fly to be found again."

"Are you a prophet now yourself?" Vesperi teased, too tired to fight.

"No, I just forgot." Janto scooted his chair back. "Father told me to tell you that. And it makes sense, doesn't it? The Silver Guard coming down from the sky, same as that energy. The same Guard that's been described as using fire in the past. And in my dream, it went to other people, commissioning them, maybe."

"So, my dear, smart husband," Vesperi mocked, while picking up on his line of thought, "the Silver Guard was sent down at your father's funeral and absconded with *my* power, delivering the magic elsewhere. But what does that have to do with the rest of the prophecy about the cantaleres?"

"The rest?" Jerusho exclaimed. The passage in the Rasselerian book was so faint, he wasn't certain there *was* more beyond what she'd shared.

She took the book and read over the passage. Her jaw fell agape. "There was more of it on my journey home, I swear. I couldn't make it out, but the ink was *not* this blurred."

More mysteries. Janto knew a person who lived and breathed mystery with every gleeful leap he took. A person who he trusted not to kowtow before a new king or tiptoe to avoid bruising his pride. A person his father had made a point of demanding he leave alone. But Janto had to follow his own vision of rulership, not merely imitate what came before. Rushing into battle against the cantaleres would be a rash choice, but this . . . this was not.

"I'm going to Braven," he announced.

The shadow flickered into its ghostly form.

"Braven?" Rynna Hullvy's voice hitched.

Janto's will solidified along with the specter. If this decision upset it, he was doing something right.

"Why?" Jerusho asked in an uncertain tone. "I may yearn for Sielban's riddles when snowed in for a week, but isn't there a murat to be held next month?"

Vesperi waited, silently and impatiently, to insist she go along, whatever his reasons.

"Because no one else is longer lived in Lansera—for all we know, he has encountered the Guard before. And he may know how they can be of use to us against this dark brother."

Nothing can defeat me. I've grown stronger than any knew I could.

The dark brother. So that's who the presence was. Did that make *them* his foe?

Janto could play that part. *Then why is your hold on me fainter by the moment?*

A hiss near his ear, and then:

I withdraw to ready myself for your failure. The world will need the guidance only I can supply when you do.

Your poison, you mean.

A pause.

Patience, child. All in due time.

It disappeared.

Janto gulped, then reached for the pitcher of mead. It had run dry long ago. He must leap into the peril of reignited hope without the help of alcohol. "Sielban knows how to use the fissures, and how to avoid disappearing into them. And maybe how to find people who've done just that."

He glanced at Vesperi, thinking of their daughter. Her luminous smile took away any doubts Janto'd had that this was the right choice. But doubts that he could face what Sielban's answers might bring? Those persisted, sure as he'd never feel comfortable standing in the shadows again.

CHAPTER FIFTEEN
SERRA

Two pairs of horse hooves clomped their way through the kratom-wood forest where Serra hid behind a large tree trunk. Napeler crouched behind another nearby, his bow drawn in anticipation of the riders catching up to them. They'd first heard their movements about a mile back.

They'd been trying to locate the path to the Perch for a day now. But finding the way to the renowned home base of the Ravens was not proving an easy task. That was how it should be, but being tracked was not. Maybe Janto had alerted Ser Swalus, the Ravens' chief, to her expected arrival and he'd sent a few spies out to guide them.

If they *were* spies, they weren't trying to hide.

"Oh, Serra Gavenstone! Come out, come out, wherever you are!"

A man with a high-pitched voice called out, and she flashed Nap an exasperated glance before abandoning the tree. She brushed its needles from her vest, as a mounted man with a medium build and shoulder-length, fawn brown hair came into view. So did a woman who wore a long black-and-gray braid and the finery of the Albrechts' household guard.

"Flivio," Serra said, embracing the man as soon as he dismounted. Flivio of Urs, in Meditlan, had been another of Janto's fellow muraters, and he was ever fond of injecting his unique brand of levity into any situation. For once, Serra welcomed it.

"And Sar Mertina." She gave the older knight the same treatment soon as she had the chance. Sar Mertina was one of the most respected warriors in Lansera, and a lovely person.

A lovely person who forced Nap into a hug despite his discomfort. Flivio followed suit with a hearty laugh and a back clap. All four had ridden together on the road to Qiltyn, where Mandat Hall had stood, and in varying configurations as the years of claren culling had gone on.

Beside Nap's squat and solid frame, Flivio appeared slender and spry. Serra asked him, "Did Madel's hand guide you here to lead us to the Perch? Or is your presence in our same patch of wood mere coincidence?"

"I don't know about Madel," Flivio laughed, "but Janto sent us here. I hope Sar Mertina knows how to get to the Perch, though, because I haven't a drasmo's ass of an idea about it." Occasionally, Flivio wrestled his wits into telling a good joke. That was not one, though he'd claim they were all brilliant. Good thing he was fast as an arrow and great at shooting them, too.

"The king sent you?" Nap asked, the question also on Serra's lips. "Is something wrong?"

"You mean beyond King Dever's death and a caravan's worth of cantaleres and jurgens gallivanting through the realm?" Sarcasm was Flivio's native language. Well, besides ale. Serra had no idea how he'd managed to be elected as a member of his town's council.

Sar Mertina produced a rolled scroll from one of her saddlebags. Her white stallion, a majestic beast, got a carrot for its trouble. "King Janto sent me with a letter, Lady Serra. You can read it as I hunt for the feathered path."

She began poking around the pines and shrubs clustered nearby. Serra cracked open the swan seal.

Dearest Serra,

Apologies for not sending word sooner to warn you of your new companions—Flivio always requires an apology. But I didn't want to trust this news to a pigeon. Nay, it should not leave the lips of anyone in your group. We are in greater danger than we realized. Vesperi has lost the flame. It disappeared the same day Father died, the same day Esye shrunk and Onsic enlarged. Jerusho arrived this afternoon, and he brought terrible tidings—cantaleres are raging

*through Neville, too. Lanserim have died. We have reports of jurgen
damaging property from Meditlan to northern Rasseleria.*

We have learned two new lines of the prophecy:

*"The Guard must ring the beastly lair
Where battles end their roam."*

*I think the Silver Guard is rising to challenge these threats, and
we're doing what we can to ascertain if there's truth to that. Lorne
was right to advise you to bring Uzziel back, along with any others
you encounter who may possess the flame's echo.*

*Head to Queen Drustalla's ruins once you have Uzziel—the plain
of Orelyn is the only place I know where a battle ended in recent
times. I am pronouncing that anyone possessing such magic meet
there to help defend the realm against the cantaleres, though I do not
know how they—you—will manage it. I trust you'll do your best.
Hopefully, we'll have more guidance for you by then.*

*That's not all, Serra. You were right—the 'shimmers from heaven'
are multiplying. And people may be disappearing into them. It fits.
Serra, it fits.*

Your dearest friend,

Janto

How could so few lines of text be so full of horror and hope in equal
measure? Serra knew what "it fits" meant. Izzy may still be out there.
They may get her back yet. And Lansera be ravaged in the meantime.

"I've found it!" Sar Mertina waved from about twenty feet away,
and the group led their horses to her. Serra rolled the parchment back
up and stuffed it in her saddlebag.

Mertina led them through the chaparral for a good hour. The
path was easy to follow once they got started, though less evident
than a deer trail. Occasionally, Mertina hesitated before continuing
to another trampled grass patch behind prickly thornberry bushes or
bare thrushberries, whose branches bore streaks of dark indigo and
a few shriveled fruits of the same hue.

After the third or fourth such stoppage, Serra asked, "How do
you find it? The path?"

Sar Mertina drew the sword from her back and pointed it up, to the kratomwood boughs. Serra craned her neck, used the sight for a hint, but found no clue.

Luckily, Flivio's patience burned faster than her own, so she needn't make a fool of herself. "Are you sure you're not chasing drapian seeds on a breeze?"

The knight left the question unanswered for a moment, then winked at Nap, who schooled his features, having figured it out, apparently.

Flivio's face paled. "Madel's hand, *are* we following drapian seeds?"

The knight broke the suspense with a well-timed laugh. "There are raven feathers tied between some of the cone clusters. See?" She pointed the sword again at the one above. Sure enough, a pair of black feathers hung a couple inches below the faded brown seeds—seeds of a much larger size than the ones Flivio had suggested.

Serra shook her head. The flags seemed so obvious once found. "You'd think I needed seeing glasses."

"For the seer? We *are* in trouble," Flivio amused himself.

She smiled, but Serra wondered if he were close to the mark.

‡

In another hour, the horses' ears drooped, and Serra agreed that it was time for a rest. The Ravens' fortress before them appeared to be a single tower, easily mistaken for a hunting blind had they not been searching for it. Slatted, wooden walls branched out from the tower. A lush, evergreen vine, encouraged by a series of metal loops, gave it structure. The plants rose over the tower, forming a façade of an overtaken cliff face. As they drew closer, open slits carved into it came into view, no doubt filled with arrow tips pointed their way.

A shiver of fear traveled through Serra, as she became aware of a group of Ravens creeping their way. She pressed a smile on her face.

"Who are you," demanded one with a silky voice despite the force it wielded. The Raven clung low to the ground, a small bow in her hand.

Serra made to speak, but Sar Mertina raised a hand.

"I am Sar Mertina, of the king's guard. I'm protecting Lady Serrafina Gavenstone at his command." Serra raised her elbows to acknowledge her introduction and Mertina continued. "This is Ser Napeler, the king's right-hand, and there is Councilman Flivio of Urs, one of his murat companions."

"Can you prove that?" the Raven challenged. "Wouldn't be the first time someone pretended to be kings' guard here."

A man answered from a thick wooden door that had opened quiet as snow could fall. "No need, Marabil. I'd recognize Sar Mertina and Lady Serra anywhere."

Chief Raven Tirlon Swalus let the door to the tower shut behind him as he stepped outside. His slim build was hidden within a black cloak lined with raven feathers. The Ravens surrounding Serra and her party stretched out of their crouches, with permission granted by Swalus's hand wave. He raised his elbows to Serra, but amusingly held them higher and longer for Sar Mertina. Serra couldn't begrudge anyone for granting the knight such deference.

Ser Swalus welcomed them to the Perch, and they handed off their horses inside its walls. A great hall opened beyond the entryway, its presence concealed by the ivy. A sparring section was roped off near the back, though the weapons of choice within it were thin clubs and fire pokers rather than maces or swords. A spy often had to use what was on hand, Serra supposed.

Closer to the hall's median, a cloaked woman spoke to a group of recruits, a peek of her wavy blonde hair exposed. At least Serra assumed they were recruits, as they were the only people other than her group who did not have a Raven's cloak draped across their shoulders. Nearer to the entrance was a great table made from Wasylim lemonwood, a surprisingly light wood for such a large piece. Likely so it could be moved around depending on the day's activities.

Ser Swalus guided them to the table. As they took seats, a Raven came up with a steaming pitcher that gave off the telltale earthen scent of tachery.

"Yes, please." Serra lifted one of the overturned cups. The vessel was nicely shaped, smoothed inside and out, and carved out of kratomwood.

The Raven poured each of her companions a serving, and Swalus spoke, his voice low. "Do we need to be in another room to discuss this visit?"

Serra was surprised by the question. "Should we not trust your Ravens, ser? Surely our spies can be depended on to keep quiet."

His gray-blue eyes twinkled. "One would hope. But in times like these—"

"Times like these?" Serra should stop speaking out of turn, but his manner concerned her. "Should I be warning the king of potential plots from his spies?"

"No. I can't imagine a single one ever betraying their country. But without an enemy to spy upon, we sometimes spy on ourselves, so to speak. And if the Meduans are let in our ranks, as has been rumored . . ." He let the sentence hang in the air.

Serra had heard no such rumor. But she could imagine why it would cause concern. Surely Janto wouldn't take the Conjoining so far as that, to trust Meduans with their security. At least not for another several years. But even distant goals might draw suspicion from a Raven, she supposed.

A man with white hair parted down the middle and dust muting the black of his feathers entered the room.

"Ser Werbose!" Ser Swalus stood and raised his elbows to his second in command, perhaps the longest-lived man in their ranks. "I did not expect you back from your visit home so soon. How are the grandchildren?"

Ser Werbose sunk into a chair at the table, knowing the relief of distributing his weight from the legs to his ass. A hearty smile revealed his sharp mental acuity.

"The grandchildren are all older than this fine young lady you've brought here—they have little use for their old grandad." He winked at Serra, and she laughed.

"*That* young lady is Serrafina Gavenstone," Swalus filled in.

Ser Werbose sputtered then raised his elbows high as he could, an unnecessary flattery. "My apologies, my lady. I can't help but be overcome with compliments whenever someone of your beauty is in my presence."

Serra waved away his concern. "None needed. It's a pleasure to meet you Ser Werbose." She raised her elbows in turn.

"Are these the visitors needing beds?" Ser Werbose directed the question to Ser Swalus. "I'm not sure we've ever had a lord other than Xantas stay here in my years of service. We don't have anything up to Callyn's standards. Oh my, what will the royal family say when they hear we've put you up on bed rolls filled with pine needles?"

"They would say thank you for being kind enough to host us with scarce notice."

Flivio leaned an arm onto the table. "Oh, I don't know, Serra.

Perhaps we should write back to share our dissatisfaction, see what else they can throw into the deal."

She rolled her eyes. "Pay Councilman Flivio here no mind." She paused. "Actually, pay him plenty of mind. He's as like to make off with these beautiful cups as he is to behave overnight."

Flivio mimed an arrow straight to the heart, and the others laughed, though Sar Mertina confirmed it was true. Flivio's sticky fingers were notorious, as was his skill with a lock pick.

Ser Swalus appeared bemused, though Serra would bet Flivio's door would have a guard posted on it tonight. "To your rooms, then?"

Ser Swalus extended an arm that Serra intended to take, but Ser Werbose gestured for her to linger. She obliged, curious if he wanted to try out a few more rusty come-ons. But he took her hands in his as she approached and examined them. When he looked up, tears flooded his eyes.

"I was in command when your brother's ashes were tossed in front of the Perch in that viper's box. I am sorry for your loss."

A generic thank you spilled from Serra's lips, a result of her training as a lady. She scrambled to find words of more significance. It had been a while since she'd thought of the letter Ser Werbose had written to accompany the box carrying her brother's ashes—the rosewood box marked by Sellwyn's viper sigil. His words had been kind, she remembered.

"That was several years ago now," she said. *And several versions of myself ago.* "You are good-hearted to think of it."

"How do you do it?" he asked with genuine wonder.

"Do what?"

"Work beside the Meduan who killed your brother. Who stole your fiancé. Who sits on our throne." His tone didn't change, but the hatred in his voice weighed heavy, a humid draft through a great hall. She couldn't blame him for feeling that way, though such bold disrespect for Lansera's queen surprised her and he was wrong about Janto. Serra left him, not the other way around.

Yet she had also felt the same once, had despaired that she couldn't do what Madel asked of her if it meant abiding Vesperi's presence. "I forgave her. With Madel's help."

"I'm not sure Madel wants us to forgive those who've hurt us. That She'd consider it just."

Serra considered *him* then. His rheumy eyes contained a hint of lavender, marking him as a descendant of the Deduins, who'd been under Meduan rule, as much as the Deduins let anyone rule them. The lineage may have been a century ago in his blood, but she would bet he'd been teased mercilessly for it over the years. Did his eyes glow now with hope she might have an answer for him or denial that anything she could say would ever satisfy his prejudice?

"The Madel who's guided my life isn't so concerned about justice." Serra measured her words. "She's concerned with protecting Her children."

"Hmph." He frowned. "The Madel I know protected me from Meduans for a generation, and now I find the country I love and serve is overrun with them. You'd have me believe that's Her will?"

"I'd have you remember that they're Her children too. And we bear some responsibility for how the Meduans behave. We abandoned them to the whims of horrible, cruel leaders for two generations."

"Did we now?" His smile returned, a knowing one. "Ah, the wisdom of youth. May you never have to fight such neighbors as I have done."

"May Madel's hand guide us both to such a future."

He kissed her hand before shuffling off to watch the training in the hall's far end. Serra hurried down a corridor to find her party, her thoughts consumed with a solitary question: could forgiveness be both a blessing and a curse? Many Lanserim had, with caution, accepted the Meduans' return to their lands, seen their potential for becoming good citizens, welcomed them into their lives. *And their beds.* For others, it appeared, the forced proximity bred resentment and fanned the flames of their prejudices ever higher.

‡

After rereading Janto's letter, Serra wondered if staying overnight at the Perch was perhaps more of a luxury than they ought to grant themselves. She should screen the Ravens right away, find out which one possessed the wisp of silver flame. The sight might detect it, and her sense of foreboding was strong. Lansera's societal balance felt more at peril the more tangible these threats to the kingdom grew.

She paused, waiting with dread for that unfamiliar voice that had been dogging her to confirm her fears. When it failed to speak, she sighed with relief. She'd seemingly left it in Mova with Lorne.

Once freshened up and in a new shift that spilled over a pair of flannel leggings, Serra headed back to the great hall. The moment she opened the door, a thunderous roar echoed through the hall and its corridors. The ground shook. Serra braced herself against a wooden wall and strained to make sense of the reverberation.

Her blood chilled. That roar was the resonance of a hundred galloping hooves, and the sounds of screaming rabbits and bleating deer accompanying them. A swarm of Ravens equipped with bows sped past her and out a side exit from the complex.

"They're cantaleres!" she shouted after them, knowing how outlandish that might sound. But they needed to be prepared.

A nearby spy gave her a gentle nod. "We know. They've been coming around these parts for the last week or so."

Janto's words were proving truer than she liked, Lansera more dangerous by the moment. She marched into the great room. The lemonwood table had been moved to its center and its length extended by at least three others, with clever joints that allowed the wood to fold.

Apparently, training was done for the evening, at least for those not rushing out to hunt cantaleres in the forest. Flivio waved to get her attention. Serra took a few breaths to calm her endorphins and headed over. The table held heaping mounds of the evening's dinner. After assembling a plate for herself of grilled winter onions and a stew of what she hoped was *not* cantalere, she joined him. More tachery waited in steaming pitchers on the table.

"Are you worried to be fighting cantaleres?" she asked a Raven seated nearby, beginning her informal examinations.

The young woman replied. "Oh no, Father won't let me."

The stranger dipped back her hood, and Serra realized she wasn't a woman yet, but a girl of about fifteen.

"Felia Swalus," Serra exhaled more than guessed. The Ravens had no need for recruits younger than adults, so this must be the chief's daughter. No one else had family at the Perch, and Felia had lost her mother a decade earlier, if Serra recalled correctly.

A charming blush splashed the girl's face with crimson. "You know me?"

Flivio raised his elbows to her. "Well, I didn't before, but I do now." He winked. "Flivio of Urs. May Madel's hand guide you, Felia." He opened his pouch to reveal fallowent and swallowed the customary fingerful.

"And you also." She returned the gesture, as did Serra.

A commotion stirred at the back of the hall. The Ravens' hunting group already returning?

"They were too fast," one said as the party dispersed to warm themselves at the fires in the rooms' four corners. Serra's portion of the table cleared to hear their news. "Probably got a whole forest's worth of rabbits slaughtered by now."

"I don't know how we're supposed to make a dent," said another. "The pack's growing. Or it's a second one, just as big and also passing south. I'm not sure what's worse."

The cantalere caught at Mova had also been galloping south. And what was south of both?

The plain of Orelyn.

Serra pivoted to ask Flivio if he'd heard of any cantaleres traveling north from Meditlan, but a glint of silver drew her eye back to the table. Might it have been a flare from the candles? The spoons and forks were made of polished wood, like the cups had been, and the plates and bowls were ceramic. No fish had been served; though there were streams this high in the mountains, few people enjoyed their native fishes' oily flesh. *I must have imagined it.*

Except it gleamed again, and Serra engaged her sight in time to catch a small smatter of silver flame lick its way up from beneath the table. It poofed, incinerating a dust bunny perhaps . . . a dust bunny, right below Felia Swalus's bench.

Serra examined the girl, unbeknownst. The teenager peeked under the table, her attention taken up by something other than the commotion in the hall. She supposed Felia was used to carrying on in her own way in a room full of adults concerned with consequential matters. She watched bemused as Felia ignited more sparks. They fizzled before their dining companions returned to their meals.

Serra's party could leave the very next morning, Serra realized, which suited their need for haste. But that came with a fair bit of regret. Life was about to change for young Felia Swalus, whether she wanted it to or not. What would *she* have to sacrifice for the sake of their people? An adolescence?

"Felia," Serra started, and the girl startled up straight. She tucked strands of her hair, radiant brown as a tawny port, behind her ears, a nervous habit.

Serra aimed for a smile wide enough to convey her genuine delight at Felia's presence. "Do you have friends here? Perhaps an instructor or a maid servant?"

Felia's head shook, and a smile sprang deep dimples. "Oh no, my lady. I mean, the Ravens are nice to me, especially the women. They've taught me to braid my hair and how not to get pregnant when I'm older and all that."

"That's good." Perhaps more information than Serra needed, but good. "Would you miss any of them terribly if you went on a trip?" *And if you didn't know what the trip was for, exactly, and couldn't understand how much was asked of you until it was too late to change your mind?* Serra wouldn't change how things had gone for her after claiming her sight—she, Vesperi, and Janto had saved Lansera from the claren, after all, reunited a country—but there were other choices, more recent ones she was beginning to reconsider.

Felia bit her lower lip while gazing at the people in the room. She shook her head. "Just my father, of course."

"How close are you?" Serra also knew what it was like to leave someone you loved behind. She didn't relish telling the girl what was to come next, though perhaps she'd like the adventure.

"Very." Felia emphasized the word by jutting out her chin. "I've only ever been away from him when he goes to visit the king. He says I can come next time, to see the new one."

"And is that something you'd like to do, travel?"

All of Serra's party was listening now, Flivio with one eyebrow cocked and an amused grin. She cast him a warning glance to keep his mouth shut.

"Oh yes. It gets so boring here." Felia flung her hands on the table with the exasperation of youthfulness. "I've been asking to go with him for ages."

Ser Swalus placed a bowl of stew on the table and slid into place beside his daughter. "Go with me where?"

"Yes, Lady Serra," Flivio feigned ignorance, "where is the young woman going?"

Someday, she'd figure out a good way to harass Flivio half as much as he did her. He might be worse than that voice had been.

But not tonight. Not when separating a child from her father was a task given to Serra tonight. *Separate one to rescue the rest.* The irony didn't escape her that she was now about to do exactly what the Brotherhood had done to her six years ago.

She suggested they move the conversation to Ser Swalus's quarters. The next hour was spent sharing Janto's letter with him, how she knew Felia had the flame's echo, what the threats were, best as they understood, and that Felia had to go with them right away. Serra empathized with his anger, confusion, and desire to know things would turn out for the best before saying yes. But there was no guarantee, never had been, never would be. Just the knowledge you had given your all for everyone else, that anything less was a selfishness no Lanserim could live with.

The Raven chief couldn't argue against protecting the country—it was his life's purpose. But he tried every possible defense before agreeing. Only when Serra gave him her most precious belonging to keep safe until she returned Felia home, did he relent.

"It's not a person," she said, fishing her handkerchief from her pouch. Stone gray and embroidered with the grapes of Gavenstone, it meant so much to her. "It's a memory of the last time I saw my brother alive. Before he came to *you* for safekeeping."

The move was a calculated one. Serra treasured Agler's handkerchief, yes. He'd left it in her care so she would think of him during his penance, when he'd decided to join the spy force to give something back to King Dever as thanks for the king's forgiveness. But she also knew invoking Agler's name would remind Ser Swalus that many Ravens hadn't returned from their missions to Medua during the divide, that some had been murdered or lost their minds. Yet they went, nonetheless.

The next morning, Serra's party set off for the riverlands of Lorvia, with an excited Felia Swalus in their stead. Red highlights gleamed from her hair in the golden light, and her smile was fixed ear to ear. Serra prayed it would remain that way.

CHAPTER SIXTEEN

VESPERI

Hamsyn's younger sister was attractive, though she wouldn't survive a year in Sellwyn's kitchens. How odd to think Terella was the same age Vesperi had been during her time in Qiltyn's convent, servicing the raunchy, old advers after her father had sent her away. Part of Vesperi wondered if such a cushy way of life made the Lanserim soft.

The gardener was showing Janto cuttings of some sort of plant with black blossoms and a rainbow sheen. Vesperi wanted to be on their way already. If visiting that Sielban bloke on Braven would help them find Izzy, she wanted to be there. But Janto just *had* to stop and greet every town council along the way, and each one insisted on a night's feting to celebrate their new king. Vesperi was certain her arms would fall off from the constant elbow raising. If she had to take another swallow of fallowent or bestow one more "May Madel's hand" blessing, she'd insert "lose your child in the swamps then steal your power" at the end.

If they remained in this greenhouse any longer, those cantalere herds might stampede right over this delegation of plumped up Nevillim and royal guards. They were prime for a carnivore's feast.

"Do you need anything, my queen?" One of the servants riding with them expressed concern.

"Can you force the king to pay more attention to our progress overland than those plants?"

The woman stammered, and Vesperi laughed. Then she paused,

trying to come up with the servant's name. She ought to know it; her face was familiar, with those cheeks puffed as a cheese pastry. Vesperi ought not chasten the woman for doing her job, either, but she must have some amusements. Being the better person was such a bore.

"Darling husband," she called out with saccharine sweetness into the glass house, "will you be much longer?"

"You should come have a look at this plant, Vesperi." Janto held a branch aloft, his grin wide. "It's truly unusual. Terella says it comes from near the sea."

"I'll pass. It's probably grown from sheven leavings." She stamped her foot with impatience, couldn't help it.

Two fingers pressed against the fabric on her ankle. Vesperi peered down to find a child's hand darting back under the plant-covered table. She stamped down hope that the hand was the one she so longed to see, and went to her knees. Her eyes met those of a young girl, maybe six or seven, who trembled, realizing she hadn't hidden well enough.

"Why did you touch me?" Vesperi asked, leaving out some of her annoyance's sting. This child wasn't the reason for it, though she could provide a distraction.

"I . . . I . . ."

"Speak up. I don't have all day."

The sentence spilled out, words tumbling into each other along the way. "I wanted to touch a queen."

"Ah." Vesperi offered her hand, and the girl took it, eyes unblinking as Vesperi drew her out. "And how was it?"

The girl gaped at her, and then again as she took in how many people surrounded them. Terella employed a fair number, but not as many as a king's consort, nor the town's citizenry who'd come to gawk as the girl had done.

"How was it?" Vesperi repeated. "Touching a queen?"

Her voice must have carried farther than she'd meant it to, as a man came running toward them down a row of rutabagas. His cap flew off and he caught it without missing a step. Vesperi wondered how limber he might be in bed.

"Koren," he shouted. "Koren, come here!"

The little girl, who wore a matching cap and the thick canvas overalls such work required, glanced back and forth between Vesperi and her father, torn on who to obey. He reached her before a decision could be made.

"I'm so sorry," he said, breathless and falling to his knees. He hugged the girl close before scolding, "What were you thinking? You were supposed to be harvesting the fallowent! What are you doing here?"

Smart, using a child to harvest such delicate seeds. And somewhat surprising that this Koren was allowed to work. Children didn't need as much distraction in Lansera as they had in Medua, tasks on which to focus their energies so they wouldn't ask questions of their mothers about which of the men who dropped in were their fathers or—

Oh, *these* were Meduans. She should have recognized it right away. Lanserim commoners retained a modicum of self-respect before nobility, rather than prostrate themselves as he had done. Still, the man's affection for his daughter flummoxed Vesperi all the more coming from a Meduan. Had her people come so far over the past six years?

Tears overwhelmed Koren as she gasped her way into a crying fit. "I just wanted to . . . *hic* . . . She's so pretty. I . . . *hic* . . ."

Oh bother. The child's torment was off-putting. Vesperi kneeled back down as well. "Don't fret," she reassured Koren, soothing her with a back pat. The girl recoiled, curling farther into the man's chest. Instantly, he swooped her up and spun his back to Vesperi, raising an arm to shield them both. Such a reaction to her attempt to offer comfort was almost offensive, but Vesperi recognized such behavior—they were not used to kindness, having been hurt and victimized many times. The silver flame had aided Vesperi in overcoming such simpering tendencies. Knowing no one could harm her when she possessed such power had been liberating.

It pained her to look at them. She didn't want to see herself in such people. She'd rather not see them at all.

"I'm going to wait by the carriage." Vesperi hurried away, her boots falling fast against the sodden floor. Some guards moved to accompany her, and Janto's concern-laden voice called her name, but she raised a hand that silenced them fast as the flame would have.

Why couldn't they be on the road already?

The horses had been well-tended during this sojourn by two stable hands in their company. Vesperi eyed the animals, contemplating how far she might make it if she mounted bareback and galloped off. But she wasn't a good rider, and the embarrassment of being "rescued" later would be far too much to endure. Maybe she could convince the carriage drivers that the king wanted her to get a head start?

A pavilion had been set up outside of the glass houses for lunch. By its entrance flap, a faded brown swatch of cloth conspicuously flashed. It waved again, and Vesperi glimpsed yellowish-white twigs adhered to it.

Not twigs. Bones. An adver's robes. Vesperi hadn't seen one since the fall of Mandat Hall, though she'd recognize them anywhere. The advers decorated their priestly garb with the bones of slain adversaries. They were clever enough to know they couldn't don the robes after the Conjoining, not if they wanted to avoid Callyn's jail cells. Janto had spared lives when the Hall burned, but he would not be so understanding if they tried exerting power again.

So why would someone be using it to gain her attention now?

The busyness of lunchtime preparations kept eyes off Vesperi as she snuck toward the pavilion. Curiosity drove her feet forward. Did this person know she was queen? Or just recognize a fellow Meduan as she had done with Koren and her father?

As she reached the folded-back flap, two violet eyes on a pale face, dripping equal parts disdain and fear, peeked out. Oh, this man knew whom he'd waved over.

"Adver Votan," she steamed. He had guided her and her companions into the claren trap where Hamsyn had died. "I'm surprised you've slithered up from the depths of obscurity."

"Vesperi—*Queen* Vesperi, it is a delight to see you again."

She squelched a laugh. No doubt, it curled every fiber of his being to watch how far she'd risen. "To what do I owe this"—she coughed—"pleasure?"

"We have an answer for your husband."

Janto had conversed with Votan and his fellow fiends? It was shock enough to discover a cell of advers plotting, or at least existing, here. Janto was aware and allowed it to happen? The notion was ludicrous, outrageous. He was bluffing her into doing something dangerous.

"An answer to what?" she demanded.

"We have word of your daughter."

Votan, a much taller man, crouched low in a show of respect. He sniveled, lips curved up. She hated those unearthly Deduin eyes, Votan's especially. At least the life had returned to them. They'd been vacant, Votan under a wizard's thrall, last time they'd met.

Trusting an adver's word would be as idiotic as petting a sheven in Thokketh's moat and expecting not to get bitten. But if there was any truth to what he said, nothing would stop Vesperi from learning more. Nothing.

"What do you know?" She nearly begged, but forbore, keeping any hint of desperation from her voice.

"Come, I'll show you. It's not safe for me to linger here."

She couldn't argue with that. But . . . "It wouldn't be safe for you to disappear with the queen, either."

"Oh, I'm certain you'll be able to persuade your guards otherwise." He blinked, slowly. "Or we friends of the crown can forget what we've learned. The king will be disappointed, but . . ." He shrugged, a devilish frown in place.

"Shush," she warned him. "I'll come." A dangerous move, and she a right fool, but if he truly had word of Izzy . . .

They slipped around the pavilion's backside. Votan guided her, descending enough of a hillside in this land of meadows to keep them hidden. He straightened to his full height, and if she looked past his Deduin traits, she'd admit he was an elegant man. She considered her own as they furtively made their way wherever Votan led. *Had* Janto reached out to the advers to locate Izzy? If so, it was a desperate act. This past year, his *lack* of desperation had provoked her so. That even-keeled manner, the months of him going back to the swamps to search—he hadn't ransacked the whole country like she'd wanted to, hadn't searched every hovel, drained the swamp, any of the things in his princely power to do.

Yet he'd been doing things that weren't in his power to openly pursue? Parlaying with advers—news of that could ruin him and the reunification he hoped would be his legacy. Was he willing to risk all that for the mere chance they might know something about Izzy? Vesperi doubted it.

Adver Votan led her into a large grass hut on the outskirts of Tilayne. Refusing his hand for the hop into the shelter was an act of self-preservation. She may be walking into a trap with no means of defending herself, but at least Janto would have to stew in his worries for a bit. Vesperi could take care of herself, had survived her whole life doing so. It was taking care of others where she fell short.

The room was full of men, more than Vesperi had seen congregated together in the absence of women since, well, since she'd burned down Mandat Hall. Fifteen lounged in various states of recline in the main room, on pillows on the stone floor or at tables playing cards. They stiffened up as she and Votan entered.

"Who's that?" One man leered, and oh, how Vesperi had not missed this revulsion. Another leaned in, baring teeth and breath that stank of milkwine.

"Queen Vesperi of Lansera," she declared unwisely, but she wouldn't cow herself before such men again. *Not even if they know where Izzy is?* Janto may have done so, lowered himself to their level to seek their daughter out. That made her feel . . . consoled, somehow.

She scanned for exits—at least three other rooms fed into the main one, but whether any of those boasted windows or outside doors, she couldn't tell. One window opened high against the back wall.

A surly man, who probably spent his free time spitting seeds, spoke. "You said you were going to talk with the king, Votan, not his wife. What good is she to us?"

"Yeah, how's she going to get our fellows released?" said another, dry beige skin peeling from his bald head, or maybe from his all-around rottenness. Six years, and they still couldn't grasp the power a woman might hold.

Vesperi spoke through gritted teeth. "My daughter. I have no patience for any other topic." She flicked her eyes to the window, imagined Esye shining through it. And flipped her hand.

Her implied threat was enough to get the conversation back on track. The way these wretches scattered into the room's corners spoke volumes—they knew they'd invited the weapon into their hut. If only she had the power to follow through.

Votan spoke. "Yes, we know the princess's location. But we require a show of good faith to share it."

She laughed at the idea of such men being capable of keeping faith. "How am I to believe you know anything about Izmareld? You want us to release prisoners who will no doubt join you in whatever *this*"—she waved her hand dismissively at the room—"is for the mere chance that you *might*?"

"The new king seemed willing." The seed-spitter clomped the legs of his chair to the ground. "We should be talking with him, not you."

Vesperi brooked no argument. "I am queen. I speak with the king's authority."

A few of the men had a good laugh at that, but she extended her hand again and they quieted soon enough.

"The world doesn't work the way it used to, o' most glorious priests of Saeth. Or did no one tell you your false god has lost his cock?" Vesperi imbued her voice with as much disdain as she could, which was to say, a lot. "The sooner you get used to it, the easier it'll be for you to stay out of our way. What's to stop me from smiting you now for wasting my time?"

Faces paled, except on one troublemaker in the back who seemed more concerned with a knife he sharpened.

"Go on then." The sand-colored man with the knife raised it up, a challenge on his face. "Smite that stand over there. We'll wait."

Vesperi cursed him internally while pretending to draw forth the silver flame.

"Can't do it, can you?"

The other men whispered. She knew her hand was played, but thrust her palm toward them anyhow, hoping to cause a panic. Votan blocked her way as she aimed to slip out the entrance.

"That's right," the knife-sharpener said. "That magic wasn't yours, was it? It came from the moon that's gone and disappeared sure as your daughter. You're as dangerous as a bee that's lost its sting. Wonder if the king would bother trading any prisoners for a childless whore like you."

Others crowded in on her in the small space by the door. Vesperi raised her finger to the window, hoping, praying, and—

—and silver flashed, setting a chair ablaze beneath it. The curtain next to that caught fire, and the room erupted into chaos. Water was thrown and the fire stamped.

A woman peeked her head out of a side room and discretely waved to Vesperi. She would not look a gift horse in the mouth. Fear reflected from the men's faces as she went, and she relished it. None tried to follow. They didn't know the power hadn't come through her, that her connection to Esye was as dry as before. It had been an echo, like the flame Lorne Granich possessed and Janto had dreamed of so recently. An echo of her power grown into a roar to perform that well.

The woman, with stark white hair, held open an exit door, but the queen paused long enough for a thank you.

"Weren't nothing," she said. Rheumy eyes glinted with amusement. "I'll have me a good laugh at the tavern later."

"You'll have the king's gratitude as well," Vesperi insisted. Then she remembered, "We are gathering people with your skill in Queen

Drustalla's ruins on the plain of Orelyn. You should go, rather than serve these men. Surely you can see they aren't worth your time?"

"Never you mind," the woman said. "I have my reasons. Now on with yourself."

Vesperi couldn't fathom any reason good enough to spend time with that den of fools, not by choice. But her window of escape was closing fast, so she made her exit.

Not ten paces farther, she found the royal company making its way down the path toward her, fewer than a hundred yards away. If any of those advers poked out a head, they'd swallow their tongues. Janto had positioned himself at the front of the coterie, quite handsome and regal, even with his tousled hair. She would *not* admit to nearly being kidnapped in front of all these people, would lash him right off the saddle if she could to avoid it.

Vesperi marched to her husband. "What are you doing, coming after me?" Her voice simmered with rage. "I can take care of myself. I'm a grown woman, you know." She knew full well this was not queenly behavior, but an emotional whirlwind had just spit her out. Far as she cared to see, Janto was responsible for it all.

"I know." He stayed high in the saddle while she pommeled the leathers covering his calves. "And I know you would have found a way to catch up with us. But I couldn't bear to leave you behind."

Vesperi paused her onslaught, and Janto caught one of her flailing forearms. His eyes asked permission, then he hoisted her up behind him once she acquiesced.

The coterie tittered at her behavior, and she refused to let *that* be her companion on this journey. "I heard a rumor Izmareld might be here," she offered by way of apology, though her tone was brash. "I had to come see for myself."

By that last word, she was crying, though she kept her chin up.

"Did you find anything, my queen?" called out one of the guards. It felt as though the group held their breaths, waiting and hoping with her.

She shook her head to palpable disappointment.

"I am so sorry," said the servant from the greenhouses with the puffy cheeks. A gentle chorus of yesses agreed with her sentiment, and Vesperi nodded in acknowledgment of their concern.

Janto pulled her handkerchief up above her neck, ostensibly to keep out the dirt once they continued on. She wiped her face against it before sinking her head into his back.

"Ready?"

She nodded against his riding cloak. "I'm sorry," she whispered. "For that show, and the one back at the greenhouse. I'm not sure I know how this queen thing works."

"Nonsense." Janto gave her right leg a squeeze. "What I saw there was a queen baring herself to her people. I can't think of a better model."

Vesperi thought on that as the horses moved to a trot. Perhaps there was more than one way to be queen.

A good amount of time passed before Janto slowed the pace enough to ask, "So what *did* happen?"

He cocked his head to hear her against the wind, so she spoke loud as she might. "Word from the advers."

His body tensed. So he *had* inquired with them about Izzy. It hadn't been just a ploy. "And?"

"And they know nothing. But they're keen to have their compatriots released from our prison."

"I'll send Captain Wolxas an alert to double their guards." He paused, breathing into the wind a moment before twisting to face her. "Should I send soldiers to capture the men back at that hut? They'll scatter once they realize we were there, but if they're plotting something, they're sure to regroup—"

"No," she decided, though she'd relish taunting them in the prison at Callyn. But advers weren't known for keeping their mouths shut. "They'd tell everyone that you were sending them birds. Most won't believe them, but the rumor will still spread . . . it's a risk, but better not to open that well."

Janto sighed. "I was a right fool to contact them. I didn't hear back—it's been months, since before you went to Elston. Didn't even know to whom I wrote, but I thought . . . I thought . . ."

She reached her arms around his chest and held tight. "Thank you."

"There's something else I should have told you," he said.

She encouraged him with a caress to his stomach.

"Something was haunting me in Callyn. Something pretending to be my father, but with a soul dark as these Esye-less nights. It didn't want us to go to Braven."

"The dark brother?"

Janto's breath caught. "I think so, yes."

"We'll figure it out, Janto. What it was, how to defeat it. Together."

His lips briefly met her brow. Their world was missing a moon and a daughter that outshined it, but Vesperi took more comfort in Janto's presence than an ocean of Elstonian hot springs. She kept her eyes on the horizon and the answers Braven might bring.

CHAPTER SEVENTEEN

SERRA

On the way to Granich Manor, Serra's party grew to six. In the Durnish lands near the mountains, they collected Ryn Colini after seeing something flashing silver through the trees. He'd been using his newly acquired magic skill to toast chestnuts for his supper.

Serra had been delighted to see him. Colini had been at Temple Enjoin with her, training to become a priest as she'd trained to become the seer. He'd not seemed put out by putting off his reassignment to Kallon, either. Serra gathered that placements in the Meduan regions were not prime pickings for the Order, whether or not the people living there were also Madel's children.

As they reached the riverlands, Serra was reminded of the first journey she'd taken in Medua. That group had been seven to start and six to finish, and it shared several members with her current crew: Sar Mertina, riding high on her marble-white horse; Flivio, riding less high but no less alert; and Napeler, whose sword hilt gleamed. Serra wondered if Hamsyn's death crossed their thoughts as it did hers. She'd seen many deaths over the years; indeed, she'd discovered some of the clarens' first victims by the banks of Lake Ashra, a father and his daughter reduced to dried skin and bone. But Hamsyn's death was the first time someone she'd journeyed with had fallen prey to them.

Terella had been twelve then. The young woman had grown a thriving enterprise since her brother's death, done so much for her country while losing so much herself. Serra knew how to exist in that space, how to bury herself in the task at hand rather than grieve for what she'd lost. Whether her decision to avoid Gavenstone Manor, and its empty rooms holding ghosts of a family she hardly knew, constituted the same, she couldn't say. *Or won't admit.*

The horses neighed, and Serra's hesitated to take its next step, throwing her off-balance. She righted herself in the saddle and cast the sight over their surroundings. Even the colors from Madel's realm felt dimmer this side of the mountains. If the claren's shimmering red and black wings were there, she'd have picked them out easily. None of those pockets of darkness, either.

"All clear."

Mertina, Flivio, and Nap nodded back at her, though Felia and Colini froze in their saddles.

"All clear from what, Lady Serra?" asked Felia, her ponytail tucked into her riding tunic.

"From the claren," Serra answered, perhaps too readily, for Felia and Colini pushed whatever material they could up to cover their faces—a smart impulse, though unwarranted.

"But you wiped them out, you and the prince." Felia's voice was muffled and her pupils dilated with the potential of a horror she'd considered banished. Had there been claren present, they'd have already entered her body through an open orifice. And other terrors walked their lands now, ones with spiked hooves and tails.

"With our king and queen, yes, I did. But when you've seen horrors like the claren?" Serra shuddered. "You don't stop looking." She tilted her head at Sar Mertina, knowing the knight would have taken this interlude to conduct her own search for what may have spooked the horses. "Mertina?"

The great warrior shook her head. "Nothing I can see, Lady Serra. Maybe some rabbits we missed?"

"Let us hope." Taking in the covered faces of her charges, Serra reconsidered. "Let us pray. We don't know what lies ahead, but we do know Madel has a plan, and you two are part of it. She will not abandon you now."

Ryn Colini was brave enough to lower his blue woolen shawl back over his airy priest garb. He led them in a simple prayer:

"Madel, mother of all, keep your servants safe and guide us with your hand."

Serra detested having so little understanding of what Madel wanted of this Silver Guard she assembled. May she be more than a shepherd leading lambs to slaughter, and about to add the queen's brother to her flock.

‡

The sun set over Lorvia's rolling hills, painting the riverlands below in abstract pink hues. The view reminded Serra of Qiltyn's spire-topped buildings. Granich's were utterly lacking in charm, flat with a utilitarian construction of yellowed mud bricks. She couldn't imagine Lorne, and all his vivaciousness, in this place.

From a distance, they glimpsed a single horseman setting out from the manor house, which loomed three times as tall as the surrounding cabins. Scouts, Serra realized, had been the cause of their horses' trepidation. Cavallen Granich was a Meduan liege-lord—he would not let visitors approach without gathering information to use against them first.

A good thirty minutes of riding passed before the herald reached their party. Nap galloped ahead to gauge the threat level. Once cleared, the herald declared, "Welcome to Granich," and pulled his reins and horse to a stop. "Lord Granich is preparing to receive you for dinner. I'll guide you the rest of the way."

He circled his horse and set off, but Serra did not accept invitations so easily these days.

"A pleasure to meet you, Mer . . . ?"

She waited until he swiveled back around with a quizzical expression. This man was not used to being addressed formally.

"My name is Serrafina Gavenstone," she supplied. "And you are?"

"P-P-Pedir."

"Pedir," she continued, infusing her smile with welcome, though she was the guest. "Have you always lived in Granich?"

"I-I have." He relaxed some into the saddle, though his hands fidgeted with the reins.

"What's it like living in Granich? Has it changed since the Conjoining?"

He cleared his throat and loosened his cloak's knot. "Granich Manor is a wonderful place. Very pleasant and all our needs are met."

Flivio released a short, loud "Ha!"

Serra silenced him with a glance. "And your Lord Granich?"

"Fair and kind, as he's always been."

In other words, the exact opposite. Serra had so hoped Lorne's resentment had exaggerated his father's two-facedness.

"Let's go on, then," she smiled sweetly. "I can't wait to meet such an agreeable man."

Flivio could not suppress his laughter.

‡

As they approached the manor, Serra tried to guess which room Lorne had snuck out of as a child to find a beloved doll that his father had ordered thrown away. That night, Madel had appeared to young Lorne and given him a glimpse of the world outside his father's reach, indeed, outside of Medua.

Serra had imagined Granich Manor would be much like Sellwyn Manor, when she'd seen it years ago: a mansion in decay after decades of neglect from a ruler more concerned with building his cruel reputation than infrastructure. Yet Granich Manor was in good repair. Its main house was joined by multiple longhouses connected by passageways, made of the same yellow bricks as the surrounding town. Measures had been taken to defend against claren attacks: solid wood covered the windows, the people milling about wore kerchiefs, and modified fly masks hung in the stables, should the horses and other animals need full-head protection. They'd likely been attacked before and were wary to let go of such precautions, even years later.

Pedir led them straight to a dining hall. They'd agreed along the way that nourishment was a more immediate concern than bathing. Serra scanned for claren as they walked, delving into the rainbow-hued brilliance of Madel's realm. No sign of their tenebrous glimmer, but the dark pockets had reappeared and grown in size, obscuring more of her vision.

Focusing back on this world, she admired a delicate centerpiece made to resemble the bird of creation. It had been laboriously constructed of blue feathers whose fine quill tips were inserted into small sacks filled to the brim with sand.

"Isn't it lovely?" Sar Mertina brushed a feather with an ungloved hand.

"Yes." Serra would ask about the artisan later; to craft such an exquisite item in the mere hours since the scouts reported on her identity? Meduan cities needed more such craftspeople to usher beauty back into their lives.

A door at the far end of the room creaked open. Lord Cavallen Granich stepped inside, the mirror image of his son in coloring and graceful movement. He led with his long legs first and beamed at his guests.

"Welcome!"

His melodious tenor brought a smile to her face. She'd need to guard against such obvious charms.

"I am honored to host such a distinguished group of westerners in Granich Manor." He beelined to Serra and took a hug, which she responded to with practiced warmth. "The seer!" he exclaimed, raising his elbows high and holding them for a good ten seconds. "I cannot imagine what my humble manor town has done to earn a visit from you."

Before Serra could find the words to answer, he had moved on to Sar Mertina and had a servant open an ornately embroidered bag of fallowent seeds. They each swallowed a helping before the warrior received a hug as well. She squeaked at his tight hold and then smoothed down her tunic.

"I've heard so much of your prowess, Sar Mertina! You'll have to tell me about that uprising you squelched in Yarowen. I always told Gion Clardill that he aimed too high for a man of his deficiencies."

Lord Granich winked, then hurried around to the other side of the table, bypassing Felia and Colini to greet Flivio and Napeler next. "And two of the king's own murat companions! Councilman Flivio, do you know some of the old advers still talk about how you lockpicked your way into Mandat Hall? Now that's a story!"

Surprisingly, Flivio did not rush to tell it. "A lot happened that day," he said, his voice solemn enough to confirm that yes, Serra had not been the only one with Hamsyn on the mind. And likely not the only person who found it revealing how prepared Granich was for these introductions.

He distanced himself from the awkwardness Flivio had engendered and placed one hand on a shoulder each of Colini and Felia. "And who are these two fine companions? I'm not certain the manor is ready to house our own servant of Madel yet, but if the king wills it—"

"Ryn Colini is here as my personal spiritual advisor," Serra interrupted. "I can see Madel's realm, but Her instructions are not always clear to me in the one we live in."

"Ah," Lord Granich smiled at Colini and Felia in turn, then returned to the table's head to take his seat. His guests followed suit and servants entered, half-standing, half-crouching as they laid platters of food on the table. Their semi-cowed statures gave away the type of treatment Lord Granich typically bestowed upon them.

The food was plentiful. Serra took a generous portion of smoked tartine, a yellow fish marbled green-blue where the bones had been removed. She layered it onto a wedge of soft bread and piled grape leaves on top. One bite took her back home to Meditlan, where the washing and pickling of such leaves was a continual summertime task. Had he intended it as a reference to her homeland? She doubted he'd had *that* much time to prepare.

"Where's Uzziel Sellwyn?" Serra asked, not wanting to give Lord Granich the time to lower her defenses. Straight and to the point was the ideal mode of operation here. "Does he not take his meals with you?"

Lord Granich put down the sausage he'd been about to bite. "Ah, yes, I'd thought perhaps the queen was concerned about her brother at last. It's only taken six years for her to ask." His mouth twisted. Did Serra share his scorn for Vesperi's disinterest, that gaze asked. Yes, she did, though she'd learned to avoid the topic during their hunts.

"The king sent me to personally invite Uzziel on a palace visit." That wasn't sticking straight to the point, though Drustalla's ruins had been a palace once. Sometimes lies were needful. "He would like to get to know his brother-in-law."

"Hm," Lord Granich relaxed into his chair. "Is the king aware his brother-in-law is a cripple?" He cocked a brow, amused.

"Like Vesperi wouldn't tell him that," Flivio muttered. His lips parted, and his eyes met Serra's, opened wide as a cat's that'd gone for a bird and got feathers instead.

She mouthed, "It's okay," before responding, "Of course, the king knows. He sent us with a special harness for the journey. Uzziel will be strapped to Sar Mertina and Sar Napeler's mounts, sharing duties for his transport." They'd improvised the contraption along the way.

"Hm," Lord Granich repeated. Clearly, he had not expected Uzziel to leave the manor. If Lorne were correct, letting Uzziel go would throw years of his careful plotting into disarray.

But Serra was prepared for that hurdle. "I have a letter from the king, granting you provisional power over the Sellwyn lands in the queen and Lord Uzziel's absence." A world of pain awaited Janto once Vesperi found out, but it was necessary.

"That sounds like a smart arrangement," Lord Granich drawled, revealing none of the satisfaction he must feel. Serra wondered how many times Lorne had pulled off that same act, his desires close at hand. "But I can barely afford to keep Granich Manor running. How could I possibly support the rebuilding efforts at Sellwyn as well?"

Never mind that he'd been supporting them for as long as he'd sheltered Uzziel Sellwyn, six years and counting. "The king is prepared to grant you a thousand souzers a month for its management."

"Hm." Lord Granich plopped the sausage in his mouth, which the dining party took as their signal to move on to the more pleasurable business at hand: filling their stomachs after a few hard days' riding. Negotiations were far from closed, but Serra was content to let Lord Granich ponder them for a while.

Felia's gaze darted around as she ate, the barest of smiles evident beyond the edges of her sandwich roll. She flexed and unflexed her right palm, fighting the impulse to play with her flame. Nap examined the exits every few seconds, while Sar Mertina ate cured craval beast and drank from her own water flask. Colini wore the same expression as Felia, though he was at least twenty years older. But Serra knew life experience prepared no one for their first time breaking bread in a Meduan stronghold.

She wondered if Lorne would still feel at home here. *And if not, where would he?* Why did it bother her that the answer might be nowhere at all? Gavenstone was ever open to Serra, if she chose to return, and Callyn. What a privilege, she realized, to have such options.

After a time, Lord Granich called a servant for more wine, and everyone but Mertina took a glass. Serra would make sure Felia drank no more than that; she couldn't imagine Ser Swalus let his daughter often partake of the Ravens' ale, and no hint must get out as to why they'd really come. The advers had planned to use Vesperi's power for their own purposes once; Serra had no doubt Lord Granich would do the same with members of the Silver Guard if he could, even the one he fostered. *Especially the one he fostered*, she realized, the thought coming to her in Lorne's tenor.

"To my unexpected guests!" Granich raised his glass high. "May

Madel's hand guide your journey home—and your conversation with Uzziel, when he feels ready to see you." He winked again, and Serra bet that "when" could mean an hour, week, or year from then. That would not do. "You'll find he's more of a challenge to win to your side than I am," the lord said.

Serra saw an opening, but Ryn Colini found his voice first. "I'm surprised to hear you invoke Madel, Lord Granich." He blushed as he spoke, unused to conversing with nobility. "Have you given up on the religion of Saeth?"

Unused to conversing with nobility, though not unpracticed at needling them. Serra choked back shock that Colini dared such a subject in a Meduan holding. Madel *did* like Her servants to have some backbone.

Lord Granich's laugh held a nervous edge. He had done his home-work on them, but hadn't expected questioning of himself. "I'm not sure anyone believed in Saeth, dear ryn."

The manor's servants, waiting against the walls, exchanged looks. Colini switched his focus to them. "And you, do you follow Madel now?"

They fell silent, but one poked the other, a short man who kept his head covered with a kitchen snood. "I don't know who Madel is, my lord," he admitted. His presumption that only nobility would sup with Lord Granich spoke an unsaid truth as well. "But we aren't missing Saeth much around these parts. Nor the advers who carried out his commands."

"Have your lives changed that much," Serra inquired, "since the fall of Mandat Hall?" She rested her head on her left hand, projecting pure innocence.

The same man answered, though he kept glancing at Lord Granich, who waved him on. "Aye, my lady, it has. Why, when it floods now, we can have the day off and don't have to forage for food with those no-see-ums in the marshes. We used to lose at least a dozen men each season, but now, we play Adver's Thrift in the cabins instead. It's a real holiday."

"Is it?" She spoke to the servant but kept her gaze on Lord Granich. "Tell me, mer, who was your lord when so many of you were sent out to your deaths each spring?"

Granich cleared his throat. He was not fool enough to sit through a recounting of his misdeeds from someone of Serra's pedigree, someone whose "disappearance" would not go unnoted by the king. "You must be exhausted from your travels. Please, let me show you to your bedrooms. They've been freshly aired." He smiled wide enough to catch krill.

The other servant spoke cautiously. Perhaps the presence of Serra's party emboldened her. "I don't know about deaths, but there have been some disappearances this year," she said. "I was going to tell the lord later tonight. Last week, two young men walked behind one of the men's cabins and didn't came back. This morning, one of the younger children did the same."

That Lord Granich still kept the genders separated was disturbing, but more disappearances? Serra's thoughts returned to the dark places in her vision.

"Immigrants to Lansera, no doubt!" Lord Granich suggested, raising his glass. "To their safe journey over the mountains."

"You should have that cabin emptied, Lord Granich," Serra said, brooking no dissent. "And the area blocked off. These are not your 'normal' disappearances, not men felled by no-see-um bites." For weight, she added, "My sight reveals that."

He acquiesced by draining his glass.

"And I expect we'll see Lord Sellwyn soon?" she said pointedly.

"I'll introduce you first thing in the morning." Granich raised his elbows in what Serra read as defeat. Now was a good time for that other inquiry, too. She had not forgotten the medallion in her pouch.

"And your daughter, Lord Granich? Will we meet her tomorrow as well?"

Now that surprised him. He stumbled over his words. "Cora? She's . . . she's boarding with the young Lord Riven. Your advisors are teaching them both how the Lanserim govern."

Serra didn't buy it for a second. This man was not the type to recognize his daughter as an heir, even with Lorne essentially exiling himself. "Such a shame. Her brother sent me with tidings for her."

He quieted. "You know my son?"

Oh, do I. "We journeyed directly here from where he is staying in Ertion. He will be so disappointed to learn I could not confirm her well-being personally." Perhaps that would be enough to entice him to produce the young woman—knowing Lorne yearned for some sort of familial connection meant Lord Granich could use Cora to manipulate him into returning.

"Indeed. It is a shame." He left the room with a forced smile.

Serra's group ate their desserts in silence. They could think of nothing it would be safe to discuss within these walls.

‡

Uzziel Sellwyn lay on his bed, propped up by pillows that bore fresh stains from the dribble on his chin. He was smaller than most boys his age; at twenty-three, Serra felt as though a generation separated them rather than a mere six years. Had she really been the same age when the sight came to her?

Uzziel resembled his sister, though Vesperi would be offended at the suggestion. Black curls brushed into waves came down to his shoulders, and dark brown eyes flashed with the same challenge Vesperi's often held. "Try me," they dared, and Serra wondered if he could follow through on the threat as well as his sister.

If he has the flame's echo . . .

Lord Granich laid a kiss on Uzziel's head, who grimaced. "Lord Uzziel Sellwyn," Granich began, "I have the pleasure of introducing you to Lady Serrafina Gavenstone." He paused for effect. "She's one of the bird of creation's three heads."

"*She* is? Like my sister and that king?" Uzziel gripped Lord Granich's sleeve, his voice querulous and high for a teenager. He turned to his guardian, disbelief writ on his brow. "Why would a god want her help?"

"Goddess," Serra corrected.

Uzziel pinched his nose. "Why must I talk with them? I want to practice with my bow." He did not acknowledge Serra, Colini, or Flivio, all hunched inside the small room that strained to fit the oversized bed. A long line of drool dripped down to his pillows, and Lord Granich blotted his chin.

"Because they are very important guests," Granich explained, turning his voice to sugar syrup. "And Lady Serra is here just for you."

"She is?"

Serra hadn't thought someone could have worse manners than Vesperi, but Uzziel proved her wrong. "I am. Pleased to meet you, Lord Sellwyn." She extended a hand and tried not to imagine how dirty his might be. Uzziel's disabilities were one thing, but his arms moved freely enough. He ought to be able to manage his own hygiene.

Patience, she scolded herself. *You have no idea what life is like in his body.* "The king and queen have sent me to invite you to visit them. What do you think of that?"

He sunk into his pillows. "I think it makes sense Vesperi would miss me. But why should I go to her? Her place is by *my* side, that's what Father said."

Serra began to understand Vesperi's loathing of her own flesh and blood. "Being invited to the king's home is a great honor, Uzziel—"

"*Lord* Sellwyn," he corrected with a sneer. "Women aren't to call me by my name. Father said so. Only *he* could. And the Graniches, of course, for doing me this service."

"It's been our honor, Lord Sellwyn." Granich soothed him like a courtesan, smoothing his wrinkled tunic. "I would love nothing more than to keep you here at Granich Manor forever."

How had Lorne found the willpower to rescue this child from Sellwyn? Lord Granich clung to his side like a parasite. Serra needed Uzziel alone to probe for the echo. She kicked Flivio's shin, the best signal they'd come up with.

"Oof!" Flivio straightened up.

Uzziel laughed.

"Are you all right, Mer Flivio?" Lord Granich quirked his eyebrows.

"Fine," Flivio said, giving Serra a quick and hidden kick back in protest. "Ow! Ow!" he feigned a leg cramp. "Lord Granich!" He leaned forward, falling into the older man, who backed into the bed.

"Do you have any milkwine in the house?" Flivio moaned. "My leg does this sometimes if it's been too long since I've had a nip—you must know how that goes. I started drinking it as a babe and cannot go long without it." He hopped on the other leg, wiped nonexistent sweat from his forehead. "Oh, I'd be ever so grateful if you had some. I'm useless to Lady Serra like this."

Uzziel laughed his way into a coughing fit, and Colini gave his back a whack as Flivio dialed up his performance. Serra moved to the other wall to give Flivio room, then watched as Lord Granich flitted from Uzziel to Flivio and back again.

The noise in the room reached a fever pitch. "Of course," Lord Granich said, frustration winning out over his desire to control their time with Uzziel. He grabbed the Meditlan by the hand and dragged him into the hall. "Come with me."

As soon as the door closed behind them, Serra leaned over the rails of Uzziel's bed. The boy had stopped coughing, though his coloring was bright red.

"I'm so glad they left," she whispered, conspiratorially, as Ryn Colini saw to the young man's needs.

"Wha-why?" His features battled between gall that a woman addressed him and inquisitiveness about what she had to say.

"Because the king wanted me to invite you to something much more exciting than just a visit."

She paused, waited until Uzziel's building curiosity caused him to demand, "What? What does he want me to do?"

She imagined herself as their dear old cook, Mar Pina, sneaking lemon cakes to young Janto from the castle's kitchen. "The king wants you to go koparin hunting with him."

Uzziel trembled with excitement. "Yes! What are koparin?"

"Only the hardest animals to hunt in the kingdom!" She was surprised he'd never heard of the ferocious furballs. They must not stray to this side of the mountains.

"Are they giant? And scary? I could kill them if I had my tornian, I bet." He leaned forward, spittle churning.

Serra narrowed her eyes as though peering at a candle flame, so she might peek into the sight without him catching on. "Koparin aren't big like giants," she kept talking to distract him, "but they *are* scary. Their claws are thick as your big toe and sharpened to fine points that can slice a vein if they catch one."

"Ew!" A pause. "That's incredible!"

Vivid colors filled her senses, oversaturating the forms around her, like their essences spilled out of coloring lines. She homed in on Uzziel. "Have you ever seen a cat?"

He nodded, and the version of his head she saw moved sluggishly, his aura hanging in the air for a split-second before following his movement. The coordination delay made sense, but not the lack of what she searched for.

She observed Colini, saw the faint outline of silver around him, and wondered if Lorne had been wrong about Uzziel. "Well, koparin are like cats," she explained. "Except they're as tall as your bed, and they have long, springy back legs that help them take great leaps. And they're vicious."

"I haven't been hunting before," Uzziel considered. "Is it hard? Can I . . . can I do it from a bed?"

How little he knows of the world outside bedrooms. Serra doubted he was the dark brother of that prophecy. The kept-in-the-dark brother, perhaps. "The king has commissioned an inventor to make you a camouflaged dais that'll be just perfect. It should be ready by the time we meet him at the plains." She hated the lies, but they were necessary—Uzziel needed to want to come, if they were to get permission from Lord Granich. But did he even have the echo? Maybe . . . maybe he was more like Vesperi than anyone had thought. And Vesperi used to need a certain something to fan her flame.

Provocation. "But I don't know that you're capable enough."

Colini gasped at Serra's untowardness, but she got the reaction she'd aimed for. Silver glinted over his head as Uzziel lashed out, "You don't tell me what I can do! You're a girl!"

He has it. Perhaps it hadn't manifested yet, but it would. And better he be with their group when it did than here at Granich Manor.

She returned to her normal sight. "I am a girl. And if you come with us, I won't be the only girl telling you what to do sometimes. Can you handle that? It takes a strong man to take direction from women."

Uzziel cringed, and his face blushed as he considered what must be the most absurd advice he'd ever received. Teaching him the ways of the world post-Conjoining had not been high on Lord Granich's to-do list. "Why?"

"Because those are my conditions." And because his yowling otherwise would draw raiders sure as the sunrise once they left Granich village behind.

"Okay," he said, trembling again. "I want to kill the kitties."

Footsteps sounded down the hall. Serra leaned over the rail and gathered him up in a hug. "We'll get you the finest fur coat made of them. But," she wiped his mouth with a nearby cloth, "you'll also be wiping your drool off yourself from now on, young man."

Lord Granich knocked and swung open the door in the same movement. Flivio tumbled in after him.

"Apologies for my long absence," Granich proclaimed in a too-loud voice. "Your companion needed quite the dose of milkwine to cure his ailment."

Flivio winked at Serra from behind Granich's back. "Indeed, your lordship!" He hiccuped. "It's hard to get just the right amount, you see."

Rising to an upright seated position, Uzziel puffed out his chest.

"I'm going to Lansera to see the king," he declared, jutting out his jaw. "He's my new brother."

Lord Granich froze, but raised his elbows to Uzziel. "As you wish, Lord Sellwyn. I'll make sure your party is well-provisioned. I can even send some guards along for extra protection on the highway—"

Serra silenced him with a raised hand. "I know you don't mean to insult the prowess of Ser Napeler and Sar Mertina." She paused. "Extra guards would slow us down. For Uzziel's health, we wish to make the journey as fast as possible."

"Of course," Granich acquiesced.

Uzziel sunk back against his pillows, eyes fluttering. The exchange must have tired him out, and he struggled to keep his eyes open even as his hands began to shake against the bedrail. The journey would be a challenge for him, and for the whole party, Serra feared.

Then she realized something else both Sellwyn children had in spades. They were very, very brave.

As she and her companions took their leave of Uzziel, Serra spied a length of long, riesling-blonde hair disappearing around a corner. She waved Colini on then tiptoed to follow.

In a back stretch of hall, a woman swabbed the earthen floor with a mop, her back turned. Serra touched her shoulder, and the woman spun around before flattening herself against the wall. Fear vaulted from her blue eyes—eyes the twins of ones Serra knew very well.

"I will not hurt you, Cora," Serra whispered, careful to watch the hallway's points of egress to ensure they were alone. She dug the Granich medallion out of her pouch. "Your brother wanted me to give you this."

The too-skinny woman's mouth fell agape. "You know Lorne?" She stowed the medallion in her apron's pocket.

"Yes."

"He is well?"

"Very," Serra assured her, deciding to leave the heartbreak out. Now was not the time.

Tears welled in Cora's eyes, and she swallowed air with a relieved gasp. Serra didn't think—she pulled her close for a hug, tried to squeeze her own strength into Cora's pores. Her party didn't have the time, room, nor defenses to steal Cora away from her father, but Serra wanted nothing more than to ferry her from this miserable place, to bring her home to Lorne. It did not matter how bright the walls or well-provisioned the feast, Lord Granich was the same cruel man he had ever been. That Cora was not recognized as his progeny, years after the Conjoining, was proof enough.

"We will come back for you," Serra promised, kissing Cora's crimson cheeks. "You will not languish here for much longer. We will not allow it."

Cora sniffed. "I can manage."

An understatement. Serra shuddered to imagine what she'd managed in her twenty-odd years. She gave Cora another hug. Mindful of her party's need to depart before Lord Granich changed his mind, she retrieved her pouch of fallowent and pressed it into Cora's hands.

"Take a tablespoon daily," she implored her. "Just in case." If anywhere in Lansera was likely to breed the claren again, Granich Manor was it.

As she took her leave, Serra scanned the room. She found none of that pestilence but felt haunted by the ghosts of tiny fluttering wings, nonetheless.

CHAPTER EIGHTEEN

JANTO

Mount Frelom's cloud-covered peak soared over a dark blue sea, the sole indication from the port town of Jost that the isle of Braven was within reach. For a moment, Janto fancied approaching it the way he had for his murat: by canoe. Odd how time shaped memory into nostalgia; the paddle had not been fun, and in late winter, it would be freezing. Plus, Vesperi hadn't been on a boat before, much less in a canoe. Though her home had straddled the river Sell and was no more than a day's ride from the ocean, the region had been in drought for years and her father had never allowed her a day of pleasure at sea.

Janto didn't think she'd call it a pleasure now, either. On the dock, she stared down the eagle carved into the hull of a two-masted caravel. The boat would ferry them across the water with a few companions. They'd arrive at Braven in a couple hours if the winds stayed the same.

"You're going to lose," he came up behind her to kiss her neck, and oh, how good it felt that he could do that again. "It's wooden."

Vesperi pushed him away with a mocking frown. "I know that." Her gaze returned to the masthead. "It's an eagle. They kill snakes."

Ah. A bit of superstition. Fiction, Janto was tempted to call it, but he'd learned long ago not to discount old wives' tales about any sort of beast. The jurgens and cantaleres multiplying across his kingdom, as recent reports indicated, were but the newest types. "Do you still think of yourself that way, as a Sellwyn viper?"

She spoke softly. "I don't know, truly. Even my fangs are gone."

"Oh, they're there, trust me," Janto joked, but when she bristled, he doubted his instincts. "I know you meant the flame, but you're the same person with or without it. You see that, don't you?"

She cast him a doubtful glance. "And which Vesperi is that? The Sellwyn daughter who'd never inherit her father's land, no matter her worthiness? The one who took pride in her cruelty? Or the Albrecht, a bride and then a mother? And then none of those again."

Janto sighed. "I didn't marry Vesperi Albrecht. I married *you*. I love *you*."

"Whomever that is." Her words were bitter, and Janto wished he could pry her head open, truly understand what she felt. To become a father, a king . . . both roles were worlds apart from what he'd thought they'd be, yet he'd been groomed to inhabit them since birth. Vesperi's perspectives had shifted dramatically over a few short years.

And was literally about to shift again. Captain Vorpa, a buxom woman with a sunhat that engulfed her sandy brown curls, waved them onboard. "Your highness, it's just you and the missus left."

"Aye, aye," he couldn't resist saying back. "Let's go."

Vesperi landed on the deck with a firm hop. The deck responded by rolling her off her feet. Janto caught her with a laugh. He couldn't mirror her mood, not today. A fresh breeze filled him with clear thoughts and cool excitement. A whole life had passed since his murat, yet Janto felt twenty-one again. Some of the townsfolk they'd met along the journey had dubbed his return to the island a holy pilgrimage. Few murated men ever went back to Braven, perhaps wishing to preserve their experiences in a nostalgic haze, a luminous butterfly kept under glass, never touched. Or maybe they, like his father, had the better sense to leave Sielban alone with his work.

But they didn't have the knowledge Janto did of the spreading disappearances and rifts, and the dark brother himself.

"For your stomach, my queen." A sailor offered Vesperi a mug of fizzing water, its bubbles a ballet of water skaters. "It's good for settling it."

"Thank you," she replied, accepting the courtesy with a curtsy. Vesperi might claim to hate the trappings of royalty, but she enjoyed being addressed as such, whether or not she deemed herself suitable.

She has a lifetime to get used to it.

Janto smiled into the wind as the sails were loosed.

‡

Janto threw himself onto solid ground and kissed the black sand of Braven's shore. Sailing on a caravel was nothing like sailing on a canoe. Not more than ten minutes at sea, and his face had turned greener than mangrove moss. The sailor who'd taken pity on Vesperi wordlessly offered him a pitcher of the concoction, and Janto had drank it straight down. A few minutes later, he was forced to ponder what constituted a privy for a king on a caravel.

He cared not how cold the wind felt or that water lapped at his boots. Nor was the sand as warm as he'd remembered, but that didn't matter. It was land.

Vesperi's platinum-toed boots ambled over to his eye-line. One eyebrow cocked, a full smirk in place, she offered a hand up. "Lanserim always help their enemies to their feet, right?"

Were they enemies still? Walking the plank of their marriage had taken more balancing than he'd have guessed at their wedding day, even before the recent waves had roiled them. But oh, how it gave him insight into the dynamics challenging their peoples as well.

He scooped up a handful of the black sand, scattering it between his fingers. "This is where I met Hamsyn," he shared, "where we searched for Terella's lost fallowent seeds together."

"Not likely you found them, then."

Her tone was frostier than the climate, and he wondered what his misstep had been this time. "Vesperi, I—"

"Ah, the little child has brought friends."

Janto spun to find Sielban already greeting them. The first time he'd met the ancient Rasselerian, Sielban had been camouflaged and on the run from their band of excited boys. He'd led them on a chase for hours through the island. Janto had half-expected they'd do the same today, but he should have known better. This was no murat arrival.

"Sielban!" He hugged the revered teacher, then apologized for getting him wet. Vesperi stood to the side, unimpressed, while their guards and most of the caravel's crew wore matching dropped jaws.

"We need your help," Janto raised his elbows, though he noted Sielban held his own a trace higher. That this legend granted him such an honor blew Janto's mind.

Not that he would ever point it out.

"It is a few weeks until I expected visitors," Sielban said. "But we'll find some use for those cases on your boat, Captain."

"I figured you'd want them," she winked, and Janto felt an idiot for not considering provisions. Par for the course for his Braven preparations.

Captain Vorpa directed some men to bring out a half-dozen boxes about half Janto's height. As they finished loading a cart, Sielban snapped his fingers and the crates disappeared. That drew some gasps, even from Vesperi, no stranger to magic. The riddle of it was precisely why Janto had insisted they come here despite his father's advice and his mother's protests.

Janto took Vesperi's hand. "My wife, Queen Vesperi Albrecht of Sellwyn."

"We'll have lots to talk about," Vesperi said, elbows raised. "I've never seen such a well-muscled Rasselerian." She dragged a finger down Sielban's chest to get a reaction. Clearly, her self-control for the day had run out.

Strawberry specks appeared on Sielban's forest green skin. Janto was impressed by Vesperi's skill.

"A pleasure to see your island," she drawled.

Sielban coughed, and in a flash, his typical twinkle of mischief returned. "This is not your first time, silver one," he said. "We are better acquainted than you remember."

He winked, and this time Vesperi was the one to blush. Janto laughed. No doubt Sielban referred to the connection between the weapon and the silver stag.

"Come," Sielban invited. "My home is around the bend."

Janto bid the captain and her crew farewell, asking them to stay near Jost so they could return quickly once needed. His party followed the imp of a man toward the wood. They hurried to match his pace.

Soon, Sielban raised a hand to bid them stop, and a familiar rustling indicated they'd reached "a bend," his preferred method of traveling on Braven. Manipulations of the rifts between Madel's realm and here, Janto'd bet, that allowed Sielban to shorten distances. In less than a second, the dune grasses nearest the Rasselerian grew taller than the height of two men and formed a bough for the group to walk through. Janto didn't hesitate, knowing it a safe path from past experience.

Neither did Vesperi, from sheer audacity. She would not be left behind, and he loved her for it. They stepped through into a clearing in a dark, thick forest. Where exactly on the island, Janto couldn't say, but he recognized the cabin in its midst. He had slain the silver stag right beside it, and dared hope for a glimpse of the creature nearby. But the stag was dead, and some things stayed dead no matter how much he might wish it otherwise.

Taking Vesperi's hand, he strode up the cabin's stairs. Sielban walked inside, but Janto hesitated, searching for something to the left of the doorframe. The daylight revealed a simple depiction of the three-headed bird etched into the ebony-stained wood.

"I saw that carved," he whispered to Vesperi, "by a lightning strike the day of my hunt." He paused, reconsidering. "By Madel, more like."

Vesperi traced it while the others caught up with them.

"Come on in, children." Sielban waved them inside. The nickname had chafed during the murat, until Sielban had granted the boys the honor of "men" instead at its completion. But the way Sielban used it now felt as though an endearment.

Janto had not been inside Sielban's cabin before. He expected it might be full of clutter from the many decades Sielban had resided there. Rather, its sitting room was sparse, though Sielban soon conjured up enough chairs and ottomans for the group. He even pulled a change of clothes for Janto from thin air, having noticed the shivers Janto tried to suppress.

"Clothes for a king," Sielban said, holding plain gray woolen pants and a tunic.

"This king is grateful," Janto responded. He changed in Sielban's washing room off to the right of a kitchen not nearly large enough to cook a murat feast. Yet the boys come to the murat were always well-feasted. Sielban had plenty of secrets left.

When Janto returned, feeling much better with fresh clothes, a large pot of water was boiling over the kitchen's central fire pit. That had happened far too fast, or Janto was a much slower dresser than he thought. Best to take such mysteries in stride here.

An equally large teapot sat on the counter, filled with curled, dried tea leaves. Their edges sparkled with iridescence, like a magnifying glass catching a sunlight beam. There was something familiar about them that Janto couldn't place. He ladled the water into the pot so the tea leaves could steep as Pic entered the kitchen. The lad had begged to come along, and Janto had agreed, remembering when his father had taken him on a cross-country visit at about the same age. Being around someone who displayed such wonder was heartening.

"That way," Janto directed him to the washing room. By the time Pic returned, Janto's wet clothes in a bundle, the leaves had unfurled and Janto had filled a tray with mugs.

"I'll get that," Pic offered, scandalized Janto had dared to plate his own provisions.

Janto waved him off. "I want to." The serving boy followed with the teapot.

In the sitting room, Janto's companions had arranged themselves around Sielban, who was telling a story and gesticulating. He had even Vesperi's attention, who glowed with beauty as she relaxed into an old leather chair.

"What did I miss?" Janto passed out the tea, receiving grateful smiles in return.

"Oh, your teacher was telling us about the time you wound up flat on your ass rappelling down the mountain." Vesperi's chin rested innocently in her hands.

"Was he?"

The skin around Sielban's eyes crinkled. "Not all tasks are fit for a king."

"I can't argue with that." Janto took a sip. The tea's herbal tang pleased his taste buds, though something in it made him sneeze.

"So what has brought the king and his coterie to Braven?"

Janto recognized the sparkle in Sielban's eyes; he was asking for his own amusement, not because he needed the answer. That was heartening. So Janto dove right in.

"I think we're headed to a crisis, Sielban, something to do with Madel's realm, maybe like a tear between our worlds? But not just one—many. The seer has seen more fissures open, and cantaleres and jurgens have come through. I think . . . I've seen the Silver Guard rising, though we don't know what for." He leaned forward, stared Sielban straight in the eyes. "And I dreamt of a Mount Frelom without clouds, its peak exposed. I think . . . I think that was a sign to come here to seek the answers we need to protect Lansera, rather than stumble around in a fog elsewhere. And—"

He looked to Vesperi, who nodded her encouragement.

"—and something tried to stop me from coming. A shadow that pretended to be my father."

Ser Irven and Pic gasped at that confession. Sielban sat cross-legged in his chair. His suit's colors shifted between the rusty brown of the forest outside and the thrushberry purple of the chair's cushion. Janto let himself hope—the boundaries between Madel's realm and theirs already constantly shifted on Braven, if Janto's theories proved true. Surely, Sielban would understand what was happening, more so than anyone else could.

"Hm." His tongue flicked out. "For this you disturb my preparations for the murat?"

Janto's stomach sunk to his feet.

Sielban laughed, a sound not unlike a rhini's unearthly hoot. "A joke, king child." He winked. "Your dream was not of Mount Frelom here, but the one that exists there." He walked to a drawn curtain near the cabin's front door. Sielban moved it back, exposing a second carving in the same exact spot as the one outside the door. It depicted Mount Frelom, or at least the one in his dream, a snowcap evident.

"This appeared the same day you captured your stag, slayer."

"How is that possible," Janto gaped. The lightning bolt couldn't have created two different images on both sides of the same log. A mirror of the three-headed bird, he might have understood, but this? Like the bird, the mountain's outline was deeply burned into the wood. Hundreds of tiny hash marks filled the space between its borders. They formed trees, birds, deer, even squiggly wisps that reminded Janto of the angels Nap had reported seeing the day he'd climbed the peak.

"It's like the marble carvings in Sellwyn," Vesperi exclaimed. Janto had seen the one on Sellwyn's bridge. It had depicted a circle of worshippers sending the bird of creation into the sky. "Same style of craftsmanship," Vesperi enthused, "though I don't remember any mountain peaks."

"They are two sides of the same coin," Sielban said. "One cannot exist without the other."

Ser Irven, a longtime guard at Callyn and also a murated man, offered a simpler explanation. "Are you saying, teacher, that the three-headed bird caused this realm rupture?"

"He speaks truths all will soon see." Sielban tented his hands.

Janto pondered Irven's words, tried to find a deeper meaning in them. Was Madel's realm infringing on theirs somehow? Was that a problem? Wouldn't being closer to Her presence be more of a blessing than a threat?

Pic gasped, and Janto reached for Vesperi's hand. He blinked furiously and gasped himself. The whole room had been bathed in a supernatural glow, an intensely golden hue not from their sun. It was as though the moon Oro had taken over, its radiance amplified as it reflected through the atmosphere. The edges of Vesperi's form grew fuzzy, as though Janto needed a reading glass. He patted her arm, making sure she was solidly there.

Wordlessly, the group left the cabin, Sielban leading. They walked into the forest of pine trees, though the tree trunks were a bolder brown somehow, and a carpet of ultra-green moss peeked up from the forest floor through fallen needles golden as the light. Just ahead of them, a section of much darker, dimmer forest contrasted sharply with theirs.

In a blink, the whole forest became that dimmer version of itself, and Janto realized they'd reverted to normal, that they'd been in Madel's realm, staring through a rift between their worlds. Is that how Serra's sight worked? How could she stand it, catching glimpses of that glorious existence and remaining in this one? Their surroundings felt drab, stripped of vitality.

Sielban raised his elbows to the group. "My apologies for not warning you of the tea's side effects. It was the quickest way to bring understanding."

"Can you do that anytime you want?" Vesperi asked. "Can you search that world from here?"

Janto knew what desire formed that question.

Sielban shook his head. "I am not the seer. But Madel sees fit to open channels to me that assist Her work." He walked near to Janto, stuck his hand in the air and parted it, revealing a glimmer of the other realm drenched with color. Then he ran a finger in a half-circle, creating an archway that dragged the snatch of Madel's realm with it.

A bend, not on a pathway, but in the fabric of reality.

"And is that what's happening with the animals coming through, the jurgen, the cantalere? And the people disappearing?" Janto asked.

Sielban's face paled. "Disappearing? Already?" He hurried past the others who were taking seats again. In his kitchen, and under his breath, Sielban muttered, "Time is short, it is."

Worry displaced the awe Janto had felt. He didn't want to know what could rattle Sielban. The teacher returned as Pic was hesitating to take another sip from his mug, which prompted Janto to peer at the rainbows reflecting from the dregs of his own half-drunk cup. The leaves conjured the sight's properties, somehow.

"Go ahead," Sielban said to Pic. "There won't be enough left for another journey. And you will need its sustenance."

Pic's eyes grew large as he raised the cup to his lips, while Sielban drew out a medallion from his pocket.

"That's like my father's!" Vesperi reached to touch the blue glass. Lorne Granich had destroyed the Sellwyns' pendant to rescue the hunting party from Mandat Hall, on the day Hamsyn had perished.

Sielban held it by a candle flame. Its pearlescent shine marked the glass as a relic of the ancient days. The same shine coated his tea's dregs, Janto realized.

The pendant displayed Lansera's moons, but something seemed off about their representation. Before Janto could peg it, Sielban flipped the pendant over, revealing Madel's hand as it appeared on the apex of Lansera's temple domes.

"When this is seen," Sielban turned the medallion back to the moons, then back again, "then this is hidden."

A sense of dread came over Janto, nearly as strong as the one when his first "Izzy? Where are you?" went unanswered ten months ago. He did not want to give voice to what Sielban's illustration portended. But a king must be brave. "What do you mean?"

Pic was the one who answered. "It's like heads or tails. Only one side can come up at a time."

Janto examined the medallion more closely. The moons . . . only three of them, and one dwarfed the other two. *Esye gone, Onsic looming.* That wasn't far off from how the sky looked now.

Ser Irven's adam's apple bopped. "Then . . . then you mean Madel has withdrawn Her hand."

Janto sputtered. "What? Can She . . . She would do that?"

Sielban explained. "It is not a matter of *doing* but of *being.* The balance must be restored for Her to return. She cannot exist among such disturbances. It's against Her nature."

"So your sweet little Lanserim goddess has left us alone?" Vesperi said. "When we're missing a moon and my power?"

Janto felt just as frustrated. "Sielban, what are we supposed to do? How do we fix an imbalance in Madel's realm? Is it even possible?"

"The realm of which you speak is not Hers," Sielban explained, "but theirs."

He hurried out the front door, and Janto followed. Above them, three moons were visible. Copper Tansic hung close to golden Oro, so close they almost eclipsed. Onsic's darkness was crowned with a halo shimmering brighter than Janto recalled, and fuller, too. The cobalt hue had drained from it, leaving searing white light.

May he rest in the cobalt flame, Vesperi had pointed out of the funeral chant. Not rest in Madel's realm. Because the realm they'd been thinking of as Hers, the one that Serra could see into, wasn't Hers at all, while the flame was.

"The moons? We have to fix the moons?" he said.

"Never 'have to,' king child."

Sielban's chiding tested Janto's forbearance.

"Or what? We let Lansera be consumed like Esye? Like our daughter? That's not a choice, Sielban. Don't act like it is." Was there some way to *get* to the moons? More fissures had appeared; could Serra lead them through one if Sielban taught them how?

"The Guard must act fast." Sielban acknowledged Janto's unspoken thoughts. "But they will make the way. Madel has not left Her children without a rope."

Vesperi paced, likely to keep her voice as measured as it was. "So we're to move to moonland then, after their creatures take over ours?"

Sielban shook his head. "Neither realm will survive if balance is not restored."

Janto was at his wit's end. "Sielban, none of this explains what we need to *do*. Are we to trust it'll work out?"

The great teacher flicked his tongue into the air. His words were grim. "I do not know that it will. Only that the Guard has ever been one of Her tools, and She stopped speaking to this one months ago."

On Sielban's face just then, Janto learned how a thousand years of loneliness might appear. Sielban's own connection to Madel had been severed. He was as helpless as them to understand what came next.

Janto's father was right, and so was his shade. They shouldn't have come here.

CHAPTER NINETEEN
SERRA

When she aimed for grace, Serra reminded herself that Uzziel had been strapped to the front of either Sar Mertina or Ser Napeler for the past three day's riding. Tight leather belts left welts on the boy's scrawny arms. She knew how red and painful they were, treated them each morning and evening with a libtyl leaf balm. Yet the longer he screamed at the top of his lungs, the more grace eluded her.

Sar Mertina had tried explaining that his cries might draw bandits, but Uzziel's curiosity about such men spurred him on. Freed from manor walls, he was proving to have plenty of that, and plenty of his sister's temperament as well.

The Lanserim army, keeping the peace as they had for six years, patrolled the main Meduan roads their party had traveled before now. But their path had shifted northwest through the Durnish foothills, where silence mattered more.

"But I want to meet other people!" Uzziel yelled. "Father always said to know your men, and I'm the queen's brother. They are my people, too, aren't they? Come here, come here, little Lanserim!"

"It doesn't work like that, Lord Uzziel," Ryn Colini tried. "It would, if the queen were an Albrecht, but she's not. The people aren't loyal to houses that—"

"Sellwyns aren't good enough for the throne? I know that's not true, because I know my worth, Father told me. So stop your lies, priest beast." Uzziel crossed his arms after wiping spittle from his chin and tucking the cloth into the collar of his tunic. *Small victories.*

Colini sighed, and Serra gave him a baleful "thanks for trying" glance. She determined that teaching Uzziel how Lanserim society worked would wait until . . . forever, maybe. Any understanding of Lord Uzziel's proper place must begin with the knowledge that Sellwyn Manor had fallen into ruin along with the renown the Sellwyn family had once carried. Lanserim considered such events a sign Madel had withdrawn Her favor from the noble line. If ever repopulated, the king would appoint a new family in place of the Sellwyns, no matter that his wife came from them. Lord Granich had been angling for the spot, all these years of caretaking Uzziel. It had never been for the boy's benefit.

That was why Serra had entrusted her Aunt Marji with Gavenstone, and thus, Meditlan, after Agler's death. She couldn't picture another family in those halls. The thought of someone else sitting in her father's chair by the fire or tending her mother's spice cellar? She shuddered and rubbed her fingers over her clove necklace.

"Come here, come here!" Uzziel's voice rasped as loud as it could. His throat sounded wetter than Serra liked, but he carried on.

Flivio sneered from atop his bay mare. "Keep that up. Mayhap we'll learn jurgen come when called."

"I'm not afraid of those rats," Uzziel insisted, sticking out his chest with bravado, though the harness hid most of the effort.

"Aye?" Flivio said. "And what will you hit them with?"

Uzziel jutted his chin forward but kept silent. Nap had confiscated the lad's parlous tornian within the first hour they'd left Granich—even strapped in, he'd managed to swing one of the weapon's spikes into the shoulder of Nap's palomino steed. The horse had its own bandage of salve to change each morning. Almost healed now, but alarming nonetheless, due to Uzziel's complete lack of concern for anyone's needs but his own.

"I will hit them with this!" Uzziel opened his palm to reveal the echo sparking in his hand. He directed it to a nearby grass patch, which burst into flame but fizzled out, damp from an early spring thaw.

Felia drew up beside Uzziel and Flivio, her face screwed up like she'd bit a chili pepper. "You will not! That's for saving people, not hurting them! We are being heroes, Uzziel, not assholes." The ride had worn on her, too. She'd been sulking in the saddle the last two days. Uzziel had rebuffed her overtures, even her attempts to get him to flick their flames together. How Lorne had developed something like camaraderie with the boy, Serra had no idea. *Madel help us.*

"Help! Help please!"

Two voices cried out from a pine tree thicket up ahead, and a thunderous crash resounded. The horses' neighed, and Serra calmed hers from rearing at the unexpected distress. The trees had grown more numerous, but they'd passed nothing else of interest since the last band of soldiers, a good two hours' back.

They circled their horses close, Serra taking hold of Felia's reins as well as her own.

"Don't you dare use it again," Felia scolded Uzziel, pressing his hand closed.

Nap and Mertina exchanged glances, and Mertina waved him on. Serra reached a finger to her lips, noticing Felia's uneven breaths. The girl nodded, trying her best, but Serra could read the fear in her eyes. Why didn't she feel it herself? Too many days on roads like these, too many attacks from things that were worse than humans.

Nap inched forward, then clicked his horse into a gallop into the thicket. He disappeared from sight and Serra held her breath.

Raucous laughter bounced off the boulders, and everyone visibly relaxed. A few minutes later, two men emerged from the thicket, prodded along by Nap's sword. They wore rags for clothes, tattered tunics and pants made more of frayed burlap patches than spun black wool. Stained capes that may once have been green covered their shoulders, and the stink of milkwine wrinkled noses among Serra's party. She did not want to be around these men for long.

One of them, with a stomach bulging over his bread-loaf legs, pointed a finger at Uzziel. He let loose a long, high laugh that hurt Serra's ears. "Saeth's fist!" he declared, "who'd have thought Lord's Sellwyn's crippled whelp would survive the claren." He elbowed his companion, whose eyes lit up with amusement, and they shared another good laugh. "What'd you do, suck your sister's teats to plug your holes?"

Uzziel reddened, and Serra was grateful he didn't try his flame, as his sister might have. He screamed instead, "You cannot speak to me like that!"

"Oh, did no one let you know you're not a little lordling anymore? Might want to check with your father—oh wait, you can't, can you?"

The man's sneer deepened his red nose's glow. "I saw him consumed myself, just a man like us, 'cept we're still breathing. And you are too."

His companion gripped a dagger's hilt Serra had failed to notice. "We can change that, if you'd like, fine folks." He examined Nap and then Mertina over Uzziel's shoulder, deferring to those who had the obvious power here, the ones with weapons. "You'll travel much faster without the deadweight. Might be we'd go with you, too. Extra protection."

Sar Mertina gave Uzziel a reassuring squeeze. No harm would come to anyone under her care. Uzziel's trembling intensified, but his fear could not deter his affront at such treatment, much less from men who'd once served him. "When I return to Sellwyn and regather my father's forces, I will have you strung up on Father's tree!"

They found this to be the most amusing claim yet and clutched each's other backs before bending over with laughter. "Nobody's going back to that hovel, boy. The claren did us a favor. Sure, I lost my favorite litter of sluts, but not living under your daddy's leash is the best thing ever happened to me. The Lanserim king makes sure we're fed, and we don't have to report to anyone but his soldiers for bread."

His friend nodded, the movement exaggerated. "Ain't never living under a lord again, that's for sure. Even the ones still around won't be for long."

That perked Serra's ear. "Is Lord Riven expected to abandon Durn?" Riven, like Lord Granich, was one of the few Meduan noblemen who'd been inclined to hunker down in their own homes while taking stock of this new world order, rather than try to force a power play. Was that about to change? Janto would need to know, right away—

"Now, how much would news like that be worth to you all?" The man leered greedily, though Serra would guess he thought himself sly.

She let loose an extravagant sigh. "Why would we bother traveling with money? As you've said, the king's soldiers see to our needs."

"Aye, but they aren't here, are they?" He licked his lips with what he interpreted to be a lascivious gesture. Serra tried not to gag as Nap drew his sword and pressed it against the man's neck, faster than his tongue could slide back in.

"We are," Sar Mertina said with pride. "Did you want to test yourself against the royal family's guards?"

The slender man gaped, scanning the ground for a good place to drop and roll if needed.

Serra laughed. "Did you not know Vesperi Sellwyn is your queen?"

His friend's eyes grew large as a full moon. "No, no, we didn't know. Just that the queen was a Meduan. Vesperi? I can't believe it. I've bedded a—"

Nap gave him another sharp poke. Serra swallowed vomit at the thought of the horrors Vesperi had underwent.

"That's right," Uzziel pronounced with a tremor. "I'm the queen's brother, you curs." A wracking cough rattled through him.

The men exchanged mortified looks. They were no challenge to Serra's party of three armed riders, and they knew it, even with an invalid, a girl, and two noncombatants among them. But there would be others less lost in their wine, Serra knew, and more apt to pursue the "good life" the Meduans had fought for before the divide. The life that meant they could take and kill at will if they were strong and greedy enough, no matter what pedigrees stood before them.

"We need to be off," she said to her companions. To the men, she leaned into a threat she knew they would respect. "We don't have time for your feeble bribery attempts to buy your silence. You know there's more going on here than the queen's brother on a joy ride, no matter how drunk you may be." To Nap, she commanded, "Leave these men some souzers for their time."

Nap's stoic face didn't reveal what he thought of the decision. But the only way such people understood value was through these transactions. Opening a stuffed-full pouch of the Meduan coins would leave them a lingering impression of power, the true currency in their eyes.

Serra and her companions left the Sellwyn guards in their dust, and yet, her disgust grew. Those men were true Meduans, the type who'd never see the value in other's lives. The majority of Meduans could, and even wanted to, become the people Madel intended them to be, like Lorne and Mer Drenyl in Terella's employ. Even their less attractive traits were more a testament to the diversity of Madel's people than an indictment of their innate goodness. Despite her occasional doubts, Serra believed that.

But how could the Lanserim root out the rot of true Meduans without being tainted by it? *Maybe the cantaleres were sent to ram them through.* The thought died on her lips; they might deserve it, but she wouldn't wish such a grisly death on anyone.

Her party had barely traveled an hour's distance when Uzziel began convulsing in the saddle. Sar Mertina's horse lurched as the reins jerked, but the seasoned warrior regained control fast enough. Uzziel's fingers caught in a plait of her braid, and Mertina screamed with pain. She and Uzziel lurched to the right as the horse leapt again.

A few heart-pounding moments passed until Felia caught up with them. The girl managed to soothe the horse as Flivio drew up parallel and pushed Uzziel and Mertina back to an upright position. Paroxysms rocked the lad. Mertina hugged his arms close to his sides after slipping one of the leather reins between his chomping teeth. How the guard managed not to tremble was beyond Serra's comprehension.

Serra dismounted and dug through her pouch for a salve to soothe the boy's bloody lips. The smell of urine prompted her to search for fresh clothes in her pack as well. They'd need to stop to bathe him at the very least, which meant this glade of thick pines would be their stopping point for the evening. Mertina would need rest as well—Serra was not about to continue the journey without the warrior at her best.

Felia gave Uzziel her rapt attention as his torment passed. The boy slumped in Mertina's arms, and Nap held his arms open from the ground, ready to take him once Mertina unlatched the straps. Serra spread a blanket on the forest carpet, and Nap laid him over it. Uzziel's eyes fluttered open as she undid his pants. Flivio held him up enough that she could slip them off.

"Felia," Serra directed the girl who gaped as though a fish on a hook, "fill up the washing bin, would you? Add a few drops of this," Serra handed her a tincture she'd made from the symphony bush's leaves. Hopefully it would restore some harmony to his system. The water would be cold, but the temperature shock might help Uzziel regain his senses.

It took a few hours' nap for Uzziel to rouse from his daze. Camp had been made in the interim. Flivio regaled them with a tale of a certain tumble he'd taken with his town's winemaker after drinking down a vat of unintentionally fermented grape juice. Felia's cheeks gained color, and Serra and Nap exchanged concerned glances. But Nap wiggled his eyebrows and Serra laughed. At Felia's age, Eddy, head stableman at Callyn, had told her a bawdy joke about two mares in heat. Being old enough to be included in such tales had been more exciting than their content. And Ryn Colini didn't seem troubled by it, so why should she? Serra felt free, letting such concerns lift off her mind and blow away in the breeze.

If only Uzziel's complaints were so weightless. He grunted with a bear's consternation and moaned as though a spirit unable to find its release. As she talked herself into an herbalist's duty to tend their charges, he quieted. That concerned her more.

She rose swiftly, but Colini caught her elbow, nodding at where they'd laid Uzziel to sleep outside their trio of tents. A dim lantern's light reflected from Felia's bucolic cheeks, where she kneeled in the grass beside him.

Serra dipped into the sight. A radiant haze of colors glimmered around Felia as she passed Uzziel something to drink that gave off a metallic sheen of moonslight—more symphony plant tincture. She ought to have asked first, but Serra found she didn't mind as Felia whispered something to Uzziel that made him laugh. The sound was delightful, a wiry blend of childlike glee with a deeper resonance hinting at his delayed adolescence.

But what made Serra smile was watching the tincture's essence flow into his body then seep back out and surround him, pulsing as Uzziel laughed again.

She lowered back onto her rock by the campfire. "What do you see?" she asked Ryn Colini.

"I see a young woman extending grace to a young man who's never felt any. And I see a young man, scared, alone, but awakening to a world outside himself. It's not so different from what most of us went through at his age."

No, Serra thought, remembering when Callyn's walls and the duties of being a someday princess had consumed her awareness. *No, it's not.*

"Do we have any milkwine," Serra asked. "I've a hankering to taste it."

The adults gathered around her laughed.

"My lady," Sar Mertina answered, "there are some thing's best left unexamined."

She filled Serra's cup with another helping of ale.

CHAPTER TWENTY

VESPERI

In Braven, Vesperi lay on a tree stump by the side of a stream, reading more of the Rasselerians' chapbook. Sielban had finagled some sort of mystical light to glow beside her, fireflies lassoed together by fairy tongues for all she knew or cared. She flipped through the pages, to see if any other passages had damaged sections like the prophecy they needed to parse. No smear of its letters remained, as though the words had evaporated, or been hollowed out.

Hollow. That's how Onsic appeared in the night sky, its inner core bleak within its new fiery corona of white light. The black onyx moon kept enlarging, as though it might swallow Mount Frelom's shrouded peak if it had a mouth to open. But the more it grew, the emptier it appeared.

Vesperi was no stranger to hollowness. Her womb had known fullness twice, and thus knew hollowness more intimately than if she'd never been pregnant. Emptiness's ache was familiar.

The rest of their party was off exploring the pathway "bends" at night, a last-ditch attempt at finding something that might make this trip worthwhile. Oh, Sielban was fine as far as Rasselerians went, and that tea had been a trip. But she'd learned nothing to bring her closer to Izzy. Nor anything that indicated what might happen if the Silver Guard "ringed the beastly lair."

Vesperi returned to the book. Its binding had frayed since coming into her possession, though the thin parchment showed no signs of damage. She wracked her brain trying to remember something, anything, about what else the page had contained, to recall even the appearance of the missing lettering.

When leaps the mighty cantalere,
the dark brother drains his foes.
The Guard must ring the beastly lair
Where battles end their roam.

. . .

"What's next?!" she yelled into Onsic's gaping maw.

"Tea?"

Sielban came up behind her, startling Vesperi. She tumbled off the log and caught the book before it hit a patch of mud.

The creeper had the gall to laugh, his eyes dilating in and out like a cat's. He held a silver tray with a pitcher of tea and two mugs.

"If that's the same Oro tea from before, I'll pass," Vesperi muttered, brushing the dirt off her tunic. The experience had been fun, but gold was not the color she longed for. Not the one whose ghost in the sky made her index finger twinge.

"Not Oro tea. It is from the symphony bush and enhances whatever light you wish. I use it often for Tansic's copper, which eases my body's aches."

Vesperi couldn't scoff at its effectiveness. She'd have never guessed this man had any maladies, despite his years, but perhaps that's why King Dever said his preparations before the murat were so important. Maybe his whole life was devoted to having the energy to manage them well. Her thoughts bounced to Uzziel and the possibility that such a tea might aid him. Wondering what might help her brother was a first, so she banished the thought.

"Symphony bush, did you say?" From the woods, her husband, Pic, and Ser Irven emerged as though the trees had spit them out.

Vesperi took Janto's hand, warm, though the early spring air had not touched this island. "Does this mean you conquered the fissures?" She whirled a finger in the air, but her mind was processing what Sielban had said about the tea.

Janto's face fell. "No. We could find no means of going through or even detecting them ourselves. The bends open on their own schedule. We just follow them around here."

Vesperi hadn't believed anything would come of their search, but it had cost Janto a lot to go against his father's advice to come here. Especially after his confidence that the dark brother had wanted them to stay at Callyn, doing nothing. This failure—it couldn't be easy for him to take. She rubbed his forearm.

Hair rumpled as a bird's nest, the young servant Pic mused, "The symphony plants were the ones with the black blossoms, right, King Janto?"

"That's why the leaves looked so familiar in the pitcher!" Janto hit his forehead. "Well done, Pic. Are we having more, teacher?"

"Your wife is not so sure."

"Your wife does not appreciate having strange men sneak up on her."

Sielban laughed again. "Come inside, I do not have enough cups."

Something pestered Vesperi as they walked the short distance back to Sielban's cabin and the pair of tents he'd conjured in his yard for their accommodation. If the tea gave them the sight, filtered through moonslight . . .

"Stop!" She plopped herself cross-legged on the lawn, uncaring as Ser Irven stumbled over her. "Sielban," she commanded, "how do I use your tea to gather Esye's light?"

Janto sat beside her, his tone gentle. "Vesperi, I know you miss the flame, but I don't think that'll—"

She silenced him with a hand. "The people who gave me the book told me to hurry it to you, that time was short. Those last few lines were already blurry then, but not the whole thing. What changed in that time?"

Pic perked up, pointing skyward. "Esye faded!"

"Indeed," Vesperi said. "And the letters faded with it. What if Esye's light might bring them back?"

Sielban had an amused twinkle in his eye, and perhaps a smidge of anticipation. He'd whisked three more glasses onto the tray in the amount of time it took Janto to catch up to speed.

Her husband planted a kiss on her, hands pressing against her cheeks. "You're a genius."

"Think of the moon you seek as you sip," Sielban instructed them as he poured.

That wouldn't be a problem. Vesperi had plenty of practice conjuring Esye in her minds-eye. Wielding the flame had demanded it. She closed her eyes and focused, letting Esye's form take hold, its silver light molten at full strength and power.

"Wow," Pic said, and Vesperi fluttered her eyes open. Silver light drenched the woods surrounding them. It reflected off bark and grass alike, a miniature firework display with no sign of fizzling out.

If only. Their first vision with the tea had not lasted long. Vesperi gazed upon the opened page.

"This is how the light falls in my slayer dreams," Janto said with awe. "I am not certain we're awake."

"Better hope we are." Vesperi held the book aloft, its words restored. The prophecy's lines glimmered with iridescence from either the light or the ink. "And better hope one of us has another parchment and pen to copy this down."

They crowded close, Ser Irven producing the asked-for implements. Each letter had a shadow in rainbow hues. Vesperi took Ser Irven's pen and wrote out the new lines first, all four of them. Dread and awe commingled in each pen stroke:

Their force combined will call the air.
Only then will fly the doe.
Or brother be taken unaware.
By silver power returned home.

Vesperi had not appeared in Janto's murat dreams as the silver stag, but as its mate. As a doe. This prophecy was *still* about them. What affected her affected her husband, though Vesperi admitting that out loud was as likely as Serra getting over her uppity self and making an honest man of Lorne Granich.

Ser Irven hoisted the pen and paper out of Vesperi's hand and copied over the complete prophecy on several new sheets, no doubt to be sent by Sielban's pigeons with all haste to Queen Lexamy, Serra, and whomever Janto had meeting the potential Silver Guard members on the plain of Orelyn. They batted around possible interpretations, their enthusiasm undimmed, even as Esye's light faded back into the nothingness it expressed of late.

Janto smiled at her, his eyes shining with that mix of admiration and love that Vesperi reveled in. Her childhood had been spent seeking it from her father. It had taken a whole new life and a whole new understanding of herself to find it. But she had. And if this hollow version of that life she lived in now, this shell, was something she had to endure to fulfill the prophecy? So be it. Vesperi could do anything knowing her flame would return someday, and her daughter with it.

CHAPTER TWENTY-ONE
Serra

Serra's thighs ached from horse riding, her arms from the simple act of holding reins. Her body itched where moisture had crept through her clothes and into crevices she couldn't keep dry no matter how much of Queen Lexamy's perfumed powder she dabbed herself with. Removing the day's clothes had become as much of a horror as putting new ones on the next morning, peeling fabric from where she hoped skin remained. Her scent? Serra was glad she had no beaus at the plain of Orelyn awaiting her arrival.

They'd pushed as fast as Uzziel's health allowed through the mountains. Three days of hard travel before reaching this hillside that offered their first view of flat ground again. Napeler lifted Uzziel up at his midsection to see, though the boy was groggy this morning. Before them, the rolling plains of Neville shimmered, coated with frost. Tips of green grasses peeked through. As the sun rose higher, the frost would melt into a waterfall of greenery. Serra was surprised to see none of the dull-witted, lumbering craval beasts shepherded there, and that gave her a chill of apprehension—had the cantaleres already come through these plains? She shuddered to wonder what damage they may have wrought.

To the northwest, a series of lumpy bumps of greenery caught her eye. Not hills, exactly, more like knobs covered in moss and briar thickets glistening with dew. Some sort of animal could be seen darting between the thickets. A blink might miss their fast movements, if there hadn't been so many.

"Koparin." Uzziel spoke with a spell-bound quality. He knew that hunting koparin was not the trip's true purpose now, but the idea of them tantalized him nonetheless.

Ah, yes, those white glints might be from their sizable claws. "Is that the ruins of Queen Drustalla's palace?" Serra asked no one in particular.

Sar Mertina answered, "Yes. I've been there many times with the prince and the—with the king and his father."

Serra touched her arm. "You don't need to correct yourself among us."

"But I do." Sar Mertina straightened up. "Or I might slip up among the citizens. Times of transition are hard, Lady Serra. The populace gets unsettled, unsure if the king will lead in a manner they understand and agree with. Madel removes unfit rulers, we believe. You and the king and queen were Her tools for that very task not so long ago in Qiltyn. No one wants to consider it may happen with the Albrechts, but they fear it might."

"Are you saying the people doubt Janto? After all he's done for them?" The idea mystified Serra. Not even in the darkest moments of their breakup had her belief in Janto's fitness for kingship wavered.

Sar Mertina shook her head. "You misunderstand me. It's not the person; it's the uncertainty. I've often thought Madel has kept the Albrechts in power so long for consistency in the transition of power. It eases the process, reassures folks. They know what to expect from an Albrecht, don't think one will be that different from another, and they loved King Dever. But they won't know Janto's a good leader, not in their bones, until they know *him*. Until they can again raise their ales to their lips with no worries."

"Aye," Flivio concurred, stepping down from his mount to gaze upon the plains. "And the disappearances and the cantaleres so soon after the claren and the Conjoining? The people have a wealth of worries, these days."

Flivio was from Meditlan, from Serra's own lands. He knew their people's everyday concerns better than she did, and that didn't sit well with her. She should share their labor to better understand, harvest spices from the coast or grapes from the vine for a season, learn what concerned them beyond the larger threats she'd had to consider instead.

Am I really considering returning to Gavenstone? The thought had flowed so naturally, which was shocking in and of itself. Perhaps the madness of the road.

Felia spoke, her hair tied back in a messy ponytail. She'd given up on the braids two days ago. "My father talked about the new swan the night before you came to the Perch. He wondered if he could bring people together as well as King Dever had." She paled, realizing she may have insulted Serra's best friend. "He didn't mean any harm by it, Lady Serra, just . . . just wondering."

Serra reassured her with a smile. "That's understandable, Felia. I guess . . . I haven't ever thought about Janto from other people's perspectives." She paused, then walked over to Napeler's horse. "What does Lord Granich think of King Janto, Uzziel?"

The boy laughed with disdain, a behavior so like his sister. She wondered if either knew how similar they were—Serra would not make the mistake of telling either first.

He answered, "Lord Granich thinks Lansera is full of idiots knocking each other senseless with wooden swords and people forced to lie down in front of women priests who steal their manhoods when they aren't looking."

How much of that was what Cavallen Granich believed versus what he wanted Uzziel to? Did such men believe in anything but their own egos?

A dribble of spit balanced on Uzziel's chin. Serra made a subtle wiping gesture, and Uzziel fished his handkerchief out.

"Well," she said, "we best continue on to Drustalla's palace. Never doubt that the king trusts us to protect his people, even if they can't say the same of him as yet."

And even if the Silver Guard hasn't the faintest idea what to do with that trust.

‡

It was well after lunch, the sun dipping in the west, before they reached the ruins. The moss-covered knobs had morphed into ivy-drenched remnants of old walls. Cracking, dusky red stucco peeked between browned leaves. Occasionally, they passed old windows, where the ivy had grown around and through the frames and surrounding supports. They gave the impression of one-eyed goblins petrified where they stood.

As long as Serra's party had remained a safe distance away, the koparin had continued their leaping through the thickets. They'd had to shoot two of the animals on the way in, ones that had lunged at them, either spooked or hungry enough for a taste of human flesh. Once felled, the koparin stretched no longer than her legs, and their muscled thighs took up a good bit of that length. But their frontal fangs and claws were as big as her thumb and plenty sharp. They were quiet now, keeping their fur-covered forms hidden within the dried, prickly briars. Or maybe they'd run off to the outer reaches of the ruins, flanking their approach. That potential unsettled her.

Soon, their party had to walk the horses. The ruins grew more tightly packed and better preserved as they reached the center of Drustalla's once-grand palace. The sun lowered farther and the shadows it cast created patterns curving at odd angles around the ivy walls, making Serra feel as though trapped in a labyrinth.

"Why is there no one to greet us?" Uzziel asked, perhaps having expected a feast in his honor or at least a spectacle greater than their journey had provided thus far. Janto said he'd send others here who had the silver power, and he would have named someone to manage their camp. She'd assumed some sort of welcoming party, too, if that had come to pass. Perhaps something had hap—

Silver orbs and strikes flashed and fizzed all around, followed by a familiar sizzle. Momentarily blinded, Serra closed her eyes. But her party's nervous gasps gave way to chatter and the sounds of people introducing themselves to their neighbors. As her eyes opened, someone's hand came up from behind to cover them. An arm pulled her tight around the waist, dragging a thumb along as it encircled her. Serra froze, though this contact felt the opposite of threatening.

Uzziel shouted "Lorne!" and Serra relaxed as her captor whispered in her ear.

"You smell rancid, my lady."

She whirled around and socked Lorne Granich in the chest. Leaves crunched as he barreled back into the nearest ruin.

"Been spending more time with Meduans, I see," he winked.

She'd punch him again, but Madel's hand, he smelled amazing. Like soap. Oh, she could live in that smell. Of course, Janto had asked

Lorne to organize their recruits. She'd been dense not to consider it. Or in denial. Or hoping and not wanting to give the wish substance.

Uzziel's whine broke in. "Lorne! Come here, I command it!"

Serra sighed and Lorne rolled his eyes for her benefit only. "Did you have to bring the brat?" he pouted.

"Did you have to tell me he had an echo?" she countered.

"Lorne! Lorne!"

"His lungs," she laugh-sighed, and Lorne's smile spread. Then she batted his ass, perhaps feeling another kind of dirty after this journey. "Go on, greet your little lordling friend."

Lorne obeyed, making his way over to reunite with Uzziel while Serra took in their new companions. Their silver flame demonstration had been informative: none had the power Vesperi had possessed. Maybe if they worked in synchrony, combining their streams, they could knock down a few cantaleres before being gored. *Not promising.*

A trio of Rasselerians smiled as they introduced themselves to Ryn Colini, who was talking animatedly about his time at Temple Enjoin. The patterns on their body suits matched the walls behind them, leaves seeming to flow between their outfits. Felia Swalus spoke with a boy about her age, though he was shorter by a few inches. He kept glancing down to his feet, and Serra chuckled—the lad was already smitten. A couple wearing knitted travel caps, a man with a defined jaw and a woman patting her stomach, stood alone. Serra went to meet them, but Lorne's tenor called her back to Uzziel, who spoke with a few rynnas gathered near the patch of grass he'd been laid upon. Serra wondered what the young man made of seeing "evil women priests" in the flesh. He looked more dazed than frightened by such fearsome creatures.

"So few," she said as she stood beside Lorne. *Enough to ring the beastly lair?*

"Oh no, there are twice as many of us back at camp." That reassurance eased some of the worry she was carrying. "We should head back before it gets too dark," he continued. "The koparin don't stay shy for long. And Councilman Ferin's sight isn't great at night. He'll want to meet you himself."

"You aren't in charge?" Lorne was a trusted friend of Janto's, and a nobleman's son. He ranked higher than council member.

"Maybe I would be if I'd been born on this side of the mountains," he filled in. Serra tutted at that.

"It's nothing new," he continued, perplexed by her reaction, though his facial features switched to smugness fast enough. "I'm surprised you're so concerned, Lady Serra. I thought you agreed with my suitability, or lack thereof, to oversee Lanserim."

Did she, though? Or had that been but part of her excuses, a reason to leave when it had become too much? Better not to dwell on it with higher stakes at risk than her future plans. She needed to meet this councilman, see the rest of the camp, and praise be to Madel, take a bath. "Lead the way."

Lorne took up one of the ropes for Uzziel's carrier and Napeler did the other. The Rasselerians followed close by. Uzziel was so shocked by their appearances, for once he had no words at all, his eyes darting between them. Serra guided her horse safely as she could, gladdened they had more experienced guides to lead them out of the ruins. As the path sloped down, she realized the portion they'd traversed was part of a larger expanse. Drustalla Albrecht had constructed a massive retreat indeed.

Soon, Serra could see over the ivy-covered walls and around the thickets, which weren't as closely grouped together this side of the plain. A faint glow came from a few fires beyond the ruins' outer limits. By the time they reached them, darkness blocked the ruins from view. *Remind me not to go for an evening stroll.*

Lorne and Nap situated Uzziel by one of the fires, and Serra promised she'd come back to see the boy soon. But she needed to meet this councilman and learn what news Janto had sent, if any.

She ducked through the canvas doorway of a large tent set up in the center of the camp. Another dozen tents surrounded it—whether they housed enough Silver Guards to get the job done, she had no idea. Knowing the job would help too.

"Councilman Ferin," she started, addressing a thin man who sat behind mostly flat pieces of wood that had been erected as a table. He peered up, but so did his three companions, one wearing the light, breathable tunic of the ryns of Temple Enjoin. The priest smiled widely.

"Ryn Gylles!" Serra was delighted to see her old mentor from her time as a novice in the Order. He rose to meet her, arms open and waiting for her to rush into them, which she did, dirt be damned. She held the embrace for a long minute, and Gylles took her face between his hands as they separated.

"You appear well," he said. "Not the frightened, angry girl the

Brotherhood forced on me back then. Though maybe a little too tough around those eyes." He spoke with tenderness, and Serra lapped it up as though parched.

"You don't look too bad yourself, though I don't remember those wrinkles," she teased.

He raised a hand to shield his face in mock offense.

"What are you doing here?" she asked.

"We receive the king's pronouncements at Lake Ashra, same as anywhere else, you know." He laughed. "I have the flame's echo. It showed up one day over morning gruel. I nearly singed Ryn Islon's whiskers."

Serra laughed. It felt good to be among friends, to know she wouldn't have to win over everyone who'd gathered here. Figuring out what Madel wanted them to do would be hard enough as it was.

"Lady Serrafina Gavenstone of Lansera, I presume?" The thin man raised his elbows to her, as did the two other people at the table: a woman shaped like a short, squat vase who wore a baker's apron modified with sleeves, and a man whose top-heavy arm muscles made it seem he might fall over. She recognized him a soon as she registered his fine, pale blond hair. "Rall!"

Serra rushed over to hug the Wasylim. Like Flivio, Jerusho, and Nap, Rall had been one of Janto's murat mates. Serra had met him just the once, however, right after he'd lost his wife and daughter to the claren. "Did Madel call you to this service, as well?"

He shook his head, his expression grimmer than she liked. "Not I."

"Evon," Serra gasped. Rall's son Evon was all he had left, and the lad had been the last person to see Izzy before her disappearance. Would Madel really have called the boy for this purpose? Hadn't the Basilos been through enough? "How old is he now?"

"Ten." Rall flashed a pride-filled grin. "He's at one of the camp-fires, listening to some of the tall tales going around. I think he'll be a writer or maybe an actor someday."

"Well, we'll work to make sure he does." She didn't know what else to say about Madel depending on a child for a cause such as this. They were flying blind.

"Councilman," Serra shifted her attention back to their leader, "can you fill me in on who else has gathered here. How many? From where?"

"Gladly, my lady." He pulled up a seat for her at the "table," and the courtesy made Serra grateful—she would not need to exert dominance over this man as she had with Lord Granich.

The councilman's eyes shone bright on a face heavily stubbled with salt and pepper growth. "But you ought to know we got a new bird in from the king."

News had been nonexistent since she'd left the Perch. No matter how smart the pigeon sent out, risks were too great on the other side of the mountain for any sensitive messages to fall into the wrong hands. "Go on."

"The rest of the prophecy—Lorne filled us in—has been discovered on Braven. And the king has had word of more disappearances, and . . . well, we should bring you the letter, shouldn't we?"

If Madel could wait this long to make Her desires clear, they could wait another half an hour. "Yes, I'll read it before dinner. But first—"

"A bath," Ryn Gylles and Rall said in synchrony, noses wrinkled.

Serra's cheeks colored.

‡

It took until her second bath the next morning, when dirt no longer ringed the wash bin, for Serra to feel clean. She mulled the words of the full prophecy over as she dried off.

When leaps the mighty cantalere,
the dark brother drains his foes.
The Guard must ring the beastly lair
Where battles end their roam.

Their force combined will call the air.
Only then will fly the doe.
Or brother be taken unaware.
By silver power returned home.

The multiple baths, and sleep, had given her time to consider what Janto's letter had contained. Per Sielban, a dissonance between Lansera and the other realm—not Madel's, the letter had been clear on that—was growing like Onsic in the sky. She'd also learned that Councilman Ferin served in nearby Trop, and the town had been evacuated. They'd been experiencing a rash of disappearances by the town's square. "A slit in the sky opened," he'd described it. *A fissure*, Serra had kept to herself. Then four dozen cantaleres had come from the north and stormed through the city. Thirty citizens dead or disappeared, and his flame's echo had done nothing but enrage the beasts.

Four miles away from Trop, the Guard Glen, as Evon had named their encampment, housed thirty people, twenty-seven of whom possessed the flame's echo. Serra was pleased so many strangers seemed to be getting along so well, though a few folks, like the couple who'd come to greet them at the ruins, hung back. She'd need to ask the councilman about them. But Serra needed to do a lot of things, like figure out how a "guard" full of people who couldn't shoot a flame farther than four feet could destroy the cantaleres or maybe herd them back home through that fissure. Maybe if they practiced, they could strengthen the flame?

That was about as likely as lighting up Esye again. Make a moon shine—anyone could manage that, right?

Serra groaned. She laced up her boots then headed in search of tachery. Felia and Uzziel were laughing by the farthest morning fire and Serra felt a pang that she hadn't checked up on the Sellwyn boy since they'd arrived. But his laugh was a warming sound, a dip in hot cocoa. She hadn't known he could sound so typically like a teenager.

"What are you two up to?" she asked.

Felia raised her elbows and Uzziel repeated the gesture. A smile spread on Serra's face—it was nice to see him try. Maybe all Uzziel Sellwyn needed to become a real boy was some fresh air and a lot of dirt.

"I'm hoping you enjoyed your baths as much as I?" Serra said.

Felia giggled. "Yes, Lady Serra. My father calls me a tomboy, but I've never been so happy to be bathed and clean as I am today."

"Me too," Uzziel agreed from where he reclined against a tree trunk. "Father had me bathed twice a day back home, in case of infections. He said the outside was so dirty, I shouldn't want to be there anyway."

Had Lord Sellwyn been so fastidious out of concern for his progeny or had he been protecting his legacy by keeping his invalid son out of sight? Knowing Vesperi's stories, the latter. Serra would check on him again in a bit, make sure he was comfortable here. Though Felia seemed to have taken on that task. It was good for him to be around others his age, people who viewed him as more than a duty to be completed.

She wandered off toward the ruins. A walk made her thoughts flow faster than any amount of sitting and staring at parchment might. Somehow, the Guard would need to combine their powers to "call the air" and once they did, the "doe would fly." But how does one call air? And what would happen if they managed it? Perhaps the doe, Vesperi, of course, would regain the full strength of the weapon and cull the cantaleres as easily as the claren. But what of the dark brother? Clearly, he was not Uzziel, no matter how dark Vesperi's thoughts toward her brother had been in the past. The boy was a pain, but not a horror.

How much simpler the silver stag prophecy had been to understand! Ryn Gylles would laugh to hear her claim it. She'd resisted his and the Brotherhood's manipulations toward fulfilling it for so long.

From this direction, the ruins towered over Serra, and she thought better of exploring them too far on her own. So she found a comfortable ivy mound and sat cross-legged upon it. When Lorne eased himself beside her on the too-small seat, she was hardly surprised. He wrapped an arm around her waist and squeezed her right hip.

"I'd fall off if I moved," he claimed, a reason readied for his hold. "You wouldn't wish such harm on me, would you?"

Serra blinked rapidly at his sorry excuse but thought better of making a point of it. "No, I wouldn't." Maybe it was how long she'd gone without the comfort of someone's affections, but Serra couldn't think of anything she wanted more right then than Lorne around her like this. *Is this how it always begins again?*

He played with the hem of her belted pants, and she found she didn't mind that either. But she should, shouldn't she? She was beginning to forget why it had been so important to push him away.

Lorne didn't take advantage of her lowered resistance, merely hummed to himself. "You smell like yourself again," he said, taking a sniff of her hair. "Cloves and lemon."

Serra ran a finger under the clove-studded yellow ribbon ringing her neck. It had been a gift from her mother when she'd been young. Had her mother known it'd become a constant reminder of where home truly was?

"What do you think?" she asked without preamble. Lorne knew better than anyone here what challenges they faced. He had the echo, had captured a cantalere. He knew what her sight could do, how it might help. He knew her in ways even Janto didn't.

Was that nostalgia pressing her to take his hand? Lorne gave a startled look when she twined their fingers together, but again chose not to make a thing of it. "I *think* we've got a lot of Lanserim here who haven't lived in close quarters with Meduans before."

"Really?" She hadn't considered there were Meduans among them beyond himself and Uzziel. The couple who'd kept themselves apart. Who else?

"Really, you say?" Lorne chuckled. "Have you forgotten what scoundrels we are? You've told me so often."

She blushed. Half those times, she'd been angry. The other half? Pressed next to him naked and making full use of close quarters with a Meduan.

"I've half a mind to draw a moan out of you right now, if you're going to keep flushing like that, thrushberries on your cheeks."

"Lorne—"

"We can't, I know. Broken up for good, I know. In another world crisis and a few stones' throws from a mob of people, I know. I'm just not quite sure why you're letting me get away with this." He kissed her earlobe, moved down to her neck.

Serra moaned. Oh, it had been a long journey. She turned her head to meet his lips and sparks coursed through her, brighter and bolder than any glimpse of that other realm. She moaned again when he stood up and moved away.

"Lorne . . ." Her tone might be considered begging.

"This is cruel, love." He faced away from her, and his waterfall of perfectly brushed hair covered his well-toned ass. "The Meduan in me is wondering what you hope to get out of me after letting me come on to you like this. And I don't mean sex." He paused, and Serra hated the tinge of self-pity in his voice. "You've made it very clear you don't see me as a fit partner. I shouldn't have come out here, but like a dog's tail, I've followed after you so long, I can't break the habit. Jerusho's rynna says I can't keep subjecting myself to this, and I can't help but think she's right."

Disbelief warred with anger. Her voice was louder than she meant it to be. "You've talked about us with a rynna?" Him seeking advice on how to process their breakup was unbelievable. She'd have thought he'd merely sleep his way through half a town and wake up refreshed.

"Don't worry," he said bitterly, "I didn't name you."

"That's not what—"

"Isn't it, Serra?" Tears of anger glistened on his face. They pained her deeply, and she rose, wanted to make this right, but had no idea how or even what *right* meant around Lorne Granich. "Isn't it about your reputation as a liege-lady?" he continued. "The king is *married* to a Meduan, and you still consider being with me an impossibility. You couldn't do that, oh no. Being with me is but taking a roll in the dirt to amuse yourself before ascending back to your higher calling."

"I don't think of you like—"

He spat at the ground, disgusted with himself or with her. Maybe both. He shook his head, a wry smirk appearing. "It's not going to be easy bringing this Guard together. I'll help, of course I will, but you aren't the only Lanserim who holds themselves above their supposed brethren, us muck-loving Meduans."

Was that what she'd been doing with him? Certainly, she'd been raised to despise the Meduans, everyone had—they'd been at war! And they'd beguiled her brother, led him to commit treachery against the king. It hadn't been easy forgiving Vesperi for her brother's death, but Serra had accepted the need for it. If not, the claren would have spread. That pestilence's very existence was proof of how much hurt the Meduans caused others, and themselves the most. They were wretched monsters, and she was right about that.

Oh Madel, do I truly think so? That inner voice she'd somehow silenced would have had her believe so. Her breath caught, and she felt unbalanced. Lorne caught her hand to steady her. Even after she'd spent so much time in Medua, after having met so many people who'd been born into that system and had no choice but to follow it to survive, people like Lorne, like Vesperi, she'd painted them with the same brush unless she knew them personally.

Yes, the advers deserved scorn and hatred for what they'd done to the Meduan populace. Yes, sometimes Meduans still committed atrocities that strained her ability to forgive—she need not think farther back than Granich Manor and Lorne's sister Cora for a reminder of that. But so many of the Meduans had just been staying alive the best they knew how. They were people, same as she, and she'd been viewing them differently, separately—Lorne was right.

And he hadn't asked in the last day about the one thing weighing on his mind most. He'd let her see to her own needs first.

"I spoke to Cora," she said.

His eyes lit up, though he appeared cautious.

"I gave her your sigil. She was so relieved to hear you are well."

He did not hesitate and wrapped Serra up in his arms, nuzzling a thank you into her hair.

"I told her we would go back for her, when this is over. I promised her. Your father's still treating her like a servant, and he's still treating servants like they're less than people. Lorne, how did you—" she choked on the words. Some would say losing one's parents was the worst thing a child could experience, but for others, keeping those parents was the greater cruelty. "How do you survive?"

"Like this." His lips encircled her own, her body flush against his. She welcomed his tongue into her mouth, placed her hands on his ass. Lorne smiled against her lips as she squeezed, drew his fingers over her arms, her hips, her thighs. Her body moved with them.

"All that riding did wonders for your muscles," he teased, and she reared back enough to give him a good-natured whack. She wanted to give him a lot more, her body ached for it. But it wouldn't be fair, not with what he'd said, what it had made her realize. Whether Lorne Granich made her desire peak was not in question. But she needed to be sure what else she wanted from him before she could give into such longing again. This wasn't the time to figure that out. Lansera's safety came first.

"I'm sorry," he said, simultaneously bashful and proud. "It's near impossible not to comfort you when you look as forlorn as you did. That's the best way I know how."

Serra leaned in for another lingering kiss, ignoring a rustling at her back. "I wanted it."

"Oh, I know that," he grinned, giving her left breast a flick.

She squeaked, and then did so again as Lorne lifted her by her waist onto a high ruin and jumped up behind her. The rustling she'd heard had loudened into a din. Dry ivy leaves loosened and whirled in the air, and vines flew as though whipped by an unseen windstorm.

The koparin were running.

Thousands of them, leaping, jumping, sprinting fast as they could. They bounded off the ruins, off each other, a beige blur of speed. Lorne shielded her, and she hid her face in his back. The fleeing animals used them as a base from which to dig sharp claws to gain purchase to push off again. She stiffened, tensing her legs to maintain her foothold, refusing to scream as multitudinous claw jabs and tears pummeled her. Lorne had her hands clutched in his, clinging to his waist and she imagined how much worse this was for him.

Minutes passed, and Serra didn't dare open her eyes for fear something would puncture them. The scrapes of claws and fury of leaves quieted, and yet she waited. Once both she and Lorne had relaxed enough that their breathing synced, she felt safe enough to take a peek.

All around them, exposed ruins gleamed, quartz flecks reflecting the sunlight from their grayed marble and granite stone. The ivy filled the channels between the walls like a river of torn and trampled brown, yellow, and green leaves.

"They're gone," she whispered. Lorne gave her hands one more squeeze before releasing them. She stretched her fingers; he'd clenched them so hard, they'd gone white. Then he tiptoed his way around the wall's width to face her, his head torn like a craval roast scored for a feast. His black tunic fluttered in shreds, reminding Serra of the mourning ribbons she'd stopped wearing after the Perch.

She took a shaky breath. He was here, he was okay, though he would need plenty of the queen's salve. He hugged her close and grimaced but didn't let her go. Her head fit readily under his own. He kissed her forehead, kissed her lips, then helped her off the ruin.

"We'll talk about all this," she said, holding onto his arm as they approached the camp. "I promise that too. This time, I promise."

Lorne stopped, turned her by the shoulders. He gazed into her eyes, and she latched onto his, saw silver within the blue. Whether that was from the adrenaline of their close shave or his flame's echo, she couldn't say.

"But not yet," he said, shaking his head. "The cantalere herds are coming, and that comes first to Lady Serrafina Gavenstone."

Was that so wrong? What other reason could there be for the koparin to flee but the approach of the cantalere masses? They were coming, and the Silver Guard must end their roam. Her heart, and her and Lorne's future, if there was one, would have to wait.

CHAPTER TWENTY-TWO

JANTO

Spring had come early to Neville's plains. Mud encased the horse hooves and the lower thirds of their clothing. Jade- and ivory-speckled woranbirds made rounds in pairs, examining scrub bushes for sturdy holds in which to make their nests. All around, craval beasts feasted on tender green weeds. The yellow gleam of the herd animals' ever-smiling teeth could be seen from many yards away. Luckily, the winds took care of their accompanying stench.

Lucky the herds were there at all, with what Janto had learned of what had happened in Trop. At the dock in Jost, the news that a third of the village's residents had been slaughtered or disappeared had awaited him, along with that of Serra and Uzziel's safe arrival and the growing Silver Guard. It made Janto nervous to have them so close to the amassing cantaleres, but it seemed the right choice if they were to be effective.

Most of the royal coterie had dispersed from Jost. Many had been civilians excited to accompany the new king on his first journey. With spring's appearance, and the ever-spreading tales of mythical creatures running amok through fields, they'd headed home. Spring planting would soon be cast into doubt, and famine join the laundry list of threats the Lanserim faced. At least jurgens could be calmed with enough easy food, reported Lady Farami from Carafin's Market.

Something whizzed through the air.

A horse screamed.

Another arrow flew.

Janto's mount reared, nearly hit. He had the Old Girl in hand in less than a second, an arrow notched on its string.

Two royal guards flanked Vesperi. More completed a circle of defense around them. Even with his back to her, Janto could sense her frustration at not having anything to defend herself with.

"Pic! Get in here!" Janto commanded.

The child's horse had fallen, and he'd been tossed into a patch of purple alyssum blooms.

More arrows glanced overhead.

The lad rolled head over foot through the legs of the mounts. "I've got him," Vesperi confirmed.

Janto scanned their surroundings. A Meduan raiding party? Would such opportunists be so reckless as to attack an armed group this large? And with so little to hide behind? Their attackers could be in only three locations: two small groupings of trees in near range, or an inclined hillside that might serve as enough of a trench to hide a handful of men.

The eastern grove was most likely, as the angle of the arrows' flights made clear. But there could be attackers in all potential spots. Their best option was to wait them out. Raiders would give up the game soon enough. If this was someone else . . . well, they'd find out.

Ser Irven had reached the same conclusion. "Shields stay up, guards. Let them reveal themselves."

Silence for long minutes, minus the whines and fear of the hurt steed.

A sudden shout came from the eastern grove, followed by groans and screams and the grotesque squish and crunch of flesh-covered bone. Anyone who could land repeated blows like that with such force had to be formidable.

Janto observed their environs—no arrows flying from the other potential offensive positions, no one running out to aid their compatriots. Likely someone had surprised the attackers, and the lack of reinforcements meant they'd been hidden only in that grove.

Ser Irven caught his attention, and Janto nodded. Irven tapped four guards on the shoulders with his sword. They steered their horses toward the trees, swords drawn. Out of caution, the rest kept watchful eyes on the other potential hiding places.

Janto kept his arrow at the ready.

Three minutes later, Ser Irven called out, "All clear, my king."

Janto released his breath, then gave Vesperi a squeeze of relief before riding over to the trees. Drapians, he realized as their dried, filigreed seed pods fluttered down from the disturbance. Izzy liked to catch them in autumn, when they danced throughout Callyn's hillsides. *She will do so again.*

The peaceful memory contrasted starkly with the sight before him. Two men's heads had been bashed against the motley tree bark. They wore the brown velvet robes of advers, though with no bones affixed to them to attest to their cruelty. They appeared young from what remained of their heads. One had a patchy sprinkle of stubble on his chin. The other, baby-faced cheeks.

Three more had been caught alive and sniveled for mercy at sword point in the mud, none older than twenty. *New recruits,* Janto realized with horror, *from Lanserim.* They'd not yet experienced what the "virtues" the advers taught could result in. Unlike the lone Meduan beside them, gripping a hammer that dripped blood.

If any man could do that much damage with that rudimentary of a weapon by himself, this was the one. Built like a grindstone, he was. But as he looked up toward Janto, his eyelids fluttered rapidly and shock took over his features.

"My king," he kneeled while awkwardly raising his elbows. An overcompensation for not recognizing Janto immediately? Or perhaps he was still addled from having killed two men.

"That's not neces—" Janto started, but changed his mind. The living advers needed to see this, if they stood any hope of reformation. They needed to see how the warrior who'd taken them and their mates down all by himself still respected his king's authority. The advers taught that might was right, but maybe these recruits could still learn that character grew out of other wells.

"May Madel's hand guide you," Janto said. "That was brave of you," he commended the man.

"Nay," the man responded. "It was self-defense. None of us are safe with these fiends about."

Wisdom from lived experience, no doubt.

"What's your name?" Janto asked.

"Cid."

"And do you live in Tilayne, Cid?"

He shook his head. "I stay in Elston these days. But the winter lingers overlong there. I don't like to be inside so much anymore."

Cid pinched his sides, perhaps a way to keep himself in the present after the rage he'd mustered moments ago. Janto wondered if this had happened before, if Cid had defended others under attack during his life in Medua before the Conjoining. Or maybe it was a more instinctive response, maybe the mere glimpse of an adver's robes reminded him of horrors he'd experienced then. Whatever the reason for his aid, Janto was glad of it.

"I heard the Green Lady was building a new glass house," Cid continued, "so I came with my hammer and thought to help."

Green Lady? Terella will like that name. "We are very lucky you did. You have the thanks of all Lansera."

Cid stared down at his tool then, as though seeing it and the blood and viscera covering it for the first time. He wiped the hammer against a pile of wet leaves with uneven, jittery strokes.

Vesperi surprised them both, approaching with soft steps and removing the implement from Cid's hands as she rubbed his back.

"We'll take care of that for you, valiant Cid," she said. "Such a weapon deserves a knight's shine, don't you think?"

She'd been practicing her courtesies during her time in Elston, it appeared. Something akin to awe filled Cid's countenance as she handed the hammer off to a guard, who pulled a cloth from her pack along with some polish.

Janto turned his attention to the advers. "Did you know your leader sent you on a suicide mission? You are alive now because Cid found you first. Our arrows and swords work just as well as his hammer; do we have more reason to use them?"

They shook their heads. "The great Adver Votan said—"

"'The great Adver Votan'?" Vesperi scoffed. "Bet he'll be calling himself 'the Guj' next." That was the moniker Medua's former ruler had bestowed upon himself.

What a fool Janto had been to try and bargain with such men for news of Izzy. What a fool to have not routed them after their attempt to kidnap Vesperi. And this was too easy. Perhaps another ambush lay in wait farther down the road?

"Have the rest of your masters gone underground?" he asked.

"The great—Votan's expecting a report by evening on how it went."

Janto nodded. He would send the report personally.

"Lulled into a false sense of security by our letting them go after the Conjoining," Ser Irven mused. "They do not think you'll come after them. Probably think you're as much of a lapdog as their King Ralion was."

Janto seethed. "They are about to learn the Albrechts rule because Madel has chosen us, not because false priests of a fake god need a puppet." He would not make a similar mistake again, even if it meant exposing that he had contacted them months ago. Not if he hoped to be the man his country needed during tumultuous times like these.

"This isn't how the advers attack," Vesperi advised, adrenaline pulsing a vein on her neck. "They prefer a subtler approach."

A distraction, was it? "Ser Irven, ride out for Carafin's Market—Captain Wolxas should have a unit passing through it by now on their way to Trop. Bring back enough warriors to take our prisoners home. These ones, and the—" he looked to Vesperi.

"Two dozen," she supplied.

"And the two dozen other men we'll be arresting in Tilayne." Janto waved over Pic. "Fetch a pigeon. We must warn my mother to screen every package, potion, and pitcher in Callyn."

Pic's head jerked up, surprised at the request. But he did as he was bid.

Janto was grateful for the practicality of Meduans like Vesperi and Cid, of people who'd had to develop sharp instincts. The advers *were* typically subtler. Except for their personal power plays, their favorite weapons had been whispers and rumors during their reign, leaving violence for the nobility to carry out.

But once, they had tried something else. Janto remembered it vividly. The day your fiancée's brother tries to poison your father is hard to forget. Janto would root the advers' poison out, whether in words or in deeds, in Tilayne and everywhere else they'd spread it.

CHAPTER TWENTY-THREE
SERRA

The town of Trop lay in a natural alcove formed by the forested foothills. A grove of Wasylim citrus trees, yet to spring new leaves, marked the market square. Serra was surprised they grew in this climate, but perhaps they were ornamental. If only she could say the same of the creatures rambling between them.

A great herd of cantaleres, five hundred at least, wakened with the sun. If there was any lair the Silver Guard might ring, it was here with the aid of that alcove. The cantaleres sharpened their horns on those tree trunks and against the mountain rock. From the still-standing village homes, creaks and groans of wood came as the cantaleres within them rose from their dens. After scavenging through the countryside, the animals had returned to Trop. By the decrepit looks of the buildings, they'd done so for several nights.

Serra touched Councilman Ferin's arm, and he gave her a sad smile in exchange for the comfort. He, Serra, Sar Mertina, and a few others from the camp had journeyed to Trop this morning to observe the enemy.

Right behind the ransacked market square, the largest portal Serra had ever seen offered hope. At least twenty yards long and the height of two horses stacked on top of each other, it was their joker card. At that size, no wonder Trop's citizens had begun to disappear. If there was any chance of sending the cantaleres back where they came, the Guard would have to make its stand here.

Their combined power was not enough to physically threaten the creatures, but the Guard might herd them through to that other realm by scaring the beasts into the fissure with silver pinpricks and firelights. It didn't seem enough, but they would need to try something soon. For the sake of Lansera, yes, but also for the sake of camp cohesion. Lorne hadn't been wrong about those undercurrents, either.

As they rode back to their base, another strange sight greeted Serra and her companions. From a crest of hills, an expanse to the south opened up. Two people were walking toward the Guard Glen through it, not more than three miles away. They wore white clothes and dragged a laden sled over the ardent green of the new spring grasses.

Deduins. No one else would wear white for such a long journey, as the fabric would be ruined by mud from traveling. But Deduins wore only white at home, in their iced-over peninsula. What could they want here? They rarely asked for aid. The sole exception Serra knew of was when the hunting party had twice swept their tunnels, killing the smattering of claren that had spread their way.

Those few weeks weren't ones she wanted to remember. She'd been so cold, always frowning as the Deduins did. It didn't help that their mere appearance was enough to cause her to recoil. Indigo eyes were their most distinctive feature, and the one most likely to be passed down through the few Deduins who had married into the greater Lanserim populace. But what repulsed Serra most was how those eyes flickered with a light not born of Madel, or anything Serra equated with Her presence. Something different animated them.

Her grimace dug frown lines into her cheeks. Agler had teased her, when they'd been children, claiming her dour expressions would freeze on her face if she made them outside in the wintertime. As her party arrived at the Guard Glen, Serra called Ryn Gylles over from a morning campfire. He secured a cloak over his breezy rynnic garb.

"And what calls me from a warm fire this morning, dear leader?"

His ready humor was a balm for Serra's apprehension. She clambered up a ruin wall and gestured for him to follow, then pointed to the two forms continuing their way, slowly but with intention.

"Two Deduins are coming to our camp."

Gylles blinked his eyes, not believing her words. Then he examined the horizon. "I suppose they must be."

"You've always been so fond of mysteries," she said. All those mysteries had caused her great frustration during her time with the Order. "What do you suppose brings them here?"

Ryn Gylles observed their approach. "Perhaps they want to lend their aid to the realm?"

Not likely. No Deduins had fought in Turyn's war, nor did she remember any tales of their gallantry. Their seeming neutrality was why King Turyn had ceded the region to Medua as part of his peace.

"Madel doesn't keep as close of confidence with me as she once did," Gylles admitted. Serra detected a note of wistfulness in his voice. "I'm afraid I don't have an answer for you this time."

"Like you'd give it to me if you did," she teased, glad she had her old adviser around during this quest.

Gylles adjusted his hold on his cloak and did not return her glance. "Right you are."

Oh. He felt guilt over his part in getting her to accept the seer's gift? "I understand, you know," she said softly, "why you and the Brotherhood had to poke and prod me into fulfilling the prophecy."

Gylles examined his clay-brown hands.

Serra continued, "I had to get to that understanding myself. I couldn't just be told my choices, then be expected to make the right one. I had to feel my way there, figure out for myself how important my choices were for Lansera. No amount of words could have made it happen."

"Maybe," Gylles drew out the two syllables into a donkey's bray. "But maybe too much was asked of you, Serra. I often wonder."

"We wouldn't be standing here if it had been too much, Gylles." She pressed his hands. "None of us. The claren would have devoured us. By now, our skins would be nothing more than dried husks drifting in the wind."

Once, picturing such a horrific image might have given her convulsions. She had come such a long way from the girl Ryn Gylles had known, and she was stronger for it. "Madel knows what She asks of us. Surely, She would not give us more than we could bear. You must believe that, as a ryn."

"Must I?" He chuckled. "I believe doubt can be as important to faith as mere acceptance. If we just fell into it, faith would not be as rewarding. Instead, maintaining it requires a constant rediscovering and reshaping of what it means." He stroked his chin. "Maybe that's what Madel is doing, allowing these creatures to come wreak havoc amongst us. Maybe She is sharpening our faith. Hm."

"Maybe She has nothing to do with why they are here." Serra couldn't imagine Madel spurring on anything that might harm Her people.

"They come from Her realm, do they not? You, more than anyone, can see that."

"They come from what we thought was Her realm."

"Oh, I doubt any existence, ours here or theirs there, can be truly separated from Madel's presence."

"You read Janto's letter. The other place I see may not be related to Her at all. Or maybe it's one She protects like our own."

"Another She rescues when their needs exceed their capabilities?"

Serra had no more appetite for pondering the finer points of religion right then. Whether or not that other realm was connected to Madel, the claren had proven it was connected to the Lanserim and that their moral shortcomings could be made flesh within it. Thus, it was a very present threat, not a philosophical one, especially not with cantaleres on their doorstep. "We have to focus on survival, Ryn Gylles, certainly you agree with me on that?"

"Surely I do. But that doesn't mean I must agree that you sacrificing your happiness should be the price of it, then or now."

"Really, ryn?" She spoke wryly. "You don't understand dedicating a life to the service of others?"

He tugged at his cloak's collar. "You have me there."

"And I'll have you back with me at camp, trying our best to ascertain how we can channel the Silver Guard's power into ridding us of these mythical mysteries."

"Yes, my lady." He raised his elbows, but lest she think him too reproached, gave her a playful wink. Serra followed him to the glen, needing to seek out breakfast. Facing Deduins on an empty stomach wasn't the wisest choice.

‡

A thorough inspection of the camp's gathered stores failed to yield dried sheven flesh or any spices from the Yarowen region. Deduins had an assortment of those they liked steeped in hot water. *Perhaps anise seeds would do. Or pine needles.*

Nonetheless, Serra met the travelers about half an hour later. Their white hoods flopped onto their shoulders as Serra approached, Sar Mertina by her side. One Deduin was a woman short of stature and the other a man tall enough that Serra grimaced to imagine him traveling through his people's tunnels beneath the ice, back bent. Their eyes' purple light was luminous. Fine blond hair grew over their ears, and their skin was a shade pale enough to blend in with snow, had there been any left on the plain.

"Welcome, citizens of Deduin," she greeted them with a fingerful of fallowent. Though the Deduins did not raise their elbows, they did consume the seeds—some concerns transcended cultures.

Serra considered starting with an "I am pleased to meet you," but lies were rarely a good way to begin a relationship. "May we grant you rest and food? You have come a very long way."

The woman spoke, her voice light and friendly, though her mouth remained straight as a line. "We sailed through the Steps, so it was not as long as it might have been. We rode a cart through your vineyards and walked once grass took over from grapes."

They had sailed the Giants' Pathway? No one had done that in Serra's lifetime. "Isn't it dangerous, sailing there?"

"Oh yes," the man said, "but I'm one of our best fishermen. I've sailed worse waters south of the Deduin peninsula."

"Impressive." That was pure honesty.

Some curious members of the camp drew close. Serra spoke loudly, so all could hear: "And what has brought you here? It must be important to tear one of your people's best fisherman away so soon after the ice has thawed."

Each catch was dear to the Deduins. A fishing party's return was the only time Serra had heard one laugh. That laughter had sounded ghastly from where her hunting party had stayed in Thokketh, a great ice palace and former prison on the peninsula. It sounded like a drasmo's cackle rising from their tunnels.

The woman's eyes shimmered, purple highlighted by the blackness of her pupils. "We've come to join your Guard, Lady Serra." Silver specks shined in her eyes and she opened her palm. A ball of silver spun within it, no bigger than a marble but controlled, contained. "Esye's flame has come to us."

The man opened his palm as well. A silver tendril flashed and went out.

Why had she not considered they might be part of the Guard? She ought to be well past the point that the forms Madel's help took befuddled her.

"Then you are doubly welcomed," she said, "to our camp and to the Silver Guard."

Some of their audience clapped at the reception, though Serra heard a few whispers—Deduins were always a spectacle. This pair opened their palms again, perhaps as a hello, and other Guard members followed suit. The flame's echo sparked from their palms then jumped from person to person, arcing between hands and delighting their owners to the point that laughter broke out. The Deduins joined in, and though the sound raised the hackles on Serra's neck, it felt right, like adding a missing note to a melody.

Lorne slipped up beside her as was his wont. He whispered, "I didn't know ghouls could talk."

Serra laughed. "You're horrible." She wouldn't admit to having thought the same, at least not to anyone but him.

He smiled as he moved closer, flipping his own hand and uncurling his fingers. The flame shot out of his palm and arced, veering toward Ryn Gylles on her left. It swooped down to combine with Gylles's magic that had already united with his neighbor's.

The group formed a circle and a few other magic wielders hurried over from the tents to join in the display. The strengthened flame's curvature bent around Serra and Sar Mertina. Serra took a step back, and the flame smoothed together where she'd stood. Sar Mertina followed suit, and it became a completed circle of silver energy.

It was beautiful. Serra wondered if Vesperi would think the same.

"What's happening?" Uzziel whined from back near the tents. Serra rushed over, surprised no one had brought him out. By the time she reached him, the circle was fizzling, running out of energy.

Uzziel was not alone. Several people remained around the campfires, either too cold to be drawn toward their new arrivals or too tired to think them worth much of a fuss. It had felt like so many more had joined in with the Deduins in forming that circle. Serra counted. Maybe a third of the Guard had gone out. And if that had happened with only a third . . .

"A circle is a ring, is it not?" Serra said excitedly.

"Yes. That's a stupid question." Uzziel's forehead wrinkled as Ryn Colini refilled his plate.

"And how many of us are there, counting these two new recruits from Deduin?" Serra asked.

"Deduins?" Ryn Colini gasped. Others nearby shushed him, likely reacting to how Serra was jumping foot to foot with excitement.

"Thirty-three, Lady Serra," answered Felia Swalus, drinking a mug of tachery. "I've been keeping a mental list."

"That's great, Felia." She gave one of the girl's braids a playful tug, and Felia squeaked. Serra did so herself, with excitement. "Thirty-three is enough for a guard, wouldn't you say? It's about time to see what thirty-three members of the Silver Guard can do together."

"Right now?" Uzziel asked. "I haven't finished my breakfast."

Serra observed the Guard Glen and each of its inhabitants. Most were gathered by the fires now, glancing at the Deduins with either interest or set jaws of suspicion. The Deduins talked animatedly with a trio of Rasselerians. Lorne stopped mid-sentence to meet her gaze, though he swung back to Ryn Gylles. The Meduan couple stood by them, the woman, Lari, rubbing her womb.

Serra was surprised to realize the Meduans had been part of the circle . . . and that was the problem, wasn't it? She knew better than any Lanserim how trustworthy most Meduans proved if given the chance, and she repeatedly doubted it. Everyone here had volunteered despite age, despite pregnancy, despite physical ailments. They were united by the desire to aid their country, a new magic skill most had not possessed a few weeks ago, and a healthy dose of fear about what might happen if they did not.

Yet the peace between the Guard would only last so long, unless they could fight down their biases. Serra was proof that years were sometimes not enough time for that.

Neither would the cantaleres last long in Trop. They would not patiently wait to be herded into the portal. This was their window, the sole chance the Silver Guard had. The Deduins' appearance was the final piece falling into place. Serra knew the pain of delaying destiny, a mistake she did not wish to repeat.

"Better eat fast," she instructed Uzziel. Then she raised her voice loud enough to make him spill his eggs. "Silver Guard!" she said as many heads turned her way. "Eat well! We travel to Trop this afternoon. In a few hours, your powers will unite to rout the cantaleres. In a few hours, you become the fulfillment of prophecy."

And their lives would never be the same. She knew that well, too.

‡

"Are we ready?"

Serra walked the line of Guard members waiting for her to begin deploying them around Trop's ridge. Two groups of ten would head to the elevated forests to the north and south of town. At the last moment possible, their third flank would close in, forming a north-south line in the meadow west of town, once the cantaleres returned through it for the night.

A good number of the animals were already back, scuffing up dens with their many legs and tossing various carcasses into the air before gulping them down. Blood seeped from those horns and dried over their flat snouts, staining their brown, moss-tinged coats with mini lava flows.

Was the fissure wider than before? The cantaleres stood clear of it, though its presence must be why they'd gathered there. Perhaps for a whiff of home in a strange land.

The Guard waited on Serra's word. They ranged in age from Rall's son Evon to seventy-three-year-old Mar Koma, who'd arrived from Tilayne the same evening as Serra's group, claiming the queen had sent her. Though she found the woman distasteful, Serra had seen her flame's echo for herself and welcomed her in.

Several Guard members wore the garb of Madel's Order, reverence glowing from the blue orbs dancing atop their heads. They'd been meditating for the last half-hour in the hopes of increasing their focus and their echoes' strength. There were also farmers and merchants, Lorne, and nine Rasselerians. Uzziel was strapped to Flivio's chest, and his new confidence brought dimples to his cheeks. The change in location had been good for him . . . if he survived it.

Which wasn't a certainty. Serra remembered Hamsyn's sacrifice, the result of the hunting party's foolhardy rush to action at the base of Mandat Hall. Did she know that the Silver Guard deployed to the meadow could withstand the ruthless creatures that would try to escape? *No.* Did she know what would happen when their flames' combined, how that might call the air? *No.* But she knew the cantaleres had to be dealt with now before more tragedy befell their people. Lansera had to be defended.

Serra prayed the Guard's power would hold for however long it took, and that the cantaleres would stampede through the fissure rather than through them.

A great rustling of leaves and needles came from the woods. From the ridge overhanging the town, koparin spilled out. They leapt to the ground among the gathered cantaleres, a desperate act. Such animals knew when they were outnumbered—more cantaleres were coming.

Serra cursed. They'd thought the cantaleres would return from the plains, not the forest.

"They're coming from the hillside!" she yelled. "Retreat into the trees!"

Whether the other flank leaders heard or not, she wasn't certain, but Nap led his group of ten guards up into the northern trees and Serra's in the south also ascended. *Climb faster,* Serra prayed. As far as she could see, the forest was full of koparin. The fastest ones blasted through the town, a few of their young abandoned and trampled while others careened to the grass. The ground rumbled with approaching hooves.

Lorne reached a hand down to help Serra up higher. Would the flame ring work through the branches? They'd soon find out. She reached one she could sit on and heard Flivio talk Uzziel through panicked breathing. Nearby, Rall had Evon in a death grip, balancing them both on a shaky limb.

The trees shook, knocking down pine cones that had failed to fall in winter. It snowed pine needles and bark. When all had fallen that could, the world was a vista of charging cantaleres. They surged beneath the trees, over and around the ridge as they pursued the koparin. If their bulk continued past the town's western border, who knew how long they would take to return. Yet she couldn't send Sar Mertina's flank out to hold the line—they'd be mauled where they stood.

Lorne gave her a wink, and called out, "Fire's on, pass it on!"

His flame burst to life in his palm, then strengthened as Colini extended his own. Felia next, then Flivio dodged Uzziel's effort with a "Whoa!"

All down the tree line, the flame snaked out and wrapped back around itself into a small ring. A Rasselerian's tongue flicked out in rhythm with the flame's pulse, and the rays thickened. Wonder exploded on their faces.

Serra leaned out of her tree and whooped—Nap's group had seen their silver and done the same. She held her breath as the silver banded between their two groups and waited for the third to join in.

And waited.

The first of the stampeding cantaleres had reached the town's outskirts.

One small silver beam plunged into the ring from that direction. Serra could barely make out the line of people at its source. They had repositioned themselves out of harm's way, but that would create a lopsided ring at an angle that would miss a large portion of the cantaleres.

The third flank's first weak beam thickened, and more of the remaining echoes joined it as though spiders tossing out their webs. Silver arcs rebounded from the original ring between Nap and Serra's groups, then formed a larger one, with a band thick as a kratomwood trunk—the fruits of all thirty-three members of the Silver Guard working together with intent.

But the changed angle meant a portion of the cantaleres had already gone past its perimeter. Both inside and out, the nearest monsters reared as the flame singed their fur, sending others stumbling into it. The air filled with hissing, roaring, and noises Serra couldn't name and the oh-too-familiar smell of grilling meat. *It'll have to be enough.*

"We need to press them toward the rift," she advised Flivio, the only person nearby not focused on sending their echo into the bonded flame, as he had none. That would take shifting the west side of the ring closer into the town center and its citrus grove, and then shrinking the size of it down. It would also mean moving Mertina's group closer to the cantaleres loose outside the ring's boundary.

Flivio cupped a hand to his ear. No one could hear her above the caged animals' roar. Her message wouldn't be communicated down the line.

Serra gulped. Then she jumped off her branch.

Lorne's free arm grabbed onto her, yanking her shoulder hard. His eyes filled with fear and his head swung side-to-side.

The silver light beyond the trees flickered.

She fixed him with a gaze as furious as the one she'd flashed the night they'd last broken up. "Don't you dare lose your concentration, Lorne Granich!" she yelled. "I'll be fine."

Face ashen and lip trembling, he shouted, "You better," and dropped her arm.

Serra rolled onto the ground to break the fall then rose as fast as she could. She ran down the sloping hill through the wood and to the town's western edge, dodging cantaleres more and more the closer she got. It felt like forever but was probably three minutes at the speed she managed. Evening frost slicked the grasses, and she focused her will on making it to Sar Mertina, mounted high on her horse as she slashed at the cantaleres threatening her group.

"Close in!" Serra yelled loud as she could, near as she dared. "Tighten the ring!"

Sar Mertina didn't hesitate, though she doubtless knew precisely what Serra's command meant. She kicked up her horse and shouted, "Follow me, Silver Guard!" The ten people mounted behind her did as she ordered, holding their palms out while advancing south toward the city.

The cantaleres within the ring shimmied away from the encroaching boundary. Some backed into the fissure at the square and disappeared.

"It's working!" Serra encouraged Mertina's group as she ran to the tree line, where it was safer. As she reached for a branch to climb, she heard a human scream. But something else caught her eye before she could react.

In the center of the ring, a thick beam of silver light coalesced above the heads of the cantaleres. It shot straight up into the sky. *Just like in the king's vision,* Serra realized with a gasp. The brightness blinded her, and it must have blinded the Guard, too, because the ring blinked out into darkness.

The agonizing screams continued. Someone had been tossed from their horse. *No no no.* Serra ran at them across the meadow. She would *not* leave her people out here to be trampled, not if she had fists to rage with. Sar Mertina tried to hold the creatures back, and a scan revealed Nap galloping his way from the forest to aid her.

Two other Guard members buttressed the fallen Mar Koma, who heaved on the cold, muddy grass. Serra slid onto her knees beside her, checked for wounds. Oh, were there wounds; she'd been gored in at least four places. That she could open her eyes was a testament to her strength.

Mar Koma clasped Serra's hand as a spasm of pain went through her. "It's okay," she said, and laughter rattled her chest. "I wasn't sure I wanted to come help you folks, but that was a jolly good time."

"Shh, keep your strength," Serra cautioned, digging around in her pouch for wound dressings.

"Never you mind that," Mar Koma said. Her short white hair was matted to her head by mud and blood where she'd struck her head from the fall. "You tell your ex, the king," she rasped, "those old advers are a damned mess of villains—they're working on some of the poison your brother used. Plan to slip it to him at the coronation. Think it'll make the Lanserim revolt against the Albrechts, him without an heir, you know. Tell him," she gripped Serra's wrist, "and tell him these Meduans, they aren't all like them. Not the ones I met here at least. I wasn't so sure before, but now . . ."

"I will," Serra promised.

Mar Koma nodded her head and closed her eyes for the last time. A silver wave of that larger beam swept past them, lighting grasses aflame off to their left. The cantaleres' squealing reached a fever pitch. The Guard had scattered, yet the beam went on shining, far stronger than Vesperi's weapon. It did not waver as it herded the cantalere, spilling flame into the circle the Silver Guard's ring had burnt into the ground. That flame whirled up into a wall of burning energy.

Sar Mertina lifted Serra by an arm, and she mounted the horse behind the warrior. As she did so, the beam shined down again from the sky, bright as any moonslight.

A screech unlike any she'd heard rolled across the great plain. A caw followed, and then a squawk. The calls interacted with each other, speaking a code Serra couldn't break.

Nap gathered Mar Koma's lifeless body onto his horse. A great shadow fell over them. Serra raised her eyes heavenward and what she saw took her breath away.

The silver flame expelled forth from a maize-colored beak, itself as big as a cat. The beak was attached to a head made of feathers and rainbows. Two more just like it fired from their gullets, their flames combining into a central beam.

Three heads. Three heads attached to a great flying bird that grew larger and larger by the second as it descended from the heavens.

It's real. The three-headed bird was no mere prophetic allusion. It was a physical reality.

"It's working!" Evon's delighted laughter shifted Serra's gaze. The cantaleres, in a great green-brown wave, rolled into the rift, the flame herding them on. The great bird shrunk the circle in on the town square and the cantaleres disappeared by the dozens into the bright riverland beyond the rift.

The bird flew overhead, its velocity fluttering her hair. That sent ripples through the cantaleres that had escaped past the ring's boundary. The ones farthest away dashed across the meadow, and the bird chased after them. Some of the animals were dazed, jumping erratically from one curve of fire to the next. Ghastly squeals joined the bird's war cries when they failed to negotiate well.

"Should we join in, do you think? Try to cast from here?" Lorne asked, suddenly by her side.

Serra threw her arms around him—she'd been so enrapt watching the bird, she hadn't seen him come. No more scrapes on his face, other than the ones the koparin had left. After a moment of relief, her attention returned skyward.

The bird adjusted its speed, gliding on a breeze she could not feel. The creature wasn't made of rainbows, not really, but its feathers shone like those of a chorna moth in the light, reflecting colors of many hues. Its heads were each a different shade: one a beautiful light umber, another shimmering silver, and the third as tawny red as Meditlan wines left to age.

Is that last one mine, I wonder?

"I think the bird's got it," Ryn Gylles answered Lorne, Ryn Colini grunting a yes beside him. All the Guard members had gathered close.

A Rasselerian flicked her tongue out, and her cheekbones raised on her bulbous face. "It tastes sweet, of the grasses nearest Lake Ashra when the moons are full." She closed her eyes, drinking in the bird's scent again. "I think we have taken the first step, my lady. It tastes of Lansera's future, not its past."

Serra felt it too, an infusion of hope on a day when she'd been everything but convinced she'd live through it. The environment around them felt crisper, the flame's presence adding back shades that had gone missing with Esye. Serra was lucky, they all were.

But not everyone in her charge had been. And though she dared to hope all the cantaleres here had been sent through or burnt, she knew better than to rule out their continued presence in smaller packs. "Do you think we can use your echoes to find other cantaleres? We could send riders to scout the countryside—"

"Serra, shh." Lorne placed hands on both sides of her head and aimed it to her left.

Six pairs of eyes were trained on her from heads connected to swanlike necks—if swans grew as big as mangrove roots. Silver, fine as pounded thread, striped their irises. One pair was blue bright as a fire's heart, the second gold and shiny as newly minted coins, and the third the same burnished copper as Queen Lexamy's hair.

The immensity of the creature overwhelmed her up close, and the others too. Serra heard not a sound, not even from Uzziel, gaping from Flivio's horse. The bird's body was the size of the briar throne. Its wings spanned the length of five men as it hovered above the ground.

Its eyes blinked slow as a meditative breath, each in turn, and the left and right heads snaked forward to inspect her. Serra stared at the bobbing head in front. Its eyelids closed, two marbles being polished with care. Once reopened, the blue had intensified, emanating power. The irises' silver stripes paled in comparison with that hue, and boiling red third eyelids, like cats possessed, rose partway. Serra felt as though she stared into a volcano's cone.

She jumped back, startled, and the three heads withdrew. They pointed westward, and the bird took off fast, steering into another ethereal wind. It shrank from view, the Silver Guard watching it depart in silence. Not until the speck of it disappeared from the horizon did anyone speak.

Serra wondered if she'd passed or failed its examination. Lorne squeezed her hand, and she realized she'd been clutching it for the past few . . . minutes? Hours? Time had lost its meaning.

"What just happened?" One of the rynnas half-laughed through her astonishment. That broke the spell. Soon, they were chattering, amazed at the bird's appearance, that they had called it to them, that they'd succeeded at sending the cantaleres back through to the other realm.

A cast of the sight confirmed no hidden glimmers of copper radiance from cantalere horns amongst the town's buildings. The portal had almost sealed behind them, which Serra had never seen happen. The thinnest thread of light from the other side spilled through.

"Do birds like that hunt cantaleres over there?" Evon's young voice was filled with awe.

"I think there's only one of those." Ryn Gylles held a hand to his chest, whether from amazement, hunger, or exhaustion, Serra couldn't guess. "Or the prophecies have been lying to us."

"They've been lying to us a little," Lorne proclaimed, raising Serra's hand high before withdrawing his own, "because there are two at least. One in the flesh, and one born of spirit from you, Janto, and Vesperi."

He stepped aside, leaving her in the center of their group. She missed his warmth beside her instantly. Perhaps the Guard had called a late winter wind down along with the bird.

"Do you think it wanted you to ride it, Lady Serra?" Felia mused. She also grimaced, and Serra reached for her salve to soothe the gash the girl's arm had received from tree branches.

"I doubt anyone's ever ridden that bird," Serra said, pouring some water on to a cloth to clean the wound. *At least not yet.*

Astonishment and the exhaustion of adrenaline's release would soon overtake them, and of course, letter writing to Janto would commence post-haste. But that blue, Madel's blue, within the bird's foremost pair of eyes, had reminded Serra of Her presence and how it had re-energized the Brotherhood ghosts until their service was no longer needed.

It reminded Serra of the dead.

She reflected on the faces turned to her, most smiling through deep breaths of exhaustion. Evon was falling asleep where he stood, clutching his father's waist, despite the excitement. These people knew so little of what following destiny meant, here in their first taste of it. Even Ryn Gylles, who had guided her to her own through dark caves and darker meanings, hadn't experienced it for himself. They hadn't spent years of their lives protecting Lansera, so this was all new, fresh, and thrilling.

But with responsibility came a cost. The proof of that was all over Trop. Their cage of flame had scarred the ground and a few dozen creatures no words could describe were now heaps of ash. It included their own dead comrades like Mar Koma, who didn't know they'd succeeded, couldn't see the proof of it in feathers long as the bodies they lay beside.

Serra bandaged Felia's injury, the salve's mint and grassy notes clearing her head. She was grieved to have to break the group's reverie. But destiny did not wait for celebrations, either.

"Let's take care of our dead and see to everyone's wounds," she announced. "And then we'll take the time to remember this night and why we're doing this, before others try to tell the story for us." She paused, took a deep breath. "Because we're not done yet, Silver

Guard. Not until every jurgen's been tossed back where it came, every fissure's been sealed off, and Esye glows again. We've work to do yet."

"And the bird will lead us," Lorne whispered in her ear.

Serra didn't respond. She was already counting heads.

PART TWO
MOONRISE

When leaps the mighty cantalere,
the dark brother drains his foes.
The Guard must ring the beastly lair
Where battles end their roam.

Their force combined will call the air.
Only then will fly the doe.
Or brother be taken unaware.
By silver power returned home.

CHAPTER TWENTY-FOUR
Vesperi

In the town of Tilayne, Vesperi watched as the advers were taken away, each in shackles, by the Lanserim army. Fear shot Adver Votan's violet pupils through with a deep purple hue, as he was loaded onto one of the wagons. Vesperi remembered how vacant those same eyes had appeared under the thrall of the Guj's wizards. Nothing the Lanserim would do to him could compare to that terror. Likely, they wouldn't hurt a hair on his head, just his pride, by keeping him in those cells.

She resented that. Briefly, she pictured what she might do to elicit further confessions, had she still possessed the weapon. How easy it would be to massage the silver flame into a fine tool of torture for humans. She'd been raised to prize such ruthlessness. But when she imagined Izzy watching her . . . Vesperi shuddered.

As they returned to Terella's glasshouses, the path was lined with villagers, some who prostrated themselves with elbows raised so high, she feared they might tip over. To smile at them convincingly, Vesperi pretended they were all Izzy, presenting her with a stick figure drawing or painted rock. It didn't matter what it was—imagining that Izzy had made it just for her was what brought the smiles forth. Someday their affection would be Izzy's by right, and Vesperi's performance helped ensure that reality. She knew she had little to offer these people herself.

It had been four days since she'd used Esye's light to reveal the full prophecy. Four days, and no sign that doing so had accomplished anything except give her a momentary superiority complex. She was growing anxious, no matter how certain they would find Izzy, bring her home. But doing so did not depend solely on herself, and Vesperi wasn't so good at trusting others. There had been no news from Serra—the Silver Guard might not succeed at their task. What then?

I will gather the Guard and compel them to try again, cantaleres and dark brothers be damned.

Hamsyn's sister and her staff awaited their arrival outside the glass-houses. Terella's long, grayish-blond hair parted over her shoulders. Over her pants and tunic, she wore an apron with gray levere and silver threads embroidered into a sparkling portrait of a full Esye—Vesperi was not the only one who hungered for the moon's presence.

Janto dismounted first and extended Vesperi a hand. She considered rejecting it but knew the villagers would view that as more of an affront than an act of gender parity. Lanserim were all about helping folks to their feet, not throwing women down on theirs.

"Terella." Janto gave her a warm hug. Vesperi went for her fallowent to avoid doing the same—she'd never feel comfortable exchanging affection as openly as Janto did, though she did like the Green Lady.

Terella's cheeks pinked as they swallowed their fingerfuls, and Vesperi remembered that feeling, the pride she felt at observing her own handiwork whenever she cleared out a claren wave. Terella had disseminated fallowent bushes throughout Lansera, saving many.

She was about to add another trophy to her collection.

"The plant with the black blossoms," Vesperi said, "you'll need to grow many more of them." Vesperi might not feel a queen, but giving commands came naturally.

"Symphony," Terella said, her eyes lighting up. "Why is that, my queen?"

Janto filled her in on its properties. "And I suspect brewing a cup may help folks deal with the lack of Esye's light, until we discover how to restore it. It certainly helped us appeal to the advers we sent on their way to Callyn's prisons. They'd been—"

The crowd reacted to that word—adver—with dismay, and Janto raised a hand, much like Vesperi had seen his father do many times to command quiet.

"The threat has been contained," he said. "Do not fear—the advers here have been removed." In a whisper for her and Terella's ears only, he added, "Perhaps we need more of that tea now . . ."

With a note of hurry in her voice, Terella waved them in. "We'll discuss how to propagate it." She closed the door behind them. To her staff, she ordered, "Wait here."

Vesperi ignored a tingle of apprehension; they had just disposed of a plot against the king, after all.

"The blossoms didn't used to be black," Terella said, heedless that she ran her fingers over her apron's embroidery. "They used to be transparent, before Esye went dark." She walked fast, and Vesperi folded her riding cloak over her arm to avoid tripping over it. "You could hold them up to the sunlight, and it would shine right through."

They reached a table full of the symphony plants. The leaves did possess an opalescent tinge of colors like the tea, but the blossoms . . . they pulled at her, made Vesperi feel nauseous.

Terella cut off a snip and held it up to the light. Nothing shone through. They left a void, a visual trick like those paintings of concave angles—Vesperi had tried to duplicate one once with her topiary experiments and failed.

Terella rubbed her finger over the cutting's stubby petals and the black came right off. She held it up again. The sunlight came through, highlighting each of its many delicate veins with a sparkling rainbow. The petal itself was translucent, minus the barest kiss of cream.

"A fungus," Janto exhaled, reaching for another blossom with which to do the same.

"A parasite," Vesperi offered, "draining its host." She withdrew further from the bushes. They made her uneasy, much, much different from Sielban's tea. As though, if she observed the blackness too long, she might see herself within it.

"Closer to that," Terella said. "No success, right, my king?"

Janto held up the still-black flower he'd touched, his expression puzzled.

"Your teacher's tea must have been harvested before Esye disappeared," Terella mused. "We stumbled upon this discovery—young Koren did actually, you remember her?"

Vesperi nodded.

"Koren had been collecting water from a pool that had formed out there—" Terella pointed at a fenced-off area outside the glasshouses, and then she blushed, a surprising reaction. "Serra told me to block the area off, and I did, but I didn't think a child would sneak beneath."

Janto patted her hand with reassurance. "Why did Serra ask you to do that?"

"A portal had opened up, she said. It wasn't safe."

"And Koren did like any child might and slipped through to play with the mysterious new pool of water in the middle of a field with no melted snow?" Vesperi offered. Perhaps Izzy had done the same in the swamplands and fallen through.

Terella nodded. "I had to wring that information out of her when I noticed what happened to the symphony bush she'd watered with it, that the black coloring went away when touched. But only on the one bush."

More things than the symphony bushes thirsted for what could be found in the other realm. Vesperi had half a mind to run out to that area, bounce around it again and again until she went through, though she was as apt to break her neck falling down.

A muffled clamor made its way into the glasshouse. They spun to find the crowd in disarray. Two-thirds of their necks were craned toward the sky, though another third was sprinting fast back to the town in retreat.

A shadow fell across several rows of Terella's seedlings, and Vesperi found herself sprinting to the door. She flung it open, Janto on her heels.

Awe filled his voice. "They did it."

Vesperi felt a different emotion, almost a choking sensation as she realized she *could* feel pride in her brother, that Uzziel had played a part in this prophecy fulfillment.

The scene played out like a mirror of the day Esye went dark, everyone's heads trained skyward as the shadow grew. Tears filled Vesperi's eyes. They did not burn like the many she'd spilled over Izzy and her miscarried child. Rather, they sent release through her body, her muscles and limbs relaxing for the first time in months. Was this what the rynnas felt when they meditated, this floating exultation?

No. It couldn't be this. Because Vesperi was completely sure no temple ritual had called forth the three-headed bird of creation before. That had been the work of the Silver Guard.

"Crr-owk!"

The sound coursed through her, and she shielded her ears as the bird passed low overhead. Janto squeezed her hand, but she could not say if he pivoted her way, too enraptured with the sight before her.

The bird landed near the fenced-off section of meadow and tucked its wings to its sides. It was the size of an Elstonian fishing boat, each tail feather a different hue of colors she'd never seen before, except for the ethereal sheens on Braven, under the tea's spell. She'd name them red, yellow, blue, and white but the words were not strong enough to convey their hues. No wonder the Lanserim used so much metallic thread in their craftsmanship, if only to capture a reflection of this. She felt she might go blind if she stared too long but could not force herself to look away.

Its three heads inspected her and Janto, whose eyes had gone large as watermelons. The crowd parted as they approached it. One of the bird's heads nuzzled another, releasing a flurry of pearlescent down.

Close, Vesperi could hear the creature purr, feel it in her core, and a laugh of delight sprang out of her. Janto broke his gaze at last, and he gave her a brilliant smile as the creature took a step toward them. Vesperi raised her elbows in welcome, and the middle head rubbed its feathers against her forearm. It felt softer than Izzy's skin at her birth, a feat she would have declared impossible once. How many times had she cried, unsure if she'd ever feel it again?

"Go on then," Janto said, and he kissed her lips like a parting gift. "Get on it."

"What?" Vesperi turned to him with disbelief.

The bird tucked its legs beneath itself and purred louder. *It cannot want me to mount it?* She did not understand what was happening.

"The flame must fly to be found again. That's what my father said, remember? And the prophecy, *then will fly the doe*." Janto whispered in her ear, "You are still the weapon, my love. Now wield it."

Vesperi felt a charge akin to the flame's churning, though no silver sparked in her hand. She thought, instead, that it may have in her heart.

Then she rolled her eyes at her own sentimentality. "And what am I to do with it? How will riding this . . . this thing—"

The bird chuffed and shook its middle head.

"—bird, I'm sorry, bird," she eyed it cautiously for any further signs of displeasure, "how will riding this bird accomplish anything?"

"I trust no one more to find out."

Vesperi found she believed him, and maybe, maybe she believed in herself a little too. She remembered the Rasselerians' gift, that glass carving of a swan rising to the sky. But—"Your coronation?"

Janto smiled, and in it, Vesperi could see their future again. "It can wait. You won't be long, will you?" He winked.

She kissed him in return, holding his head between her hands as she took her fill of his love and desire. Then she blinked in awe at the shape her new destiny took before bridging the distance between herself and it.

Three heads bobbed as she neared, each neck thick as she was round, yet able to gracefully curve. The feathers covering them were dense and tipped with silver that shined with welcome. Vesperi planted a foot on an outstretched wing and began to climb.

"Let's go, Three-Headed Bird." She grimaced. "Oh no, that won't do. Three-B, how's that?"

The three heads gave her three disdainful reactions.

Janto laughed from below.

"Three-B it is," Vesperi declared, not one to give ground to others' silly pride. Only her own.

When she'd settled herself between its shoulder blades, the middle head arced round to her and clucked.

"To Izzy," Vesperi said, "whatever it takes."

The head lolled up and down in seeming agreement. Its mass, and Vesperi, rose higher.

"I'll bring her home," she called out to Janto as the bird began to run.

"I'm counting on it," he yelled back.

The wind blew through her hair as she flew.

CHAPTER TWENTY-FIVE
Serra

On the meadow outside Trop, three pyres stood ready to burn. It felt appropriate for the Guard to use their united flames for the act. The Meduans among them had put forth the idea; secret fires had often been used to memorialize their loved ones, as the lords of Medua did not allow commoners funeral honors. Ertions also practiced burial by fire. There was something elemental about it, something lingering in the zeitgeist from before Madel's defeat of the ancient gods.

Though the ryns and rynnas had searched, no appropriate bell could be found in the town's ruins to use for the ritual. They would make do. Nap and Flivio came to collect Serra once the wood was piled high enough. They approached the gathered Guard circle with solemnity. Two Rasselerians made space between them.

Guard members spoke in turn about their fallen compatriots, at least those who knew them well enough to contribute a "mighty fine Sloshed Ryn player" or "not a bad sort, for a Meduan," superlatives gleaned from the two weeks they'd spent together. Serra shed a few tears before they'd all had their say, touched by the homespun tributes.

The Guard waited on her once the remembrances fell silent. Pride welled in her chest, that she was granted the honor to see these heroes to their rest, an honor given to those who had earned their people's respect. She had not known she still craved that.

Serra waved her hand, encompassing the side-by-side pyres. The

Guard raised their arms as one, flipped over their hands, and extended their pointer fingers.

Nothing happened. Not a lick of the flame passed over a single palm.

"What?"

Nothing, except for an explosive unease.

"What's going on?"

Felia shook her hand as though it'd gone numb. Ryn Gylles stared at his own, his face blank.

"It's just . . . gone?"

Others tried again with no success. Flaring tempers and frustration threatened to break the reverent mood they'd cultivated. Perhaps, their task done, Madel had withdrawn the power from the Silver Guard. They were no longer needed.

But a glance at the sky confirmed Esye's continuing absence, as did the dullness of the nighttime glow. Mar Koma's warning for Janto replayed in Serra's head. Lansera was not out of danger. Most of the cantaleres were gone, but how long would that last? They hadn't sealed the fissures they'd come through. Nor had the disappeared people returned. And when Serra used the sight, the dark pockets advanced, clouding her vision as though a shifting pattern glimpsed through a dirtied kaleidoscope lens.

A golden glow, reminiscent of Oro's moonslight, drew Serra's attention back to the pyres. A torch ablaze in his hand, Lorne stepped away from the second one, the first already lit. Wordlessly, the pregnant Meduan, Lari, stepped forward to light the last. The flames' radiance accentuated her belly's curves.

The rest of the Guard stopped arguing, the spell of their unity holding them together a little while longer. The trio of flames took Serra back to a childhood memory of Gavenstone. She'd sat in front of the fireplace in their parlor, playing a game with Agler. She couldn't have been more than five, and in her minds-eye, their parents were no more than a blur on the chaise behind the children, drinking wine. But she remembered the delight of making it to the opposite end of the board and Agler turning her piece into a princess. He must have let her win; she'd never have beaten him at that age.

The thought conjured up a warmth she had long missed. Serra had loved her big brother, but couldn't remember a time when they'd gotten along, when he had shown her kindness. His later irritation, whenever she came home for a visit, was what lingered in her memories, and the malice and desperation of the man he'd become.

A longing to walk those halls filled her, to find that game and run her fingers over the hash marks etched on each square. She smiled and couldn't remember ever doing so before when thinking of Gavenstone as home.

The group dispersed, each lost in their own thoughts. Uzziel rested beside her on a stretcher. Sar Mertina had made it of rope and branches bound together by elaborate, strong knots. His face pale, he drank a warming broth she'd prepared to boost his constitution after last night's events.

"I saw them in town, in Sellwyn," he said. "Bonfires like this. From my window. I didn't know why they'd been lit, just that they had a dreadful smell that made me wretch. Father told me the village women did it to punish their children who refused to leave for the labor camps when they came of age. They'd burn them for bringing such dishonor to their wombs, Father said.

"I demanded the women be hung for such a thing—building fires without permission and for denying my father the right to use his hanging tree instead." Uzziel paused, and shame flushed his face. "I was just angry they made me ill. Father ignored my request, and when I challenged him, he said, 'There are lines we cannot cross with our thralls, if we want to keep them in our grip.' I didn't understand what he meant then."

"Do you now?" Serra prodded, wondering if his shame stemmed from the request he'd made or his father's denial of it. Would Uzziel grow up to become one of the Meduans Mar Koma had detested or one that had renewed her faith in their humanity?

Uzziel lowered his head. That was answer enough for now.

The sound of rock clanking against rock brought them back to the present. Ryn Gylles had fashioned a sort of bell from a bowl-shaped stone and another rock, long enough to bring forth a sound, any sound, against it.

Words flowed from Serra's lips.

"May they rest in the cobalt flame."

The chant repeated from one member of their group to the next, ending in rounds that evoked the power the Guard had displayed the night before.

"May they rest in the cobalt flame."

"May they rest in the cobalt flame."

The Meduans mouthed the words, eyes darting about like hers used to when she'd been too young to behave during rituals. That memory amused her, and she wondered what their childhoods had been like, whether they too had once had an older brother who loved swinging them by the arms.

"A penny for your thoughts," Lorne asked, as the group began the walk back to the Guard Glen. Napeler and Mertina hoisted Uzziel up on the stretcher, taking care to avoid the muddiest patches of clover and grass that had sprung up overnight.

By way of an answer she asked, "Would you have taken your sister with you from Granich Manor, if you could have back then?" *Are we the same people we always were? Was the Agler who let me win the same who tried to kill the king?*

Lorne took her hand and drew her away from the others. He grimaced as he talked, his wounds still painful from the koparin stampede. "If Madel had asked me to, yes, I would have. But I'm not sure I had a moral compass back then, not without Her guidance."

"And you do now?"

The pyres' light flickered in his eyes. Again, she found silence to be answer enough.

"Do you think Vesperi will welcome him?" she asked softly.

No name was needed. "I think, if Izzy returns, she will want to know her uncle. And I think Vesperi cannot resist anything that child asks."

"May Madel's hand guide her home."

"May we all have homes to be guided to." Lorne lifted Serra's chin, and though he made no move to kiss her, Serra moved away from the intensity of his gaze.

"Serra—" he started.

She held up a hand to stop his impulsive plea. She was not ready to handle it, not with the rest of the Guard wondering what their next move should be. Not when her duties remained with them. "We have to figure out next steps. The dark brother . . ."

Lorne gave her an exaggerated curtsy. "Just so, my lady. The country first, of course."

She ignored the bitter edge of his words as they walked. Awhile later, she found it mirrored in the pine resin notes of a warmed ale someone passed her as they neared the camp.

They gathered around campfires to share bread and more ale. Ryn Colini spoke, "I think the Guard has been decommissioned. We are of no use rounding up stray cantaleres or jurgens without the silver flame."

"The army should be able to handle that," Sar Mertina said. "With the main herd gone, they'll be less of a threat."

"I wonder," Rall mused, Evon sitting on his knee, "if we can be so sure our mission is complete. The bird is out there, who knows where. And it's not as though the kingdom is without threats."

Lari's husband Sim used sharper words. "And what threats would you say those are, *Lanserim*? Have we not served faithfully with you here, responded when called by our shared king? Lari and I could have remained in Kallon, minding our own business, and letting her rest until our child was born. But where would your precious Guard have been then?"

Serra groaned at Rall's misstep. "He did not mean to imply—"

Lari cut her off. "That's part of the problem, Lady Gavenstone, this make-believe. Because he *did* mean to imply it. Did you not, Rall Basilo?"

Rall stared over the top of his son's head and gave a slight nod, chagrined.

The Deduin man picked up the argument. "If you Lanserim would admit to your prejudices, we could make a lot more progress understanding each other. And I say that as a person not so well tolerated by Meduans, either. By any of you in these lands where leaves turn green."

Serra's cheeks colored. "Your point is taken." She took another sip, considered how the ale's kick of cinnamon and calming lavender scent brought balance to the cup. "I will try to be more honest myself."

Lorne gave a sharp laugh at that. "I'm sorry," he lied, "a koparin just caught its own tail." He pointed into the darkness. Flivio spun to look, but Serra knew Lorne was covering for his brittleness.

"Regardless," Serra said, "I do think we achieved our purpose here. I think it passed to the bird the moment your flame came out of its mouths."

"So we disband?" Felia asked. Serra did not miss the disappointment in her voice, nor the wistful look Uzziel cast her way.

"Yes," she agreed. "You are no longer a full complement. I'm not sure the Guard can exist, or should exist, if missing any of its components."

A Rasselerian leaned forward. "I think learning that lesson was also part of our purpose here."

Others nodded, and Serra let those words sink in. Each of these people, disparate yet united by the barest of threads, had come when the kingdom needed them, and they formed a greater whole together.

"You should be proud," she said, raising her voice. "Of what you've accomplished here, all of you. And of who you were before the Guard. They are one and the same—*you* are one and the same, then and now. I hope all Lanserim will learn the truth of that in the days ahead. Including myself. I hope the Silver Guard will spread that message wherever they go."

She peeked at Lorne, but he had removed himself from the gathering, off "watching koparin," no doubt. At least he committed to his untruths. *Can I blame him when the truth can hurt so much?*

Serra finished her mug, clinking it down on one of Drustalla's broken columns. "Let's figure out in the morning who needs a guard for the journey home and who might travel together."

Felia asked, "Where will you go, Lady Serra?"

"To Callyn." Serra hadn't considered another option. "The king and queen need to know about the bird's appearance and your success. The pigeons we sent last night may not find them before they return home for the coronation. And I will want to share my report of what happened personally as well." *And make certain no poison makes its way there first.*

"And then?" Felia, no doubt, was simply curious, but the prodding cut like little knives at Serra's flesh. She glanced at Lorne's shadowed form.

"Where the king directs me, I guess. Lansera still needs protecting."

The group disbanded, some folks rising for bed, others for another mug of ale. Felia hesitated a moment longer, before swinging in close to Serra and whispering, "What about the younger Lord Granich, my lady? Won't you . . . won't you be going back with him?"

Serra suffered a loss for words. "We aren't . . . it's not like that."

Felia colored to a deep tomato hue that firelight brightened. "Oh, I'm sorry. I didn't mean to—"

"It's fine, Felia. Get some sleep."

The girl scurried off and Serra served herself a third round, longing for the alcohol to induce sleep before she did anything she'd regret. *Too late.*

Longing prodded her to approach Lorne. He'd withdrawn just beyond the first row of crumbling walls. She spoke fast, before she lost her nerve, "Lorne, will you come with me to Callyn?"

His lip curled into a dare, the gesture intensified by the cuts that marred it. "Why?"

Serra paused, opened her mouth.

You'll regret it, the moment you're on the road.

A third voice spoke—*that* voice, the one she'd thought she'd banished back in Mova. She glanced around quickly before remembering it was in her head.

"Serra?" Lorne's question hung in the air. "Why do you want me to come to Callyn?"

Yes, Serra, why would you lower yourself that far?

She found, even fueled by ale, that she was not yet brave enough for such a challenge. Face an invisible plague and a murderous regime? Lead a hodge-podge force through obscure prophecy and call forth a mythical creature? Yes, yes, and yes. But this?

"I would like to have another account to give Janto and Vesperi. A Meduan version to supplement my own."

It was *a* truth, just not the one Lorne had asked for. Not the one she was still too scared to examine herself.

His gaze was on her, cold in a way that pierced her core. He tossed his full head of hair. "No, I don't think so, Lady Serrafina."

He placed a hand on her shoulder to guide her back to the fire. "I'm heading to Lake Ashra. Perhaps you can take the Deduins with you? I'd bet they'd welcome further respite from the cold."

She shouldn't have been surprised he'd made plans without her, but she was. And it hurt, though she had no right for it to. "Lake Ashra?"

"Yes." Lorne made himself space between two of the Rasselerians on a log. He slapped an arm around each one's shoulder. "My mates here have been teaching me about relic hunting. Perhaps I can find another piece with the Granich sigil. Have a pair someday to share with my sister."

The Rasselerians' suits swirled with the reds and oranges of the fire. "And the meditation. Don't forget that, Lorne of Granich." An amused giggle passed between them. Serra refrained from guessing what, exactly, entertained them so.

"Oh yes, that too." Lorne smiled, bright as the day they'd met, when he'd been talking fast and charming harder to save his skin. "I thought I had my future figured out until recently. Now, I find myself in need of Madel's guidance, so I will learn how to best seek it. I'm a quick study."

Serra remembered how his lips had felt on her palm that day, when he'd kissed it in greeting despite the bindings on his hands and legs. He'd flirted with her even then, before he knew who she was or what she could do. And she'd loved it.

Lorne Granich has ever been a threat to me.

She needed no extra voice to tell her that.

"Makes perfect sense," she acquiesced, keeping her tone light as she could. She decided to retire to bed after all, though rest would only come after hours of tossing and turning. Tomorrow, they would part ways again, and for the first time in ages, she couldn't bear the thought of it.

A good choice, nonetheless. He's not the equal of you.

She could not deny those words were true, though not in the way her inner doubts supposed. Lorne deserved better than the coward she'd become.

CHAPTER TWENTY-SIX

Vesperi

After a few hours, flying on a giant bird was not quite as amazing as Vesperi had thought it might be. She tucked the fabric of her cloak around her arms for the millionth time and was grateful she'd given up skirts after running away to Lansera. Regardless, the fabric did little to resist the wind. On the ground, it had been spring and warm enough for a picnic, but up here? Cold enough to freeze the hair off Saeth's fist.

I ought to find new swear words. Knowing Saeth had been a ruse of the advers reduced the thrill of invoking his name. But she couldn't imagine calling out for Madel's hand in anger, not when she knew Madel brought blessings and safety rather than suffering. *At least on the whole.*

A squawk from the bird's central head sent Vesperi scrambling for a better grip. She must have started to doze off. Who'd have thought such a thing possible on an adventure like this? She needed to believe in the impossible right then, needed to continue having every faith this bird would take her to her daughter.

Right now, it was taking her over the bare plateaus of Ertion. The mountains loomed close, though the sun bouncing off their snowcaps made her vision blurry . . .

Another squawk, this one accompanied by the bird's right head swooping up and lassoing her to its body with its long neck. She gave the head a solid scratch of thanks. It cooed at her, flipping almost upside-down.

"Can you talk?" Vesperi hoped. "It would keep me awake." She licked her lips; they were cracking from the brisk winds.

The creature said nothing in response. Vesperi sighed. "Three-B, this won't do." It blinked, revealing a third eyelid that gleamed red as a polished ruby. Its gaze had a calming presence, like Serra's, and Vesperi laughed while considering which of the heads was hers. *The central one with silver crown feathers, of course.* Anything else would deal her pride a mighty blow.

Her eyes ached from the sun's brightness in this atmosphere, but she thought she could make out something on the horizon. Something shimmering same as the rift at Dever Albrecht's funeral.

The bird picked up speed, maybe re-energized by the sight of a portal to its realm. Why couldn't it have used the one in Tilayne and spared her this bracing journey? Maybe this one would take her closer to where Izzy had disappeared.

Her heart beat faster. If they were truly going in, then Izzy was closer than she'd been in so long. Vesperi prayed it true, and she swore she saw a flash of deep blue within the fissure. They headed for it at an alarming pace. Or maybe—Vesperi couldn't be sure—maybe it was coming closer to them as well.

They flew through. Humidity bathed her arms, a shock after the coldness of the high atmosphere. The bird kept flying, dodging the treetops of the forest they'd flown into. The greenery felt alive, like she could feel it breathe while zooming through the tree trunks. The colors were gorgeous. She imagined Izzy naming each hue. The grove of smaller trees they'd passed? Teeny green! The flowers dotting the trees now, enormous ones to appear so detailed at this height? Radical red! Vesperi had thought the colors glinting off the bird's feathers were too vibrant to be real, but here, they fit right in.

They flew at a more moderate speed now; perhaps the creature felt content being home, but Vesperi would not be until her daughter was back in her arms. She raised a hand and stroked the neck keeping her secured. Its head made a sound like a chortling purr and the neck twisted around her way. Eyes the size of her fist, striped silver and gold with black pupils, attended her. They were positioned about six inches apart, the eyes of a predator.

The thought made Vesperi feel safe—she was among her kind.

But she didn't know how to communicate with it. "Izzy? Daughter?" She sounded like an idiot, but how was she to know if the bird preferred complete sentences?

The look her clipped phrasing drew was clear disdain; Vesperi was certain she could reproduce it perfectly. Sentences, then. "My daughter, Izzy. Do you know where she is, Three-B?" Merely asking the question raised her spirits.

Not that it mattered. Three-B narrowed its eyes, as though daring her to say whatever she wished—it would not answer. Vesperi huffed. "The moon Esye is gone from Lansera, Three-B. We need to get it back, and my daughter, and the silver flame. I think you're here to help. I have no idea how we'll do it, and I have no idea where they might be, but I'm hoping you have flown me between *worlds*," she emphasized those last two words with a motherly glare, "for more than a joy ride."

Third eyelids closed in like a lens shuttering. *The nerve.* Irritated, Vesperi flipped her right hand over and jabbed it forward, palm up, as if she could compel the silver flame to express her frustration. Of course, nothing happened. She groaned, feeling stupid for the habitual instinct, for trying to get a bird to understand what she needed. But as she hid her head between her hands, Three-B responded from deep within its chest, letting loose a sound closer to a roar than a chirp. Its leftmost head twisted back to join the right one, those eyes a bold copper. Then the head opened its beak with a stream of fast chatter.

The explosion of sound nearly caused Vesperi to lose her grip. She opened her palm again, rolled her finger out and . . . the heads bobbed up and down like ducks fishing on a pond. Three-B had some sort of connection with the silver flame, liked it when she called for it, even when nothing came out. Vesperi was dumbfounded.

The heads swung fast into a streamlined position around the central one—they were about to move fast. She grabbed on to a clump of skin beneath the feathers and held tight.

‡

In the haze of a golden morning, Vesperi woke to find herself on a bed of damp, grassy material. Had she fallen off the bird? A scan revealed Three-B a few feet away, its heads curled in on itself, and she remembered landing, barely. Remembered she had searched groggily around for Izzy, through the surrounding foliage and its faint bioluminescence that dimmed as the sun rose. And she'd fallen fast asleep.

Vesperi yawned, stretched, and went to relieve herself behind some nearby bushes, if these fuzz-covered globs of flora could be called bushes. Her stomach growled, but she was not fool enough to eat plants unknown to her in Lansera, much less this realm. At least not since she'd run away from Sellwyn, desperate and alone.

The canopy was covered in the same blossoms they had passed overhead the day before. They hung from the trees like blankets airing out in the sun. She plucked one, and plopped it on her head, entertained that it was large enough to pass for a hat. Perhaps she would start a new fashion craze back home in Callyn. The queen decrees flower hats for everyone!

Vesperi was becoming aware she felt a tad loopy.

Something shuffled off to her right, and she also learned she was farther than she'd like to be from Three-B and its mighty claws and curved beaks. She took a deep breath and ran past whatever jurgen or giant spider might be about to snatch her head away along with the flower.

Three-B raised itself from its pseudo nest, its feathers revealing their rainbow luster once it fluttered its wings. The bird squawked as she drew close but not at her. At the something beyond her. Something that probably had fangs and stingers and—

"Hello!"

Vesperi turned fast as a spinner. "A human?" And then, "Oh, I said that out loud." Finally, "I need breakfast."

Her legs gave way beneath her and she plopped to the ground.

Pleasant laughter spilled forth from the woman who'd come out from within some ferns. She looked of age with Vesperi, or perhaps a little older. Her garment's hue, ruffled as though a cloud of gauzy fabric, was much drabber than their surroundings.

"You're from Madel's realm, aren't you?" the woman said.

Vesperi's mouth fell open. "I'm sorry? This is closer to Madel's realm than where I'm from."

The woman laughed again, clasping a hand over her mouth. "Oh my," she said. "I suppose it is from your perspective."

Vesperi rummaged through her pouch, certain sustenance would stop this hallucination. Scratchy leather and a coil of string met her fingers, nothing else. Her mind hadn't been on supplies yesterday, when Three-B flew down from the heavens to get her.

"Here." The woman held out a rounded baked good that was a brighter yellow than a lemon. A strip of tantalizingly purple jelly ran through its middle.

Vesperi's suspicious nature made her hesitate. The woman took a bite from one end, and Vesperi remembered Janto doing the same to a sandwich when they'd first met and she had been his captive.

She took the item and bit into its spongy dough in the same movement. *Orgasmic.* She wouldn't be telling Janto about this.

"Do you have another?"

The woman nodded and a second appeared in her hand like a magic trick. Or maybe it *was* magic.

"Lansera," Vesperi said, once she'd paused eating enough for breath.

"Pardon?" The woman cocked her head.

"Where I'm from? Lansera. It's not where Madel lives, but She visits us, sends us Her hand to help." Vesperi likewise held the baked good to Three-B, but its heads lifted their beaks to the air. The bird chuffed its disapproval.

"Oh, I had forgotten the name!" the woman said. "Lansera flows so nicely from the tongue, doesn't it?"

Vesperi wasn't awake enough for such bubbliness. Neither was Three-B, if its wandering away into the woods was any indication. "I guess."

"Well, why are you here, Lanserim? Are you searching for Madel?"

Vesperi choked on her bread. The idea that she might stumble across the goddess here hadn't crossed her mind.

"I'm afraid She's been gone a while," the woman continued. "You might try checking with one of the others—they keep better track of Her comings and goings than I've been able to. Why Onsic's been practically holding court lately, he's gotten so strong. People can't help but be drawn to him."

She was smiling, though it was faint, as though she'd forgotten how not to. Or maybe it was the vacant stare of someone who referred to the moons as though they were people. Things were strange here.

"Do find a better coat if you go to see him," the woman continued. "The absence of light, you know. Gets cold."

She performed an exaggerated shiver, and Vesperi doubted the smile was genuine. It reminded her of the ones Serra gave when they'd gone on hunting trips and she'd rather have been canoodling with Lorne, their relationship still new, than chasing down claren.

"You're funny, the way your thoughts jump all over," the woman said.

"You're reading them?"

"Oh, sorry. I didn't mean to be rude."

"More like . . . unexpected."

"You must not be one of the ones Madel blessed then. It's so hard to know what's happening through the gossamer between our realms, you know."

Not blessed? But Vesperi was one head of the bird, the fulfillment of prophecy! And that bird was right over there, roughing up dirt to find worms. *Okay, maybe not so blessed.*

The more this woman talked, the more Vesperi's confusion grew. "You speak as though Madel's a friend, not a goddess. Is She not so powerful here?"

The woman opened and closed her mouth. "Oh. Oh, I'm sorry. I'm making things worse, aren't I? That's what Onsic's been saying. I should have kept resting, but I heard you shuffling about, and it's been so long since I had the energy to talk with anyone else, and . . . Yes, Madel is powerful here, the most powerful force there is. But it's *your* world She protects, not ours." She touched her head. "Well, that's not strictly true, is it? It just feels that way sometimes. I'm sure Onsic could explain it to you—he always does make a lot of sense."

"I'm not sure we're talking about the same moo . . . person." The wonder of this experience had dimmed, and Vesperi had made no headway finding her daughter. She didn't want to hear more of what this woman had to say, not if it took her off target.

May as well get to the point. "That's why I'm here. We need Her to come back. It seems the curtain between our worlds is dissolving. People keep disappearing, and—"

"Oh, isn't it exciting? We haven't had so many new people here in so long. I haven't gone out to meet them, of course, not with how I've been feeling, but—"

Finally, some validation for their theory! "So there *are* others, here, other humans? Not just me?" Hope pricked Vesperi's skin like she'd dipped into an Elstonian hot spring.

"Oh yes! They've been gathering near Tansic and Oro—too many of our creatures here might harm them, you know, and their light is so calming. Unlike—"

"How do I get to Tansic and Oro?" If there was a chance Izzy might be there, the slightest potential, Vesperi had to go, no matter the absurdity that her daughter might be spending time with a moon. *Believe it's possible. That's what the Rasselerians told you when they gave you the swan carving. Have you not now flown, too?*

"Oh, that's easy." The woman came closer. With the full sunlight now on them, Vesperi noticed the bags under her eyes and the way she held herself gently, as though she might break with a breeze. It was a mirror image of how Vesperi had felt for months, the handiwork of the soul-sapping grief she'd experienced.

Whatever this woman was going through, Vesperi hoped it would get better for her soon.

"Oh, thank you," the woman said, reading her thoughts again. "I'll be fine. Don't worry about me. I'm not worth worrying about." The woman smiled wider, which strained her lips. "You head out of the woods about a mile that-a-way"—she pointed into the forest—"and then follow the moonslight."

The speaking seemed to diminish her. Compassion, one of those emotions so new to Vesperi, prodded her to ask, "Would you like to come with me?"

The woman withdrew a few steps, shaking her head. "Oh no, no. That's sweet, but . . ."

Vesperi waited as the woman gazed wistfully at the colors blazing through the trees.

". . . I'm not up for it just yet." She hugged herself, revealing hands pockmarked with black spots on her pale skin.

"Thank you," Vesperi offered, "for the information, and the food, and the company."

"Oh, it was almost like talking to myself." This time, the smile reached her eyes.

Vesperi raised her elbows in farewell and walked to Three-B, who'd made fast work of preening itself. A pile of rainbow-tipped feathers lay at its feet. Vesperi supposed three heads made the task easier. She grabbed hold of enough skin to give her purchase, but the three heads wagged left to right.

Hmph. Apparently, she would need to find Tansic and Oro on foot. Well, it wouldn't be the first time Vesperi walked alone through a foreign land.

"You better be here when I come back, Three-B. Izzy and I will need a ride home."

All she got was a *chrrrumph* in reply.

CHAPTER TWENTY-SEVEN

JANTO

When Vesperi took to the sky, Janto almost halted the journey home, ready to wait right there until she returned with Izzy. He had no doubt it would happen—all doubts Izzy was alive, that Vesperi could find her, had vanished the moment he saw that glorious creature in the sky.

The bird's appearance was a good omen, indicating that the Silver Guard's quest had gone well. But he'd had no confirmation. Word would come to Callyn, so he'd continued on. A day after his return, Serra, Flivio, and a pair of Deduins had arrived to fill him in. Serra had confirmed the advers' threat of poison, and Janto made sure everything in the castle would be screened, especially gifts for the coronation.

Back in his quarters after their report, Janto's room felt as murky as his next steps. The prophecy spoke of the silver power returned home, and Janto had no doubt Vesperi would do that, hopefully soon. But how would they take the dark brother unaware? Could they do so of a spectral presence? And how would that restore Esye and bring the balance Sielban spoke of, not to mention Madel Herself?

"I don't have the first idea of what to do, Father," Janto spoke into the empty room. The closed velvet curtains swallowed his words.

But not entirely.

"Do you think your father always did?"

Had the voice not been as familiar to Janto as his own, he might have startled, thinking it the dark brother again. But Janto could make out Ser Allyn's form in the armchair to the left of his bed. Were he not completely sapped of energy after the last few days . . . weeks . . . months, he would have given him the courtesy of greeting. Instead, he flopped back onto the bed.

"Can I kick you out of my bedroom until I get a night's rest?"

Ser Allyn laughed, a remarkable sound because it was rare. "You can. But—and this is not about your grammar, my king, though we can speak about that another time—you *may* is more apt. Ruling is not about following a strict set of rules."

Janto bathed Ser Allyn with his astonishment. "Everything I have ever learned from you has been about the strict set of rules governing me."

"Hm, I can see how it would seem that way."

He flipped onto his side. "*Can* you?" Janto's sarcasm rivaled Flivio's. Seeing his friend had reminded him of its benefits.

Ser Allyn was amused, much to Janto's consternation. "Why yes, I suppose so. But those *cannots* you've been taught were meant to help you decide what you *may* do when you took command. If being the ruler of Lansera were a simple set of guidelines to follow, well, it wouldn't matter who followed them, would it?"

Janto let the weight of those words sink in. "I suppose it wouldn't. But my parents could have had another child, perhaps a sister, who'd be queen right now. Or maybe a brother, far wiser than I, who could better manage combining two peoples who've been so long at enmity."

"Perhaps," Allyn allowed, "but have you ever considered, Slayer of the Silver Stag, King of the Silver Guard, Architect of the Conjoining, that no other Albrecht could have been quite as well-suited for these particular times as you? Your father kept a country together in the aftermath of civil war and built it back to flourishment, which is a remarkable achievement. But he did not live to see cantaleres running through the woods, nor rips in the fabric between worlds, nor, if the rumors preceding you are correct, the bird of creation in the flesh."

A smile rose to Janto's lips. "Three-B."

"What?" Ser Allyn drew his hand to his brow.

"That's its name. Three-B. Vesperi named it before taking off on its back."

Ser Allyn breathed in very deeply, holding his hand at his side as though he had a stitch. "The queen is flying around on the bird of creation . . . whom you have named Three-B?"

Janto sank his head onto the bed, splayed his fingers over the pilling fabric. "I know. We shouldn't have—"

"Shh." Ser Allyn leaned over to rub a hand on Janto's back. "I am certain you did what you thought best. And while it may not be the most conventional"—he paused for emphasis—"choice, I'm certain it will work out. What's the other possibility? That slaying the stag, and your and the queen's complementary temperaments, and your continued closeness to the seer . . . that's all merely happenstance?"

"No, of course not, but—"

"Janto Albrecht, you are not king because you were the sole Albrecht heir left to fill the throne. You are king because Madel knew She needed *you* in that place for *this* here and now. The sooner you realize it, the better for us all."

Janto caught Ser Allyn's arm as the advisor made to leave. He wasn't certain he believed him, but he was glad of his presence. It made his father's absence incrementally easier to bear. "Thank you, Ser Allyn."

The man nodded as he straightened to his full height. On the way out, he peered back. "You have faith in the people around you, don't you, my king?"

"I do."

"Then have faith in the person who chose them to support him." He exited with elbows raised.

Janto considered those people: Napeler, who had served as his right hand for years with honor and friendship; Jerusho, who had dropped his own concerns as Mova's council head to see to Lansera's needs first; Mertina, who had guarded the royal family for decades with grace and strength and was now protecting Uzziel on his overland journey to Callyn, a half-day behind Serra's faster riding pack. And most of all, Vesperi and Serra and his mother, the people who knew him best in this world, including his faults.

They were people he respected, people he loved, and they readily pledged themselves to him and not just out of patriotism. Maybe, just maybe, they weren't fools. Maybe Janto was the right man for the job. Maybe he would find the best strategy for moving forward, help the Lanserim and Meduans come to respect and love each other, learn how their cultures best complemented each other. Their wounds would heal with time.

And I shouldn't be afraid to rock the boat, if the shoreline's in sight. Visiting Sielban did not turn out so badly, after all.

A crack of light snuck past the curtains, falling on the mate of the armchair Ser Allyn had used. High on its back, a carved swan and river snake swam harmoniously in a pond. The chairs had been a wedding gift from Lord Sydley, carved from soft Wasylim cypress. The Old Girl rested beside it, near the door leading to the family's secret outer passageway.

Compared with the ornate handiwork, the bow looked plain, but Janto knew she was anything but. He reached for the weapon and his nearby quiver, thinking some target shooting would help him figure out his next step. But he must have tripped, because his head hit the chair's rim. Or rather it passed *through* the chair's rim, and all of Janto followed, spiraling down, down through a rainbow-tinged hole . . .

. . . he tumbled over his bow and his quiver, as he rolled from what felt like a very tall hill indeed. Janto curled his body around the Old Girl as they spun, to protect it from damage. Something wet and cold glanced against his side before launching him into the air. A spring? A spring made of vegetation?

At least I am not in my sleeping clothes. Janto's thoughts were uncomplicated as he collided with something that felt like a net. The propulsion lobbed him back the other way, but tiny, sticky cilia held him tight. They were made of the strangest material; it rubbed to pieces between his fingers, and thus, he worked his way off. Once safe on the ground—if the spongy moss his body sank into could be called that—he examined his former captor. Not a net, but a formation strung between the trees. Threads thick as his arm composed the web, their coloring greener than the young, thumb-sized limes that would soon bud in the queensgarden.

Janto had no desire to stick around long enough to discover what might have spun it into being. As he rose, the world spun with him. All around, colors as vivid as those threads assaulted his senses. He spun in confusion, their brilliance hurting his head, and landed over his feet again on the spongy ground covering. The brightness of light forced his eyes closed.

A few morsels of grass touched his lips, and Janto bolted upright on tasting their sharp sweetness, like a sugar-dipped lemon wedge. The shock opened his eyes, though the light's intensity made his head pound.

At least the spongy stuff smelled okay, kind of like steamed milk. He stayed where he was, fleetingly content to contemplate how similar the moss was to cauliflower heads, if those were a dazzling green. When his senses calmed, Janto remembered his bow . . . then being in his room in Callyn . . . and that Serra had arrived, and he bolted upright.

His fingers grasped in a panic, reaching for the Old Girl but coming to land instead on a scaly root . . . a root with a thick, sturdy claw coming out of it that clinked against his wedding ring. Something else pecked at his cheek.

Janto locked eyes with one head of the bird of creation. It chittered and bobbed, examining him before something else caught its attention. Three heads swerved, and the bird began running at it with a loping gait.

Janto scrambled to his feet, yelling, "Vesperi! Izzy? Izzy!" but there was no answer, no sign of his family. What else could he do but follow the bird—Three-B. Perhaps it meant to lead him to them. Janto ran. One of Three-B's necks slid up and under him, then rolled him unto its back. Another had the Old Girl and his quiver grasped securely in its looping folds. That one regarded him with something like contempt in its silver and blue eyes.

Ah, yes, he recognized its shared spirit with Vesperi. Janto chuckled.

"Thank you," he managed, grasping for purchase through the feathers. "And what am I doing here, Three-B?"

The bird chuffed at the name. It released a series of grunts and clicks that Janto was certain expressed its sincere consternation. Which was entirely unfair.

"*You* brought me here." His appearance right by the bird could not be a coincidence.

Janto took Three-B's three-toned *crr-owk* as acknowledgment.

"Where's Vesperi? My daughter? Do they need help?"

In response, Three-B took a few steps back, then launched itself into a gallop and then the sky. Once they'd cleared the hill Janto had slid down, Three-B soared over a valley. Janto knew then for certain that he'd passed into the other realm, this world so closely connected with his own, yet so little understood. The horizon was indistinct, shifting if he tried to focus too hard on any one point of it. The valley below reminded him of the view of Braven from the cave he and his fellow muraters had slept in. At times on the island, they'd shifted between Lansera and here, though Janto hadn't understood that then. The treetops' edges were fuzzy as piled cotton balls. Their colors were anything but: thrushberry indigo, the brightest orange egg yolks, and others he could not place.

"Are we headed to Vesperi, Three-B? Or Izzy?" *Please, Madel, may the bird be taking me straight to them.*

Three-B dipped in the air, and the temperature warmed a few degrees. Its wings clipped the tree's edges, which rustled delightfully. But Janto's high spirits shriveled as they sped past the topiary and the temperature dropped fast. The problem wasn't the giant herd of cantaleres beyond it, copper sparking from their horns as they ran toward a distant shore. It was something within a broad glen lined by multitudes of fern and skinny trees with long, narrow, and glowing green leaves.

He didn't understand what natural laws governed this land, but he knew, sure as his hackles raised, that the giant shifting hole at that glen's center was *not right*. An oval, it spanned perhaps the width of four horses and height of his father's tower study at Castle Callyn. It possessed no color, just a void. Beyond, or perhaps within it, Janto glimpsed a dimmer version of the brilliant environment surrounding him. A mirror, maybe, except instead of reflecting their surroundings, it took them in, as though the brilliant vivacity of this world drained into it.

It felt wrong, askew, out of place. Yet the void tugged at Janto, nonetheless.

No, not a void. An abyss, like in Father's dream.

"Can't you attack it? Like the canteleres?" Janto demanded of Three-B. The bird was surely more capable of beating back the abyss than he—it was Madel's weapon, one of Her first creations. It belonged in this world, unlike him. "Why haven't you? Why is it allowed here? It's . . . it's wrong."

Janto felt nauseous. He was barely aware he'd been pummeling Three-B's shoulder blades. The thick layers of feathers absorbed his frustration. But the bird registered his rage, because it swerved, mid-wingbeat, and flung them around to observe the abyss from the other side. And that perspective yielded something Janto hadn't thought he'd see again, outside of his dreams.

Two silver stags flanked the abyss. Their antlers blazed with the silver flame. An arc of it came from a great stone that also shone with silver. Oblong and domed, the stone's arcing power fed the stags, which in turn channeled streams of silver into the abyss and the nothing that was something beyond it. From this side, that something dazzled like a galaxy reflected from the surface of a lake.

A breath passed, and Janto gasped as a small area of the void puckered, letting sunlight through. A man stumbled out of the pocket, dressed in a ryn's tunic and mourning ribbons. His head slowly took in his new environment. Dazed, the man collapsed onto one of many stone benches arrayed before the silver stone. Stone benches full of other humans, half a gross at least.

The disappeared, Janto gasped. He glanced, but his daughter was not there.

"Why are you showing me this?" Janto yelled against the wind. Three-B didn't answer, except to shift again when Janto felt himself leaning forward, straining over Three-B's head toward the void, the presence that called to him without saying his name. *My people, I must go to them.* And likely be sucked in and spit out in just the same way, if he did.

Warmer air bathed him as they journeyed away, breaking whatever attraction the void had held. Janto had felt ensorcelled, like Adver Votan at Mandat Hall, when the Guj's wizards had tormented him with an unseen needlestorm. He shuddered to think what might have happened if Three-B hadn't flown away when it did.

They hit the earth, jostling Janto's senses more than they'd already been. The bird landed in an area beyond the fern glades and the Braven trees. Somewhere far from the abyss, Janto hoped, though knowing it existed inspired a primal horror. Whatever it was, it had to be stopped. If it wasn't, then it didn't matter if Vesperi and Izzy returned to him. They would be lost, in the end, with every soul in his kingdom if *that* advanced on them.

A sea's waves lapped at sand that was not sand but mounds of squishy turquoise stones.

"Tell me what to do," Janto implored the bird. "I'm ready. Whatever I can do, the Old Girl and I will."

Not what you can, *but what you* may.

Ser Allyn's words rose to the forefront of Janto's mind. He pondered the lesson. What did it mean when he didn't know his options? When each step in this strange world felt like tumbling forward into darkness? Had Janto created that abyss somehow by letting the advers remain free as long as he had, just as their evil deeds in Medua had created the claren? A stronger ruler might have wiped the false priests from the world, recognized that no good could come from allowing such men to spread their poison. But he and his father had done not what seemed sound, per se, but what had seemed right. Bringing the Meduans back into the Lanserim fold *was* right. Not easy, but right.

Maybe doing what he *may* meant trusting his decisions. Second guessing himself stirred up confusion and resentment. That wouldn't destroy the abyss—it would add to its power that came from such imbalances. That much he sensed.

Janto stroked Three-B's green-eyed head. "We will solve this, I promise."

The bird nuzzled Janto's hand, and he felt its rapid pulse, another life so interconnected with his own. Janto would do nothing to jeopardize it. He felt confident he hadn't. Confident as a king.

The bird ruffled its wings. The copper eyes blinked lazily at him, reminding Janto of a contented cat. He returned the gesture, then slung the Old Girl over his shoulder, quiver already on his back, and climbed up the bird's body.

Three-B settled into a dipping lope before launching into the sky again.

CHAPTER TWENTY-EIGHT

Serra

In the queensgarden, Queen Lexamy sat below a statue of Ginla Xantas, an ancient heroine of Lansera. She mourned alone on the bench, her back to Serra. Tansic's copper light seemed especially bright this morning, granting the queen's jasper-toned skin a rosy gold aspect that made her appear a creature of legend herself.

She raised a handkerchief to her face, and Serra regretted having to disturb this private moment, likely one of few the queen had allowed herself since the king's death. But life's demands did not always allow for private moments.

Before Serra took a forward step, Queen Lexamy called out in her strong contralto, "Come on over, daughter." The queen directed a convincing smile her way. "I'm near done with my sobfest."

Serra lifted her skirts to avoid dragging them over the dew-covered ground. As she neared, she noticed the queen's lashes were likewise frosted. "How long have you been out here," Serra asked, wiping down a seat on the bench.

"Since sunrise." Queen Lexamy's smile was wistful. "I've been coming here every morning since we sent Dever to the cobalt flame. We used to love mornings out here."

Serra hesitated, remembering the stolen moments she and Janto had also shared on this bench, when they'd been betrothed. The nature of their relationship had changed, but their love had not. And now . . .

"Just tell me what it is." The queen cupped Serra's face with a hand cold enough to send a shiver through her spine. Or maybe that was the news Serra needed to share.

She gaped at her feet, gulped a breath. "Janto's disappeared."

The queen's hand fell back to the bench like a brick, her rings clinking against the marble. "More fissures opening."

"Yes." Serra stared elsewhere to give Queen Lexamy space to digest the news. "Pic woke me as soon as he found the room empty."

"So no one saw it happen?"

"No, but there's no way Janto would leave Callyn, leave us, without a word." Unless Madel demanded it. Not for the first time, Serra wished Lorne were here to assure her of Madel's goodness. Sometimes, those who hadn't been born worshipping the goddess found it easier to see the purpose in Her ways.

Queen Lexamy was silent for a long while. Then she reached an arm around Serra's shoulders and pulled her close to lean back against her chest. Flakes of snow drifted down, a passing flurry, and dusted the garden. The queen took long, calming breaths. Serra matched them and wrapped her hands around the queen's forearms, taking strength from her presence. But they both knew they couldn't stay this way long.

A cough from the statue's right side punctuated that necessity.

"I don't know what to say." Ser Allyn had undoubtedly come to fetch the queen to hold court, in Janto's absence.

"Come," the queen said. She led them back from the garden to the castle. "Make sure to evacuate the rooms nearest Janto's quarters. If a rift has opened, we must be careful not to feed it. Serra will scout it for you. After court." The queen pressed Serra's hand. "You'll join me."

She waited on a reply. Her tone had not been questioning, but her eyes implied that Serra had a choice.

Serra nodded. The Lanserim needed the Albrechts in command. *Please, Madel,* she prayed, *let me remember how to be one.* She had forsworn the duties of nobility for long enough.

The queen went on ahead with Ser Allyn, Serra trailing behind. On the way through the halls, a woman with a square face and a reddish gleam asked her, "Are you going to court?" She wore her auburn hair in a bun and a fine gingham dress belted with feathers. Not a castle servant, Serra thought, but a merchant from Callyn proper.

"I am," Serra said, quite certain this woman did not know whom she was.

"I have heard such amazing rumors of late! The bird of creation, truly, flying in the skies and taking the Meduan princess off with it? Madel sending a sea of silver daggers down at the king's funeral to protect us from these monsters running about? I don't know what to make of any of it, and I want to hear about it from the new king himself."

Well, she'll have to wait awhile for that.

The woman clutched her basket full of provisions for lunch. "I've met him, you know," she learned close to Serra, who ducked low enough to catch the whisper. "Right handsome he is, with his Rasselerian coloring and those freckles the Albrechts have."

"Indeed." Serra gave her a conspiratorial look, enjoying the moment of levity. "Why, I'd almost marry him, if I could." She kept the humor of those words to herself and nodded at the guards stationed outside the throne room. They opened the doors to let Serra and her new friend in.

"I'm sorry," Serra whispered to her, "but I can't sit with you. I have to go up there." Queen Lexamy was already speaking with plaintiffs at the front of the room. Serra pointed at the bleachers near the throne, where a space had been cleared next to Uzziel, who reclined in a chair. The teenager had arrived in the dark hours of morning.

Realization spread over the woman's face, and she beamed with delight. Serra asked Ser Irven to find the merchant a seat among the crowd. At least a hundred people were present. She straightened up and strode down the aisle to the queen. She may not be royalty, but her presence as a noble and as the foster daughter of the Albrechts would add to the air of control the queen needed to project over the proceedings. The citizens of Lansera needed to feel secure. So Serra, after years of hiding out from the public eye, would make herself seen.

The plaintiffs standing before the queen were a family of three children and two parents dressed in plain clothing. They watched wide-eyed as Serra interrupted their plea to honor the queen with raised elbows. Then she took her seat beside Uzziel, smoothing the feathers on her levere-threaded skirt overlay. Their green hue highlighted her emerald eyes, and Serra let herself enjoy feeling admired by the public for the first time in ages.

"Finally." Uzziel sounded put out as she reached him, though his chin trembled. "I was beginning to think you'd forgotten the queen's brother. She'd be so vexed."

Serra couldn't help but laugh at the absurdity of his claim. She would love to witness the immensely awkward reunion of the Sellwyn siblings on Vesperi's return.

"Is that Lady Serra of the bird?" asked the middle child of the plaintiff family, with awe in her voice. She appeared perhaps six, with a younger brother in toddlerhood and an androgynous older sibling of perhaps twelve.

"It is," answered Queen Lexamy with amusement, despite Janto's disappearance and the threats they faced. "She doesn't bite, I promise," the queen continued, as the child ducked a head of wild black hair behind her father's leg.

"Now, young Delia Farri," the queen said, "may I ask your parents for more information about what happened on your farm?"

The child nodded and took her older siblings' hand.

Mer Farri held his dark gray peasant's cap in hand. "It's not our farm," he started. "We just work it for the big lord with the bear furs—"

"Lord Xantas."

"Yes, that's it. We were told we could live and work there when we came over the mountains."

"Of course." The queen gestured for chairs to be brought for the family, whose sagging shoulders and shaky legs indicated they'd had no time to rest on their journey to Callyn. They'd been led directly into the throne room, which sent pinpricks of apprehension over Serra's skin.

The queen spoke. "If what Ser Allyn told me of your experience is true, then this matter is of utmost important to Lansera. You made the right choice, coming here so fast." The whole family relaxed with relief.

"Delia, would you tell me what you saw?" the queen continued.

The middle child nodded, and Mar Farri kneeled so she could hold Delia's shoulders as the child spoke. "I was gathering up the dollies like Mama said, and I couldn't fit anymore, so I turned around to walk back home through the field. Except I couldn't see home anymore!" She raised her arms in astonishment. "It was like a wall of shiny rainbows. And then the wall came closer! And the nothing became something, fuzzy shapes and things in silly colors, and then I screamed and dropped the dollies. And then Mama was there, but she couldn't see the wall. But she couldn't see home either, just like me."

The other realm. The pit that had lodged in Serra's stomach at Janto's disappearance grew to a boulder. There weren't just *more* portals. The ones in existence were expanding, swallowing parts of

Lansera whole. It was more than leaking through; it was consuming them like the claren did.

Queen Lexamy asked the parents, "You didn't see what she saw?"

Both shook their heads no. Mer Farri explained, "We were all outside, on the western side of the farm, digging out the old runion roots like we've done ever since Lord Xantas moved us there. When Delia screamed, we rushed over, of course. She was pointing at fields beyond where the house had been. The house was just gone."

The throne room was silent as Temple Enjoin during a meditation training. Everyone, Serra included, held their breath, waiting for Queen Lexamy to speak.

"Send pigeons at once to Ser Swalus in the Perch and Lord Xantas. All the manors and homes within two miles of the Farri's farm should be evacuated. And everywhere else Lady Serra has documented one of these fissures. Including this castle."

The throne room exploded into a cacophony of activity and alarm. So much for avoiding panic.

Uzziel tugged at her arm. "What's going on, Serra? I don't understand. Didn't we send the cantaleres back?"

"It wasn't enough," Serra answered softly, as much to herself as Uzziel.

A tremor took his hands, and Serra gestured for Pic. "Quick, take Lord Uzziel down to the healer's chambers. He will need calming herbs and restraints."

Pic did as told, though his countenance was pale as a granfaylon's belly.

The queen nodded toward Ser Allyn. "Make sure the Farri family is housed. Court will resume tomorrow in town." She addressed the crowd over the volume of their fear. "I'm sure you all realize these are pressing matters we must see to at once."

Queen Lexamy rose from the throne and hurried out the side door into the hallway. Serra was momentarily surprised she hadn't offered words of calm. But the queen knew there were none to be given. The people must protect themselves as best they could. The Guard had failed. King Janto was gone.

Why bother to evacuate at all? All will join the darkness in time.

Even in her darkest moments, Serra would not give in to despair. She had saved the world before, and she would do whatever she could to do so again. That voice—that was *not* her.

She waded through a hall full of people, some crying, some yelling, others speaking in hushed tones. They stared at empty hands, blinking in shock that a massive evacuation had been ordered. She hurried across the courtyard to the turret King Dever had used for his studies, climbed the steps fast as her skirts allowed. The glow from a fireplace lit the walls with a yellow hue.

The queen was not sitting at the desk, head hidden in her hands, as Serra had guessed. Rather, she was uncorking a bottle of fine Meditlan red.

"Have we shared a drink since your failed wedding day?" Queen Lexamy asked, her tone jarringly light, though the wrinkles at her eyes were more pronounced than they'd been an hour earlier. "I find it helps calm me when facing days like today."

"Would you say you've faced others like today, you and the king?"

The queen gave her a wry grin. "No, not quite like today," she admitted.

Serra could hardly believe Queen Lexamy was taking time for a glass of wine rather than overseeing evacuations. Then the fragrances of sweet balac blossoms, astringent jalif berry, and piquant clove filled her nostrils.

Queen Lexamy held a glass of claret wine beneath her nose.

"See?" she said as Serra breathed it in and felt her panic subside. "It helps."

"It does." Serra took a sip, rolled it over her tongue as her brother had taught her on one of her home visits, in his rare good moods. The wine's velvet body coated her tongue, and its berry notes took on a brown-sugar sweetness while the alcohol tickled her throat. "So a glass of wine and then where do you need me? Sweeping the kitchen to see if the rift there is growing?"

The fire's light heightened the orange of the queen's hair. Yet the hopelessness of her next words put Serra on guard. "Why bother to map these portals if they can pop up anytime, anywhere?"

"My queen, I don't understand. You just asked me for a list."

"For show," she said, reaching for another glass.

That shocked Serra. "But I can see them. I can help." She'd never heard the queen speak with such bleakness.

What has she to hope for? All will soon be lost.

Serra grit her teeth.

The queen continued, "You are but one person. The portals are everywhere, Serra." She paused. "How long did it take you to round up your Silver Guard? A whopping three dozen people took what, two weeks? And you did not do that alone."

Serra's cheeks flushed red with embarrassment. "I get your point." She held the wine in her mouth to feel its bite.

"I'm not chiding you, Serra." Queen Lexamy gentled her tone. "We don't have time for you to scour the whole country. Not with the walls of the other realm pressing down on us. We need faster solutions. May Vesperi and Janto find them. May you and I and our people survive until they do. If we're lucky."

The resignation in the queen's voice troubled her deeply. She closed her eyes, imagined Vesperi riding the three-headed bird. The weapon was so strong—Serra had seen the proof of it more times than she could count. But she was also impetuous, prone to anger and lashing out, and dealing with so much loss. Janto had to have been sent there to aid her. His disappearance was not an accident, nor a tragedy. She had to believe that and push forward—push the queen forward too, if she must.

But who is here to aid me? To see that she wasn't fine, as Lorne had done in Mova and Orelyn?

No one. They have all abandoned you.

Worry churned within her fierce as the winds against Thokketh's ice walls. Her pulse raced and a cold sweat sprang up.

A knowing smile peeked around the queen's wine glass rim. "You'd be stronger with him by your side." She wiped a red drop from her cheek. "Serra, don't worry about us. You should go to Lorne, take solace in him while you can."

Serra shook her head.

"Why not?" The queen took another sip.

Because Queen Lexamy Albrecht would never press me to run away from a fight. It was time for Serra to take a leap of faith.

"Have you been hearing voices, my queen?" she asked.

The queen dropped her glass. It clattered and rolled to a stop on the platter.

"A voice has been inside my head," Serra continued. "Gnawing at me for weeks. I think it's been inside yours, too."

Hearing voices? You are crazed.

The queen's pupils grew large.

"I heard it in your words," she continued. "Just now, and in the throne room. It's stripped the hope from you."

The queen took a seat on the bed, fanned herself with her handkerchief.

She doesn't believe you. You are grasping at feathers.

Serra was shaking, but she pushed through. "It tried to do it to me, too—is trying, right this moment. But you've known," she bore down on the queen with a look, impressing all her sincerity into it, "something isn't right about it. That's what it does—latches so strongly onto your doubts, your fears, that you forget how wrong it feels."

Madel's hand! The dark pockets, they'd started appearing just before that voice began speaking to her. "The voice is part of this all somehow, I know it."

She reached for the queen's hand, and the queen pulled away, but Serra could see a spark of longing in her eyes.

"Be gone!" Serra shouted into the emptiness. "You have no power over us, foul spirit. I have stood with the Silver Guard, released the three-headed bird! Your fate awaits you."

As does yours.

A prolonged, bone-chilling hiss. And then silence. Blissful, beautiful silence.

The queen's countenance lifted. Her features relaxed, like a prune plumped with brandy. "I . . . I think you may be right. It's been so hard to tell, with Dever gone, and I . . ."

She dove her head into her hands.

"Hey, hey," Serra moved to embrace her. "I know what you're feeling. It did the same to me. I only just now realized it. If I weren't the seer . . . If I didn't have you to depend on, and Janto and . . ."

"And Lorne?" Queen Lexamy managed a mischievous grin despite the bewilderment of what she'd just experienced. "Do you love him?"

Serra choked on air, more out of sorts than she'd been at the voice's reemergence. Her body trembled with the stress of admitting the truth.

"I think about it, sometimes," she answered, "what it might have been like introducing him to my parents, to Agler. I can't picture it. Lorne Granich raising his elbows to the Gavenstones? Going out into the countryside, visiting our townsfolk?"

"You want to go back to Meditlan. That's new." The queen's eyes glinted. Her mood had improved so much already. How resilient she was.

And it was true, Serra realized. She *did* want to reclaim Gavenstone, to learn from her aunt and take care of her parents' people, of their lives' work.

"I do."

"Then your parents would have loved him too. I know I do, as did the king. Certainly, Lorne gives us plenty to raise an eyebrow at. But what he's done for Lansera? What he's become in the years since the Conjoining? Serra," Queen Lexamy took her hands and squeezed them. "That svelte minx of a man is a Lanserim hero. I'll be surprised if he isn't called to attend the murat once we achieve some semblance of normalcy again. You best not lose him," she scolded. "I'd like to stare at his handsome face more myself and sigh a bit, wishing I were younger."

She winked then dragged Serra up by the arm. "Now go to him— that encouragement didn't come from . . . from my depression. We all need someone to rely on, share our burdens with. Leave me a list of everywhere you know of a portal before you do, so I can properly evacuate the castle and the affected areas." She shook her head. "I can't believe I almost stopped bothering just then." She leaned forward, flared her irises. "Do that, but then go, daughter. Take what happiness you can, because you'll need it to get through, so we can get them"—Queen Lexamy moved to a window that opened above the courtyard, where the din of the citizens' panic poured steadily in—"through."

Serra pressed her hands. "Don't give into the despair again, my queen. Lansera needs you. As do all your children."

"I know." The queen cupped her cheek. "I will do my best."

Serra's bones congealed into jelly, and she wasn't sure she could move. Could she . . . could she do this? Take this? Have Lorne? And it would all be all right?

The sky was already falling, or spreading, at least. What was the worst that could happen?

She flew through Callyn's stone halls, veering from the turret's stairwell. The crowd was thick, so she decided to take the family's secret passage via the queen's quarters to save some time navigating to her own. The guards allowed her in without a word. Her pulse raced, and not just from the exertion. She imagined the surprise on Lorne's face when she arrived in Rasseleria, how the creases of his cheeks would rise high before deepening into dimples as she placed her lips on his, pushed him into the door. Oh, how she wanted to place her hands on his muscled arms, to lift herself up over his hips and—

Serra tumbled forward onto soft, spongy stones a turquoise shade that she'd glimpsed before with the sight. They seemed tarnished, muted under an intense blend of golden and copper light. The turquoise dusted her hands.

This wasn't the passageway. This was somewhere else. But she'd just been outside Janto's quarters . . . the new rift must have been there, in the passageway and seeping through into his bedroom. Serra hadn't even considered that potential, her mind on finding Lorne and telling him how much she loved him and wanted to be with him. That wouldn't be happening now.

She flopped onto her back against the soft stones, allowed herself a sob of exhaustion. For a good five minutes, she lay there, shielding her eyes from the radiant light while she cursed fate and whatever else had caused her to lose the one moment of happiness she'd granted herself in so long.

"Oh, hello there."

A woman spoke, and Serra lowered her hand. The woman had muted gray hair and drab gray clothes that hung loose in billows. She seemed about to fall over, like the life itself had been drained out of her. Yet she offered Serra a hand and then a carafe filled with a pearlescent golden liquid to sip. It tasted like creamed honey.

Once Serra's thoughts shifted from an imagined happy ending to the reality she was in—*to the other realm, and it has people in it, not just the disappeared Lanserim*—Serra raised her elbows in greeting.

"My name is Serrafina Gavenstone of Lansera," she said. "What's yours?"

"Oh, how delightful. A name!" The woman returned the gesture. "I can't remember the last time someone told me theirs. Mine is Esye."

CHAPTER TWENTY-NINE

VESPERI

Vesperi had never walked this far in a day before. For one, she wouldn't allow it. For two, she should have been winded hours ago, but the ground had a spring to it. Still, the seams of her boots wore on her flesh. Yet, she felt certain she was going the right way, as each step brought her deeper into a metallic haze, which gave her a heady feeling. That, combined with the hope she was so close to Izzy, created a potent vainglorious mood.

The Vesperi of before, the one who hadn't flown into this other realm on the back of a gigantic bird, knew she should be far more suspicious of these unfamiliar surroundings. She'd passed plenty of greenery in the form of glades, like the one she'd left the strange woman in. There'd been trickling brooks and rows of trees with fruit hanging heavy on the branches. Also fields of bold fuchsia and fiery orange plants, but no people working them, and nary a bee buzzing by. All she recognized were great bushes of fallowent, the plants growing taller than herself here, rather than up to her knees as they did in Lansera. The seed pods could be seen without a magnifying glass, even the milk seeping at their seams.

A peculiar, compelling music drifted over the fields. Izzy loved music; surely, she would have also followed its call. Each step felt like walking farther into an unending sunset, an orange-tinged light joining the glorious gold. Seeing through the haze was difficult, but Vesperi continued toward what appeared to be a pavilion a few hills farther away. Once she reached it, she dragged a hand over its terra-cotta walls, found an arch, and entered.

The pavilion's scale was impossible to grasp; Vesperi gave up as soon as she started. Size didn't matter. What stood at the center of its roofless amphitheater did.

A crowd surrounded two extraordinarily tall individuals. The crowd appeared to be human: some wore the Rasselerians' camouflage suits, others the heavy furs of Ertion. She even glimpsed the Sellwyn viper's green on a man who might have been one of her father's guards once. She determined not to head his way.

The energy flowed from the two giants—they, a wheel of light and the rays its spokes. Those light waves undulated like a brook's currents rather than a riptide. Yet Vesperi could feel the power they possessed, a power she'd had a taste of with the silver flame.

One of them had a man's form, slender as a reed. His head almost reached the top of a wooden bough under which they stood. When he shifted, his golden clothing moved as if made of metallic filigree, one long, tinkling robe.

The other person's appearance was womanly, her hair a brighter copper than Queen Lexamy's. It fell straight and fierce over her shoulders, its tips sharp as daggers. She wore the same garb as the man in her own copper coloring. A rainbow of quartz-dusted feathers crowned her hair, with more daggers of hair strung up within it.

I want a crown like that. Vesperi hadn't seen anything like them before, or anything else she'd witnessed the past few hours. If it had been mere hours—time felt slippery here. But she had a more pressing quest than trying to make sense of this unreality.

She moved quietly as she could, scanning the crowd for Izzy. These other humans also needed to go home, and a good queen would help them. She would be a good queen, someday. But Izzy came first. What mother could be faulted for that instinct?

A Meduan one would have been, before. Vesperi had scoffed at the idea of maternal love growing up, seen it as a foible of the Lanserim. Now, she grasped at hands and clutched the heads of children she couldn't see clearly through the haze. Why did they all sit here, mouths agape as though fish in a pond? The pavilion didn't feel threatening, but shouldn't they be desperate to get home? She couldn't imagine Izzy complacently accepting such a circumstance, hadn't raised her to.

A silky alto and deep bass spoke in unison, their voices as

intertwined as their speakers. The light people had practically melded into each other, fingers and arms laced between them. Just as Tansic and Oro so often did in the Lanserim sky.

Vesperi froze in disbelief. These were *moons*. This was no mere "other realm." It was a celestial one.

"Who moves among the lost?" they called. "Do you also need to be fed? Drink of our moonslight, and we will do our best to sustain you."

Caught, Vesperi chose defiance. "Moonslight? I have been in great need of it this past month."

The light intensified, and a warm stream of it sought her out, making the hairs rise from her skin. Vesperi twisted her palm up, hoping to tap into that power, but no spark came. They were not Esye.

The two people—moons—spoke again with excitement. "The weapon! We are honored to have you in our abode. May Madel's hand guide you."

Oro and Tansic raised their linked elbows as though they shared a body.

"And you also," Vesperi chorused, though it came out as no more than a whisper. The moons knew of her? She was speechless, one of the few times in her memory.

The gathered Lanserim were not, and they shifted to face her with expressions of awe and worry. "Have you fallen through also, princess?"

"Queen! She's the queen, now, you know."

"Is she? How long have I been gone?"

"Have you fallen through also, Queen Vesperi?"

"Is the king with you?"

"Have you come to take us back? I want to go back."

The last voice was a child's, and Vesperi darted, grasping through the light for it. Her hands came upon a young girl, but she wasn't young enough, more like eight or ten. Vesperi stroked her skin mindlessly anyhow, tried not to let her disappointment show.

"What's your name?" she asked.

"Imil, your highness." The girl raised her elbows, but the poor child shook, with either nerves or hunger. Likely the latter, if the moons' words could be trusted. Vesperi was not the type to assume so.

"Imil, are there any other children with you? How long have you been here?"

The girl took a big gulp of metallic light. "I . . . I think it's been a couple months, but it's hard to say. I haven't seen any other little girls, not since home. Can you take me home?" Big, brown eyes gazed up at Vesperi, and she wished she could tell this child yes.

But that would have to wait. If these people were starving, and Izzy had been here so much longer than anyone else . . .

"Is this heaven?" Imil asked, and Vesperi shook her head. There could be no heaven without Izzy by her side.

The light reddened. Tansic leaned over Vesperi and the girl, Imil. Up close, the moon's crown of feathers was not a rainbow of colors, just the dust shining differently depending on how the moon's light reflected from it.

Tansic touched a hand to the child's cheek, which blossomed like poppies in the sun. "For us, this *is* heaven, or at least it was before Madel withdrew Her hand. It is not meant for humans, though. That's why you were drawn to our moonslight. The food here cannot nourish you."

"Not even the fallowent?" Vesperi asked. She'd eaten plenty of that, they all had, in the years since the claren purge.

"Can a poultice defeat an infection? No, it merely wards it away until true care is given. Those of your people who've been here long are waning."

That sounded like a reproach. "I didn't bring them here. Where is Madel? Isn't She responsible for this?" Vesperi raged, out of panic at Izzy's absence as much as chagrin that this moon was placing some sort of blame at her feet for not seeing to their needs. "People keep saying She's withdrawn. What does that mean? What did we do to have our goddess abandon us?"

"What did your people here do, that you'd abandon them now when you could lend them aid?"

"What can *I* do? My daughter—"

The moon Oro twined his arms back together with Tansic's, a coiling rope. "Actions have repercussions, weapon. Your people and the evil they manifested in the clarens' form took much of Esye's power to defeat. In her time of weakness, Onsic preyed on her, and the balance shifted."

The dark brother drains its foes.

Oro continued, "Madel had to withdraw. Her nature cannot abide such disharmony. Onsic grows stronger, and the firmament between our worlds waver. He may have the child of the slayer and the weapon. But these people here need—"

"Where is he? Where is Izzy?" *Bring on the dark moon*! Oro and Tansic's radiance gave her a headache anyhow.

"Onsic is too powerful for you to face alone. His essence is folding in on itself, compounding. He cannot be found unless he calls to you."

Vesperi shuddered. It was the same in her world, darkness always seeking her out. That darkness might reach for her, but Izzy? Izzy would never give in to such evil.

But it might hold her hostage. "Will you guide me to him?"

Tansic waved her hand over the heads of the nearest humans. "We are needed here. We cannot leave."

If she wanted to find her daughter, she'd need to help these starving people first. Something within her had known that already, and she'd resisted, for Izzy's sake. But Vesperi was more than a mother. She was a queen, the Lanserim queen. And the weapon, the fulfillment of prophecy. She had a destiny, was one head of the very bird of creation.

The bird. "Three-B! You better be listening!"

Silence. Yes, she had ignored Three-B's consternation when she chose to seek out Oro and Tansic here, but it wouldn't abandon her, would it? They were practically soul sisters!

"Three-B! Come to me!" she tried again.

A great flapping of wings was her answer. The humans gasped and scrambled away to make room for its monstrously large body. They could hear, more than see it, through the glare.

"Would you mind?" Vesperi asked the moons. They breathed in, dimming their light enough that the others would be frightened less.

Three-B landed with a squawk that ruffled everyone's hair. It looked rather pleased with itself despite making her think she'd been abandoned.

Then she saw her husband on its back.

"Need some help?" Janto grinned, holding the Old Girl and a quiver of arrows.

Vesperi lunged into his arms before he'd reached the solid ground. Why had she ever thought his presence a curse?

"Did you find her?" he asked, once they, and the bird, had caught their breaths.

She shook her head. "Three-B took me to a glen of ferns at first, but I didn't find her there, just a strange woman who gave me even stranger juice. And then it bedded down for a rest. I nearly broke my boot trying to kick it back into action, but that creature's worse than Lord Xantas after too much drink." So sue her for a little embellishment. She was helping the people, wasn't she? "So I took off here instead."

Janto's dimples deepened with hope. She hated to squash it.

"She isn't here, either. But some of the others who've disappeared are. And we need to get them home, as soon as possible."

Vesperi gestured at the Lanserim around them and asked Three-B, "Can you take them back?" The bird had seemed to know where to fly when bringing her here, so it must sense the rifts between this realm and Lansera.

Three-B answered by folding its knobby legs beneath it so it could be mounted.

Vesperi kneeled beside Imil. "Are you ready to be brave, young one?"

The child hesitated, her mouth hanging open. But she nodded very slowly, and Janto lifted her up and placed her on the bird.

"Who's been here longest?" Vesperi asked, trying to determine some sort of system. The bird could fit three people and fly with ease. But it would take at least ten trips to ferry everyone out of here.

In answer to her question, two men boosted an older woman onto the bird's back. "Hold on tight," she instructed. Another possibly related man scrambled up behind the woman.

The bird raised itself to its full height. It gave a few warning *crr-owks* as its passengers gripped the skin beneath its feathers.

"Is it safe?" the woman asked Vesperi.

Having second thoughts after heading feather first into adventure was something Vesperi could empathize with. "Safe enough for your king and queen," she said, exuding confidence. "It brought us here to rescue you."

The woman smiled and spread her mouth into a determined line. Vesperi smiled back, proud she'd been able to provide this stranger with reassurance, and amazed she'd wanted to. She gave one of Three-B's heads a swift pat, and the creature responded by digging its claws into the ground before pressing off at a run then leap. Soon, it appeared no larger than a tadpole swimming through a golden-copper sky. Vesperi wouldn't have believed the sight possible a day ago.

"What *do* you believe in, Vesperi?"

A voice, disembodied, spoke into her ear. Onsic calling to her? *No.* Something reaching to her from that same sky that Three-B had disappeared into. In seconds, it grew large enough to wrap around her and scoop her up—a giant hand that flamed blue and held her tight. Vesperi could see nothing through its majestic blaze.

"What *do* you believe in, Vesperi?" The voice came again, a woman's voice, *Madel's voice.* Her question teased but challenged Vesperi to produce an answer.

She found she had several. Vesperi centered herself, amazed that she only wanted to speak truth. "I believe in my husband, that he's a good man, the best a man can be despite his shortcomings. I believe in my daughter, that she is good too, and that You've kept her safe. I believe we will find her soon." No speeding pulse or twitch to convey a lie. Vesperi believed it fully. "And I believe in You, Madel, in Your goodness and love for Your people." Flattery could get you everywhere, that Vesperi also knew.

"And I believe . . . " she gasped as tears bubbled up from somewhere deep within her. She pushed through them, knowing her words to be true. "I believe I will bear more children, because I wasn't . . . I didn't kill my baby. It wasn't my fault. It was no one's fault."

She felt a great release. Had she really been holding such guilt inside? "And I believe in myself. I believe that I can be a good queen. That I am enough, with or without the silver flame."

Blue energy caressed her face. She could hear Janto's voice, as though from a great distance, and those of the others in the pavilion. But she could not see them. And if she never saw anything again but this glow, she might not complain.

Madel sang into her ear, "Good. Because I believe in you, too."

The blue light flashed and Vesperi was blinded. *I didn't mean it—I would complain if you took my sight away!* People around her scattered, she could hear them and feel Janto's hands on her cheeks, holding her head firmly as he repeated her name.

Then she could see again and found her voice had disappeared instead.

A crown of blue orbs danced above Janto's head. It reminded Vesperi of the day King Dever had visited her in Callyn's prison. Their radiance was but a pale reflection of Madel's presence, and she was amazed she knew that now—that she had been cupped in Madel's own hand. What a way to mark this moment, the one in which she remembered how capable and powerful she was all by herself. She didn't need a silver flame to prove it. A goddess believed in her.

"You're glowing." Vesperi smiled at Janto.

"So are you," Janto laughed, pointing at her arm. Vesperi raised it and gasped. Her skin was lined with that same blue, the mark of Madel's presence.

But what took her breath away was the silver flame arcing within her palm.

She knew just what to do with it. And Onsic would soon find out.

CHAPTER THIRTY

SERRA

Taking one's destiny by the throat was a more understated affair than Serra had imagined. Perhaps that came from stumbling into this celestial realm rather than mounting a mystical bird and soaring there, as Vesperi had. But having a stroll with a moon? Serra would make the most of that. Assuming their worlds did not collide, she couldn't imagine having another opportunity to do so.

She took a whiff of the ambrosia Esye kept offering and Serra kept drinking. "Do I call you 'Lady Esye?'" Serra wondered out loud.

The moon whirred around, glancing at herself as though a bug had gotten loose in her gown. "Oh, am I a lady? I always wondered. How delightful. I suppose if I am a sister, I would be." She laughed. "But just Esye will do. It's all I've ever known as a name."

Yet Esye's delight couldn't pierce the gloom that followed her and what it portended. Often, a sister had a brother. Sometimes a dark one. *I should know.*

Though she kept her distance, undulating away when Serra drew close, Esye led her to the banks of a stream no more than two hops wide. The moon stopped intermittently to touch a flower or fluff up a sprig of springy moss. She was not forthcoming, but maybe she didn't know why Serra was there, either.

Serra's stomach growled, and she realized ambrosia might not be substantial human fare. "I'm sorry, it's rude of me to ask, but do you have any other food here?"

"Food?" Esye stopped her careful advancement. "I had some, but I gave it away. No more meant for you, I think."

Fine, that's fine. Serra would learn what she could from Esye and subsist on ambrosia in the meantime. She tilted the cask back for another sip and followed her companion's wanderings away from the stream and its jewel-hued reflections. They passed into a glade with a ceiling of braided boughs, formed from bushes whose branches had plaited together over the years . . . bushes with see-through blossoms and green leaves veined with copper, silver, gold, and onyx.

"Symphony bushes!" Serra was delighted to see their coloring in their natural state.

"Balance boughs," Esye corrected, though she paid them no mind.

The blossoms' edges had blackened with some sort of fungus. *Like my sight at first.* The effects of the imbalance would be felt here soon enough.

A few yards away, Esye tended a line of holes covered with their leaves. The moon used a stick to poke underneath one, revealing a trio of scaled eggs.

"Jurgen nests," Serra guessed. "You breed them?"

"They breed themselves, but I help. Or I used to. I cannot take care of them as well as I once did. Except tuck in the leaves to make sure they are snug." She demonstrated, raking another pile of the leaves on top of decomposed ones. "Onsic said he would help." She squinted her eyes, shook her head.

"Why would you want to take care of such miserable creatures?"

Esye considered the question, perhaps for the first time, Serra realized. "They have a place," she said, "like all of Madel's children."

Serra couldn't imagine how creatures causing so much destruction, like the cantaleres and jurgen, were part of Madel's plans. But then, Serra doubted Madel had planned for the realms to overlap and interact.

Serra took a step toward the moon. "Does Madel care for you like you do Her creatures?"

Esye projected positivity as she moved away from Serra. "Of course." The moon's smile did not reach her eyes. "When I'm worthy." Her voice filled with sorrow, and more distressingly, acceptance. She settled back into a frown.

Serra's throat clenched. "You're not worthy anymore?"

Esye stilled. "Onsic said, once I'm healed . . ."

Onsic's said a lot. "May I ask you a personal question, Esye?"

She nodded.

"Why *has* your light dimmed?"

Esye resumed her leaf raking. "I don't know what you mean."

So a moon could lie. "I think you do. It's affected us, your absence. It's affected us a lot in Lansera. The plants aren't growing right, the heavier minerals in them concentrating and turning dark. Our people are on edge, mistrustful of what they see with their own eyes—it looks different to them without you, doesn't feel right. Your jurgens and the canteleres are spilling through to us, and they aren't meant for our world. Yet here you are, raising more. Do you know they're destroying us?"

Are you working with your brother or against him?

Esye moved to another nest, her knuckles white as she gripped her stick. "Madel will take care of you. She always does."

"I'm not so sure She can, Esye. Something is blocking Her from fixing the rifts between our worlds. I think that something is you."

Esye sucked wind through her teeth, reminding Serra of a storm brewing on a dark night. "I am not so important as that."

Serra knew this woman's strength, would gather it for her if she must. Lansera needed a storm of silver raining down upon them. "You are important to *us*, Esye, all the moons are. Your light gives us hope on dark nights, lets us dream on the good ones. Not to mention how *your* energy, in particular, saved us from the claren."

"Oh, how they sizzled." Esye's eyes flashed with momentary delight. "I do miss your weapon's anger. It energized me so well. And the flame is so good at sealing off these nests from predators."

Serra determined right then and there not to ask what might prey on jurgens.

"How do we get your flame back?" Serra asked gently, worried Esye might spook like a bird on a branch.

"It's gone," the moon moaned, a hollow cast around her dim gray eyes. "Burned out."

"But that's not true. I've seen it."

"Yes, in the past. I used to shine, shine, shine with such—"

"No," Serra faced her, grabbed her shoulders.

The moon shrieked, a piteous sound, and backed several feet away.

"I'm sorry," Serra said, concerned she'd harmed her somehow. She was so fragile. "It's just, I've seen it since the king's death, since you dimmed in our sky. The flame was in Lansera, divided among the Silver Guard, and then it went with the bird."

"How . . . I . . ." Esye paused, speechless. "The Guard has returned?"

"Yes." Serra smiled widely. "The thirty-three had the flame, and it passed to the bird when they called it down."

Esye's voice trembled. "I didn't know." The moon bit her lip and spoke soft as a breeze, something her light had never been. "It's been drained from me."

The dark brother drains his foes. Esye was not their enemy. Whomever had done this to her was.

Serra had a hunch. "By Onsic?"

Esye sputtered. "What? No . . ." She stopped speaking, and her eyes flashed. She spit something from her mouth—a brown blob that filled the glen with a wretched smell. "My brother, how could he?"

Serra didn't ponder if one could hug a moon, simply slung her arms around this one. Esye quivered from the contact.

"We will return it to you," Serra repeated. "Now how do I find Onsic?"

The moon's bantam radiance blanched. "He will find you soon enough. You are something new here, something special. He will want a taste, and once he's had it, he will thirst for more."

"Do you think he can be stopped?"

"If he is not, he will ultimately consume himself."

Serra filled in the blanks. *And all of us well before that.* She moved toward the moon again. Esye ducked to the ground and withdrew into herself as though a cocoon.

The leaves on the bushes and nests rustled, and something glinted off the back of Serra's neck, its touch ticklish as butterfly wings.

Serra yelped, but a swift "*Shh!*" from the sky quieted her.

"Climb on!" Vesperi whispered from the back of the three-headed bird.

Serra was rendered speechless, to be so close to this majestic creature again. For the first time in her life, she wanted to follow a command from Vesperi blindly. *How far we've come.* But going elsewhere would delay the actions they needed to take. Those actions had to involve Esye, who'd faded into the shadows amidst the commotion of the bird's arrival.

"No." Serra ran a hand over the feathers ringing one of the bird's heads. "You two come down. We need to talk now."

Vesperi fixed her with a glare fiercer than any Serra had seen. "We can't delay again. We must go to Onsic. He has Izzy."

Serra took a step back before she realized why. Silver sparked from Vesperi's hand. "Your flame came back?" Oh, it was comforting to see it in Vesperi's experienced hands! And she knew someone else who should be comforted by its light.

Serra approached the moon who hugged her arms firmly against herself.

"See, Esye? The flame is not lost. The weapon has it."

The moon lifted her head, and hope spilled over her countenance like dawn over the horizon.

CHAPTER THIRTY-ONE
Janto

"Esye?" Janto asked, stepping down from the bird. "What do you mean?"

He'd spent the last few hours in the company of the moons Tansic and Oro, though whether it had been hours or minutes or days, he could not say for certain. Yet he had not considered that the woman behind Serra, who'd almost melted into fern fronds, might also be one.

Vesperi grabbed at his arm as his foot hit the ground. "Did our flight shake the sense out of you? Our daughter is not here."

"Neither was she among the people Three-B ferried home. Yet you knew they needed the help more." He'd been proud of Vesperi's actions. That Esye also needed whatever aid they could lend was self-evident—nay, monumental. He'd not been granted supernatural powers like Vesperi and Serra had, but Janto could sense that well enough.

The moon quavered less as Serra made her way over to them and away from Esye, he noticed.

Serra ruffled the bird's crown feathers. "You named it Three-B?"

The bird gave a chorus of playful chirps, either at the name or her touch. From her hiding place, the moon gazed up at Vesperi, or rather, at the swirling energy in her palm.

"I didn't realize." His wife's lips parted. "Three-B brought me straight here, and I didn't even consider you were her. That's why you're so sad, isn't it? Because this has been taken from you? I know . . . I know a bit of what that feels like."

Esye was silent, though she took a few steps toward the energy, circling around to the other side of the bird from Janto and Serra. She shrank back rather than touch the flame. Would it burn her, though she was its source?

"It's been drained from her by Onsic," Serra filled in. "She spoke to me about it. I think he—it?—he's the dark brother in the prophecy. He's been stealing her essence, or whatever it is that powers the flame."

Onsic the dark brother—it made sense that he'd been haunting others beside Janto. And doing more harm, too.

Like Tansic and Oro, Esye's voice didn't have a human's resonance. Nor did it hang in the air like Onsic's had. Rather it leapt at Janto as her lips twisted, forming words. Or maybe that was simply her anger propelling them on. "I'd thought it gone. He told me it was, that I'd done too much. All this while, he's been stealing it from me, storing it in that temple he's staged by my glade. No wonder he's stayed so close."

"Three-B took me there," Janto said. "It was an awful place, and there were silver stags, two of them. And some sort of large silver stone feeding them energy. That must be where he's keeping your essence."

Esye crossed her arms and rocked in place. She muttered something he could not make out.

Janto continued, "I thought it the abyss in Father's dream. The energy was oppressive, nothing like the flame, yet it compelled me forward. Three-B took us away from there, and I was relieved."

Vesperi asked, "And Izzy? Did you see her?"

Janto answered quickly, before her hopes could rise. "No Izzy—I'd have told you right away. But there *were* people and children. I may have missed her, but I don't think so."

"*May have* was enough to keep us going every time you went to search the swamps again." Vesperi rubbed her hands together. "We have to go to Onsic, if there's the slightest chance."

If. Janto gazed upon Esye. She seemed a shell of the might and radiance Tansic and Oro had possessed. If Izzy had been so long with the person who did this to a moon . . .

Janto's hand gripped his bow. "We don't know how to fight him, how things work here. I can aim arrows at him, but what if they just go through? You could strike him, Vesperi, but if he has Esye's power, too, couldn't he strike back?"

"Janto's right," Serra agreed. "We don't know what Onsic can do. We haven't had much luck rushing in places unprepared before."

Recalling Hamsyn's sacrifice at Mandat Hall felt like a cheap move, but Serra was right to bring it up. If anything like that happened to her or Vesperi . . . he strummed his fingers against the Old Girl's frame. His foot tapped with nervous energy.

Vesperi dismounted. "Would be nice if Madel gave us a clue," she grumbled, absent-mindedly arcing the flame between her palms. Esye's eyes followed their journey, glimmering with longing.

Janto leaned the Old Girl against Three-B. Its closest head veered around to investigate. The beak's sections clasped together, but it returned to picking through its feathers.

Janto paced. "She has given us each other, hasn't she? That has to mean something."

Vesperi groaned. "Love, this is not the time for a motivational speech."

He ignored her. "It's more than that, though. Think of the glass relic Sielban showed us, the two sides. Only three moons equals a Madel withdrawn."

Serra nodded. "And Her cobalt hue is gone from my sight as well. We're much more interconnected than we know, us and the beings here. Like the Lanserim and Meduans, even after a generation apart. The claren taught us that."

"Yes," Janto agreed, "but I think this is a different problem now. This time we must fight the battle here."

"Yes, we know, Janto." Vesperi rolled her eyes as her arms opened to their surroundings. "But how?"

Janto stopped pacing, noticing the symphony bushes above his head. They were much healthier than the ones in Terella's glasshouses. He pulled a cutting of the latter from his pouch. "Vesperi, would you call forth your flame?"

Vesperi and Serra exchanged looks.

"I hardly think we need to be building fires right now, darling." Vesperi crossed her arms, an echo of Esye's protective stance, though Vesperi's held defiance, too.

"No, just your palm. I want to see what happens when I expose the symphony to it."

Vesperi sighed, but she sparked the silver to life. Immediately, the black fungus that had overtaken the leaves shrank back. Though dried, he could see their metallic veins sparkle in the light.

Janto yelped. There it was! A silver band reappearing among the other veins, and the dark dust coalescing into a band of its own rather than an encroachment.

"Balance boughs, Esye called them," Serra gasped. "May I?" She blew on the blossoms, and black fungal dust flew from them like dandelion spores. The transparent blossoms were likewise veined, with all four moons' colors.

"See how the black remains?" Janto said with excitement. "It's not overtaking the rest of the colors. It's part of the structure, like the others."

"I'm stopping now." Vesperi closed her palm into a fist. "Or do you still need the visual aid to explain how we're not just composed of one thing or another? How our elements weave together to create a better whole?" She tilted her head sideways, flared her eyes wide.

"Well, yes, there's that." Janto deflated, but would not let his wife's cynicism deter him. "But I'm talking more about how everything must come into balance for the plant's true form to appear. Only then is the symphony released."

Okay, he deserved those chuckles of derision. At least he recognized the fondness they conveyed.

Serra did not appear to find much humor in the situation. "Janto, your point. There's a lot at stake. We have to correct the balance, but how?" She skirted Three-B's frame to give Esye a reassuring touch. The moon slipped away toward the ferns in response, and a kernel of a plan unfurled in Janto's mind.

He beheld Vesperi, remembered the day he'd met her. She'd been wild, struggling to survive. But also trapped, literally. By a net after she'd tripped a farmer's wire in the mountains. Arrows had secured the net around her, fired with such force into the tree trunks that her thrashing did not disturb them.

"Esye," he said, "why do you keep running from Serra?"

Serra's head jerked up, and she withdrew the hand she'd reached toward the moon.

Esye pointed at Serra's skirt. "Those fibers do not yield to me."

Of course. The levere thread. Levere repelled the silver flame—that quality had been essential to their victory at Mandat Hall. It made sense it would have a similar effect on Esye herself.

Janto gave thanks that Serra had been at Castle Callyn when she came to this realm—she never dressed so formally on the road. This skirt's overlay had multiple layers of levere threaded into its construction, twisted into intricate designs. Multiple layers he could take apart and knot into a net. Janto had not forgotten the pair of stags Onsic kept. They would need to be disabled, and he doubted an arrow could twine its way through their elaborate antlers well enough on its own. But with a levere net . . .

"The silver stags aren't Onsic's, right, Esye?" Janto asked. "They come from you?"

"They are my children," she said. Familial pride flushed her face. Janto recognized how it felt when he wore it himself.

"Your children?" Vesperi flashed Janto a worried glance, and he realized she thought he meant to slay them. That had been his role, but Janto was not one to seek death when he could find another way. And he was beginning to think he had.

"Your children," Serra asked, "like the other creations you tend? The jurgen? The symphony plants?"

Esye shook her head. "The stags are made from me. When my essence grows too strong, if it has been years since Madel last needed it, I cut part off, lest it overcome me and I disappear into it. That's why they are so few—I am not often overcome." Those last words made her seethe.

Vesperi pieced part of the puzzle together. "That's why Madel created the flame and its wielders, too, isn't it? She can't send you directly to help us, because your might would blaze through us."

"Just so." Esye smiled with a wicked glint. There it was, that spark of fury within her that they needed: her confidence.

"How could someone so powerful," Janto wondered aloud, "that she must cut parts of her power away lest she burst, ever come to believe her strength could run out?"

"He took it," Esye spit out the words, "scooped it out of me with his insults and his probing touch and his *remedies*. I was so tired, I thought it concern. I did not notice all the pricks and missing bits that had taken hold." Her eyes narrowed to a dagger's glint. "My own brother."

"And now, he wants more," Serra gasped. "His own power wasn't enough to satiate him, so he's been stealing yours. But that won't be enough, either. He's already advancing on us, too. The fissures were expanding when I left, out of sync because of him."

Expanding? Janto needed to return to his kingdom. But this— helping Esye, defeating Onsic—was the only way he could see how.

Esye rested her head on interlocked fingers. "Power should be given when asked. But he"—her rueful glare sparked with silver energy, though that failed to last—"*took* it. Put it in that sphere, fed my children with it so they might hurt others rather than protect them. That is not our nature. That is not balance."

If Esye were anything like her power's current conduit, Janto knew anger was the best time to focus her. "Esye, you must know how we can fight Onsic, counter what he's done to you."

Her brows, barely discernible against her skin, knit together. "I could overtake him, I think, if . . ."

Janto flashed Vesperi a look of apology. She returned a perplexed frown, which exploded into a glower after his next words.

"If you had your power back?"

CHAPTER THIRTY-TWO
VESPERI

No. Janto couldn't mean that. Her husband could not seriously be suggesting Vesperi yield the one thing taken from her that had been given back. That Madel had restored to her mere moments ago. *He can't.*

"If Vesperi gave you the flame, could you defeat him?"

He meant it. *That absolute bastard.* The flame roiled in her palm, grew jagged edges.

"I . . ." Esye hesitated. "That was some other person, the one who was silver. *She* could have, yes, but I . . . I was so stupid, I did not notice it being stolen from me."

"Those are Onsic's words," Serra guessed, and Vesperi wished she'd stop talking too. "You are the same person, Esye, whether or not you possess your flame. Don't let him tell you otherwise. Don't let him have that power over you."

There was truth in Serra's words—Vesperi had felt the same when she'd lost the magic, that it was her fault somehow. Onsic's direct torment hadn't convinced her of it, but so much else had, that had built up inside her. The loss of her children, her grief over King Dever's death, her utter unpreparedness for being a queen, a mother, a wife. But she was more than those roles, more than what they expected of her. Vesperi Sellwyn had never let others define her place in the world. Queen Vesperi Albrecht would not let a flame do so, either.

Still, she did not want to relinquish it.

She circled Esye, took in this rather plain woman with whom

she had shared so many of her innermost longings. Had Vesperi sculpted Esye's representation in topiary, she'd have opted for a warrior's figure, with Sar Mertina for a model. Her helmet would have been topped with a soaring flame and her shield would reflect her inner strength.

This woman before her seemed the opposite. Her shoulders hunched down and in, making her appear diminutive. Her feet held the same angle, and they were wrapped in that monotone fabric, itself fragile as lace. The billowy gown was wrinkled and torn in places.

She wondered how long it had been since Esye had been out in the sunlight before meeting her and Three-B in the fern glade. She wondered if, a short time ago, when Vesperi had felt stripped of her might and her family, of all she'd thought made her who she was, Vesperi might have judged herself the same.

Esye cupped a hand over the flame swirling in Vesperi's palm. Her eyes reflected it back, the spark within them enlivened. "It's beautiful. More than I realized."

Vesperi could empathize. "It is."

Esye met her eyes. "I miss it so much."

She recognized that hunger. It frightened her, how sharp and brittle it could be. How familiar she was with it.

The moon swept her hand cautiously through the flame, sending an energy disruption hiccuping through Vesperi's body. A shimmery band marked Esye's skin where her fingers had passed through it.

"Did you hear her?" Janto asked, impatience in his voice, though his eyes were full of compassion—couldn't he try to let her resent him? "Vesperi, please, we need her help."

"Oh, I heard her well enough, dear husband." Vesperi smirked. "And I remember what she said: 'Power should be given when asked.'"

"Well," Vesperi examined Esye, "are you asking?"

"Yes."

The moon's irises were no longer dim but flecked with silver radiance. The flame hadn't burned her skin but been absorbed into it. Vesperi hoped she'd realize someday that she'd had her essence within herself all along, that she could start renewing it at any time. But time was not something they had.

"Then you shall have it." Not that Vesperi knew how to give it. But it must be done. "We must defeat Onsic, and you're the only one of us who can. Come, take your flame back."

Esye drew close, brushed her hand over the flame's licks. "Are you certain?"

Vesperi nodded.

Esye opened her lips in a wide smile and took a deep breath. Hazy, twinkling orbs of silver floated from Vesperi's palm, as though the energy had birthed a tiny galaxy. Esye dove her hand through it and gripped Vesperi's own in a hold that started soft and unsure but grew stronger by the second. Vesperi closed her eyes, felt pain where Esye's grip solidified, firm as fired pottery. She shook, the energy swimming in channels beneath her skin, surging as though a sea had called up the low tide all at once.

A hot blaze seared Vesperi's palm while a flash of light blinded her. She and Esye stumbled away from each other, coughing as a cloud of steam surrounded them.

"Vesperi!" Janto shouted, and she warned him away.

Her cells rang with the effort of the flame being pulled from her. Sweat poured over her skin, and the world was one singular, radiant silver ball of energy between herself and Esye. A corona surrounded it, growing lighter and brighter and stronger and Vesperi couldn't see anymore, felt weightless. Her knees buckled as she screamed, knives prickling her skin and her hand, slicing into it. Her throat clenched; the flame hadn't burnt *her* before. Her eyes hurt down to their nerves.

Not until the moist heat she'd felt had cooled and evaporated, did she open them. Janto's arms encircled her, and six heads peered down at her: two human, three avian, and one, a moon with a pulsing halo.

"She's coming to." Serra touched a hand to her head, worry creasing her brow. "She's hot, cold—it keeps changing. But I think it's stabilizing."

"Oh, thank Madel." Janto's lips pressed against Vesperi's hair, and he repositioned his hold on her. "That was terrifying." He hugged her, rubbed her skin as though making sure she was there. "We could see right through you, like you'd been caught in time, the flame burning you, but not. Vesperi," he hugged her to him again, "I didn't know it'd be like that." His warm tenor sang with reverence, a tone Vesperi associated with him addressing his father. Or her, after sex.

"I—" she coughed, and it wracked her ribs, "I'm fine." It wasn't easy making words after being jolted by a lightning flash. She tried to raise herself, but her legs felt like molten lava. "Okay, almost fine.

I need to rest, maybe." Was that the treatment for recovering from having magic ripped from you?

"You can't yet. I will need you." Esye's voice sounded strong and sure, like her earlier self had been but a dream. Vesperi hoped it a nightmare they'd banished.

"You just had me." She groaned as she tried to take a deep breath, but the pain felt less. She could feel her skin again. That was nice.

"I am not at my full strength yet. I will need your anger to overcome Onsic." Esye's voice conveyed command, rather than request. She regarded Vesperi with confidence, implied expectations and demands, and Vesperi trusted her implicitly.

"Then you shall have it." Vesperi's well of anger never ran dry. "But in a few minutes, please."

She leaned back against Three-B, one head of whose stopped searching for insects long enough to nuzzle her cheek with a cold beak. Janto slipped an arm around her for support.

Somehow, in the time since Vesperi had passed out, Serra had stripped the overlay off her skirt. The seer ripped at its levere threads with a satisfying sound. They'd yielded perhaps ten yard's worth of length, tripled in on itself.

"Do you think this will be enough?" Serra asked Janto as she dug out shears sharp enough to slice through the metal. Vesperi quirked an eyebrow at those.

Serra pursed her lips. "An herbalist needs to treat many wounds. Nothing cuts better than these."

"They'd be good for cutting through some leather ties for Lorne, too," Vesperi quipped.

"Feeling better already, dear?" Janto sighed, waving his hands in acquiescence at the thread. "It will have to do." He retrieved his arrows from his quiver and squinted one open eye into a slit between their fronds. Then he licked his fingers to smooth them down. Vesperi could churn up whatever anger Esye needed to power herself, but Janto's arrows would need to prove fast and well-aimed. They would not have time for do-overs.

Her husband reached down for Serra's levere thread and began tying it with crown knots into a pair of nets.

Vesperi reached down to gather some herself.

"You're resting," Serra scolded, her fingers fumbling over the necessary loops.

Vesperi rolled her eyes. "And you're failing. I practiced a lot with Mertina. I can help."

Serra handed over the remaining thread. Vesperi and Janto made quick work of the materials they had. The misshapen net wasn't pretty, and was barely wider than five feet and higher than three, but the double-threaded metal was sturdy enough. It would hold, if Janto aimed his arrows well.

Serra had taken on a far-off look as they worked, but she gave them one now that had hardened with determination. "What worked for us before," she asked, "when we knew the claren outnumbered us and would only grow the more we poked at them from the shadows? When we'd been trying to stem our losses rather than cut off the flow?"

Janto clenched his arrows, a determined grimace on his face. "We took the fight to them."

"Just so." Serra took a handkerchief from the pocket of her skirt and wrapped it around her neck. Then she pushed it up to cover her face. An unnecessary precaution for this fight, but it was the surest signal of battle readiness any of them knew.

Janto and Vesperi did likewise. "Let's go."

Esye led the way, with the humans filing in between her and Three-B. The moon had masked herself, not appearing much different than before, though Vesperi caught silver glinting through her skin, when the light hit just right. That she could lead them was proof enough of the change—it, and the ache of loss in Vesperi's bones.

‡

It did not take long to find Onsic. Perhaps the smell led them to him: the sweet heat of boiling tar. Its pungency was overwhelming, so out of place in this realm of such beauty. The air was cold too, prickling Vesperi's goose flesh.

Both disappeared from mind as Vesperi peered ahead at a clearing between trees. After having met three moons, she'd thought herself prepared for a fourth, but her first glimpse of that indistinct, wavering void revealed how mistaken she was.

A sense of infinity beckoned to her from within it. It was beautiful, mesmerizing. The stars in the abyss shifted and swirled in iridescent, dazzling hues. Energy tendrils poked out from it, only to be pulled back in again in seemingly endless loops.

"Vesperi!" Serra whispered loud as she dared, grabbing on to her arm. Vesperi stumbled over her feet, and Serra and Janto's firm grips kept her from falling. She hadn't realized she'd moved forward. But the warning to stay on top of her wits was punctuated by a horrible sight: a person, facing the void, took a step and disappeared.

Vesperi held back a scream. Had Izzy gone through? She scanned the crowd of people she had failed to register at first, overcome by the abyss's presence. The unctuous smell returned, and her skin felt cold to the touch. The people were huddled close together near the void's brink, Lanserim and Meduans of many different backgrounds. Some wore lightweight tunics, likely having come through the black fissure before winter, while others wore heavy cloaks lined with fur or feathers.

They must be so weak, starving. Having just been drained herself was why she, and not her companions, had fallen prey to the void's call. Maybe four dozen individuals in all gazed at its form with reverence.

From the starscape, the suggestion of a man stepped out. A hazy outline took on a human shape as she watched—Onsic, peeling himself out from the darkness, and the darkness went with him, absorbing the very air nearby. She'd seen nothing like it—except, of course, in the night sky, where the absence of light marked his presence. As a child, when she wasn't dodging chores or her father's wrath, she'd wondered if Onsic were playing hide and seek.

He wasn't hiding now. "I am so glad to see so many of you have come to me," he addressed the disappeared people. To Vesperi's left, Serra gasped.

"That voice," she whispered. "It's been in my head and the queen's, taunting us, for weeks."

Vesperi squeezed her shoulder. "Now we will taunt it back." Or crush it, more like. There was a familiar quality to the voice, now that she considered it, like a chill breeze beating against wet sand. Or desperate words piling on top of each other until they crowded a person in. Vesperi had just barreled through such darkness herself. Onsic's reach was powerful indeed, if he could infest so many minds like that.

"You must go now," Esye whispered to Janto and Serra, "before he senses me."

Janto gave Vesperi's hand a squeeze and then they were gone toward the trees. She felt a flash of fear for them, and for herself. But the weapon was made from sterner stuff than that. She set her features in a determined line.

As Onsic moved among the people sitting near him, the void gathered behind him like a cloak. The colors nearest to him dulled, and their radiance glinted briefly from his approximation of skin. Vesperi was surprised no cobalt corona surrounded him. But that was Madel's color, and She had withdrawn Herself from this madness. Instead, a bright white light ringed the void, perhaps pulled from the universe he contained.

Once the void-cloak had shrunk enough, Vesperi glimpsed the silver stags beyond it, their candelabras of antler tines tipped with a silver glow. The sphere Janto had described was also there, churning with Esye's stolen essence. They were betting on him not sensing that more had been returned to her. How else would *the brother be taken unaware, by silver power returned home*? And oh, this brother needed to be *taken*, far more than Uzziel ever had.

Onsic's head jerked suddenly, as though he'd caught a scent on the wind. "Dear sister," his voice projected far as he made his way through the people, "I did not expect you here. I am surprised to see you out and about."

He changed his path, began ambling his way toward them. Did the starscape shift with him, or was that a trick of the eye? The humans he touched on the way gasped and collapsed onto their knees, paper lanterns deprived of a breeze. It reminded Vesperi of the claren and how they'd suck the insides out of their prey. This monster deflated souls instead.

Vesperi prayed they still breathed. Why did the others not run away? What drew people to such a black hole as this, and kept them there?

Despair. She had danced with that emotion for near a year. She imagined finding herself trapped in a strange land where everything seemed incomprehensible. With no family, no friends, nothing to sustain her. These people had been drained long before Onsic had called them here.

His approach halted, and his starry head shifted to a thoughtful tilt. "Your weapon is here?"

Onsic's voice held a hint of fear, enough to keep Vesperi from despairing herself. "Did Madel send her?"

"I do not know." Esye sounded weak. Vesperi hoped it a ruse. "She may have. For all the good it'd do me. She no longer has the flame."

"Oh," Onsic's features, such as they were, twisted into a patronizing pout. "Had you thought to get it back?"

He swerved, lifted an arm and jabbed it forward, index finger pointing at the sphere. The stags huffed as a new charge of silver energy channeled into them from the stone. Electricity laced their antlers, and a low hum filled the clearing, refracting from the trees. The animals shambled as in pain, and Vesperi fumed. How dare he threaten his sister's children with her own power?

Esye's voice cracked through Vesperi's mind like a whip. *He will pay.*

The two women, one human, one celestial, shared a smile they hid as Onsic pivoted to face them again, his hubris writ large in those dazzling, star-filled eyes and the ease of his stance. Such men never failed to underestimate a woman's strength. Watching him fall would be delicious.

CHAPTER THIRTY-THREE
ESYE

Onsic's smile revealed jagged teeth, like those of the sheven fish that churned through the cold waters of the Lanserim's realm. How many of those monsters had he consumed, Esye wondered. What would it take to satisfy him?

His voice filled with condescension. "Esye, you should be resting. Why are you out and about?"

"Esye?" one of the humans gasped, a sallow man with deep green skin and a suit that mimicked Onsic's galaxy. "Esye is gone. She left us."

Esye probed the weapon. *Is that how it seems on your world?* She hadn't known how complete her withdrawal had been, how it had affected their existence. *I am sorry. I didn't realize.*

That's how he wanted it, the weapon returned, her anger churning. *You, despairing in ignorance.* Her olive skin glowed rapturously, incensed. *Us, withering as your light dimmed.*

"Yes, it's a shame she's grown so weak." Onsic stroked the man's head, and he wilted, a vine in the sun. Alive, but with too much taken from him. And the more Onsic took, the less these people would feel it. He would peck away at them, one pebble at a time.

As he had done her. Knowing she bore some responsibility for what the humans had suffered? More fuel for the flame.

"What is all this?" Esye feigned confusion. "Have you brought my stags to aid me?"

He sent another javelin of silver energy into them from the orb, tormenting them. The stags were not meant to possess so much of her essence. They grunted in agony. What did he plan for them? To release them among these people? To what end?

"I did think they'd bring you comfort," he said. "You have been so weak—I have been concerned." He pointed at the stone swirling with power—her power. One more thing he'd bent against its nature to his will. "And I have another present for you."

More lies. They tasted sour as they absorbed into her skin. So she sent them out again, reshaped to her own purposes. "You are so near my home, I had to come out, despite my waning mood." She kept her voice soft, quavering. "Was it unwise for me to come greet you?"

She tired of this charade. Yet part of how Onsic had gained the extra foot had been endurance, waiting her out. It was foolhardy to push—the slayer and the seer needed time to take up their positions.

Onsic meandered among the humans, creating thralls as he went. He'd had acolytes before, all the moons had, but this was different. The humans had come willingly in the past—and sparingly. Only ones longing for union with the bliss his nothingness provided. So few humans truly wanted that. This was greed, calling them to him, manipulating their thoughts to bring them here. Something had changed in Onsic.

She felt sorrow it had escaped her notice. His fixation with consumption had grown so vast, he'd created a cosmos-wide dissonance. Onsic would draw everything into himself in time, as he'd done with her essence. She hadn't seen it coming, hadn't felt him creep into her crevices, spreading his imbalance with lies.

Sorrow was for another day. Today, she needed anger.

"Dear sister, you mistake me. I am overjoyed that you are well enough to leave your nest." He glided toward her, over moss that shriveled as he passed. The ferns—their browning had not been her doing, either, but his malevolent breath bathing them. A voice inside her argued, *but you allowed it.* She'd almost lost her battle with that voice. She would not lose this one.

She peered again at the weapon, felt her immense wrathfulness. The weapon had also felt strong sorrow in recent months, and self-doubt. Esye empathized, remembered the stomped jurgen nests. Those hadn't been her fault, either. It was his. He'd hurt them to make her more pliant. Like he was doing now, with her stags.

No more. Her sorrow crystallized into a rage that beat pure: the rage of a mother and of the dispossessed. Oh, she had missed this part of herself. With the slightest uncoiling of a finger, she drank more of it from the weapon. Such rage could be patient. She must not strike until she had enough of herself back. She would need the stags for that.

The weapon stamped her foot. *Oh, just smite him already.* Esye smiled at her impatience, bent her spirit toward it, invited it in. Onsic was not the only being that could feast on other's essences—colors were simply a better choice.

She stepped forward.

"I wonder," Onsic shifted to block her movement, "if you can resist your own power when it's turned against you." Concentrated starlight flashed in his eyes and he raised an arm to draw forth the stags' power.

The game was up. No more pretending. "You've had enough of tricking me, brother? Now you would twist my own force against me rather than my doubts?"

Onsic laughed, and it rattled the trees. "Ah, you have stopped bluffing. A few hands too late. I am well-versed in tricks."

"You bastard!" The slayer's voice rang out from the tree line. Something whirred in the space beyond Onsic's cape—an arrow aimed straight for his back.

Before it could strike, a depression formed in Onsic's being. The arrow caught in it as though a fly in tar. A sickening *thlip* absorbed it into Onsic's universe.

"It was you, pretending to be my father!" the slayer charged from his hiding place. "You said those same words at the foot of my bed!"

Oh, clever. Another arrow winged its way toward Onsic, who swerved toward its origin in the bushes far off near the trees.

"Slayer!" Onsic said, relish curving his comet's trail of an eyebrow up. "A delight to have you here. Oh, how it disappointed your father when you disobeyed his orders."

Worry surged from the weapon as more arrows flung Onsic's way. But the slayer was not wasting their chances at securing the stags. He'd already known the games Onsic played with him.

This was a diversion. A way for Esye to catch her brother unaware.

"You curse his memory!" taunted the slayer.

Onsic chortled. He slithered toward the ferns from whence the arrows came. The emptiness of his void-cloak folded in on itself as he reversed directions.

Esye slipped closer to the stags.

With a loud twang, a pair of arrows shot wide of Onsic, the levere net held between them. They dug deep into the tree trunks above her children.

Onsic bore down on the slayer. The next two arrows deflected against the same trees, leaving the net hanging limp above the stags.

Esye rushed toward them. Her window was closing.

Onsic reached into the ferns.

Two more arrows shot out in quick succession, securing the net. Caught within it, the silver stags tramped in circles, panicked. The net repelled her too, and she cowered down. Then she glimpsed a gap through the bottom that she might use.

Onsic's hands clasped around the slayer's neck, dragging him from the bushes.

"Saeth's fist," the weapon swore, running toward her husband. The dark moon swerved toward her, the slayer choking in his grasp.

Esye focused on the gap, pulled her essence through it. Veins of power flowed from the antlers' tines and into her skin. Oh, *that* was what she'd been missing.

A plop—the slayer dropped to the ground. Onsic swerved toward Esye, one palm up.

No! If he drew the stags' energy out through the net, it would merely rebound against the levere threads, burning the animals.

Esye flung herself between them. With his other hand, Onsic called forth power from the orb and cast it toward her. She jerked in the air. He pummeled her with his own magic. Twin fires shocked through her, a channel of stars, half her essence, half Onsic's.

Onsic grabbed her arm, his fingers mere extensions of his great expanse. They burned cold like her flame, melted the skin where he pressed. She imagined becoming a moon in his new starscape, wondered how long it would be until Oro and Tansic also hung on its endless horizon, if she gave in. She wondered, too, if he knew that when his thirst ran its course, he would swallow himself the same.

"Brother," she gasped through the pain of his touch, "brother, you can stop this. You can return to yourself, release what you've claimed before it is too late."

How much simpler it would be if he did. But Onsic laughed in her face, his maw swimming with the vast nothingness that thought itself everything.

"What power do you have over me, sister? Two worlds I consume in tandem! Even Madel Herself could not stop me. She did not withdraw; I have pushed Her from our existence!"

Esye spilled a few tears for her brother's foolhardiness—she could not help it. He must have deceived even himself to believe Madel unable to stop him.

The weapon's anger sparked with sheer madness. That woman would punish anyone who would subject her family to such a fate—a world where Madel could be overcome. She cradled her husband, who lay near motionless on the ground. Esye extracted more of her anger, used the arrogance of Onsic's words to stoke her flame.

Onsic focused his assault on her physical being, and the sphere pulsed. Power crashed through Esye's flesh, and her skin caught fire. But Esye was so much more than her physical being, so much more than any limitations others forced on her. As his darkness continued searing her body, she focused her will on the sphere's coil of energy, arrested its progress.

Was it not also made from her? Did not like things attract each other as much as opposites could repulse?

She cast the weapon's anger at the sphere in one mighty burst, calling to her essence within it. That electricity met the sphere's in the air, coalescing with it into a thick, strong beam of her magic. Buoyed, she channeled *herself* back out from the stone that had sucked her power away, reclaimed what she had been tricked into relinquishing. Thus, she ended Onsic's claim on her, a claim he'd not been entitled to stake.

Esye glowed and her essence renewed. A silver haze emanated from her innermost self and it grew, intensifying as she took all the emotion from the people around them into herself. Anger, so much anger, but also the horror and injustice of what she'd been through, of what the humans had endured. Her consciousness bounced among them, and she pulled from their experiences, too. A man with blond hair had loved his mother despite her continual rejections. An elder had lost her place on her town's council to a youngster who'd laughed too much while insisting his way was better. A child's mother and sister had perished in the mountains as they'd tried to cross over into a new life, a life he didn't know how to seek on his own.

Esye felt Onsic's fury too, found she could feed on that as she directed her renewed strength at him. His nebulas sparked and sizzled, burning themselves up as she focused an energy stream on him. His actions had weakened himself as well as the worlds, and he hadn't even known it. Her power battered him, and his feelings of resentment, of injustice, grew.

He opened his mouth to swallow her, and she let him, pushing her power through into that abyss. Her strength surged, and he recoiled as her might curled around the stars in his void. The silver flame wrestled and pulsed, jostling those stars, reminding them there was more to this existence than mere shining, that they had been robbed of the fullness of living.

In his mind's pit, Esye channeled the wrath of being lied to, fooled into thinking she'd ever been less than enough. She poured it into Onsic's universe, and the lights blinked out of it. Stars returned to their skyward placement. People tumbled away from his form, released from the despair they'd given in to.

Esye hurled her emotions onward, found them rich and full and worthy. Her hair rose like a halo, every tress a dazzling conduit of silver. At some point, the weapon came to her. It may have been minutes, days, weeks later—Esye knew not.

The weapon said, "I think you've got him," and Esye calmed her anger enough to gaze upon her brother again.

He lay on his back, his suggestion of limbs twitching like a cockroach in the pool of liquid avarice that his essence had released. Her own flesh had reformed around her, fully restored.

"Do you yield, Onsic?" She was not sure if she wanted to hear a yes. She wanted to blast him out of this existence—he deserved to meet his end. But she must exercise restraint or risk becoming him. Without Onsic, balance could not be restored, and his plan might still work.

"Yes." The word plummeted from his mouth, which had narrowed to a thin, shimmery line. "I am defeated, destroyed. Sister, please stop." He drew his limbs beneath him.

"Finish him," prodded the weapon. Esye understood her desire, could talk herself into believing it wisdom. But as sure as anger fueled Esye's existence, hunger drove his. Such hunger had a place in their worlds, like the jurgens and cantaleres, if it remained in check.

"Madel knows his worth," she said. "For how can Her children learn and grow without the doubt that his nothing that is something engenders?"

Onsic twitched beneath her feet in that puddle congealing into tar.

Embers glowed from the tines of the silver stags' antlers. They posed no danger any longer, unless she wielded it.

The weapon asked, her voice faint and the slayer's hand gripped in hers, "Where can I find my daughter?"

"I do not know," Esye said.

She rolled her shivering brother over and sopped the filth from his form with her now luminous dress.

CHAPTER THIRTY-FOUR
SERRA

"You must go up the ridge," Janto had told Serra as they sprinted toward a grove of trees opposite the silver stags. "Observe what happens in case it goes wrong. Find another way to fix the imbalance."

"No, I can help!" Serra had gripped the levere net. She would not simply watch the other members of her hunting party be attacked—could not. The Silver Guard's stand had taught her that.

"Watching *is* helping, Serra," Janto had implored, his amber eyes glistening. "No one else can see better what we may miss."

Only once before had she said no to those eyes, and that act had nearly destroyed their relationship. She handed over the net and scampered up a low ridge, glad the spongy grass softened her footfalls. She climbed one of the farthest trees. Its verdant green leaves dripped something viscous that the grasses stretched to reach. The battle was over so fast, she'd barely been able to follow it. Or was it so slow, she'd caught every silver flash? It mattered not. What did was what she soon glimpsed through the tree's branches: the dark moon quivering on the grass.

No color danced within the outline of Onsic's body, as though a vat of oil had smothered him. A faint halo of white light ringed his form, the balance re-asserting itself perhaps. Had they done enough to restore it?

Esye glowed anew. Her essence pulsed around her, a silver coat.

The stags pawed the ground and bleated as she drew close, bending to release them. Their silver had dulled, but as she stroked their fur, a soft shimmer returned to them, more heartening than the sharpness they'd worn before. Serra wished Lorne were here to see it. What had become of his echo now?

The disappeared people, near where the shattered abyss had hung, appeared stunned, not sure what to make of the cosmic display they'd witnessed. Janto rose to a seated position, rubbing his throat.

Vesperi had begun her interrogations already. "Have you seen my daughter? Princess Izmareld? She has hair like mine and freckles like her daddy's and she's always giggling, and . . ."

Serra slipped down from her perch and made her way to the clearing. The people stared vacantly as Vesperi spoke. Her voice pitched higher when they failed to answer. She wasn't angry—Esye had drained her of that for now. But the fear beneath her anger was clear enough.

Serra touched Vesperi's arm, and she whirled around, eyes frantic.

"We will find her," Serra squeezed both her arms to provide support, "but these people are in shock. Onsic enthralled them. That will need to wear off. They can't help you yet, can't even make sense of your words."

Janto fetched out his branch of symphony. "The balancing has already begun." Four small, new leaf buds had sprouted from its vines. When the light hit the transparent blossoms just right, a bluish tinge could be seen.

Serra sighed at its beauty. "Madel will return."

Esye's smile was as radiant as her anger had been moments before. "Yes. And She will restrain my brother so this can never happen again."

Vesperi glowered over Onsic's form. "What have you done with my daughter?"

His body shuddered, spent. But he managed to turn his head toward them and form lips again. "I do not have her. I never did."

Serra's mind raced. Could he be telling the truth? "Janto," she asked, "what did you mean earlier, that he had pretended to be your father?"

Janto took a deep breath, and his pain at recalling the details made his voice waver. "Like a ghost. He appeared a few times, preying on my doubts about how to handle all this." He gestured toward the scores of people around them, people Onsic had weakened and fooled, through his vile words, into letting him steal their energy.

Serra came to her knees beside the dark moon. She could almost see the green moss through his body, as though he were no more substantial than a looking glass. The cape twisted around him, puckering in spots, and she realized that those dark patches in her vision, they too, had been him.

"How did you do it?" she asked. "Open your pockets to bring all these people here?"

His lips creased tight against each other, but Esye pricked him with fiery silver energy. It surged through him like an electric shock.

Perhaps Serra has misjudged the silver moon's tenderness toward her brother.

"Fine," he gasped, raising a limp hand to call her off. "If the seer wishes to see more clearly, I'll spell it out for her." Rage boiled in those eye hollows despite his defeat. She did not trust that he'd learn from his failure or that his thirst had been quenched.

"I have always seeped into your thoughts," he said, "made your fears more real by suggesting they might be true. But drinking of your emotions only when sadness overwhelmed no longer satisfied me. So I pressed more, took more. You humans are so easy to control."

No matter how menacing, the sting of his words was dulled after Esye laid him low. His confidence was too battered to give them weight, and the voice scratched rather than soothed and suckled as it had done before.

It grew fainter, too. To hear the rest, Serra was forced down to his level.

"When they gave me enough of themselves, felt they had no way out of their despair, I found I could open one for them, just as Madel's servants are guided through Her rainbow path."

Serra could see it in her mind's eyes, a fold between here and home whose emptiness beckoned to those who'd lost hope. Maybe they'd given into it after a loved one's death, a sickness, or too many years spent suffering under the advers' thumbs. Or too few of feeling as though they belonged anywhere or with anyone.

Serra shuddered to recall how close her own battles with the slippery sound of her doubts had come. How easy it might have been to follow Onsic's call, not realizing she'd been pulled rather than made a choice.

But she could not imagine her goddaughter, full of joy and life, falling prey to him.

"I believe him," Serra said. "I don't think he has Izzy."

"Then where is my daughter?" Vesperi clutched Janto's side, and he wrapped an arm around her. Both were as drained as Onsic in their own ways. Tears welled as Serra recognized the anguish her friends felt. A very real possibility reared up: Maybe Izzy had never been here at all. Maybe she hadn't disappeared like these people, maybe she was really and truly—

One of Three-B's heads squawked, and the other two answered in unison as it shuffled through ferns into the clearing.

"Where have you been, Three-B?" Serra went over to ruffle the great bird's feathers. She hadn't noticed its absence.

Three necks twisted into a braid, or perhaps a coil—into something stronger than they were on their own. The head with gold eyes ended up on top, and it stretched back toward the grove. The other heads jerked forward fast, pecking at the empty air. And then a hole appeared, about the size of a coin. With it came a rush of warm air and the scents of wet dirt and rotting leaves.

The heads angled slowly downward, the topmost beak rending the fabric between their worlds as it went. A peculiar, familiar blend of sulfur and the herbal greenness of spring wafted through.

"It's a rift," Serra said, unsure if the others could see it without the sight on this side of reality. The earthy tones of a Lanserim swamp had never felt so inviting.

Home, it's home. A rush of images came over Serra as to what that meant. In Meditlan, the first grapevines would be budding soon, like the balance branch. The spice bushes near the shores would need pruning, and as their parents worked, the children would dress up in giant sacks and pretend they were ghosts, bumbling around to avoid the thorns. She thought of Aunt Marji, arms open and ready to embrace her, and the dark wood halls of Gavenstone filled with books Serra hadn't read since she was a child. Home was what Serra had *not* explored in her years of travel. It was Meditlan and the roots she hadn't put down, the ones she wanted to. With Onsic's voice out of her head, she could see it so easily.

"That's the border swamp between Wasyla and Rasseleria," Janto said. "I've been there so many times, I know every bend. Vesperi," Janto reached for his wife, hope flaming in his cheeks, "it can't be a coincidence that Three-B chose this location. It's letting us know that *it* has her."

"What?" Shock deepened Vesperi's wrinkles.

Serra considered the idea, as Three-B finished off the new fissure with a quick snip from its topmost beak. "Maybe Madel brought her through," Serra theorized, "before all this started, to get us to come after her."

"What?" Vesperi repeated, finding her anger again.

"Think about it, Vesperi. Would you have flown off to this realm if your daughter were safe at home? *Especially* if she were safe at home while the world around us was being invaded by cantaleres and jurgens and disappearing Lanserim?"

Vesperi spit at the ground. Then she rushed at the bird, which squawked and jumped back. "Why didn't you take me to her straight-away?" She flung her fists against its girth. Her voice grew in volume. "Where is my daughter, you foul, tick-infested beast?"

All three heads *crr-owked* in Vesperi's face, and she fell, repelled by the force of sound. But Serra recognized the light in her eyes, her anger replenished. Hopefully, she'd recognize the value of taking a more circuitous path, once it wore off and Izzy was warm in her arms again. Hopefully, Serra's own love would do the same.

Soft sounds of confusion and moaning came from the disappeared people. Serra moved between them, offering sips of ambrosia from Esye's flask and calming salves. Three-B came along, though the people scrabbled away from the bird like crabs from a sea wave. The bird squawked again and flung its heads back toward the portal, then back and forth again between it and the people. Then it pointedly fluttered its wings and tucked its heads beneath them.

"I think it wants us to return these people home ourselves," Serra ventured. The fissure opened on solid ground—there was little risk of harm. "I'll go with them, make sure they're tended to until we come upon a village."

Janto and Vesperi would find Izzy; Serra could free them to do that. It wasn't her family that needed tending in this realm. And as much as she loved the Albrechts, it was time for Serra to claim her own.

"Of course," Janto took a deep breath, and turned to his wife with regret. "I know where the nearest villages are, how to get to them through the swamp. I have to go with Serra—"

"Go with Serra? What about our daughter?"

Serra was glad Vesperi possessed no flame right then.

Janto took Vesperi's hand in his. "I trust you will bring her home,

Vesperi." He gave her an extended look, one so fraught with shared emotion that Serra felt abashed watching it. "Just as I did when you first left with Three-B."

Vesperi calmed, then leaned up to give him a kiss. "I promise."

Serra helped a young woman up from the grass, gave her an ambrosia sip. "Let's go." She nodded to Janto.

They passed Esye, who had kneeled beside Onsic on the grass. She soothed him with a wordless tune that might pass for a star's lullaby.

"Take care of him," Serra advised, having had a fallen brother of her own. "And of yourself," she cautioned. "Do not allow yourself to fade away again."

A silver haze veiled Esye's expression, but Serra could hear her confidence well enough. "I will take care, dear seer. May you see your own way as plainly."

For once, Serra thought she could. She took the young woman's hand and guided her through the fissure, holding her breath until her boot clomped down into the mud and mangroves on the other side.

CHAPTER THIRTY-FIVE

Vesperi

Janto and Serra disappeared into the infuriating new fissure, leading the others back into their proper world. Just as she and Janto had overseen Three-B shuttling the wayfarers home from Oro and Tansic's court. All the while, that bird had known precisely where her daughter was. The limitations of animal-to-human speech hardly seemed an excuse between creatures of prophecy such as them.

"You couldn't find a way to let me know my daughter was safe?" Her voice pulsed with controlled fury. "Couldn't take me straight to her instead of tromping around with all these moons and their drama first? Fine."

Maybe Three-B had done as Madel directed. Maybe if she'd listened to its consternation when she left Esye in the first place and remained to help her, this would have been over faster. Perhaps she should be grateful Izzy had been kept safe until the true dangers were averted.

"Fine." Vesperi knew all that, but she didn't have to like it. "Now, bird," she mounted Three-B without warning, grasping its feathers harder than required for safety, "take me to my daughter."

Blue, gold, silver, and copper eyes examined her. For a moment, Vesperi worried she'd been too harsh—when would she learn that making demands of those with the upper hand rarely ended with her desired result? Yet Three-B dug its spindly legs in the dirt before leaping into a running stride.

"I'll see you in the sky, Esye!" Vesperi called back to the moons.

She had no advice on caring for an ailing brother. Her relationship with Uzziel, or lack thereof, proved that.

A surprising smile rose to her lips as the wind hit her face. Her daughter would soon have an uncle to meet. Did she actually look forward to that? Vesperi could handle anything, if it meant Izzy was home.

‡

In a glen twinkling with lights like a firefly gone into heat, Vesperi waited. Three-B had deposited her there half an hour ago, with a demanding *crr-owk* she interpreted as "Stay put." Every second spent in waiting for Izzy was agony. The cheerfulness of this realm's oversaturated colors was too much to bear while her arms remained empty.

Vesperi closed her eyes, clenched her fists, and waited.

A loud rustling of leaves and crack of overhead branches signaled the bird's return. Twigs fell against Vesperi's face, dislodged as Three-B made its way through the canopy.

Vesperi held her breath. If she dared to peek, her daughter might not be there, on its back, and she refused to admit that possibility. So she breathed, counted backward from ten like Serra had taught her, and waited.

Until a child's fingers slipped into her own and the question, "Mama? Are you okay?" was spoken with the tender concern Izmareld had learned from her father.

Vesperi trembled. Tears spilled as she released the dregs of doubt. She blinked them away so she could see her daughter there, truly there.

She was.

Izzy had grown a head taller. She was dressed in a pair of shiny pants speckled with metal paillettes and a down shirt of ruffles lined with feathers of the brightest, boldest blue.

My daughter.

Vesperi stared, speechless. Tears threatened to overtake her vision, but she wouldn't let them, wouldn't let anything take her daughter out of her sight again. She went to her knees, rubbed Izzy's arms up and down, as though doing so would commit the lines of her body to memory and she'd never lose her again. Then she placed her hands under Izzy's armpits and lifted her, twirling in the air.

Delighted giggles filled the holes in Vesperi's heart, holes that only this joy could patch.

After peppering her face and hair with a million kisses, Vesperi collapsed to the ground, taking Izzy with her. They lay in the springy moss, and Vesperi reveled in her daughter's brown irises, as warm and inviting as the day she'd been born.

"What does the mama snake say to the baby snake?" The remembered words slipped from Vesperi's mouth, unbidden.

Izzy hesitated, and in the half-second before she answered, Vesperi endured a hurricane of fear. Might this be a trick of her imagination, or another evil plan? Such cruelty was not beyond belief, not according to her lived experience.

Then Izzy gazed up at her, starry-eyed. "Ssssnuggles, ssssnakelet!"

Vesperi launched into a tickle attack. Izzy's giggles redoubled, filling more than Vesperi, also the glen and the sky and the realm. Turquoise dust showered down on them from the canopy as Vesperi joined in, as though the leaves themselves shook with laughter. Or maybe that was Three-B searching for a snack.

When her sheer amazement dulled the slightest bit, Vesperi asked, "Are you okay?" She held Izzy close, inspected every square inch of skin she could see.

"Mama, I'm okay. The blue woman took good care of me."

Madel had her? Not just Three-B, but Madel Herself?

Izzy tossed a head of tousled dark curls that had grown past her waist. They were full of bright leaves and fluff and unbrushed—maybe for weeks, likely for months. Vesperi had never seen a more beautiful sight.

"What was She like, the blue woman?" She smoothed the spot where Izzy's hair used to part. It was a small change, one of many Vesperi noted.

"Like rolling down the grass." Izzy nestled under her arm.

"I don't remember you rolling down our hills in Callyn."

"Daddy and I rolled on them! With Pic, at home."

Vesperi *hmmed* as she combed through Izzy's hair. "What did you eat with Her?"

"Sometimes berries. Lots of times nothing, but she'd give me a big rush of air whenever my stomach growled and told me to drink it up. It was so funny."

"What else would She do? Were you always together?"

"No." Izzy's voice quieted, and Vesperi's heart clenched. She held her tighter and tried not to imagine what Izzy might have gone through, trusted that Madel had made sure she felt safe and loved, though Vesperi felt not a small bit used by the goddess who'd reduced her daughter to bait.

"But it was better when She was there. I missed you though, Mama."

"Oh, sweetheart, you have no idea how much I missed you. Daddy too."

For a time, Vesperi thought of nothing else but the presence of her daughter in her arms. If she could spend the rest of their lives right here, she would. But a giant bird soon pecked its three heads between and around their legs like a cat begging for breakfast. Others waited on them, too. Izzy was not Vesperi's joy alone, much as she might wish it so, if only to extend this moment.

"Do you want to go home, Izzy?" After spending a year with a goddess, Vesperi didn't know what her answer would be. How could she and Janto compete?

Izzy sat up, nodding faster than Janto saying yes to lemon cakes. "Is Daddy home? And Grandpa and Grammy?"

Vesperi wouldn't let the sorrow of King Dever's death touch her just yet. There would be time. *There would be time.* That alone was worth praising Madel for.

"Yes. And if you're not afraid to ride this fine steed again"— Three-B chuffed and shook its feathers—"then we'll head home as soon as you're ready."

Izzy leapt up on skinny, strong legs. "Can we go right now?"

Vesperi smiled and tried not to cry again. "Yes, we can. Whatever you want."

Three-B bent its knobby self down and Vesperi clambered up, trying not to grip feathers too hard this time. "Jump!" she instructed her daughter once she'd got a good seat.

Izzy leapt high and Vesperi caught her, swinging her in front. "Let's go home to Daddy, okay?"

"Yay!"

Izzy screamed into the wind as Three-B sprang back through the hole in the canopy it had created. Not for a moment did Vesperi wonder if Janto would be there when they made it back. She was done with doubt for now. Her most important dream had come true.

CHAPTER THIRTY-SIX

JANTO

To say Prince Janto Albrecht had never thought he'd watch his family return to him on the back of the bird of creation wouldn't be saying much. Prince Janto Albrecht had never thought much of what life had brought him in his twenty-seven years was possible.

But King Janto Albrecht knew to expect the impossible.

His smile widened as Three-B flapped steadily over the hillsides near the Mount. It had been near a week since he and Serra had left Vesperi in the celestial realm, enough time to leave the disappeared people in the capable hands of the Wasylim herbalists and return to Callyn and reports of halted evacuations from his mother. Serra had marked the fissure outside his quarters; it, and the others she'd seen on the journey home, had begun to recede, thankfully.

That it had been a week was further proof time did not pass the same way in Lansera as it did in the celestial realm. As much as Vesperi may have wanted to keep Izzy all to herself, Janto knew his wife wouldn't have done so for long.

Three-B grew larger in his field of vision, and Janto maintained his father's kingly demeanor for a few more minutes, holding his arm proudly across his chest. His mother stood beside him. He flashed her a grin, and her eyes glimmered before she let out a whoop. Taking her hand, they ran up the nearest hill and down the next.

Queen Lexamy's curls bounced as they loosened from the bun on her head. Laughing, they yelled excited welcomes at Three-B, until

Janto could hear his daughter giggle in return. He had thought himself ready, had known Vesperi would bring her back, but the sound of Izzy's laughter yanked the breath from him.

His mother clutched his hand and they stared up in wonder until Three-B's claws stretched out for a landing grip. Janto shielded his mother from the backdraft but waited only a half-tick before running to his family and whisking his daughter up and around. That couldn't have compared to the ride she just took, but her cheeks bloomed with delight and Janto's heart twirled in sync with her long-flowing curls.

"Look at you." His eyes filled as Izzy twisted her head around to do as he asked. Oh, this was her, the same sweet wonder she'd always been, though taller and skinnier, and with a near years' worth of tales already spilling out, give or take a few units of celestial timekeeping.

"Can Grammy get a hug?" His mother held her arms open, and Izzy jumped into them, knocking them both back into the grass. Janto couldn't speak, watching them. His legs folded of their own accord, and he sat back, amazed.

Vesperi sat beside him and rested her head on his shoulder.

"You're trembling," she said.

He hadn't noticed. Time had slowed as he took in his daughter now poised on his mother's knee, talking animatedly about drinking the wind. Izzy gestured at Three-B, who was picking at the grass, in search of energy replenishment. The image coalesced with the last sight he'd had of her in the mangrove swamp, black curls swaying as she'd run beyond the meadow.

He leaned toward his daughter, as compelled as he'd been by Onsic's pull.

"Go on," Vesperi nudged. "She's real. I promise you that."

So he did, taking his wife with him. Janto gathered his whole family tight within his arms and squeezed them into a lasting hug until Izzy complained, "Daddy!" He released his hold with reluctance, declaring, "We are never moving from this spot. None of us. We shall live the rest of our lives right here. Three-B will bring us sustenance, and—"

"—and I think Ser Allyn might have something to say about that." His mother winked and gestured for him to look over his shoulder.

The rising din of his responsibilities crested the hill. It sounded an awful lot like the footfalls of the castle's servants crunching the thick spring grass.

"Pic!" Izzy screamed with delight and ran to her friend, already moving past the thrill of her return to her parents. Janto didn't know if he could do the same. He stood stunned, barely blinking, as Pic whirled her in the air again. Ser Allyn grimaced at their undignified comportment, but even he could not resist complying when Izzy reached up for a hug.

"Oh my," said Mar Jeffyr, flour on her cheeks, as Izzy found her next. "You look skinny as a skeleton!" She rummaged in her apron pockets and drew out a lemon cake. Then she pinched Izzy's cheek as the girl swallowed it whole. By then most of Callyn's staff and visitors had reached the hillside, and yet, Janto had no words to explain her return, nothing in him but gratitude and awe. He took comfort in the feel of Vesperi's hand in his and thought, what a gift to share such a feeling with so many others. What a gift to partake in and witness a reunion such as this.

The words came.

"Captain Wolxas!" Janto called over the commander of the army, who'd filled him in on their success thus far in rooting out the advers' cells. "Send out word with your forces: All citizens whose family has returned home from the celestial realm should send us a report. I would like to offer them a token of our shared joy."

"What token, Daddy?" Izzy had returned, having made her rounds. Lemon sugar speckled her lips.

Janto lifted her onto his shoulder. He remembered the way his people at Onsic's abyss had looked, the despair on their faces at having been so far removed from all they knew and understood. He thought of the Meduans confronted with a world order so different from their own after the Conjoining. Circumstances had improved for most, but such changes took an ongoing adjustment—in time and frames of mind. Hope was something everyone could use.

He spoke loud enough all could hear. "Six years ago, myself, my wife, and my dear friend, Serrafina Gavenstone, went together to Mandat Hall. We toppled it and the advers' control over the Meduans. My father declared a Conjoining of our countries, a reunification of what had been sundered generations before. That word, *conjoining*, conveyed his intentions to welcome the Meduans back into the fold, not just to coexist.

"In the years since, we've learned a few things. Simply declaring we are one people does not make it so. Nor is that a desirable outcome.

Each of Madel's children brings their own strengths to the whole—not by blending, but by contributing their richness to a fuller song.

"Nor are we humans the only beings in this existence. The claren were our first proof of how our actions can affect people in other places. The cantaleres and jurgens we've struggled with are the most recent examples. Our people used to know such things, but we've lost sight of them. We must relearn how precarious, and precious, is the intricate interweaving of our lives with those in the other realms.

"So we will send a token to the families who have paid the price of our ignorance: the fallen members of the Silver Guard and those whose loved ones were taken from them through the fissures. This token will help us remember better in the future."

"From the royal family," he placed a heartfelt kiss on Izzy's knee, "an assurance we will not forget their pain and sacrifices, because we know them ourselves."

He dug into a pocket and retrieved a new cutting Terella had sent of the symphony bush, a fresh shoot from one of the previously ailing plants. Its leaves were a healthy green, and when the light struck just right, a rainbow of moonslight reflected from them. Janto held it high.

"They shall be sent a seedling of the symphony bush. This plant provides a measurement of our health as a society. Clear blossoms foretell clear sailing, but black ones reveal inner sicknesses we must shine lights upon. The moons taught us that."

Janto lowered Izzy back to the ground—her eyes were drooping. He chuckled, but had a few words left to share so handed her over to Vesperi's waiting arms.

"We are not the same Lansera as we were before the Conjoining. And we no longer aim to be. We do not seek to remake our neighbors in our own image but endeavor to join with them in harmony."

"Look, Daddy!" Izzy pointed skyward, trying to wrest excitement from her sleep-sluggishness. "I was on it!"

Three-B had taken to the skies again, evoking peals of wonder. It flew a figure eight around Callyn's faithful servants and then skidded to a stop on the ground. Once still, it maneuvered its three heads into a suggestion of a viper's strike. Janto wondered if it had practiced moves for aping swans and grapevines, too.

"Thank you," Janto said, stroking each head in turn. "Thank you for everything."

Three-B bobbed and fluttered its wings.

"Don't take this the wrong way," Janto continued, "but I hope not to see you again."

Each head released a simulacrum of laughter before twisting up toward the sky. *One . . . two . . . three . . .* bounding strides, Janto counted before Three-B launched into flight, ascending fast and steady.

"Good riddance," Vesperi said, though her smile belied the sentiment.

His mother took his arm. "I think you've just been coronated."

Janto laughed. "And deprive the nobility of a spectacle and Vesperi of a crown? Mother, you taught me better." He raised his voice. "Captain Wolxas, your scribes took all that down, right?"

Captain Wolxas let loose a belly laugh. "Best work on an abridged version, my king. Our pigeons can't take to the air quite like that one can."

Vesperi held Izzy over her shoulder, and Janto teared up again, gazing upon them. He had longed so for that sight.

"Come on," he said, "let's get this sss-snakelet home."

Serra

Sap leaked from the cracks on a reed-covered cabin's front door. The humid heat surrounding Lake Ashra made the cracking a common occurrence, which was why locals coated the doors with resin before installing them, rather than after. But the man who lived here, who'd spent much of his childhood in drought, could hardly have known he should.

Though tempted to tease, Serrafina Gavenstone would not start today's conversation with anything but what mattered most. That was the woman Serra had waiting out of sight of the entrance, dressed in a light, tan slip of a dress and a smile on her face that she was not yet used to wearing.

And the man inside. Sap on Serra's fingers mattered not.

She took a deep breath and knocked, breaking some lichen off the door in the process. This was not the first time she'd planned an appeal to someone whose heart she'd broken. But it was the first time she did so knowing just how poor her behavior had been.

The door flew open. Serra gulped. Lorne's hair was shorn, falling just above his eyes, a flattering change.

"Ready, finally?" he said. "I thought you were going to wait on the stoop for hours."

Had she been balanced on the threshold that long? Serra tipped herself over it and into the room. "How did you know I was there?"

"Word travels, Serra. Your journeys aren't as prosaic as you think.

Even when it's just you, a horse, and a saddlebag weighed down with tinctures and plants, the seer doesn't ride unseen."

"But people don't know how I look—"

Lorne rolled his eyes, before dragging her to his looking glass. "One of these days, you'll see how remarkable you are."

His lute lay beside his brush on the table. Lorne lingered behind her, and Serra took in the figure they made. She imagined them at Gavenstone, sitting side-by-side by the fireplace, celebrating the ice wine harvest right before winter crept in.

Lorne moved away from the reflection. "So what brings you here? Are you gathering the Guard back together already? Are there granfaylons clogging up the waterways?"

Serra sighed. How much a mess she'd made of things that Lorne wouldn't guess *himself* the reason for her visit. Even if he rejected her now, as she fully expected him to, she pledged to leave knowing he'd never diminish himself that way again.

"How was the coronation?" he asked, ever willing to hear court gossip. He'd spent his adolescence as a courtier in Qiltyn, when it had been Medua's capitol.

"Beautiful." It had been a celebration on a scale Serra hadn't seen before, the quartz bridge over the River Call full near to bursting as Janto and Vesperi were crowned below its waterfall. "Izzy spent it on her uncle's lap. You wouldn't believe how much she makes Uzziel smile."

Lorne lifted an eyebrow. "Vesperi allowed him to attend?"

"Vesperi gifted him with a viper-green ceremonial cape."

Lorne choked on air. "Amazing."

"People change," Serra said. Vesperi was a jumble of contradictory impulses, as were they all. Not so very long ago, Serra would have considered her Meduan loved ones to be enemies, a *them* versus the *us* she grew up valuing. It had been a given, that Meduans were the lesser people. But the Lanserim hadn't exorcised their demons. They'd merely done a better job controlling them. Any person had the potential to tip one way or the other, to feed or starve their own toxic impulses.

For a moment, Serra entertained the idea of indulging her desirous ones, throwing herself onto Lorne's lap and begging her way into his bed. But that was not Serra, and she had to trust Lorne wanted *her* again, not some other idea of them. Plus, she would not leave the woman outside alone for long. Cora Granich had been treated as an afterthought her whole life.

"I'm returning to Gavenstone." Serra sat in a reed-plaited chair, letting her words sink in with no further explanation.

"To visit your aunt? Do tell her hello. And tell Jehos he best be using the levere belt I had crafted for him. Those saggy bottoms on his pantaloons are a tragedy." Lorne smiled. Aunt Marji's husband amused him. "Did you want some tachery? I can brew some up."

"I'm not going for a visit," she said.

He placed the filled kettle over his fireplace. "No? Business then, for the king?"

"I'm moving back. Permanently."

The mortar he'd been using to crush the tachery into threads clinked against the stone pestle. "Really?" He took her hands for a moment that filled her with glee, before thinking better of it. "Are you certain? You've been against that for so long. Did all the moonslight addle your senses?"

He never had bought her lies before, had he?

"One thing could make me more certain." She held Lorne's gaze. "You, there with me."

Lorne laughed, and the resentment it held twisted her innards. "Need an official jester, do you? Or someone in the village who can keep an eye on your Meduans?"

Serra took another deep breath. She leaned forward, placed her hands on his knees. "No. I want you there *with me.*"

The kettle screamed and he jumped to take it off. In silence, he prepared his tea and her tachery to steep in two separate vessels. The water poured, steam rose, and the room soon smelled of libtyl leaves and the warmth of roasted seeds. Normally, Serra would take comfort in such smells, but the seconds ticked, Cora waited, and still, Lorne said nothing. She'd never seen him rendered speechless and tapped the arm of her chair anxiously. Maybe she could pretend it hadn't happened, call Cora in, and—

Two mugs appeared on the table between their chairs. Lorne slumped back into his. Tears danced on his bottom eyelids.

Oh no. She hadn't wanted to cause him more pain. She'd already put him through so much. If he said no, if he rejected her, she'd leave him alone. But the mere thought of not seeing him again—her stomach clenched and her hands shook.

"Do you mean it?" His voice was quiet, yet it held so much hope. "I told myself I wouldn't let you in if you knocked, that I'd refuse any overtures you made. I owed it to myself. But Serra, by Madel's hand, if you mean it . . ."

"I do." She slid one hand across the table, touched her fingertips to his. "Lorne, I really, truly do." Suddenly, she was hiccuping and crying through her words. "I think returning home would be good for me, and good for Meditlan. I'll have Aunt Marji and Jehos to lean on, but I can't do it without the rest of my family. Without you."

His fingers intertwined with her own. She gazed up, daring to hope that meant what it might.

He shrugged. "So, I'm a hopeless idiot—"

She kissed him. His arms wrapped around her, hands gripping her waist and her own going up the small of his back and spreading higher. This was everything. Everything Serra had wanted since she'd learned to dream beyond the walls of Callyn, to live fully in the world. Who could please her more than this man with his loving heart, his sharp wit, and his array of Meduan survival smarts that so complemented her own strengths? She hoped they could share them with each other and with the Meditlans.

But she had more to share with him right then. He groaned as she separated and held a finger to her lips. "One moment, my love." Then she went out the sap-lacquered door and found Cora counting cattails near the path.

"I'm sorry I kept you out here," Serra said, taking her by the hand. Cora was an elegant woman, though shy. Who could blame her for that, living to the age of twenty-four within her father's halls, unable to acknowledge her place in her own family? That changed today. "It's time."

They passed through the threshold together, and Lorne's hands rushed to his mouth. He touched one to his throat, eyes filled with tears. His willingness to plainly show his feelings was one of the reasons Serra loved him so. She'd not been raised to do the same.

"Cora! How?" Lorne enveloped his sister in a hug, and both their faces flushed with emotion. But his eyes were on Serra.

"Janto sent a company to support me. We left a few advisors behind, to 'help' your father's 'adjustment' to more equitable ways of governance. A town council will soon be formed in Granich, and in the other manors held by Meduan nobility. Not doing so right away was a mistake of naivety, though Janto does want to study any positives among the old systems."

"Thank you," Lorne mouthed, before shifting his attention back to Cora.

Serra watched in silence for a time, sipping the tachery Lorne had brewed. He was so tender with Cora, rubbing her shoulders, asking her an endless barrage of questions about the ways they might be similar despite being raised apart.

"We will spend the next eternity learning about it," he assured his sister, when she found herself overwhelmed.

I would like that, too, Serra thought. Then she spoke the words that naturally followed that sentiment, though they were far from impulsive.

"Lorne Granich, will you marry me?"

His eyes flashed with surprise. "Serra?"

"I mean it. I don't know what I'm doing going home. I don't know how to be the lady of Gavenstone, how to care for my people when I'm not sure I can care for myself most the time. But I know I don't want to do it alone. I can't picture myself as Lady Gavenstone without you there, Lorne."

She took a seat beside the siblings. "Or you either, Cora. I've never had a sister, at Gavenstone or Callyn. I would love to share that with you."

Cora pushed blonde tresses behind her ears. "I'd like that too."

"And you," Serra informed the man she loved, "I want to teach you how to press grapevines against the temple's walls. I want you coming up with some sort of amazing fashionable use for grape must. I want you whispering in my ear all your theories on who's doing whom or what during a council meeting."

Lorne laughed, more boyish than when they'd first met. She wanted to learn everything he could do, to savor it over decades.

"Then I will try my best," he said.

That sounded like a yes. Was that a yes? She glanced up through her lashes.

A grand smile overtook his features, the sun surfacing from behind a cloud. Or Esye back in the sky, blooming full silver at midnight.

Lorne opened a free arm to her, keeping one wrapped around Cora's waist. Serra tumbled into his side, a flying fish taking too far a leap, and dove into depths she thought might be home.

Then he pushed her away, and Serra gulped. *He's reconsidered already.*

"Oh, no, no." The concern on his face warred with the upturned corners of his mouth. "Serra, look."

He opened his palm, and the silver flame whirled within it, bright as a needlestorm.

Cora gasped, "What's that?"

Serra's lungs felt drained. She already had so much to process, and now this, too? "How?"

His delighted laugh filled her with air. "I don't know! I felt it right then, like a tickle, and then—"

He flipped his palm, and the flame was still there.

"I wonder if Vesperi's is back, too, and the rest of the Guard. I wonder if it means something else is coming."

Serra rose to her feet and took two steps before Lorne drew her back.

"Oh no," he said. "You're not about to go rush off. I just got engaged, and you are going to celebrate with me and Cora. You're the one I'm engaged to, after all."

Serra was unable to protest, as he kissed her lips and handed back her tachery. He was right. Finding an answer could wait. There would always be threats to Lansera, things that upset the realms' delicate balance. But Serra was determined to find her own first.

As Lorne reached for his tea, her hand shot out and clasped his wrist.

"Try there," she said, pointing at a candle on the window's ledge. Together, they took aim.

CHARACTERS

Forms of Address

Nobility: *Lord*, male; *Lady*, female.
Knights: *Ser,* male; *Sar,* female.
Priests of the Order: *Ryn*, male; *Rynna,* female.
Priests of the False God Saeth: *Adver,* all males.
Citizens: *Mer,* male; *Mar,* female.

Notable Characters by Region

MADEL, goddess of all.

BRAVEN

Citizens

SIELBAN, murat trainer of ancient Rasselerian descent.

CAPITAL CITY OF CALLYN

Royalty at Castle Callyn

DEVER ALBRECHT, king. Sixth Albrecht on the throne.
LEXAMY (BRENDEL) ALBRECHT, queen by marriage and herbalist.
JANTO ALBRECHT, their son, prince, and the Silver Stag Slayer.
VESPERI (SELLWYN) ALBRECHT, princess by marriage and the Weapon.
IZMARELD ALBRECHT, their daughter, princess.

Advisors, Guards, and Servants

ALLYN, long-serving right hand of the king, a murated man.
PORCIA, his daughter.
EDDY, chief horseman.
IRVEN, royal guard, a murated man.
JEFFYR, head cook.
JYNDALA, royal guard.
MERTINA, royal guard.

NAPELER, royal guard, Prince Janto's right hand, and a murated man.
PIC, serving boy.
WOLXAS, captain of the army, a murated man.

Citizens

HULLVY, priestess of Madel and the city.

DURN

Nobility at Riven Manor

CARNIF, liege-lord.

Citizens

COLINI, priest of Madel assigned to Kallon.

ERTION

Nobility at Varma Manor

CINO XANTAS, liege-lord, a murated man.
GELLA XANTAS, lady by marriage.
JORY XANTAS, their son.

Ravens at the Perch

TIRLON SWALUS, head Raven, a murated man.
FELIA, his daughter.
MARABIL, a surveyor.
WERBOSE, second-in-command, a murated man.

Councilors

JERUSHO, chief councilor of Mova, a murated man.
DORELLA, councilor of Mova, engaged to Jerusho.

Citizens

THE FARRI FAMILY, farmers.

LORVIA

Nobility at Granich Manor

CAVALLEN GRANICH, liege-lord.

CORA GRANICH, his unacknowledged daughter.
LORNE GRANICH, the estranged son of Lord Cavallen Granich. Currently resides in Mova.
UZZIEL SELLWYN, ward of Lord Granich, brother of Vesperi Albrecht.

Citizens
PEDIR, serves Granich Manor.

MEDITLAN

Nobility at Gavenstone Manor
MARJI GAVENSTONE, liege-lady in Serrafina's absence.
JEHOS GAVENSTONE, lord by marriage.
SERRAFINA GAVENSTONE, niece to Marji, rightful heir of Gavenstone, and the Seer.

Councilors
FLIVIO, a councilor and murated man in Urs.

Citizens
YELON FORA, chief farmer of Orun

NEVILLE

Nobility at Carafin's Market
GRANSYL FARAMI, liege-lady.

Councilors
FERIN, chief councilor at Trop.

Citizens
DRENYL, a gardener.
KOREN, his daughter.
FRELLA KOMA, a local woman of Tilayne.
LARI, a pregnant woman.
SIM, Lari's husband.
TERELLA NORVYN, chief botanist, sister of Hamsyn (deceased).

VORPA, a captain often at Jost.
VOTAN, a priest of the false god Saeth.

RASSELERIA

Nobility at Elston Manor

RUFALYN, liege-lady of Elston. The Rasselerians have no liege.

Temple Enjoin

CLADIO, chief priest of Madel, a murated man.
GYLLES, a priest of Madel, a murated man.
ISLON, a priest of Madel.

Citizens

BINI, former servant of Serrafina Gavenstone, now at Elston.
CID, a carpenter at Elston.
LOURDA, priestess of Madel at Elston.
WERNO, painter at Elston.

WASYLA

Nobility at Coronith Manor

SYDLEY, liege-lord, a murated man.

Citizens

RALL BASILO, a murated man.
EVON, his son.

YAROWEN

Nobility at Qiltyn

RALION SUMA, former king of Medua.

Nobility at Garrow Manor

CLARDILL, liege-lord.

Citizens

HINTA, a craftswoman at Qiltyn
PITYR, her son.

AGLER GAVENSTONE, former liege-lord, brother to Serrafina Gavenstone.

BROTHERHOOD, THE, former heads of the Order and ghosts, now dissipated.

DIDIO ALBRECHT, second monarch in the Albrecht line.

DRUSTALLA ALBRECHT, third monarch in the Albrecht line.

GUJ, THE, aka ROMER, former chief adver of Medua.

HAMSYN NORVYN, killed by the claren at the fall of Mandat Hall, brother to Terella Norvyn.

JAHNAS SELLWYN, former liege-lord of Sellwyn, father to Vesperi Albrecht and Uzziel Sellwyn.

LADY SELLWYN, wife to Jahnas, mother to Vesperi Albrecht and Uzziel Sellwyn.

PINA, former head cook at Castle Callyn.

TURYN ALBRECHT, fifth monarch in the Albrecht line, King Dever's father.

WIZARDS, THE, corrupted Brotherhood spirits, now dissipated.

GLOSSARY OF LANSERIM TERMS

Celestial

ESYE: The silver moon and source of the Silver Flame's energy.
ONSIC: The black moon, with a cobalt halo.
ORO: The golden moon.
TANSIC: The copper moon.

Political

CONJOINING, THE: The reunion of the Meduan and Lanserim peoples after the fall of Mandat Hall, the Meduan stronghold of power. The kingdom of Medua ceased to exist thereafter.
DIVIDE, THE: The historical period during which the kingdom of Medua existed.
LANSERA: The sole kingdom. During the Divide, Lansera ceded part of its lands to create Medua.
MEDUA: A former kingdom formed after a segment of the Lanserim population rebelled against the social mores of Lanserim civil society. It was ruled for two generations by the advers, a group of ministers who established a false religion to control the population. Meduan lands have been folded back into the kingdom of Lansera.
TURYN'S PEACE: The peace agreement brokered to end the civil war and establish the kingdom of Medua two generations ago.

Fauna

BAROOL: Earth-toned worms covered with spikes. Found in the mountains.
CANTALERE: A creature of legend. They have six legs, a jagged horn, and brown hides covered in green moss. The back two legs have hooks in their hooves.
CHORNA MOTHS: Fast whirring, with black wings covered in an opalescent dust.
CLAREN: Thought to be legendary until a recent plague.

Black and red winged insects invisible to the human eye that travel in swarms. They enter orifices and drain their victims of their innards.

CRAVAL: Large, yak-like beasts with constant toothy smiles. Known to be dull-witted and spook easily.

DRASMO: A fast-moving, clawed mammal that lives in tunnels. They are known for leaving a mess.

GRANFAYLON: Thought to be legendary until Jerusho of Mova caught one on Braven at his murat. The large freshwater fish with a pale underside was thought to be thin, flat, and invisible prior to its capture.

JURGEN: A creature of legend. They lay eggs and have a broad paddle tail covered in spikes. Believed to be destructive.

KOPARIN: Large wild cats that hide in the brambles of Drustalla's ruins on the plain of Orelyn. Yellow-white coats with black tips, sharp claws.

RHINI: Furry, cat-sized rodents that climb and fly through the canopy of Braven and some areas of the mainland.

RUFIOR: Green bird with fast wings. Considered homely.

SHEVEN: many-toothed sharks found in ocean waters, particularly around Deduin. They have purple flesh and purple eyes and are known to attack humans.

SILVER STAG: Thought be legendary until Prince Janto Albrecht slayed one on Braven at his murat. The deer have shiny gray coats and elaborate antlers with many tines.

SNAVELIN: Mammals with elongated snouts and sticky paw pads. Rumored to eat babies.

TARTINE: A fish with yellow flesh, good for smoking.

WORANBIRD: Speckled birds that mate for life.

Flora

BALAC: A vining plant that takes well to trellis growth. Its white blossoms smell of honey.

DRAPIAN: Trees with light seed pods that float well. The seed pods are covered in sticky spires.

JALIF: A bush with astringent berries striped purple and white.

LIBTYL: An herb that smells of mint and eucalyptus. Pungent, calming, and antiseptic.

ROSEWOOD: Sturdy, lean trees with trunks streaked red.

Thorns on their rose-colored leaves are nearly imperceptible. Restricted to groves around Sellwyn in Durn.

SHORNAL: A groundcover plant with sweet and sour berries good for producing candy.

SOOTHPRICKLER: A thorny plant with milky nectar that soothes the skin.

SYMPHONY: A vining plant with transparent blossoms, opalescent dust, green leaves, and silver, gold, copper, and black veins.

RUNION: A long-stemmed vegetable with jade leaves, violet flowers, and a tender stem.

TACHERY: A tall bush whose seed pods and roots can be roasted, then crushed to brew an invigorating, earthy, and bitter beverage.

THORNBERRY: a prickly, low-lying bush found throughout Lansera. Its leaves are used for tea.

THRUSHBERRY: a hedge bush that yields purple berries prized for their ink. It grows throughout Lansera.

Miscellany

BOMBAL DROUGHT: A moonshine made of mint and mushrooms, common in Ertion.

LEVERE: A gray metal that repels the power of the Silver Flame.

MURAT, THE: A rite of passage for Lanserim young men. Only those who Madel anoints may attend, and they compete in feats of bravery under the tutelage of Sielban.

OLD GIRL, THE: Bow used by Janto Albrecht to slay the silver stag. Originally owned by Hamsyn Norvyn of Neville.

SOUZER: Coins that served as currency in Medua, and now, on the black market.

TORNIAN: A club weapon with a thin ring extending from its top. Used for beheading.

ACKNOWLEDGMENTS

To my husband, Ben Farrell, thank you for your cheerleading and unwavering faith in my writing. This sequel, much less my career, would not exist without you. Thank you for always being a light when doubts overwhelm.

My thanks go to Ben, Jessen Langley, and Jennifer Holbrook for sharing your thoughts on this manuscript's first draft. Your critiques gave me the confidence to realize that Esye didn't need to hide from the readers, that I could amp up the horror of Onsic's insidious methods, and that I was on the right track by bringing Three-B to life. I knew, if I wrote a sequel to *Wings Unseen*, that making the three-headed bird of prophecy into one of flesh and feathers was a necessity. Thank you for validating that feeling!

To Tricia Reeks, rockstar-in-chief at Meerkat Press, thank you for encouraging me to consider a sequel for *Wings Unseen*. It may have taken a few years for me to put fingers to keyboard and write *Wings Unfurled*, but once I started, I was so excited to discover Serra, Janto, and Vesperi's growth since Book 1 as characters, parents, and leaders up to the task of safeguarding their people once again. I'm glad they get to fly another round with Meerkat Press, and with your smart editing and publishing skills to guide them (and me).

To my many, many friends and acquaintances who've experienced depression, the pain of miscarriage, and other forms of grief, thank you so much for your transparency. The themes and emotions driving this book come from the trauma you've been brave enough to share with loved ones and complete strangers. Letting others see your struggles empowers us all to push back through the darkness that aims to consume us.

Once again, my final thanks go out to my cats, Mazu and Bemo.

May your comforting purrs be ever strong, and your reminders that
I need to take a break to play with you be ever plentiful.

ABOUT THE AUTHOR

Rebecca Gomez Farrell refuses to say "Bloody Mary" three times into a mirror, though she'll write stories about the people who do. She lives in California's East Bay with her tech wizard husband and two feline coworkers. Her epic fantasy duology, which includes *Wings Unseen* and *Wings Unfurled*, is published by Meerkat Press. Becca's shorter works have appeared over thirty times in magazines, websites, and anthologies including *Beneath Ceaseless Skies*, *It Calls From the Sky*, *PULP Literature*, and *A Quiet Afternoon 1 & 2*.

Becca is the communications director for the Science Fiction and Fantasy Writers Association (SFWA). She helms a local chapter of the national Women Who Submit Lit organization, which encourages all writers who identify as women and/or nonbinary to submit their work out for publication. She also co-organizes the East Bay Science Fiction and Fantasy Writers Meetup Group and administers several discussion groups for women, nonbinary, and Bay Area writers.

Over the past decade and a half, her food, drink, and travel blog, *theGourmez.com*, has influenced every tasty bite of her fictional world-building. Her replicator order is "Absinthe verte, one cube." Author Website: RebeccaGomezFarrell.com. Social Media: @theGourmez.

www.ingramcontent.com/pod-product-compliance
Lightning Source LLC
Chambersburg PA
CBHW030710190726
48286CB00001B/252